James Pennington Macpherson

Life of the Right Hon. Sir John A. Macdonald

Vol. 2

James Pennington Macpherson

Life of the Right Hon. Sir John A. Macdonald
Vol. 2

ISBN/EAN: 9783337095109

Printed in Europe, USA, Canada, Australia, Japan

Cover: Foto ©Raphael Reischuk / pixelio.de

More available books at **www.hansebooks.com**

LIFE OF

THE RIGHT HON.

SIR JOHN A. MACDONALD

G.C.B., D.C.L. (*Oxon.*), LL.D., Q.C., P.C.

BY HIS NEPHEW

LT. COL. J. PENNINGTON MACPHERSON, A.D.C.

VOLUME II.

"There does not exist in Canada a man who has given more of his time, more of his heart, more of his wealth, or more of his intellect and powers, such as they may be, for the good of this Dominion of Canada."—*Sir John in 1873.*

ST. JOHN, N.B.

EARLE PUBLISHING HOUSE

1891

CONTENTS

CHAPTER XXV.

CHAPTER XXVI.

1865-67.

CHAPTER XXVII.

1867-1871.

CHAPTER XXVIII.

CHAPTER XXIX.

CHAPTER XXX.

1872-74.

CHAPTER XXXVIII.

LIST OF ILLUSTRATIONS.

STEEL ENGRAVING.

FULL PAGE ILLUSTRATIONS.

SIR JOHN A. MACDONALD,

G.C.B., D.C.L. (*Oxon.*), L.L.D., Q.C., P.C.

CHAPTER XXV.

Meeting of Parliament, January 19, 1865—References to Confederation in the Speech—Mr. Macdonald moves an Address to Her Majesty on the subject—His speech—Resolutions carried by 91 to 33—Prorogation, March 18th—Deputation to England.

PARLIAMENT met again on January 19, 1865, when the following references to Confederation appeared in the Speech from the Throne :

" At the close of the last session of Parliament I informed you that it was my intention, in conjunction with my Ministers, to prepare and submit to you a measure for the solution of the constitutional problem, the discussion of which has, for some years, agitated this Province.

" A careful consideration of the general position of British North America induced the conviction that the circumstances of the times afforded the opportunity, not merely for the settlement of a question of Provincial politics, but also for the simultaneous creation of a new Nationality.

" Preliminary negotiations were opened by me with the Lieutenant-Governors of the other provinces of British North America, and the result was that a meeting was held at Quebec, in the month of October last, composed of delegates from those colonies, representing all shades of political parties in their several communities, nominated by the Lieutenant-Governors of their respective provinces who assembled here, with the sanction of the Crown, and at my invitation, to confer with the members of the Canadian Ministry, on the possibility of effecting a union of all the provinces of British North America.

"This Conference, after lengthened deliberations, arrived at the conclusion that a federal union of these provinces was feasible and desirable, and the result of its labours is a plan of constitution for the proposed union embodied in a series of resolutions, which, with other papers relating to the subject, I have directed to be laid before you.

"The general design of a union, and the particular plan by which it is proposed to carry that intention into effect, have both received the cordial approbation of the Imperial Government.

"An Imperial Act of Parliament will be necessary in order to give effect to the contemplated union of the Colonies, and I have been officially informed by the Secretary of State that Her Majesty's Ministers will be prepared to introduce a Bill for that purpose into the Imperial Parliament so soon as they shall have been notified that the proposal has received the sanction of the legislatures representing the several provinces affected by it.

"In commending to your attention this subject, the importance of which to yourselves and to your descendants it is impossible to exaggerate, I would claim for it your calm, earnest, and impartial consideration.

"With the public men of British North America it now rests to decide whether the vast tract of country which they inhabit shall be consolidated into a state, combining within its area all the elements of national greatness, providing for the security of its component parts, and contributing to the strength and stability of the Empire, or whether the several provinces of which it is constituted shall remain in their present fragmentary and isolated condition, comparatively powerless for mutual aid, and incapable of undertaking their proper share of Imperial responsibility.

"In the discussion of an issue of such moment I fervently pray that your minds may be guided to conclusions which shall redound to the honour of our Sovereign, to the welfare of her subjects, and to your own reputation as patriots and statesmen."

On Monday, February 6th, Attorney-General Macdonald moved, "That an humble address be presented to Her Majesty, praying that she may be graciously pleased to cause a measure to be submitted to the Imperial Parliament, for the purpose of uniting the colonies of Canada, Nova Scotia, New Brunswick, Newfoundland and Prince Edward Island, in one Government, with provisions based on certain resolutions which were adapted at a conference of delegates from the said colonies, held at the city of Quebec, on October 10, 1864."

He said :—" Mr. Speaker, in fulfilment of the promise made by the Government to Parliament at its last session, I have moved this resolution. I have had the honour of being charged, on behalf of the Government, to submit a scheme for the Confederation of the British North American Provinces— a scheme which has been received, I am glad to say, with general, if not universal, approbation in Canada. The scheme as propounded through the press, has received almost no opposition. While there may be, occasionally, here and there expressions of dissent from some of the details, yet the scheme as a whole has met with almost universal approval, and the Government has the greatest satisfaction in presenting it to this House. This subject, which now absorbs the attention of the people of Canada and of the whole of British North America, is not a new one. For years it has, more or less, attracted the attention of every statesman and politician in these provinces, and has been looked upon by many far-seeing politicians as being eventually the means of deciding and settling very many of the vexed questions which have retarded the prosperity of the colonies as a whole, and particularly the prosperity of Canada. The subject was pressed upon the public attention by a great many writers and politicians ; but I believe the attention of the Legislature was first formally called to it by my honourable friend, the Minister of Finance. Some years ago, in an elaborate speech, my honourable friend, while an independent member of Parliament, before being connected with any Government, pressed his views on the Legislature at great length and with his usual force. But the subject was not taken up by any party as a branch of their policy, until the formation of the Cartier-Macdonald Administration in 1858, when the Confederation of the Colonies was announced as one of the measures which they pledged themselves to attempt, if possible, to bring to a satisfactory conclusion. In pursuance of that promise, the letter or despatch, which has been so much and so freely commented upon in the press and in this House, was addressed by three of the members of that Administration to the Colonial office.

The subject, however, though looked upon with favour by the country, and though there were no distinct expressions of opposition to it from any party, did not begin to assume its present proportions until last session. Then men of all parties and all shades of politics, became alarmed at the aspect of affairs. They found that such was the opposition between the two sections of the province, such was the danger of impending anarchy, in consequence of the irreconcilable differences of opinion, with respect to representation by population, between Upper and Lower Canada, that unless some solution of the difficulty was arrived at, we should suffer under a succession of weak governments—weak in numerical support, weak in force, and weak in power of doing good.' All were alarmed at this state of affairs. We had election after election—we had Ministry after Ministry—with the same result. Parties were so equally balanced, that the vote of one member might decide the fate of the Administration and the course of legislation for a year or a series of years. This condition of things was calculated to arouse the earnest consideration of every lover of his country, and, I am happy to say, it had that effect. None were more impressed by this momentous state of affairs, and the grave apprehensions that existed of a state of anarchy destroying our credit, destroying our prosperity, destroying our progress ; than were the members of this present House ; and the leading statesmen on both sides seemed to have come to the common conclusion that some step must be taken to relieve the country from the dead-lock and impending anarchy that hung over us.

"With that view, my colleague, the President of the Council, made a motion, founded on the despatch addressed to the Colonial Minister—to which I have referred—and a committee was struck, composed of gentlemen of both sides of the House, of all shades of political opinion, without any reference to whether they were supporters of the Administration of the day or belonged to the Opposition, for the purpose of taking into calm and full deliberation the evils which threatened the future of Canada. That motion of my honourable friend resulted most happily. The committee, by a wise provision—and in order that each member of the committee might have an opportunity of expressing his opinions without being in in any way compromised before the public, or with his party, in regard either to his political friends or to his political foes—agreed that the discussion should be freely entered upon without reference to the political antecedents of any of them, and that they should sit with closed doors, so that they might be able to approach the subject frankly and in a spirit of compromise. The committee included most of the leading members of the House—I had the honour myself to be one of the number—and the result was that there was found an ardent desire—a creditable desire, I must say—displayed by all the members of the committee to approach the subject honestly, and to attempt to work out some solution which might relieve Canada from the evils under which she laboured. The report of that committee was laid before the House, and then came the political action of the leading men of the two parties in this House, which ended in the formation of the present Government.

"The principle upon which that Government was formed has been announced, and is known to all. It was formed for the very purpose of carrying out the object which has now received, to a certain degree, its completion, by the resolutions I have had the honour to place in your hands. As has been stated, it was not without a great deal of difficulty and reluctance that that Government was formed.

The gentlemen who compose this Government had for many years been engaged in political hostilities to such an extent that it affected even their social relations. But the crisis was great, the danger was imminent and the gentlemen who now form the present Administration found it to be their duty to lay aside all personal feelings, to sacrifice, in some degree, their position, and even to run the risk of having their motives impugned, for the sake of arriving at some conclusion that would be satisfactory to the country in general. The present resolutions were the result. And, as I said before, I am proud to believe that the country has sanctioned, as I trust that the representatives of the people in this House will sanction, the scheme which is now submitted for the future Government of British North America. (Cheers).

"Everything seemed to snow that the present was the time, if ever, when this great union between all Her Majesty's subjects, dwelling in British North America, should be carried out. (Hear, hear). When the Government was formed, it was felt that the difficulties in the way of effecting a union between all the British North American Colonies were great —so great as almost, in the opinion of many, to make it hopeless. And with that view it was the policy of the Government, if they could not succeed in procuring a union between all the British North American Colonies, to attempt to free the country from the dead-lock in which we were placed in Upper and Lower Canada, in consequence of the difference of opinion between the two sections, by having a severence to a certain extent of the present Union between the two Provinces of Upper and Lower Canada, and the substitution of a Federal Union between them. Most of us, however, I may say, all of us, were agreed—and I believe every thinking man will agree—as to the expediency of effecting a union between all the provinces, and the superiority of such a design, if it were only practicable, over the smaller scheme of having a Federal Union between Upper and Lower Canada alone.

"By a happy concurrence of events, the time came when

that proposition could be made with a hope of success. By
a fortunate coincidence the desire for Union existed in the
Lower Provinces, and a feeling of the necessity of strengthening themselves by collecting together the scattered colonies
on the sea-board, had induced them to form a convention
of their own for the purpose of effecting a Union of the
Maritime Provinces of Nova Scotia, New Brunswick, and
Prince Edward Island, the Legislatures of those Colonies
having formally authorized their respective Governments to
send a delegation to Prince Edward Island for the purpose
of attempting to form a Union of some kind. Whether the
Union should be federal or legislative was not then indicated,
but a Union of some kind was sought for the purpose of
making of themselves one people instead of three. We,
ascertaining that they were about to take such a step, and
knowing that if we allowed the occasion to pass, if they did,
indeed, break up all their present political organizations
and form a new one, it could not be expected that they
would again readily destroy the new organization which they
had formed,—the Union of the three Provinces on the sea-
board—and form another with Canada. Knowing this, we
availed ourselves of the opportunity, and asked if they would
receive a deputation from Canada, who would go to meet
them at Charlottetown, for the purpose of laying before them
the advantage of a larger and more extensive Union, by
the junction of all the Provinces in one great Government
under cour ommon Sovereign.

"They at once kindly consented to receive and hear us.
They did receive us cordially and generously, and asked us to
lay our views before them. We did so at some length, and
so satisfactory to them were the reasons we gave; so clearly,
in their opinion, did we show the advantages of the greater
union over the lesser, that they at once set aside their own
project and joined heart and hand with us in entering into
the larger scheme, and trying to form, as far as they and we
could, a great nation and a strong Government. (Cheers).
Encouraged by this arrangement, which, however, was altogether unofficial and unauthorized, we returned to Quebec,

and then the Government of Canada invited the several Governments of the Sister Colonies to send a deputation here from each of them for the purpose of considering the question, with something like authority from their respective Governments. The result was, that when we met here on October 10th, on the first day on which we assembled, after the full and free discussions which had taken place at Charlottetown, the first resolution now before this House was passed unanimously, being received with acclamation, as, in the opinion of every one who heard it, a proposition which ought to receive, and would receive, the sanction of each Government and each people. The resolution is : 'That the best interests and present and future prosperity of British North America will be promoted by a Federal Union under the Crown of Great Britain, provided such union can be effected on principles just to the several provinces.'

"It seemed to all the statesmen assembled—and there are great statesman in the Lower Provinces, men who would do honour to any government and to any legislature of any free country enjoying representative institutions—it was clear to them all that the best interests and present and future prosperity of British North America would be promoted by a Federal Union under the Crown of Great Britain. And it seems to me, as to them, and I think it will so appear to the people of this country, that, if we wish to be a great people, if we wish to form—using the expression which was sneered at the other evening—a great nationality, commanding the respect of the world, able to hold our own against all opponents, and to defend those institutions we prize; if we wish to have one system of government, and to establish a commercial union, with unrestricted free trade between people of the five provinces, belonging, as they do, to the same nation, obeying the same Sovereign, owing the same allegiance, and being, for the most part, of the same blood and lineage; if we wish to be able to afford to each other the means of mutual defence and support against aggression and attack, this can only be obtained by a union of some kind between the scattered and weak colonies composing the British North American provinces. (Cheers).

"The very mention of the scheme is fitted to bring with it its own approbation. Supposing that in the spring of the year 1865, half a million of people were coming from the United Kingdom to make Canada their home, although they brought only their strong arms and willing hearts, though they brought neither skill nor experience nor wealth, would we not receive them with open arms and hail their presence in Canada as an important addition to our strength? But when, by the proposed union, we not only get nearly a million of people to join us—when they contribute not only their numbers, their physical strength, and their desire to benefit their position, but when we know that they consist of old-established communities, having a large amount of realized wealth—composed of people possessed of skill, education and experience in the ways of the new world—people who are as much Canadians, I may say, as we are—people who are imbued with the same feelings of loyalty to the Queen and the same desire for the continuance of the connection with the mother country as we are, and at the same time having a like feeling of ardent attachment for this, our common country, for which they and we would alike fight and shed our blood if necessary. When all this is considered, argument is needless to prove the advantage of such a union. (Hear, hear).

"There were only three modes—if I may return for a moment to the difficulties with which Canada was surrounded —only three modes that were at all suggested, by which the dead-lock in our affairs, the anarchy we dreaded, and the evils which retarded our prosperity, could be met or averted. One was the dissolution of the Union between Upper and Lower Canada, leaving them as they were before the Union of 1841. I believe that that proposition, by itself, had no supporters. It was felt by everyone, that although it was a course that would do away with the sectional difficulties which existed— though it would remove the pressure on the part of the people of Upper Canada for representation based upon population—

and the jealousy of the people of Lower Canada lest their institutions should be attacked and prejudiced by that principle, yet it was felt by every thinking man in the province that it would be a retrograde step which would throw back the country to nearly the same position as it occupied before the union, that it would lower the credit enjoyed by United Canada, that it would be the breaking up of the connection which had existed for nearly a quarter of a century, and under which, although it had not been completely successful, and had not allayed altogether the local jealousies that had their root in circumstances which arose before the Union, our province, as a whole, had nevertheless prospered and increased. It was felt that a dissolution of the Union would have destroyed all the credit that we had gained by being a united province, and would have left us two weak and ineffective governments, instead of one powerful and united people. (Hear, hear).

" The next mode suggested was the granting of representation by population. Now, we all know the manner in which that question was and is regarded by Lower Canada; that while in Upper Canada the desire and cry for it was daily augmenting, the resistance to it in Lower Canada was proportionably increasing in strength. Still, if some such means of relieving us from the sectional jealousies which existed between the two Canadas, if some such solution of the difficulties, as Confederation, had not been found, the representation by population must eventually have been carried, no matter though it might have been felt in Lower Canada as being a breach of the treaty of Union; no matter how much it might have been felt by the Lower Canadians that it would sacrifice their local interests, it is certain that in the progress of events representation by population would have been carried, and had it been carried—I speak here my own individual sentiments—I do not think it would have been for the interest of Upper Canada. For though Upper Canada would have felt that it had received what it claimed as a right, and had succeeded in establishing its right, yet it would have left the Lower Province with a sullen feeling of injury and injustice. The Lower Canadians would not have worked cheerfully under such a change of system, but would have ceased to be what they are now—a nationality, with representatives in Parliament, governed by general principles, and dividing according to their political opinions—and would have been in great danger of becoming a faction, forgetful of national obligations, and only actuated by a desire to defend their own sectional interests, their own laws and their own institutions. (Hear, hear).

"The third and only means of solution for our difficulties was the junction of the provinces, either in a Federal or Legislative Union. Now, as regards the comparative advantages of a Legislative and a Federal Union, I have never hesitated to state my own opinions. I have again and again stated in the House that, if practicable, I thought a Legislative Union would be preferable. (Hear, hear). I have always contended that if we could agree to have one Government and one Parliament, legislating for the whole of these peoples, it would be the best, the cheapest, the most vigorous, and the strongest system of Government we could adopt. (Hear, hear). But, on looking at the subject in the Conference, and discussing the matter as we did, most unreservedly, and with desire to arrive at a satisfactory conclusion, we found that such a system was impracticable. In the first place it would not meet the assent of the people of Lower Canada, because they felt that in their peculiar position—being in a minority, with a different language, nationality and religion from the majority—in case of a junction with the other provinces, their institutions and their laws might be assailed, and their ancestral associations, on which they prided themselves, attacked and prejudiced, it was found that any proposition which involved the absorption of the individuality of Lower Canada—if I may use the expression—would not be received with favour by her people. We found, too, that though their people speak the same language, and enjoy the same system of law as the people of Upper Canada, a system founded on the common law of England, there was a great disinclination on the part of the various Maritime Provinces to lose their individuality, as separate political organizations, as we observed in the case of Lower Canada herself. (Hear, hear). Therefore, we were forced to the conclusion that we must either abandon the idea of union altogether, or devise a system of union in which the separate provincial organizations would be in some degree preserved. So, that those who were, like myself, in favour of a Legislative Union, were obliged to modify their views and accept the project of a Federal Union as the only scheme practicable, even for the Maritime Provinces. Because, although the law of those provinces is founded on the common law of England, yet every one of them has a large amount of law of its own—colonial law framed by itself, and affecting every relation of life, such as the laws of property, municipal and assessment laws ; laws relating to the liberty of the subject, and to all the great interests contemplated in legislation ; we found, in short, that the statutory law of the different provinces was so varied and diversified that it was almost impossible to weld them into a Legislative Union at once.

"Why, sir, if you only consider the innumerable subjects of Legislation peculiar to new countries, and that every one of those five colonies had particular laws of its own, to which its people had been accustomed, and are attached, you will see the difficulty of effecting and working a Legislative Union, and bringing about an assimilation of the local as well as general laws of the whole of the provinces. (Hear, hear). We in Upper Canada understand from the nature and operation of our peculiar municipal law, of which we know the value, the difficulty of framing a general system of legislation on local matters, which would meet the wishes and fulfil the requirements of the several provinces. Even the laws considered the least important, respecting private rights in timber, roads, fencing, and innumerable other matters, small in themselves, but in the aggregate of great interest to the agricultural class, who form the great body of the people, are regarded as of great value by the portion of the community affected by them. And when we consider that everyone of the colonies has a body of laws of this kind, and that it will take years before those laws can be assimilated, it was felt that at first, at all

events, any united legislation would be almost impossible. I
am happy to state, and, indeed, it appears on the face of the
resolutions themselves, that as regards the Lower Provinces, a
great desire was evinced for the final assimilation of our laws.
One of the resolutions provides that an attempt shall be made
to assimilate the laws of the Maritime Provinces and those of
Upper Canada, for the purpose of eventually establishing one
body of statutory law, founded on the common law of England, the parent of the laws of all those provinces.

"One great objection made to a Federal Union was the
expense of an increased number of Legislatures. I will not
enter at any length into that subject, because my honourable
friends, the Finance Minister and the President of the Council,
who are infinitely more competent than myself to deal with
matters of this kind—matters of account—will, I think, be
able to show that the expenses under a Federal Union will
not be greater than those under the existing system of
separate governments and legislatures. Here, where we have
a joint legislature for Upper and Lower Canada, which deals
not only with subjects of a general interest common to all
Canada, but with all matters of private right and of sectional
interest, and with that class of measures, known as ' Private
Bills,' we find that one of the greatest sources of expense
to the country is the cost of legislation. We find, from the
admixture of subjects of a general, with those of a private
character in legislation, that they mutually interfere with
each other ; whereas, if the attention of the Legislature was
confined to measures of one kind or the other alone, the
session of Parliament would not be so protracted and therefore not so expensive as at present. In the proposed Constitution all matters of general interest are to be dealt with
by the General Legislature, while the Local Legislatures will
deal with matters of local interest, which do not affect the
Confederation as a whole, but are of the greatest importance
to their particular sections. By such a division of labour the
sittings of the general legislature would not be so protracted
as even those of Canada alone. And so with the local legislatures, their attention being confined to subjects pertaining

to their own sections, their sessions would be shorter and less expensive.

"Then, when we consider the enormous saving that will be affected in the administration of affairs by one General Government—when we reflect that each of the five colonies have a Government of its own with a complete establishment of public departments and all the machinery required for the transaction of the business of the country—that each have a separate executive, judicial and military system—that each province has a separate Ministry, including a Minister of Militia, with a complete Adjutant General's Department —that each have a Finance Minister with a full Customs and Excise staff—that each Colony has as large and complete an administrative organization, with as many executive officers as the General Government will have—we can well understand the enormous saving that will result from a Union of all the Colonies, from their having but one head and one central system.

" We, in Canada, already know something of the advantages and disadvantages of a Federal Union. Although we have nominally a Legislative Union in Canada—although we sit in one Parliament, supposed, constitutionally, to represent the people, without regard to sections or localities, yet we know, as a matter of fact, that since the Union in 1841, we have had a Federal Union ; that in matters affecting Upper Canada solely, members from that section claimed and generally exercised the right of exclusive legislation, while members from Lower Canada legislated in matters affecting only their own section. We have had a Federal Union in fact, though a Legislative, a Union in name ; and in the hot contests of late years, if, on any occasion, a measure affecting any one section were interfered with by any members from the other—if, for instance, a measure locally affecting Upper Canada were carried or defeated against the wishes of its majority, by one from Lower Canada—my honourable friend, the President of the Council, and his friends, denounced with all their energy and ability such legislation as an infringement of the rights of the Upper Province. (Hear, hear, and cheers). Just in the same way, if any Act concerning Lower Canada were pressed into law against the wishes of the majority of her representatives, by those from Upper Canada, the Lower Canadians would rise as one man and protest against such a violation of their peculiar rights. (Hear, hear).

"The relations between England and Scotland are very similar to that which obtains between the Canadas. The union between them, in matters of legislation, is of a federal character, because the Act of Union between the two countries provides that the Scottish law cannot be altered, except for the manifest advantage of the people of Scotland. This stipulation has been held to be so obligatory on the Legislature of Great Britain, that no measure effecting the law of Scotland is passed unless it receives the sanction of a majority of the Scottish members in Parliament. No matter how important it may be for the interests of the empire, as a whole, to alter the laws of Scotland—no matter how much it may interfere with the symmetry of the general law of the United Kingdom—that law is not altered, except with the consent of the Scottish people, as expressed by their representatives in Parliament. (Hear, hear). Thus, we have, in Great Britain, to a limited extent, an example of the working and effects of a Federal Union, as we might expect to witness them in our own Confederation.

"The whole scheme of Confederation, as propounded by the Conference, as agreed to and sanctioned by the Canadian Government, and as now presented for the consideration of the people and the Legislature, bears upon its face the marks of compromise. Of necessity there must have been a great deal of mutual concession. When we think of the representatives of five colonies, all supposed to have different interests, meeting together, charged with the duty of protecting those interests and of pressing the views of their own localities and sections, it must be admitted that had we not met in a spirit of conciliation, and with an anxious desire to promote this union ; if we had not been impressed with the idea contained in the words of the resolution : 'That the best interests and

present and future prosperity of British North America would
be promoted by a Federal Union under the Crown of Great
Britain,' all our efforts might have proved to be of no avail.
If we had not felt that, after coming to this conclusion, we
were bound to set aside our private opinions on matters
of detail, if we had not felt ourselves bound to look at what
was practicable, not obstinately rejecting the opinions of
others nor adhering to our own ; if we had not met, I say, in
a spirit of conciliation, and with an anxious, over-ruling desire
to form one people under one government, we never would
have succeeded.

   " With these views, we press the question on this House,
and the country. I say to this House, if you do not believe
that the union of the colonies is for the advantage of the
country, that the joining of these five peoples into one nation,
under one sovereign, is for the benefit of all, then reject
the scheme. Reject it if you do not believe it to be for
the present advantage and future prosperity of yourselves
and your children. But if, after a calm and full consideration
of this scheme, it is believed, as a whole, to be for the advantage of this province—if the House and country believe this
union to be one which will ensure for us British laws, British
connection and British freedom—and increase and develop
the social, political, and material prosperity of the country,
then I implore this House and the country to lay aside all
prejudices, and accept the scheme which we offer. I ask
the House to meet the question in the same spirit in which the
delegates met it. I ask each member of this House to lay
aside his own opinions as to particular details, and to accept
the scheme as a whole, if he thinks it beneficial as a whole.

   " If we are not blind to our present position, we must see the
hazardous situation in which all the great interests of Canada
stand in respect to the United States. I am no alarmist. I
do not believe in the prospect of immediate war. I believe
that the common sense of the two nations will prevent a war ;
still we cannot trust to probabilities. The Government and
Legislature would be wanting in their duty to the people if
they ran any risk. We know that the United States at

THE FATHERS OF CONFEDERATION.

this moment are engaged in a war of enormous dimensions—
that the occasion of a war with Great Britain has again and
again arisen, and may, at any time in the future, again arise.
We cannot foresee what may be the result ; [we cannot say but
that the two nations may drift into a war as other nations
have done before.] It would then be too late when war
had commenced, to think of measures for strengthening
ourselves ; or to begin negotiations for a union with the sister
provinces.   At this moment, in consequence of the ill-feeling
which has arisen between England and the United States—a
feeling of which Canada was not the cause—in consequence of
the irritation which now exists, owing to the unhappy state of
affairs on this continent, the reciprocity treaty, it seems
probable, is about to be brought to an end—our trade is
hampered by the passport system, and at any moment we may
be deprived of permission to carry our goods through United
States channels—the bonded goods system may be done away
with, and the winter trade through the United States put an
end to.   Our merchants may be obliged to return to the
old system of bringing in during the summer months the
supplies for the whole year.   Ourselves already threatened,
our trade interrupted, our intercourse—political and commercial—destroyed, if we do not take warning now when we
have the opportunity, and while one avenue is threatened to
be closed, open another by taking advantage of the present
arrangement and the desire of the lower provinces to draw
closer the alliance between us, we may suffer commercial and
political disadvantages it may take long for us to overcome.

"The Conference having come to the conclusion that a
legislative union, pure and simple, was impracticable, our next
attempt was to form a government upon federal principles,
which would give to the General Government the strength of
a legislative and administrative union, while at the same time
it preserved that liberty of action for the different sections
which is allowed by a federal union.   And I am strong in the
belief that we have hit upon the happy medium in those
resolutions, and that we have formed a scheme of govern-

ment which unites the advantages of both, giving us the strength of a legislative union and the sectional freedom of a federal union, with protection to local interests. In doing so we had the advantage of the experience of the United States. It is the fashion now to enlarge on the defects of the constitution of the United States, but I am not one of those who look upon it as a failure. (Hear, hear). I think and believe that it is one of the most skilful works which human intelligence ever created; it is one of the most perfect organizations that ever governed a free people. To say that it has some defects is but to say that it is not the work of Omniscience, but of human intellects. We are happily situated in having had the opportunity of watching its operation, seeing its working from its infancy till now. It was in the main formed on the model of the Constitution of Great Britain adapted to the circumstances of a new country, and was, perhaps, the only practicable system that could have been adopted under the circumstances existing at the time of its formation.

"We can now take advantage of the experience of the last seventy-eight years, during which that Constitution has existed, and I am strongly of the belief that we have, in a great measure, avoided in this system, which we propose for the adoption of the people of Canada, the defects which time and events have shown to exist in the American Constitution. In the first place, by a resolution which meets with the universal approval of the people of this country, we have provided that for all time to come, so far as we can legislate for the future, we shall have as the head of the executive power, the Sovereign of Great Britain. (Hear, hear). No one can look into futurity and say what will be the destiny of this country. Changes come over nations and peoples in the course of ages. But, so far as we can legislate, we provide that, for all time to come, the Sovereign of Great Britain shall be the Sovereign of British North America. By adhering to the monarchial principle, we avoid one defect inherent in the constitution of the United States. By the election of the president by a majority and for a short period, he never is the sovereign and chief of the nation. He is never looked up to

by the whole people as the head and front of the nation.
He is at best but the successful leader of a party. This defect
is all the greater on account of the practice of re-election.
During his first term of office he is employed in taking steps
to secure his own re-election and for his party a continuance
of power. We avoid this by adhering to the monarchial
principle—the Sovereign whom you respect and love. I
believe that it is of the utmost importance to have that principle recognized, so that we shall have a sovereign who is
placed above the region of party—to whom all parties look
up—who is not elevated by the action of one party nor
depressed by the action of another, who is the common head
and sovereign of all. (Hear, hear and cheers).

"In the Constitution we propose to continue the system
of responsible government which has existed in this province
since 1841, and which has long obtained in the mother
country. This is a feature of our Constitution as we have it
now, and as we shall have it in the Federation, in which, I
think, we avoid one of the great defects in the constitution of
the United States. There, the president, during his term of
office, is in a great measure a despot, a one man power, with
the command of the naval and military forces, with an immense
amount of patronage as head of the Executive, and with the
veto power as a branch of the Legislature, perfectly uncon-
trolled by responsible advisers, his Cabinet being departmental
officers merely, with whom he is not obliged by the constitution to consult unless he chooses to do so. With us, the
Sovereign, or in this country the representative of the Sovereign, can act only on the advice of his Ministers, those
Ministers being responsible to the people through Parliament.

"Prior to the formation of the American Union, as we all
know, the different states which entered into it were separate
colonies. They had no connection with each other further
than that of having a common sovereign, just as with us at
present. Their constitutions and their laws were different.
They might and did legislate against each other, and when
they revolted against the mother country they acted as
separate sovereignties, and carried on the war by a kind of

treaty of alliance against the common enemy. Ever since the
union was formed the difficulty of what is called 'State
Rights' has existed, and this had much to do in bringing on
the present unhappy war in the United States. They commenced, in fact, at the wrong end. They declared by their
constitution that each state was a sovereignty in itself, and
that all the powers incident to a sovereignty belonged to
each state, except those powers which, by the Constitution,
were conferred upon the General Government and Congress.
Here we have adopted a different system. We have strength-
ened the General Government. We have given the General
Legislature all the great subjects of legislation. We have
conferred on them, not only specifically and in detail, all the
powers which are incident to sovereignty, but we have
expressly declared that all subjects of general interest, not
distinctly and exclusively conferred upon the Local Governments and Local Legislatures, shall be conferred upon the
General Government and Legislature. We have thus avoided
that great source of weakness which has been the cause of the
disruption of the United States. We have avoided all conflict
of jurisdiction and authority, and if this constitution is carried
out, as it will be in full detail in the Imperial Act to be passed
if the colonies adopt the scheme, we will have, in fact, as I
said before, all the advantages of a Legislative union under
one Administration, with, at the same time, the guarantees for
local institutions and for local laws, which are insisted upon
by so many in the provinces now, I hope, to be united.

   "The desire to remain connected with Great Britain, and
to retain our allegiance to Her Majesty, was unanimous. Not
a single suggestion was made that it could, by any possibility,
be for the interests of the colonies, or of any section or portion
of them, that there should be a severence of our connection.
Although we knew it to be possible that Canada, from her
position, might be exposed to all the horrors of war, by
reasons of causes of hostility arising between Great Britain
aud the United States—causes over which we had no control,
and which we had no hand in bringing about—yet there was
a unanimous feeling of willingness to run all the hazards of

war, if war must come, rather than lose the connection between the mother country and these colonies. (Cheers).

"We provide that 'the executive authority shall be administered by the Sovereign personally, or by the representative of the Sovereign duly authorized.' It is too much to expect that the Queen should vouchsafe us her personal governance or presence, except to pay us, as the heir-apparent of the Throne, our future Sovereign, has already paid us, the graceful compliment of a visit. The executive authority must, therefore, be administered by Her Majesty's representative. We place no restriction on Her Majesty's prerogative in the selection of her representative. As it is now, so it will be if this Constitution is adopted. The Sovereign has unrestricted freedom of choice. Whether in making her selection she may send us one of her own family, a Royal Prince, as a Viceroy to rule over us, or one of the great statesmen of England to represent her, we know not. We leave that to Her Majesty in all confidence. But we may be permitted to hope that, when the union takes place, and we become the great country which British North America is certain to be, it will be an object worthy the ambition of the statesmen of England to be charged with presiding over our destinies. (Hear, hear).

"Let me now invite the attention of the House to the provisions in the Constitution respecting the legislative power. The sixth resolution says, 'there shall be a General Legislature or Parliament for the Federated Provinces, composed of a Legislative Council and a House of Commons.' The Legislature of British North America will be composed of Kings, Lords, and Commons. The Legislative Council will stand in the same relation to the Lower House, as the House of Lords to the House of Commons in England, having the same power of initiating all matters of legislation, except the granting of money. As regards the Lower House, it may not appear to matter much, whether it is called the House of Commons or House of Assembly. It will bear whatever name the Parliament of England may choose to give it, but 'The House of Commons' is the name we should prefer, as showing that it represents the Commons of Canada, in the same way that the English House of Commons represents the Commons of England, with the same privileges, the same parliamentary usage, and the same parliamentary authority. In settling the constitution of the Lower House, that which peculiarly represents the people, it was agreed that the principle of representation based on population should be adopted, and the mode of applying that principle is fully developed in these resolutions. When I speak of representation by population, the House will, of course, understand that universal suffrage is not in any way sanctioned, or admitted by these resolutions, as the basis on which the constitution of the popular branch should rest.

"In order to protect local interests, and to prevent sectional jealousies, it was found requisite that the three great divisions into which British North America is separated, should be represented in the Upper House on the principle of equality. There are three great sections, having different interests, in this proposed Confederation. We have Western Canada, an agricultural country far away from the sea, and having the largest population, who have agricultural interests principally to guard. We have Lower Canada, with other and separate interests, and especially with institutions and laws which she jealously guards against absorption by any larger, more numerous, or stronger power. And we have the Maritime Provinces, having also different sectional interests of their own, having, from their position, classes and interests which we do not know in Western Canada. Accordingly, in the Upper House—the controlling and regulating, but not the initiating, branch (for we know that here, as in England, to the Lower House will practically belong the initiation of matters of great public interest), in the House which has the sober second thought in legislation—it is provided that each of those great sections shall be represented equally by twenty-four members. An hereditary Upper House is impracticable in this young country.

"Here we have none of the elements for the formation of a landlord aristocracy—no men of large territorial positions —no class separated from the mass of the people. An

hereditary body is altogether unsuited to our state of society
and would soon dwindle into nothing. The only mode of
adapting the English system to the Upper House, is by
conferring the power of appointment on the Crown (as the
English peers are appointed), but that the appointments
should be for life. The arguments for an elective council
are numerous and strong ; and I ought to say so, as one
of the Administration, responsible for introducing the elective
principle into Canada. (Hear, hear). I hold that this principle had not been a failure in Canada ; but there were causes
—which we did not take into consideration at the time—why,
it did not so fully succeed in Canada as we had expected.
At first, I admit, men of the first standing did come forward,
but we have seen that in every succeeding election in both
Canadas there has been an increasing disinclination, on the
part of men of standing and political experience and weight
in the country, to become candidates ; while, on the other
hand, all the young men, the active politicians, those who
have resolved to embrace the life of a statesman, have sought
entrance to the House of Assembly.

"The nominative system in this country was to a great
extent successful before the introduction of responsible government. Then the Canadas were to a great extent Crown
colonies, and the upper branch of the legislature consisted of
gentlemen chosen from among the chief judicial and ecclesias-
tical dignitaries, the heads of departments, and other men of
the first position in the country. Those bodies commanded
great respect from the character, standing and weight of the
individuals composing them, but they had little sympathy
with the people or their representatives, and collisions with
the Lower House frequently occurred, especially in Lower
Canada. When responsible government was introduced it
became necessary for the Governor of the day to have a body
of advisers who had the confidence of the House of Assembly
which could make or unmake Ministers as it chose. The
Lower House, in effect, pointed out who should be nominated
to the Upper House ; for the Ministry, being dependent altogether on the lower branch of the legislature for support,

selected members for the Upper House from among their political friends at the dictation of the House of Assembly. The Council was becoming less and less a substantial check on the legislation of the Assembly, but under the system now proposed, such will not be the case. No Ministry can in future do what they have done in Canada before. They cannot, with the view of carrying any measure, or of strengthening the party, attempt to over-rule the independent opinion of the Upper House by filling it with a number of its partizans and political supporters. The provision in the Constitution, that the Legislative Council shall consist of a limited number of members, that each of the great sections shall appoint twenty-four members and no more, will prevent the Upper House from being swamped from time to time by the Ministry of the day for the purpose of carrying out their own schemes or pleasing their partizans. The fact of the Government being prevented from exceeding a limited number will preserve the independence of the Upper House, and make it, in reality, a separate and distinct chamber, having a legitimate and controlling influence in the legislation of the country.

" The objection has been taken, that, in consequence of the Crown being deprived of the right of unlimited appointment, there is a chance of a dead-lock arising between the two branches of the Legislature, a chance that the Upper House, being altogether independent of the Sovereign, of the Lower House, and of the advisers of the Crown, may act independently, and so independently as to produce a dead-lock. I do not anticipate any such result. In the first place we know that in England it does not arise. There would be no use of an Upper House if it did not exercise, when it thought proper, the right of opposing or amending or postponing the legislation of the Lower House. It would be of no value whatever were it a mere chamber for registering the decrees of the Lower House. It must be an independent House, having a free action of its own, for it is only valuable as being a regulating body, calmly considering the legislation initiated by the popular branch, and preventing any hasty or ill-con-

sidered legislation which may come from that body, but it will
never set itself in opposition against the deliberate and
understood wishes of the people. Even the House of Lords,
which as an hereditary body is far more independent than one
appointed for life can be ; whenever it ascertains what is the
calm, deliberate will of the people of England, yields, and
never in modern times has there been, in fact or act, any
attempt to over-rule the decisions of that House by the
appointment of new peers, excepting, perhaps, once in the
reign of Queen Anne.

" In this country, we must remember, that the gentlemen
who will be selected for the Legislative Council, stand on a
very different footing from the peers of England. They have
not, like them, any ancestral associations or position derived
from history. They have not that direct influence on the
people themselves, or on the popular branch of the legislature,
which the peers of England exercise, from their great wealth,
their vast territorial possessions, their numerous tenantry, and
that prestige with which the exalted position of their class for
centuries has invested them. (Hear, hear). The members of
our Upper House will be, like those of the Lower, men of the
people, and from the people. The man put into the Upper
House is as much a man of the people the day after, as the
day before his elevation. Springing from the people, and one
of them, he takes his seat in the Council with all the sympathies and feelings of a man of the people, and when he
returns home at the end of the session, he mingles with them
on equal terms, and is influenced by the same feelings and
associations and events, as those which affect the mass around
him. And is it then to be supposed that the members of the
upper branch of the Legislature will set themselves deliberate
ly at work to oppose what they know to be the settled
opinions and wishes of the people of the country ? They will
not do it. There is no fear of a dead-lock between the two
Houses. There is an infinitely greater chance of a dead-lock
between the two branches of the Legislature, should the
elective principle be adopted, than with a nominated Chamber
chosen by the Crown, and having no mission from the people.

The members of the Upper Chamber would then come from the people as well as those of the Lower House, and should any difference ever arise between both branches, the former could say to the members of the popular branch : ' We as much represent the feelings of the people as you do, and even more so ; we are not elected from small localities and for a short period ; you as a body were elected at a particular time, when the public mind was running in a particular channel ; you were returned to Parliament, not so much representing the general views of the country on general questions, as upon the particular subjects which happened to engage the minds of the people when they went to the polls. We have as much right, or a better right, than you to be considered as representing the deliberate will of the people on general questions, and therefore we will not give way.' (Hear, hear). There is, I repeat, a greater danger of an irreconcilable difference of opinion between the two branches of the Legislature, if the Upper be elective, than if it holds its commission from the Crown.

" Besides, it must be remembered that an Upper House, the members of which are to be appointed for life, would not have the same quality of permanence as the House of Lords ; our members would die ; strangers would succeed them, whereas son succeeded father in the House of Lords. Thus the changes in the membership and state of opinion in our Upper House would always be more rapid than in the House of Lords. To show how speedily changes have occurred in the Upper House, as regards life members, I will call the attention of the House to the following facts :—At the call of the House in February, 1856, forty-two life members responded ; two years afterwards, in 1858, only thirty-five answered to their names ; in 1862 there were only twenty-five life members left, and in 1864, but twenty-one. (Hear, hear). This shows how speedily changes take place in the life membership. But, remarkable as this change has been, it is not so great as that in regard to the elected members. Though the elective principle only came into force in 1856, and although only twelve men were elected that year and twelve more every two years since, twenty-four changes have already taken place by the decease of members, by the acceptance of office, and by resignation. So it is quite clear that, should there be on any question a difference of opinion between the Upper and Lower Houses, the Government of the day being obliged to have the confidence of the majority in the popular branch, would, for the purpose of bringing the former into accord and sympathy with the latter, fill up any vacancies that might occur with men of the same political feelings and sympathies with the Government, and consequently with those of the majority in the popular branch ; and all the appointments of the Administration would be made with the object of maintaining the sympathy and harmony between the two Houses. (Hear, hear).

"There is this additional advantage to be expected from the limitation. To the Upper House is to be confided the protection of sectional interests ; therefore is it that the three great divisions are there equally represented, for the purpose of defending such interests against the combinations of majorities in the Assembly. It will, therefore, become the interest of each section to be represented by its very best men, and the members of the Administration who belong to each section will see that such men are chosen, in case of a vacancy in their section.

" In the formation of the House of Commons, the principle of representation by population has been provided for in a manner equally ingenious and simple. The introduction of this principle presented at first the apparent difficulty of a constantly increasing body, until, with the increasing population, it would become inconveniently and expensively large. But by adopting the representation of Lower Canada as a fixed standard—as the pivot on which the whole would turn— that province being the best suited for the purpose, on account of the comparatively permanent character of its population, and from its having neither the largest nor least number of inhabitants, we have been enabled to overcome the difficulty I have mentioned. We have introduced the system of repre-

sentation by population without the danger of an inconvenient
increase in the number of representatives on the recurrence of
each decennial period. The whole thing is worked by a simple
rule of three. For instance, we have in Upper Canada
1,400,000 of a population ; in Lower Canada 1,100,000. Now,
the proposition is simply this, if Lower Canada, with its
population of 1,100,000, has a right to sixty-five members, how
many members should Upper Canada have, with its larger
population of 1,400,000 ? The same rule applies to the other
provinces, the proportion is always observed, and the principle
of representation by population carried out, while, at the same
time, there will not be decennially an inconvenient increase in
the members of the Lower House. At the same time there is
a constitutional provision that hereafter, if deemed advisable,
the total number of representatives may be increased from
194, the number fixed in the first instance. In that case, if an
increase is made, Lower Canada is still to remain the pivot on
which the whole calculation will turn. If Lower Canada,
instead of sixty-five, shall have seventy members, then the
calculation will be, if Lower Canada has seventy members,
with such a population, how many shall Upper Canada have
with a larger population ?

"I was in favour of a larger House than 194,
but was overruled. I was, perhaps, singular in the
opinion, but I thought it would be well to commence with
a larger representation in the lower branch. The arguments
against this were, that, in the first place, it would cause
additional expense ; in the next place, that in a new country
like this, we could not get a sufficient number of qualified men
to be representatives. My reply was that the number is
rapidly increasing as we increase in education and wealth :
that a larger field would be open to political ambition by
having a larger body of representatives ; that by having
numerous and smaller constituencies, more people would be
interested in the working of the union, and that there would be
a wider field for selection for leaders of governments and the
leaders of parties. These are my individual sentiments, which,
perhaps, I have no right to express here, but I was overruled,

and we fixed on the number of 194, which no one will say is large or extensive, when it is considered that our present number in Canada alone is 130. The difference between 130 and 194 is not great, considering the large increase that will be made to our population when Confederation is carried into effect.

"While the principle of representation by population is adopted with respect to the popular branch of the Legislature, not a single member of the conference, as I stated before, not a single one of the representatives of the Government or of the Opposition, or any one of the Lower Provinces, was in favour of universal suffrage. Every one felt that in this respect the principle of the British Constitution should be carried out, and that classes and property should be represented as well as numbers. Insuperable difficulties would have presented themselves if we had attempted to settle now the qualification for the elective franchise. We have different laws in each of the colonies, fixing the qualification of electors for their own local legislatures ; and we therefore adopted a similar clause to that which is contained in the Canada Union Act of 1841, viz., that all the laws which affected the qualification of members and of voters, which effected the appointment and conduct of returning officers, and the proceedings at elections, as well as the trial of controverted elections in the separate provinces, should obtain in the first election to the Confederate Parliament, so that every man who has now a vote in his own province should continue to have a vote in choosing a representative to the first Federal Parliament. And it was left to the Parliament of the Confederation, as one of their first duties, to consider and to settle by an act of their own the qualification for the elective franchise, which would apply to the whole Confederation.

"In considering the question of the duration of Parliament, we came to the conclusion to recommend a period of five years. I was in favour of a longer period. I thought that the duration of the Local Legislatures should not be shortened so as to be less than four years, as at present, and that the General Parliament should have as long a duration

as that of the United Kingdom. I was willing to have gone
to the extent of seven years ; but a term of five years was
preferred, and we had the example of New Zealand carefully
considered, not only locally, but by the Imperial Parliament,
and which gave the Provinces of those Islands a General
Parliament with a duration of five years. But it was a
matter of little importance whether five years or seven years
was the term, the power of dissolution by the Crown having
been reserved. I find, on looking at the duration of Parliaments since the accession of George III. to the Throne,
that excluding the present Parliament, there have been seventeen Parliaments, the average period of whose existence has
been about three years and a half. That average is less
than the average duration of the Parliaments in Canada since
the Union, so that it was not a matter of much importance
whether we fixed upon five or seven years as the period of
duration of our General Parliament. In short, this Parliament shall settle what shall be the different constituencies
electing members to the first Federal Parliament. And so
the other provinces, the Legislatures of which will fix the
limits of their several constituencies in the session in which
they adopt the new constitution. Afterwards the Local Legislatures may alter their own electoral limits as they please,
for their own local elections. But it would evidently be
improper to leave to the Local Legislatures the power to
alter the constituencies sending members to the General
Legislature after the General Legislature shall have been
called into existence. Were this the case, a member of the
General Legislature might at any time find himself ousted
from his seat by an alteration of his constituency by the
Local Legislature in his section.

"I shall not detain the House by entering into a consideration at any length of the different powers conferred
upon the General Parliament as contradistinguished from
those reserved to the Local Legislatures ; but any honourable
member, on examining the list of different subjects which
are to be assigned to the General and Local Legislatures
respectively, will see that all the great questions which affect

the general interests of the Confederacy as a whole, are confided to the Federal Parliament, while the local interests and local laws of each section are preserved intact, and intrusted to the care of the local bodies. As a matter of course, the General Parliament must have the power of dealing with the public debt and property of the Confederation. Of course, too, it must have the regulation of trade and commerce, of customs and excise. The Federal Parliament must have the sovereign power of raising money from such sources and by such means as the representatives of the people will allow.

"It will be seen that the Local Legislatures have the control of all local works ; and it is a matter of great importance, and one of the chief advantages of the Federal Union and of Local Legislatures, that each province will have the power and means of developing its own resources and aiding its own progress, after its own fashion and in its own way. Therefore, all the local improvements, all local enterprises or undertakings of any kind, have been left to the care and management of the Local Legislatures of each province. (Cheers).

"It is provided that all 'lines of steam or other ships, railways, canals and other works, connecting any two or more of the Provinces together, or extending beyond the limits of any province,' shall belong to the General Government and be under the control of the General Legislature. In like manner, 'lines of steamships between the Federated Provinces and other countries, telegraph communication and the incorporation of telegraph companies, and all such works as shall, although lying within any province, be specially declared by the Acts authorizing them, to be for the general advantage,' shall belong to the General Government. For instance, the Welland Canal, though lying wholly within one section, and the St. Lawrence Canals in two only, may be properly considered national works, and for the general benefit of the whole Federation. Again, the census, the ascertaining of our numbers and the extent of our resources, must, as a matter of general interest, belong to the General

Government. So also with the defences of the country. One of the great advantages of Confederation is, that we shall have a united, a concerted, and uniform system of defence. (Hear). We are at this moment with a different militia system in each Colony—in some of the Colonies with an utter want of any system of defence. We have a number of separate staff establishments, without any arrangement between the colonies as to the means, either of defence or offence. But, under the Union, we will have one system of defence and one system of militia organization. In the event of the Lower Provinces being threatened, we can send the large militia forces of Upper Canada to their rescue. Should we have to fight on our lakes against a foreign foe, we will have the hardy seamen of the Lower Provinces coming to our assistance and manning our vessels. (Hear, hear). We will have one system of defence and be one people, acting together alike, in times of peace and in war. (Cheers).

"The criminal law, too,—the determination of what is a crime and what is not, and how crime shall be punished —is left to the General Government. This is a matter almost of necessity. It is of great importance that we should have the same criminal law throughout the Provinces—that what is a crime in one part of British America, should be a crime in every part—that there should be the same protection of life and property in one as in another. It is one of the defects in the United States system, that each separate state has or may have a criminal code of its own—that what may be a capital offence in one state, may be a venial offence, punishable slightly, in another. But, under our Constitution, we shall have one body of criminal law based on the criminal law of England, and operating equally throughout British America, so that a British American, belonging to what province he may, or going to any other part of the Confederation, knows what his rights are in that respect, and what his punishment will be if an offender against the criminal laws of the land. I think this is one of the most marked instances in which we take advantage of the experience derived from our observations of the defects in the Constitution of the neighbouring Republic. (Hear, hear).

" The thirty-third provision is of very great importance to the future well-being of these colonies. It commits to the General Parliament the 'rendering uniform all or any of the laws relative to property and civil rights in Upper Canada, Nova Scotia, New Brunswick, Newfoundland and Prince Edward Island, and rendering uniform the procedure of all or any of the courts of these provinces.' The great principles which govern the laws of all the provinces, with the single exception of Lower Canada, are the same, although there may be a divergence in details, and it is gratifying to find, on the part of the Lower Provinces, a general desire to join together with Upper Canada in this matter, and to procure, as soon as possible, an assimilation of the statutory laws and the procedure in the courts, of all these provinces. At present there is a good deal of diversity. In one of the colonies, for instance, they have no municipal system at all. In another, the municipal system is merely permissive, and has not been adopted to any extent. Although, therefore, a legislative union was found to be almost impracticable, it was understood, so far as we could influence the future, that the first act of the Confederation Government should be to procure an assimilation of a statutory law of all those provinces, which has, as its root and foundation, the common law of England. But to prevent local interests from being over-ridden, the same section makes provision, that, while power is given to the General Legislature to deal with this subject, no change in this respect should have the force and authority of law in any province until sanctioned by the Legislature of that province. (Hear, hear).

" The General Legislature is to have power to establish a General Court of Appeal for the federated provinces. Although the Canadian Legislature has always had the power to establish a Court of Appeal, to which appeals may be made from the Courts of Upper and Lower Canada, we have never availed ourselves of the power. Upper Canada has its own Court of Appeal, so has Lower Canada. And this system will continue until a General Court of Appeal shall be estab-

lished by the General Legislature   The Constitution does
not provide that such a court shall be established.   There are
many arguments for and against the establishment of such a
court.   But it was thought wise and expedient to put into the
Constitution a power to the General Legislature, that, if after
full consideration they think it advisable to establish a General
Court of Appeal from all the Superior Courts of all the
provinces, they may do so.   (Hear, hear).

"I shall not go over the other powers that are conferred
on the General Parliament.   Most of them refer to matters of
financial and commercial interest, and I leave those subjects
in other and better hands.   Besides all the powers that are
specially given in the thirty-seventh and last item of this
portion of the Constitution, confers on the General Legislature the general mass of sovereign legislation, the power to
legislate on 'all matters of a general character, not specially
and exclusively reserved for the Local Governments and Legislatures'   This it precisely the provision which is wanting in
the Constitution of the United States.   It is here that we find
the weakness of the American system—the point where the
American Constitution breaks down.   (Hear, hear).   It is in
itself a wise and necessary provision.   We thereby strengthen
the central Parliament and make the Confederation one
people and one government, instead of five peoples and five
governments, with merely a point of authority connecting us
to a limited and insufficient extent.

"With respect to the Local Governments, it is provided that
each shall be governed by a chief executive officer, who shall
be nominated by the General Government.   As this is to be
one united province, with the Local Governments and Legislatures subordinate to the General Government and Legislature,
it is obvious that the chief executive officer in each of the
provinces must be subordinate as well.   The General Government assumes towards the Local Governments precisely the
same position as the Imperial Government holds with respect
to each of the colonies now, so that as the Lieutenant-
Governor of each of the different provinces is now appointed
directly by the Queen, and is directly responsible and reports

THE EARL OF DUFFERIN, K.P., K.C.B., G.C.M.G. (*Lord Dufferin*).
(*Governor-General from June 25, 1872, until October 18, 1878*).

directly to her, so will the Executives of the Local Governments hereafter be subordinate to the representative of the Queen and be responsible and report to him.

"There are numerous subjects which belong, of right, both to the Local and the General Parliaments. In all these cases it is provided, in order to prevent a conflict of authority, that where there is concurrent jurisdiction in the General and Local Parliaments, the same rule should apply as now applies in cases where there is concurrent jurisdiction in the Imperial and in the Provincial Parliaments, and that when the legislation of the one is adverse to or contradictory of the legislation of the other, in all such cases the action of the General Parliament must overrule, *ex-necessitate*, the action of the Local Legislature. (Hear, hear).

"We have introduced also all those provisions which are necessary in order to the full working out of the British Constitution in these provinces. We provide that there shall be no money votes, unless those votes are introduced in the popular branch of the Legislature on the authority of the responsible advisers of the Crown—those with whom the responsibility rests of equalizing revenue and expenditure—that there can be no expenditure or authorization of expenditure by Address or in any other way unless initiated by the Crown on the advice of its responsible advisers. (Hear, hear).

"The last resolution of any importance is one which, although not affecting the substance of the Constitution, is of interest to us all. Is it that ' Her Majesty the Queen be solicited to determine the rank and name of the federated provinces?' I do not know whether there will be any expression of opinion in this House on this subject, whether we are to be a vice-royalty, or whether we are still to retain our name and rank as a province. But I have no doubt Her Majesty will give the matter her gracious consideration, that she will give us a name satisfactory to us all, and that the rank she will confer upon us will be a rank worthy of our position, of our resources, and of our future. (Cheers).

"One argument, but not a strong one, has been used against this Confederation, that it is an advance towards independence. Some are apprehensive that the very fact of our forming this Union will hasten the time when we shall be severed from the mother country. I have no apprehension of that kind. I believe it will have the contrary effect. I believe that as we grow stronger, that, as it is felt in England we have become a people, able from our union, our strength, our population, and the development of our resources, to take our position among the nations of the world, she will be less willing to part with us than she would be now, when we are broken up into a number of insignificant colonies, subject to attack piece-meal without any concerted action or common organization of defence. I am strongly of opinion that year by year, as we grow in population and in strength, England will more see the advantages of maintaining the alliance between British North America and herself. Does anyone imagine that, when our population instead of three and a half, will be seven millions, as it will be ere many years pass, we would be one whit more willing than now to sever the connection with England? Would not those seven millions be just as anxious to maintain their allegiance to the Queen and their connection with the mother country as we are now? Will the addition to our numbers of the people of the Lower Provinces, in any way lessen our desire to continue our connection with the mother country? I believe the people of Canada east and west, to be truly loyal. But, if they can by possibility be exceeded in loyalty, it is by the inhabitants of the Maritime Provinces. Loyalty with them is an over-ruling passion. (Hear, hear). In all parts of the Lower Provinces there is a rivalry between the opposing political parties as to which shall most strongly express and most effectively carry out the principle of loyalty to Her Majesty and to the British Crown. (Hear, hear).

" When this union takes place, we will be at the outset no inconsiderable people. And with a rapidly increasing population—for I am satisfied that under this union our population will increase in a still greater ratio than ever before—with increased credit—with a higher position in the eyes of Europe —with the increased security we can offer to immigrants, who would naturally prefer to seek a new home in what is known to them as a great country, than in any one little colony or another—with all this I am satisfied that, great as has been our increase in the last twenty-five years since the union between Upper and Lower Canada, our future progress, during the next quarter of a century, will be vastly greater. (Cheers). And when, by means of this rapid increase, we become a nation of eight or nine millions of inhabitants, our alliance will be worthy of being sought by the great nations of the earth. Hear, hear). I am proud to believe that our desire for a permanent alliance will be reciprocated in England. I know that there is a party in England—but it is inconsiderable in numbers, though strong in intellect and power—which speaks of the desirability of getting rid of the colonies, but I believe such is not the feeling of the statesmen and the people of England. I believe it will never be the deliberately expressed determination of the Government of Great Britain. (Hear, hear).

" The colonies are now in a transition state. Gradually a different colonial system is being developed—and it will become, year by year, less a case of dependence on our part, and of over-ruling protection on the part of the mother country, and more a case of a healthy and cordial alliance. Instead of looking upon us merely as a dependent colony, England will have in us a friendly nation—a subordinate, but still a powerful people—to stand by her in North America in peace or in war. (Cheers). The people of Australia will be such another subordinate nation. And England will have this advantage, if her colonies progress under the new colonial system, as I believe they will, that, though at war with all the rest of the world, she will be able to look to the subordinate nations in alliance with her, and owing allegiance to the same Sovereign, who will assist in enabling her again to meet the whole world in arms, as she has done before. (Cheers). And if, in the great Napoleonic war, with every port in Europe closed against her commerce, she was yet able to hold her own, how much more will that be the case when she has a colonial empire rapidly increasing in power, in wealth, in influence, and in position. (Hear, hear). It is true that we stand in danger, as we have stood in danger again and again in Canada, of being plunged into war, and suffering all its dreadful consequences, as the result of causes over which we have no control, by reason of their connection. This, however, did not intimidate us. At the very mention of the prospect of a war some time ago, how were the feelings of the people aroused from one extremity of British America to the other, and preparations were made for meeting its worst consequences. Although the people of this country are fully aware of the horrors of war—should a war arise, unfortunately, between the United States and England, and we all pray it never may—they are still ready to encounter all perils of that kind, for the sake of the connection with England. There is not one adverse voice, not one adverse opinion on that point.

"We all feel the advantages we derive from our connection with England. So long as that alliance is maintained, we enjoy, under her protection, the privileges of constitutional liberty according to the British system. We will enjoy here that which is the great test of constitutional freedom—we will have the rights of the minority respected. (Hear, hear). In all countries the rights of the majority take care of themselves, but it is only in countries like England, enjoying constitutional liberty, and safe from the tyranny of a single despot or of an unbridled democracy, that the rights of minorities are regarded. So long, too, as we form a portion of the British Empire we shall have the example of her free institutions, of the high standard of the character of her statesmen and public men, of the purity of her legislation, and the upright administration of her laws. In this younger country one great advantage of our connection with Great Britain will be, that, under her auspices, inspired by her example, a portion of her empire, our public men will be actuated by principles similar to those which actuate the statesmen at home. These, although not material physical benefits, of which you can make an arithmetical calculation, are of such overwhelming advantage to our future interests and standing as a nation, that to obtain

them is well worthy of any sacrifice we may be called upon
to make, and the people of this country are ready to make
them. (Cheers).

"We should feel, also, sincerely grateful to a beneficent
Providence that we have had the opportunity vouchsafed us
of calmly considering this great constitutional change, this
peaceful revolution—that we have not been hurried into it,
like the United States, by the exigencies of war—that we have
not had a violent revolutionary period forced on us, as in
other nations, by hostile action from without, or by domestic
dissensions from within. Here we are in peace and prosperity,
under the fostering government of Great Britain—a dependent
people, with a government having only a limited and delegated
authority, and yet allowed, without restriction, and without
jealousy on the part of the mother country, to legislate for
ourselves, and peacefully and deliberately to consider and
determine the future of Canada and of British North America.

"It is our happiness to know the expression of the will of
our gracious Sovereign, through her Ministers, that we have
her full sanction for our deliberations, that her only solicitude
is that we shall adopt a system which shall be really for our
advantage, and that she promises to sanction whatever conclusion, after full deliberation we may arrive at, as to the best
mode of securing the well-being—the present and future
prosperity of British America. (Cheers). It is our privilege
and happiness to be in such a position, and we cannot be too
grateful for the blessings thus conferred upon us. (Hear,
hear). In conclusion, I would again implore the House not to
let this opportunity pass. It is an opportunity that may
never recur. If we do not take advantage of the time ; if we
show ourselves unequal to the occasion, it may never return,
and we shall hereafter bitterly and unavailingly regret having
failed to embrace the happy opportunity now offered of
founding a great nation under the fostering care of Great
Britain, and our Sovereign Lady, Queen Victoria."

Many other able speeches were made by leading men on
both sides, until the whole subject was thoroughly exhausted.
The attack on the Government propositions was led by the

Honourable A. A. Dorion, who moved an amendment to the Twelvth Resolution, "that the people of this province neither wish nor seek a new nationality." What he desired to convey by this can only be conjectured, as he did not offer any argument in support, but, taken in connection with the manifesto issued by him, as soon as the proposed new constitution was made public, it was thought at the time that his desire was to alarm the jealousy of the French-Canadians, and thus create opposition to the Union of Canada and the Lower Provinces. The views of the House, however, were in harmony with those of the Government, and the resolutions were carried by a vote of 91 to 33.

On March 18th Parliament was prorogued, and in the following month a deputation, composed of the Honourables John A. Macdonald, George E. Cartier, George Brown and A. T. Galt, proceeded to England to confer with the Home Government on the matter of Confederation.

CHAPTER XXVI.

1865-67.

IN the Maritime Provinces, and especially in Nova Scotia, a determined opposition to the project of Confederation was offered by a portion of the press, and a section of the people led by the Honourable Joseph Howe, a man of great ability, and who wielded an immense influence and used every possible effort to prevent the scheme being carried into effect. To meet the arguments thus advanced, many others offered their views in the press and on the platform, and, of these, there were none whose opinions carried greater weight or received more attention than those of Archbishop Connolly in reply to the *Halifax Morning Chronicle.* Both on account of its intrinsic merit and also of the dignified position of the Right Rev. writer, the letter received a wide circulation, and did much in directing the public mind in the proper direction. We give the following extracts :—

"If one-half of what you say about Fenians and armed and hostile organizations in a neighbouring country be true, which I do not contradict, some or many of our Catholic Churches, with or without our consent, may be turned into drill-rooms—but if I know anything of the Catholic body in this country, I vouch for it, they will never be used for the purposes of pretended loyalists and sympathizers, or the foreign foe, and much less for the Fenian Brotherhood on their quixotic expedition, unless, indeed, it be to help them in finding and filling up these much talked of and mysterious coffins from which, according to you, Mr. Editor, their muskets are to be supplied.

" If half what you say be true (although I am no politician), on the strength of your own argument, I say the
sooner we are confederated the better. If the maxim be
universally admitted that Union is strength, no time is to
be lost, for in your hypothesis we will at once require all
the elements of strength at our command, and (may a kind
Providence forbid) perhaps more too.

" To leave Upper and Lower Canada and New Brunswick
to their fate, as you propose, and to fall back on the impregnable ramparts of Nova Scotia, with a militia of fifty thousand
men, and a nucleus of a British army of thirty or forty thous-
and, is precisely what an American or our worst enemy
would suggest if a war were to commence to-morrow. Wait
until Upper and Lower Canada and New Brunswick be
swallowed up one after another ; wait until we shall have
detached three millions of fellow subjects—good men and
true—from their allegiance to Britain, and added them to
the numberless hordes of the enemy already comprising the
population of almost a whole continent ; wait until we have
two or three hundred thousand men, succeeded by as many
more, if need be, on our frontier line, at Amherst, or per-
chance at the head of the Basin, or the Three Mile House,
and then what you say about the advantages of responsible
government and the blessings of isolation and the strength
of a militia of fifty thousand, will be our never failing resource
against every calamity.

" Sir, either there is, or there is not, danger, or, in other
words, either the nation on our borders has or has not the
power to pull down our flag and destroy us as a people. If
they have the power, then good intentions and inclinations
are a matter of no importance whatever. We are, then, living
only on sufferance, on mere toleration. Our lives and liberties,
and the means of paying $4.10 taxes, and everything we hold
most dear, are staked on a haphazard, on which no man can
calculate, and no nation can or ought to depend for a single
week.

" If there be 50,000 men already prepared to invade this
country, as you admit, instead of labouring to keep us in our

present disjointed and defenceless position, you should rather call on all to unite where a single man cannot be dispensed with and gird on our armour for the *rencontre*. If responsible government, which the great and good men of this country won for us, be a precious heirloom on the Liliputian scale, on which we now find it, instead of bartering it away for nothing by Confederation, as you say, we shall rather, in my opinion, add to its lustre and value, and ennoble and enrich it, and make it boundlessly grander and more secure for ourselves and those who are to come after us. We obtained responsible government from the mother country, in whose legislative halls we had not a single member to represent us. We are now, on the contrary, asked to transfer the rich and prized deposit to a place which will be a part only of our common country, where our voice must be heard, and where we will have a fuller and fairer representation than the city of London, or Liverpool, or Bristol, can boast of in their English House of Commons; and this is the great difference between obtaining from England what we had not and transferring what we now have, in order to make it more valuable and more available for our own purpose, and, by far, more secure. Confederation, therefore, instead of depriving us of the privileges of self-government, is the only practical and reliable guarantee for its continuance. We are too small to be warranted in the hope of being able to hold it always on the strength of our own resources, and England, if not too weak, is certainly too prudent and too cautious to risk her last shilling and her last man to a country where, instead of a population of 4,000,000, she will have scarcely one-tenth of that number to help her against the united power of a whole continent. To deny, therefore, the obvious advantages of Confederation, you must first prove that union is not strength —that England, under the Hierarchy, and France, under her feudal chains and Barons, were greater and stronger and happier than they now are as the two greatest nations of the world. You must prove that Lucerne, and Geneva, and Berne and the Grisons would be equally strong and secure out of the confederation of their sister cantons in Switzerland; and that Florida, and Texas, and Delaware and Little Rhode Island, in the neighbouring States, would be stronger if detached from each other. You must prove that the petty and miserable republics of Central America, with all their responsible government, and entire exemption from foreign control, are in any way benefitted by their smallness and isolation, and their reluctance to coalesce and form one strong government as the only possible guarantee for the lives and liberties and happiness of all.

" On the principle that the part is greater than the whole, you must prove that the smaller the state, the greater, and stronger, and happier the people ; and that on your own principle the repeal of the Union at the present moment would be a signal benefit to Cape Briton, and Yarmouth, and Shelburne, where they have far stronger local reasons for being dissatisfied with the central government in Halifax than Nova Scotia can ever have for being united, with Ottawa as its capital, and the boundless British territory beyond our borders. Prove all this if you can, and without referring to the financial and commercial views at all, which are completely beyond and beside the question, you will convert me and thousands like me in Nova Scotia to the policy of having a large and effective militia, and paying heavy taxes for the debt already contracted and the two contemplated railroads, and we shall contentedly settle down according to your scheme within no hope within our natural lifetime of having an intercolonial railroad or more frequent intercourse with our sister colonies and the vast country that extends for thousands of miles along their borders.

" I yield to no man in my heartfelt appreciation of the blessings we all enjoy in this country, and I ask for nothing more but to be able to calculate on their continuance—*Sed hoc opus hic labor est.* This is the difficulty, and I will say with all candour the only difficulty for me and all others who have everthing to lose. No country situated as Nova Scotia now is, with a vast area and sparse population, can reasonably hope to maintain its independence for any considerable period. Unless we are to be a single exception, and an anomaly in the history of nations, some change must come, and come soon. In a word, Mr. Editor, as you say, 'Something must be done.'

"Instead of cursing like the boys in the upturned boat, and holding on until we are fairly on the brink of the cataract, we must at once begin to pray and strike out for the shore by all means, before we get too far down on the current. We must, at this most critical moment, invoke the Arbiter of Nations for wisdom, and, abandoning in time our perilous position, we must strike out boldly, and at some risk, for some rock on the nearest shore—some resting place of greater security. A cavalry raid visit from our Fenian friends on horseback through the plains of Canada, and the fertile valleys of New Brunswick and Nova Scotia, may cost more in a single week than Confederation for the next fifty years ; and if we are to believe you, where is the security, even at the present moment, against such a disaster. Without the whole power of the mother country by land and sea, and the concentration in a single hand of all the strength of British America, our condition is seen at a glance. Whenever the present difficulties will terminate—and who can tell the moment ?—we will be at the mercy of our neighbours ; and, victorious or otherwise, they will be eminently a military people, and with all their apparent indifference about annexing this country, and all the friendly feelings that may be talked, they will have the power to strike when they please, and this is precisely the kernel and the only touch-point of the whole question. No nation ever had the power of conquest that did not use it, or abuse it, at the very first favourable opportunity.

"All that is said of the magnanimity and forbearance of mighty nations can be explained on the principle of sheer expediency, as the world knows. The whole face of Europe has changed, and the dynasties of many hundred years have been swept away within our time on the principle of might alone—the oldest, the strongest, and, as some would have it, the most sacred of titles. The thirteen original States of America, with all their professions of self-denial, have been all the time, by money-power and by war, and by negotiation, extending their frontier, until they more than quadrupled their territory within sixty years ; and, believe it who may, are they now of their own accord to come to a full stop ? No; as long as they have power they must go onward, for it is the very nature of power to grip whatever is within its reach. It is not their hostile feelings, therefore, but it is their power, and only their power I dread, and I now state it as my solemn conviction, that it becomes the duty of every British subject in these provinces to control that power, not by the insane policy of attacking or weakening them, but by strengthening ourselves—rising, with the whole of Britain at our back, to their level; and so be prepared for any emergency. There is no sensible or unprejudiced man in the community who does not see that vigorous and timely preparation is the only possible means of saving us from the horrors of war such as the world has never seen. To be fully prepared is the only practical argument that can have weight with a powerful enemy, and make him pause beforehand and count the cost. And, as the sort of preparation I speak of is utterly hopeless without the union of the provinces, so at a moment when public opinion is being formed on this vital point, as one deeply concerned, I feel it a duty to declare myself unequivocally in favour of Confederation as cheaply and as honourably obtained as possibe, but Confederation at all hazards and at all reasonable sacrifices.

"After the most mature consideration, and all the arguments I have heard on both sides for the last month, these are my inmost convictions on the necessity and merits of a measure, which alone, under Providence, can secure to us social order and peace, and rational liberty, and all the blessings we now enjoy under the mildest government, and the hallowed institutions of the freest and happiest country in the world."

Parliament met in Quebec, for the last time, on August 8th. The Premier, Sir E. P. Tache, having died on July 30th, a re-organization of the Cabinet became necessary. The Honourable John A. Macdonald was called upon to perform the duty by His Excellency, but objection being

raised by Mr. George Brown, he waived his claims, as also
did Mr. Cartier, and Sir Narcisse Belleau, a member of the
Legislative Council, became Premier. So much has been
said in these pages of Sir Etienne Paschal Tache that it is
only necessary to add that he was born in St. Thomas, below
Quebec, in 1795, and consequently was seventy years of age.
He was not a man of showy qualities or brilliant talents,
but was the most loyal and self-sacrificing of colleagues and
thoroughly devoted to the interests of Britain in America.
He was Aide-de-Camp to the Queen, held the honorary
rank of a Colonel in the army and was a Knight in the
Roman Order of St. Gregory. He had, previous to entering Parliament, filled the positions of Deputy Adjutant-
General of Militia, Government Director of the Grand Trunk
Railway, member of the Board of Railway Commissioners,
and member of the Board of Education for Lower Canada.

The despatches laid upon the table of the House
expressed the willingness of the Imperial Government to
assist in carrying out the scheme of Confederation, and the
report of the delegates being received, and the necessary
measures carried through, Parliament was prorogued.

It had for some time been very evident that the United
States Government had determined upon putting an end to
the Reciprocity Treaty negotiated in 1854.

The fifth article of that Treaty provided that : "The
Treaty shall remain in force for ten years from the date
at which it may come into operation, and further, until the
expiration of twelve months after either of the high contracting parties shall give notice to the other of its wish
to terminate the same ; each of the high contracting parties
being at liberty to give such notice to the other at the
end of the said term of ten years or at any time afterwards."

The Treaty came into operation on March 16, 1855, and
consequently the earliest date which it could be made to
expire was March 16, 1866.

In May, 1864, the House of Representatives took up the
matter with great earnestness and the debates indicated that
strong views were entertained, both as to its abrogation and

retention. Those who desired to see the treaty at an end seemed imbued with the idea that Canada had done something for which her people should be punished, that without the treaty they could not exist, but must perish miserably, or join their lot to that of the United States. They were not in a humour to settle the question upon purely commercial grounds; considerations, such as these, were, for the time, subordinate to the political interests. On the other hand the Boston Board of Trade and other commercial bodies together with such leading papers as the *New York Herald*, concurred in the view that the balance of advantage was, altogether on the side of the Americans and, therefore, that the treaty should be retained. Some idea of the arguments advanced in the House of Representatives will be gathered from the following extracts from the debates:—

"The House proceeded, as the regular order of business, to the consideration of a joint resolution (H.R. No. 56) authorizing the President to give the requisite notice for terminating the treaty made by Great Britain on behalf of the British Provinces in North America, and to appoint Commissioners to negotiate a new treaty with the British Government, based upon the true principle of Reciprocity.

Mr. Baxter—"The question before this House, as now presented, is whether a notice to terminate this treaty, called the Reciprocity Treaty, shall be given pure and simple, or whether it shall be diluted to a milk-and-water consistency. This Reciprocity Treaty, so called, is a misnomer entirely. After the people of Great Britain became dissatisfied with taxing themselves for the benefit of the Colonies, and after the corn laws were repealed, it became necessary that that Government should be supplied with breadstuffs from some other quarter. Immediately the question was agitated in Canada, and men were sent here to make proffers to our Government, pretending that they had something to give for what they asked in return. General Taylor's Cabinet, with Mr. Preston, of Virginia, in it, gave it no heed whatever, beyond a proper examination, declaring that they had no constitutional right to make such a treaty or compact; and, in the next place, to do it would be impolitic and destructive of American interests and American policy.

"Now, sir, I do not expect to shut the Canadians out. I expect that they will enjoy our markets. God knows I do not want to destroy that people entirely, because some of them have been and still are most glorious friends of ours. I wish I could say that there were a majority of such there, but they are such men as I honour. I know they have nowhere else to go but to our markets. The 'mother country,' as they call it, has failed to protect them. The markets there do not suit them and are of no account to them, but they come to us for our markets. I say let them come, but let them not come to rob the brave men of our own country, who have given their best blood for the protection of our liberties. Let them not come to the exclusion of those who have birthrights and who bear the heat and burden of the day. We will treat them as well as we do the most favoured nation, as neighbours, but we will not feed or clothe them. If they are to enjoy our markets, let it be on the same terms with other nations of the world. Why not? Is there any man opposed to giving this notice who can show what has ever been discovered during the working of this treaty which would induce us to believe that there is anything on the part of the Canadians that they can give us for what we can give them? What reciprocal advantages can they return to us? What benefits do they give us for those we confer on them? They tell us that we may go to their markets. Why, sir, they have no markets. We may go there, but what is the use of going there if there are no markets? I know there are no markets there; I was born near there, and I know what I say. Fifty bullocks from Illinois would frighten every butcher out of Montreal!

"I am much obliged to the House for indulging me, and I will detain them but one moment longer. If you are going to pass this resolution I want to amend it a little. If this commission is to be provided for, I want its name changed to 'A commission to arrange terms for continuing, in a

dignified position, the wet-nurse of the sick British Colonies.'
(Laughter).   I have done."

Mr. Sweat—"My idea is that we can revise this treaty
without abrogating it, and that we can treat better with these
Provinces while the present treaty is living than we can with
a dead treaty.

"It has been said that there exists an unfriendly feeling
between the Provinces and the United States. Sir, the
people of the Lower Provinces of Canada are friends of the
loyal citizens of the United States. However much the
Canadian papers may have given an appearance of a public
sentiment against us, it is a mistake to suppose that their
interests are adverse to ours or that the people there are
unfriendly to us.

"The question is not whether the treaty is what we would
have it—in my opinion it is not—but whether commissioners
shall be appointed to revise and improve it.   Sir, if there is to
be a revision of the treaty it will need amendments in behalf
of the interests of Maine quite as much as of the interests of
any other state.

"Now, sir, shall we be governed by such a course as this, or
shall we be governed by passion, excitement, purposes of
retaliation, or promptings of revenge? Because some Canadians have exhibited ill-feeling against this country shall we
undertake to stultify ourselves by breaking up our commercial
relations with them, and destroying the interests of our own
citizens to a large extent? I believe that some gentlemen
upon this floor are actuated more by their prejudice against
this people than by any other consideration in the line of
policy they are advocating in this matter. Now, I submit to
gentlement upon this side of the House and upon the other
side, that even if all that is alleged in reference to this Canadian people be true, whether we are justified in allowing
ourselves to be governed by such considerations in determining a national, commercial question?

"Shall we, if we can, negotiate a new treaty upon the
principles of reciprocity ? If we make the effort to revise this,
and to make it mutually beneficial and satisfactory, and fail, I

need not inform the House that we may then give notice of the abrogation of the existing treaty. It is said there is a necessity now of giving this notice, as though we could not even wait until September 11th, which will be the termination of the ten years, as though we could not even make an effort to come to a fair and honourable understanding.

" With all the defects of the present treaty, the balance of trade for the last ten years has been in favour of the United States."

On January 11, 1865, the resolution to repeal the Reciprocity Treaty was taken up in the United States Senate, and carried by 31 yeas to 8 nays. We give the concluding speeches of Mr. Hale and Mr. Sumner.

Mr. Hale, of New Hampshire, said " he was sorry the Senate contemplated the repeal of the treaty. He regarded it as a step in the wrong direction. The treaty had been productive of good to both parties, and to repeal it could effect no good. If the object in repealing it was to benefit our commercial and financial interests, he would not object to it ; but it had come from the committee on foreign relations, and no report had been made as to why action should be taken. It had been said that the treaty operated all one way. The reasons assigned by those who urged its abrogation were vague and unsatisfactory. He (Mr. Hale) had an interest in the commercial prosperity of the country, and he had taken the trouble to look at the operation of the treaty in the gross. Some special pleader might make out a case against it on a particular point, but its general operation had been unquestionably beneficial. Mr. Hale read a statement from a letter of the Secretary of the Treasury to show that, under the operations of the Treaty, the exports to Canada had been increased in a few years from $6,000,000 to $25,000,000. Both free goods and duty paying goods had increased. He had been told that Canada had altered her tariff so as to make it burdensome to American commerce. The rates had not been more than two per cent., and in the last year they had decreased. In 1861 they were nineteen per cent., only a half per cent. larger than in 1850. The statement that there had been unfair advantage taken in the way of duties was therefore a mistake. In 1853 the exports to Canada were $7,000,000. In 1854 $15,000,000; in 1856 $22,000,000; and in 1863 $28,000,000. The imports had increased from $490,000 to $20,000,000. Mr. Hale was sorry the Senate was about to act so soon upon this matter. The Chamber of Commerce of New York had taken the matter under consideration, and would soon report. He understood the Chamber of Commerce of Chicago, was averse to the repeal of the treaty. He thought we ought not to strike a blow at commerce, when we needed the sinews of war so much. In conclusion Mr. Hale said the abrogation of the treaty would be regarded in Canada and England as retaliation for wrongs which the people of the United States rightly imagined they had sustained, and he was sure the people of Canada were willing now to do anything they could to repair the wrongs that had been committed lately, and to prevent their repetition. He believed it would strengthen the rebels and weaken the Union cause to repeal the treaty. Suppose it true that the repeal of the treaty would impoverish Canada, he did not believe it would be wise to do so. We ought to wish our neighbours rich and prosperous and enterprising; able to buy from us and help our commerce. In reducing them to poverty we would injure ourselves, but he had no hope of preventing the passage of the resolution. This was a time when men took counsels of their passions rather than of the welfare of the country. The treaty had been wise and salutary, and under it commerce had grown up and improved. Until some gentleman could point out some great injury that had been done, he hoped the Senate would pause. He hoped that the merchants of New York would have an opportunity to be heard on the subject."

Mr. Sumner said : " The reciprocity treaty has a beautiful name. It suggests at once equality, exchange and security, and it is because it was supposed to advance these ideas practically, that this treaty was originally accepted by the people of the United States. If, however, it shall appear that while organizing exchange, it forgets equality and equity in an

essential respect, then must a modification be made in con-
formity with just principles. I mean to be brief, but I hope,
though brief, to make the proper conclusion apparent. It is a
question for reason, not for passion or sentiment, and in this
spirit I enter upon the discussion. The treaty may be seen
under four different heads. It concerns the fisheries, the navigation of the St. Lawrence, the commerce of the United States
and the British Provinces, and the revenue of the United
States. These fisheries have been a source of anxiety
throughout our history. Even from the beginning, and for
several years previous to the reciprocity treaty, they had been
the occasion of mutual irritation, verging at times on positive
outbreak. This is a plain advantage which cannot be denied,
but so far as I have been able to examine official returns, I do
not find any further evidence showing the value of the treaty
in this connection, while opinions, even among those most
interested in the fisheries, are divided. There are partisans
for it in Gloucester, Massachusetts, and partisans against it in
Maine. If the treaty related exclusively to fisheries, I should
not be willing to touch it, but the practical question is whether
the seeming advantage in this respect is sufficient to counter-
balance the disadvantages in other respects. Next comes the
navigation of the St. Lawrence, but this plausible concession
has proved to be but little more than a name. It appears that
during the first six years of the treaty only forty American
vessels, containing 12,550 tons, passed seaward through the
St. Lawrence, and during the same time only nineteen vessels,
containing 5,446 tons, returned by the same open highway.
These are very petty amounts when we consider the value of
the commerce on the lakes, which, in 1856, was $58,797,320, or
when we consider the carrying trade between the United
States and the British Provinces. Take the years 1857 to
1862 inclusive, and we shall find that during this period the
shipping of the United States, which cleared for the British
Provinces, was 10,707,239 tons, and the foreign shipping,
which cleared during this same period, was 7,391,399 tons,
while the shipping of the United States, which entered at our
custom houses from the British Provinces, was 10,056,183

tons, and the foreign shipping which entered was 6,455.520
tons. I mention these things by way of contrast. In comparison with these grand movements, the business which we
have been able to do on the St. Lawrence seems to be trivial.
It need not be considered as an element in the present discussion. The treaty may be seen next in its bearings on
the commerce between the two countries. This has
increased immensely, but it is difficult to see how much of
this increase is due to the treaty and how much is due
to the natural growth of population and the facilities
for transportation in both countries. If it could be traced
exclusively or in any large measure to the treaty, it would
be an element not to be disregarded, but it does not follow,
from the occurrence of this increase, after the acceptance of
the treaty, that it was on account of the treaty. The census
of the United States and of the British Provinces, will show
an increase of population, which must not be disregarded in
determining the origin of the increase of commerce. There
are also railroads furnishing prompt and constant means of
intercommunication which have gone into successful operation
only since the treaty. It would be difficult to exaggerate the
influence these have exercised in quickening and extending
commerce. I cannot doubt that the railroad system of the
two countries has been of itself a reciprocity and equal to any
written on parchment. The extent of trade before and after
the treaty may be shown in a few figures. In the three years
immediately preceding the treaty the total exports to Canada
and the other British provinces were $48,216,518, and the total
imports were $22,588,577, being of exports to imports in the
proportion of 100 to 46. In the ten years of the treaty the
total exports to Canada and the British provinces were
$256,350,931. The total imports were $200,399,786. According to these amounts the exports were in the proportion of
100 to 78. If we take Canada alone we shall find the change
in their proportion greater still. The total exports to Canada
in the three years immediately preceding the treaty were
$31,866,865, and the total imports were $6,587,674, being in
proportion of 100 to 52, while the whole exports to Canada

alone during the ten years of the treaty were $176,371,911, and the total imports were $161,474,347, being in the proportion of 100 to 94. I present these tables simply to lay before you the extent and nature of the change in the commerce between the two countries, but I forbear embarking on the much debated enquiry as to the effect of a difference between the amount of exports and imports, involving, as it does, the whole perilous question of the balance of trade. In the view which I take on the present occasion, it is not necessary to consider it. The reciprocity treaty cannot be maintained or overturned on any contested principle of political economy. I come, in the last place, to the influence of the treaty on the revenues of the country, and here the custom house is our principal witness. The means of determining this question will be found in the authentic tables which have been published from time to time on the reports of the treasury, and especially in the report made to Congress at this session, which I have in my hand. Looking at these tables we find certain unanswerable points. I begin with an estimate founded on the trade before the treaty. From this it appears that if no treaty had been made and the trade had increased in the same ratio as before the treaty, Canada would have paid to the United States in ten years of the treaty at least $16,373,800, from which she has been relieved. This sum has actually been lost to the United States. In return Canada has given up $2,650,890, being the amount it would have collected if no treaty had been made. This is a vast proportion to the detriment of the United States." Mr. Sumner then quoted from the report of the Secretary of the Treasury, showing that the treaty had released from duty a total sum of $42,333,357 in value, of goods of Canada, more than of goods the product of the United States.

All the speeches convey the idea that a feeling of irritation against Canada was the real cause of the abrogation of the treaty, and the monetary article of the *New York Herald* is very plain-spoken in its views on the subject:

"The vote of the Senate, by 31 against 8, in favour of the abrogation of the reciprocity treaty with Canada, indi-

cated the general feeling on the subject of our relations with
Great Britain and her possessions, more than a sound politico-
economic view of the question.   The arguments both for and
in opposition to a repeal of the treaty were inadequate and
without grasp ;   and very few of those who cast their votes on
one side or the other showed that they had taken any pains
to inform themselves of the facts relating to the treaty and
their bearings, so as to be enabled to draw fair conclusions,
while those who appeared to have done so failed by their
observations to view them in a comprehensive light *pro* and
con, although Mr. Hale, of New Hampshire, discussed the
subject with tolerable impartiality.   He argued that as the
exports to Canada from the United States had increased in
value from $7,000,000 in 1853, to $28,000,000 in 1863, and the
imports from $490,000 to $20,000,000, therefore the treaty had
been beneficial in developing our trade with the neighbouring
provinces.   Mr. Sumner, on the other hand, took the opposite
side, and argued like a protectionist of the last century.

" The very unstatesmanlike deductions of Mr. Sumner from
these figures are, that if no treaty had existed, and the trade
had increased in the same ratio as before the treaty, Canada
would have paid to the United States during the ten years of
the treaty at least $16,373,800, which she has been in this way
relieved of.   ' This sum,' says Mr. Sumner, ' has actually
been lost to the United States ;' and this remark alone shows
him to be but a sorry political economist.   In the first place,
he assumes almost an impossibility when he supposes that the
trade between the two countries would have increased in the
same ratio if the treaty had not been in operation.   It was the
treaty that mainly caused the increase.   In the next instance,
Mr. Sumner makes a grave mistake when he says the United
States ' lost ' the amount stated.   He overlooks the important
fact, that all taxes upon commodities fall ultimately upon the
consumers, and that by importing goods during the last ten
years from Canada under the treaty, we were saving in their
reduced cost what would otherwise have been expended in
duties.   Mr. Sumner, on the same principle, would consider
the customs duties a gain to the United States, whereas

HON. LIEUT.-COL. MACKENZIE BOWELL, J.P., P.C.

Minister of Customs.

those duties are paid by the people of this country to the Government, and the import tax relieves every citizen who consumes imported goods as directly as any other tax does."

The leading commercial papers of the great cities of the American Union—papers that were accepted as organs of the commercial interests of that country—were unanimous in protesting against the abrogation of the treaty. The policy of reciprocal trade had not been adopted without long consideration by the leading merchants and public men of the United States. As early as 1816, President Madison brought the subject before Congress in a special message. President Monroe had tried to negotiate a treaty for that purpose, and repeated efforts in the same direction were made during the Administration of John Quincy Adams and General Jackson. These attempts to secure reciprocal trade were continued, on one side or the other, for some years without much effect. In 1847 the Canadian Parliament authorized the admission into Canada, free of duty, of the natural productions of the United States, whenever the latter country should reciprocate by similar legislation. In the same year the British Minister at Washington proposed an arrangement for reciprocal trade, but the matter lay in abeyance several years. In 1852 the New York Chamber of Commerce took up the subject and pressed it earnestly. Reciprocity was supported by most of the leading statesmen of the American Union, including, amongst others, Webster, Everett, Douglas, Seward, Marcy, Dix, Clayton and Cushing. The treaty was finally negotiated in 1854, and the necessary legislation to carry it into effect adopted. Next year the treaty went into operation, and was so satisfactory, that in 1856 the New York Chamber of Commerce petitioned Congress to remove all restrictions upon the commerce between Canada and the United States, by procuring reciprocity in manufactures, as well as in natural productions, and by securing an arrangement which should open to the vessels of both countries the coasting trade of the intervening waters, with all the advantages which then existed between adjoining states.

The advantages of the treaty had been altogether on the

American side. They had diverted our foreign trade from the St. Lawrence to their own ports. Their sales to us had been much larger than our sales to them ; they had enjoyed the benefits of the fisheries on the British American coast, whilst we had scarcely sent a smack in exchange into their waters ; and they had enjoyed the use of our Welland and St. Lawrence canals, which afforded an outlet for the commerce of the North-Western States. A special report on the subject was made by Mr. Derby, the Commissioner of the Treasury Department at Washington, to the Secretary of the Department, from which the following extracts are taken :

As to the general result of the treaty, he states that the commerce of the United States with the British American Provinces "rose from $2,100,000 in 1828 to $3,800,000 in 1832; $8,100,000 in 1840; $9,300,000 in 1846; $18,700,000 in 1851; $50,300,000 in 1856 ; and to $68,000,000 in 1865.

" American fishermen are by this treaty allowed to frequent and approach, without regard to distance, all the shores of four provinces, and to land and cure their fish there without the consent of the private owners.

" The return of fish and oil from this tonnage for 1862, considerably exceeded $14,000,000—drawn from the rich pastures of the deep. We have not exact returns of the fish or oil landed on our shores, but we have proof that in 1862, and down to the present hour, the trade has paid fair profits beyond outfits, repairs, insurance and other disbursements, and that these average more than $80 per ton for the vessels and boats in service, or more than $13,000,000.

" The number of American vessels in the fisheries has ranged from 2,414 in 1850 to 3,815 in 1862, besides boats in the shore fisheries. Six hundred sail of these vessels have in a single season fished for mackerel in the Gulf of St. Lawrence and Bay of Chaleurs, and taken fish to the amount of $4,500,000.

"American fisheries are not only the chief nurseries for the mariners and petty officers of our navy, but they are the schools from which spring the most able and enterprising mates, captains, and merchants who conduct the foreign commerce of the nation.

.   .   .   .

"The St. Lawrence is a valuable outlet for our cereals, but its importance must depend in a great measure upon the enlargement of the canals and increase of their depth to twelve or fifteen feet to suit a class of vessels adapted to the navigation of the ocean.

.   .   .   .   .   .

"The goods we export (to the Maritime Provinces) are more available than those we receive, and for several years before the treaty our exports averaged in value more than twice the value of our imports. This disparity has been reduced, but still the balance of trade is in our favour, and is realized in part from drafts on England.

.   .   .   .   .   .

"The shipment of coal from the provinces to the United States has increased from 220,000 tons in 1863, to at least 400,000 tons in 1865.   ·   ·   We are not, however, to forget that we already export from 105,000 to 171,000 tons of coal to Canada.

.   .   .   .

"Provincial coal can be laid down in the seaports of New England for five dollars per ton in specie. It would seem as if nature had designed this region for the supply of our north-eastern coast. The coal from Nova Scotia is bituminous, and thus differs from the coal of Pennsylvania, and is adapted for other uses, in gas works, forges and furnaces. At least half of it is used for gas. Fifty thousand tons are annually used by one gas company in Boston. It is used, also, to a considerable extent by the steamers which run to foreign ports.

.   .   .   .

"Canada supplies us with 3,500,000 pounds of combing wool the present year, of a quality we do not produce, but which we require for our new fabrics for mousse-line-delaiues, alpacas and bunting.   .   .   .   The free wool of Canada has been an inestimable favour to our worsted manufacturers. It does not compete with the productions of our farmers, as we raise little more than 200,000 pounds long wool, while Canada consumes 300,000 pounds of our clothing wool annually. It is not possible that our production of long wool can keep up with the demand."

The treaty has "quieted strife and restored the rights secured by the treaty of '83 to our fisheries, from which spring the seamen to our navy, the mates, masters, and intrepid merchants who have guided our keels to the confines of the earth."

And to sum up the American view of the matter, Mr. Derby declares: "A treaty under which our commerce with the provinces has increased threefold, or from $17,000,000 in 1852, to $68,000,000 in 1864, is not to be abandoned, or the amity which now exists between the contiguous nations of the same origin to be endangered, without careful investigation and conclusive reasons." And again : " If, under the treaty, our commerce with the provinces has, in twelve years, increased threefold, and in that commerce the tonnage arriving and departing from our ports exceeds 6,600,000 tons ; if in this tonnage we have the preponderance ; if our country has made rapid progress both in population and wealth—is there any reason to dread the operation of a new treaty more favourable to our own productions than the treaty expiring ?"

But Mr. Derby goes further. He shows that the commerce which has grown up under the treaty is so valuable to the United States, that should it be brought to an end on March 17th, it would be suicidal to impose high duties upon the products of the provinces. He says :

"There are few of the great staples of the provinces it would be wise to tax heavily, should the chance be afforded. It would be unwise to tax the minor articles, and most unwise to tax those which would be diverted by a duty. The field of inquiry is limited to the great staples of the provinces—wheat, oats, barley, coal, lumber and fish, and possibly horses."

Commenting upon this report the Toronto *Globe* of February 3, 1866, says :

"In view of all the perplexities of the case for Poor Uncle Sam, Mr. Derby exclaims : 'What is to be done?'

"'Are we to go back, with contiguous and growing Provinces, more populous than the United States in 1783, to a system of retaliation and restricted commerce?'

"'Would it be wise to incur the ill-will of a province whose frontier for three thousand miles borders on our own?'

"'Would it be politic to stimulate illicit trade at a time when we require high duties to meet our engagements?'

"'Should we divert business from our canals and railways to a new and circuitous route across New Brunswick?'

"'It is doubtless desirable for Canada to reach our home market and to gain a direct route, summer and winter, to the sea ; but she has open to her half the year the route of the St. Lawrence, connected by a series of canals and railways, with the lakes : And is it our policy to turn all her trade that way, or through the wilds of New Brunswick?'

"And in desperation at the threatened loss of the fisheries, Mr. Derby exclaims : 'Are we to come to blows with her for rights won by the sword in the war of the Revolution, which improvident Commissioners have impaired or put in jeopardy, or shall we make a Treaty? We must either risk our mackerel fishery, treat, or annex the provinces.'

"Yes—this is the alternative—TREAT with the Provincials, or 'annex the provinces.' Which course would be the best for Uncle Sam, Mr. Derby has no doubt. He goes strongly for annexation, or absorption. 'If,' says he, 'the Maritime Provinces would but, join us spontaneously to-day—sterile as may be their soil, under a sky of steel—still with their hardy population, their harbours, fisheries, and seamen, they would greatly improve and strengthen our position and aid us in our struggle for equality upon the ocean. If we would succeed upon the deep, we must either maintain our fisheries, or absorb the Provinces.'

"No—Mr. Derby has no doubt as to *absorption* being decidedly 'beneficial' to Uncle Sam. He tells his countrymen with great gusto that it 'would bring to the Union a white population which will, in 1868, possibly before the measure could be consummated, reach four millions. It would bring to us two thousand miles of railways, and vast forests and mines, and fisheries and mariners, and nearly two-thirds of a million tons of shipping.'

"To attain that, Mr. Derby is ready for anything. But how to attain it is the question? Coercion?—prohibitory duties?—non-intercourse? There are 'gentlemen of intelligence' it seems, and possibly some American 'statesmen' who think that these would bring it about; but Mr. Derby has no such faith. 'Is there no danger,' he asks, 'that such a policy would produce "alienation" instead of Union?' 'Is the present moment,' he wants to know, 'when we are mastering a debt of twenty-eight hundred millions by severe taxation, an auspicious one for bringing in new States to share our burden?' Mr. Derby thinks not. He is of opinion that Uncle Sam is decidedly not in a condition to offer any temptation to the Provincials at this moment—but he lives in hope that 'we can offer more inducements and attractions at a future day.'

"Mr. Derby being unable to attain *absorption* at this moment, goes in for conciliation and negotiation, and a treaty. He does not believe in 'Legislative Reciprocity.' Mr. Derby, like a sensible man, goes for a treaty. 'Let us treat the Provinces,' says Mr. Derby, 'as friends and patrons, as valuable customers, and, if they join us, let them come as friends. We desire no unwilling associates.'

"The sort of treaty Mr Derby recommends, and his declarations as to the endorsal by Canadians of his views, we will consider hereafter. But meantime, we heartily recommend Mr. Derby's views to the best attention of some of our weak-kneed contemporaries, who have been seeing nothing but 'Ruin and Decay' in the abrogation of the treaty. And especially would we commend them to that class of individuals who would have the people of Canada to go down on their knees to Brother Jonathan."

The Canadian Government were anxious to keep the treaty in operation, or to negotiate a new one, and were willing to make every reasonable concession, believing that great injury would be done to the country if there were no treaty for reciprocal trade with the United States. It was said at the time that Mr. George Brown did not concur in the views of his colleagues, not being willing to yield as much as they were, and he, therefore, considered it his duty to resign his seat in the Cabinet. Mr. Brown was a man who had such faith in his own views that he was unable to calmly consider the strength and sincerity of the convictions of others, and in taking that step he acted hastily and unadvisedly. Having entered the Cabinet to carry out the great scheme of Confederation, he should have remained at his post until the project was completed.

In spite of every effort to the contrary, the treaty came to an end on March 16, 1866. The results, however, were not so disadvantageous to Canada as were expected in this country or looked for by our neighbours. What these results actually were will be a proper subject of consideration when we come to speak of efforts made in future years to obtain a new treaty with the United States which would contain elements of advantage to both countries. Suffice it now to say, that if the *New York World* can be accepted as the exponent of public opinion, the advocates of the abrogation of the Reciprocity Treaty of 1854 believed that absorption of Canada into the United States would follow as a matter of course. Here are its words, January 30, 1866 :

"As annexation seems to be the real beginning and the end of argument on this subject with some of those who oppose all reciprocity, it is well to caution the Administration against the pleasant reports of its employees. It is no new characteristic of the worst part of human nature that men are inclined to flatter those who are in power, and can give, withhold or perpetuate the emoluments and honours of office. But if intended to promote annexation of the provinces to the United States, the method which has been selected has been most unfortunate, and has thus far produced results exactly the reverse of those desired by its originators. Not one influential representative of public opinion among the Canadian journals—nor, we believe, one newspaper of an inferior class—

now advocates annexation to the United States. The common sentiment is more opposed to it than for many previous years. Even those who, six months ago, contributed money to promote union, now unite in defying the system of commercial coercion, and ask us to consider what we should feel if a similar pressure was applied to us to induce us to change our allegiance to our own country. To this, of course, there can only be one answer. It enables us to see ourselves as we are seen by others. The Canadian journals speak of Potterization as an effort to make them part with their honour and their birthright for unworthy considerations, and they diminish the force of whatever inducements we can offer by calling the attention of their readers to our system of enormous taxation."

Another danger threatened Canada at this time. The Fenian Organization had acquired an extraordinary strength in the United States. One branch, under Stephens and O'Mahony, proposed to drive the English out of Ireland; another branch under Roberts and Sweeny, proposed to conquer Canada and make it the basis of attack. Arrangements were made for simultaneous invasions at three points. Demonstrations were made near St. Albans, Ogdensburg and Buffalo, of which the latter was the most serious. Towards the end of May it became known that large bodies of men were collecting on the Niagara frontier. Before daybreak on June 1st they had landed near Fort Erie and taken possession of all the horses and provisions they could lay their hands on. No violence, however, was offered to the inhabitants. The next day, General O'Neil, who was in command, moved his force to an elevated woodland termed Limeridge, and there erected temporary fortifications. Meanwhile the Canadian Government, who did not realize until the invasion had actually taken place, that so serious a step could be seriously contemplated, called out the militia force of the country to repel the invaders. The Queen's Own regiment composed of ten companies, under Major Gillmor; the 13th of Hamilton, composed of six companies, under Major Skinner; the York Rifles under Captain Davis; and the Caledonia Rifles, under Captain Jackson, were ordered off to the Niagara frontier

Colonel Booker, who was in command of the brigade, did not follow out the instructions received from his superior officer, Colonel Peacocke, and prematurely attacked the Fenians. All went well until, upon a false alarm of an attack by cavalry, the men were ordered to form squares. This, at once, exposed them to a severe fire from the enemy, confusion ensued, followed by a retreat from the field with the loss of about forty killed and wounded. The Fenians did not follow up their advantage, and, being hard pressed by other forces, escaped as best they could to the American side of the river. Many were killed and wounded, and a large number taken prisoners. As there were many thousands ready to follow the first comers, the matter might have been very much more serious had the leaders not so soon lost heart. Threatening demonstrations continued to be made for some time, but finally the band were dispersed by the United States Government providing transport to their homes. A most interesting account of the raid, with a detailed description of the movements of the troops, and the engagements that took place, was written by Colonel (then Major) George T. Denison of the Governor-General's Body Guard.

During the ensuing week thousands of Fenians congregated on the banks of the St. Lawrence, near Prescott and Cornwall, and on the borders of the Eastern Townships, but the remonstrances of the Canadian Government against the apathy of the American authorities in allowing so wanton an invasion of the soil of a friendly country, began to have effect and General Meade was ordered to seize the arms and ammunition which had been collected, and to send the raiders to their homes. Although the blood of Canada's brave sons had been shed, some property destroyed, and heavy expense incurred by having, at one time, 40,000 of the militia under arms, the sacrifice was not in vain. It demonstrated to the world the ability and determination to defend our land at all costs and hazards, and gave a further impetus to the military spirit already awakened by the *Trent* affair.

In Canada a feeling of uneasiness prevailed. It was said that the organization had taken deep root in our midst, and all sorts of rumours were afloat as to the aid and countenance likely to be accorded to their confederates from the other side of the border. Many prominent Irish Roman Catholics raised their voices to warn those of their countrymen who were suspected of leaning towards the cause of Fenianism, to strengthen those who, while loyal to the country of their birth, did not desire to see the land of their adoption the scene of bloody strife, and to dispel from the minds of the people at large the doubts which had arisen as to the loyalty of the Irish Catholics, as a whole. Amongst those were Dr. Connolly, the venerable Archbishop of Halifax, and the Honourable Thomas D'Arcy McGee. The former wrote to the Lieutenant-Governor of New Brunswick a lengthy letter from which we quote the following :

" From all the sources of information at my command, I am convinced, if the crisis come, that the whole Roman Catholic population in this country will yield to no other class in unwavering loyalty and the unflinching performance of duty in the day of trial. Apart from the allegiance which, as Churchmen, we owe to the constituted authorities, we have here everything to lose and nothing whatever to gain by a change, be it ever so luring in the distance. What can any Government give that we have not got ? We have prosperity, law, order, peace, unmeasured liberty, the country secured against the foreign foe, trade and commerce protected all over the world at an expense one-sixth less per head than in the neighbouring republic, and a mere fraction as compared with the expenditure of any other country we know of. To exchange this condition with any other would be suicidal madness, and the thinking, reading portion of our people, the portion that have anything to lose, are aware of the fact. They, like myself, have visited the United States from time to time, and have had ample data to guide them to the same conclusion. Catholics, no doubt, enjoy many advantages in that country (and it is a blessing for millions they have such a country as a refuge), but after the experience of twenty-four years in British America, it is my deep conviction that Catholics, taking into account their numbers and opportunities, are wealthier and happier—better Christians—and socially and politically more elevated here than there.

" In Canada, New Brunswick, Nova Scotia, Newfoundland and Prince Edward Island, there has been no period since the days of emancipation, at which Catholics have not possessed that influence in the community to which their numbers and position fairly entitled them. The Legislature, the Executive Council, and the Bench are as accessible to the Catholic as the Protestant, whilst men of vast wealth and the highest business and social standing in every city, from Montreal to St. John's, Newfoundland, are to be found among our ranks. In all these particulars, according to our numbers, we stand as a hundred to one when compared with our fellow religionists in the neighbouring republic.

" Our people, therefore, have nothing to expect from change of any kind but increased taxation, diminished incomes, a decided fall in the social scale, the scathing contempt of their new rulers, as was ever the case in New England, and with these, perhaps, the horrors of a devastating war. The great Government of the United States has nothing more tempting to offer ; and what have we to expect from the so-called Fenians, that pitiable knot of knaves and fools, who, unable to degrade themselves, are doing all in their power to add another Ballingarry to the history of Ireland, and to make the condition of our poor country more deplorable than before.

" On the occasion of my recent visit to the United States many of these poor deluded people talked as flippantly and confidently of taking all British America in the course of this winter, and holding it, as if they already had the title deeds in their pockets. If they come on the strength of their own resources, it will be, indeed, a laughable scare ; and from what is now occurring in New York, we may easily foresee the glorious denouement. Two millions of Protestants and eighteen hundred thousand Catholics, who have mothers, wives, and daughters—happy homes and free altars, and a Government of their own choice—will meet them as they would the freebooter and assassin, with knife in hand on the trail of his victim.

From their success we have nothing to expect but bloodshed, rapine, and anarchy, and the overthrow of God's religion—for all this is inscribed on their banners. Table-turning and rapperism the rhapsodies and extravagances of a moon-struck brain, are to take the place of the old religion in Ireland, and the priests are to be exterminated under the fostering ægis of the new Republic. All British America is to be occupied and declared a neutral territory, wherein Fenian armies and navies are to be recruited and built up. The power of England is to be crushed. Protestants, Catholic priests, and the upper classes of Catholics in Ireland are to be exterminated, and a new Republic is to be inaugurated with an ex-lunatic, Mr. O'Mahoney, at its head! With such a programme, the Catholics of this country will assuredly accord to the Fenians, if they come, the warm reception they so richly deserve."

The Honourable Thomas D'Arcy McGee had, previously availed himself of the occasion of the annual concert for the benefit of the funds of St. Patrick's Society, held at Montreal in January of the preceding year, to express his views in equally plain and unmistakeable language, and his remarks will always have a greater interest attached to them from the fact that this denunciation of Fenianism is believed to have caused that bitter feeling amongst the conspirators which led to his assassination three years later. After speaking in eloquent terms of Ireland, and the Catholic University, for which subscriptions were then being taken up, he said :—

"There is another subject which more immediately concerns ourselves in Montreal and in Canada, which has lately occupied a good deal of the attention of the press—I allude to the alleged spread of a seditious Irish society, originating at New York, and which has chosen to go behind the long Christian record of their ancestors to find in Pagan darkness and blindness the appropriate name of Fenians. (Laughter). A statement having been made the other day in the Toronto *Globe*, on the authority of its Montreal correspondent, that there were 1,500 of these contemporary pagans in Montreal, a statement made,

I am sure, without intentional malice on the correspondents
part, I felt bound, as I suppose you have seen, to deny absolutely that statement. (Cheers). My denial was not given in
my own words, but the alleged fact was denied, and that was
the main point. (Cheers). I now, in your presence, repeat
that denial on behalf of the Irish Catholics of this city. I say
there could not be fifty such scamps associated and meeting
together, not to say 1,500, without your knowledge and mine,
and I repeat absolutely that there is no such body amongst us,
and that the contrary statements are deplorably untrue and
unjust, and impolitic as well as unjust. (Cheers). I regret
that papers of great circulation should lend themselves to the
propagation of such statements, which have a direct tendency
to foster and enhance the very evil they intend to combat.
Already indecent and unauthorized searches have been made
for concealed arms in the Catholic churches ; already, as in
some of the townships of Bruce, the magistrates are very
improperly, in my opinion, arming one class of the people
against the other. (Hear, hear). What consequences of evil
may flow from this step, should make any reasonable man
shudder, and what is it all owing to ? Why, to these often
invented, and always exaggerated newspaper reports. Observe
the absurd figure Upper Canada is made to cut in all this
business. The Protestant million are made to tremble before
a fraction of a fraction, for if there are Fenians in that quarter
of the world, I venture ro say they are as wholly insignificant
in numbers as in every other respect. (Cheers). At the risk,
however, of sharing the fate of all unmasked advisers, I would
say to the Catholics of Upper Canada, in each locality, if
there is any, the least proof that this foreign disease has
seized on any, the least among you, establish at once, for your
own sake, for the country's sake, a *cordon sanitaire* around
your people ; establish a committee which will purge your
ranks of this political leprosy ; weed out and cast off those
rotten members, who, without a single governmental grievance
to complain of in Canada, would yet weaken and divide us in
these days of danger and anxiety. (Cheers). Instead of
sympathy for the punishment they are drawing upon them-

selves, there ought to be a general indignation at the perils
such wretches would, if permitted to exist among us, draw
upon the whole community, politically and religiously.   How
would any Catholic who hears me like to see the parish
Church a stable, and St. Patrick's a barrack?   How would
our working men like to see our docks desolate, our canals
closed, our new buildings arrested, ruin in our streets, and
famine shivering among the ruins?   And this is what these
wretched conspirators, if they had the power, would bring to
pass, as surely as fire produces ashes from wood, or cold
produces ice from water.   (Cheers).   I repeat here deliberately that I do not believe in the existence of any such
organization in Lower Canada, certainly not in Montreal ; but
that there are, or have been, emissaries from the United States
among us, for the purpose of establishing it, has been so often
and so confidently stated, that what I have said on the general
subject will, I hope, not be considered untimely or uncalled
for."   (Hear, hear).

These timely and patriotic utterances of men so influential,
had a soothing effect upon the public mind, inasmuch as they
indicated, that, while the organization had taken root in
Canada, it was not so widespread as was generally supposed,
and would be opposed by some of the most eminent Irish
Roman Catholics in the country.

On December 4th the following Delegates met in London
to settle the details of the Act to give effect to the Union
of the Provinces :—The Honourables John A. Macdonald,
George E. Cartier, A. T. Galt, W. P. Howland, H. L. Langevin and Wm. McDougall, representing Canada ; the Honourables S. L. Tilley, P. Mitchell, R. D. Wilmot, C. Fisher and
J. M. Johnston, representing New Brunswick ; and the Honourables Chas. Tupper, W. A. Henry, J. W. Ritchie, A. G.
Archibald and J. McCully, representing Nova Scotia.

The Honourable John A. Macdonald was unanimously
elected Chairman.

For several weeks the Conference was engaged in preparing the new Constitution, and on February 7, 1867, the
Bill, Confederating the Provinces, was introduced into the

Imperial Government by Lord Carnarvon. It passed through the various stages in the House of Lords in less than three weeks and was brought down to the House of Commons without delay, where it was read a third time and finally passed, on March 8th. On March 28th it received the Royal assent and became one of the laws of the Empire. On May 22nd, Her Majesty's proclamation was issued, bringing the Dominion of Canada into existence on July 1, 1867.

Through the young giant's mighty limbs, that stretch from sea to sea,
There runs a throb of conscious life—of waking energy.
From Nova Scotia's misty coast to far Columbia's shore,
She wakes—a band of scattered homes and colonies no more,
But a young nation, with her life full beating in her breast,
A noble future in her eyes—the Britain of the West.
Hers be the noble task to fill the yet untrodden plains
With fruitful many-sided life that courses through her veins ;
The English honour, nerve and pluck—the Scotchman's love of right—
The grace and courtesy of France—the Irish fancy bright—
The Saxon's faithful love of home, and home's affections blest ;
And, chief of all, our holy faith—of all our treasures best.
A people poor in pomp and state, but rich in noble deeds,
Holding that righteousness exalts the people that it leads ;
As yet the waxen mould is soft, the opening page is fair,
It rests with those who rule us now, to leave their impress there ;
The stamp of true nobility, high honour, stainless truth ;
The earnest quest of noble ends ; the generous heart of youth ;
The love of country, soaring far above dull party strife ;
The love of learning, art and song—the crowning grace of life ;
The love of science, roaming far through nature's hidden ways ;
The love and fear of Nature's God—a nation's highest praise ;
So, in the long hereafter, this Canada shall be
The worthy heir of British power and British liberty.

—*Fidelis.*

CHAPTER XXVII.

1867-1871.

THE Honourable John A. Macdonald was called upon by
Lord Monck to form the first Cabinet of the new Confederacy. He accepted the task and succeeded in gathering
together probably the ablest Cabinet that Canada has ever
seen. In making his selections he announced his policy as
follows: "I desire to bring to my aid in the new Government
those men, irrespective of party, who represent the majorities
in the different provinces of the Union. I do not want it to
be felt by any section of the country that they have no representative in the Cabinet, and no influence in the Government.
And as there are now no issues to divide parties, and as
all that is required is to have in the Government the men who
are best adapted to put the new machinery in motion, I desire
to ask those to join me who have the confidence, and who
represent the majorities in the various sections of those who
were in favour of the adoption of this system of Government
and who wish to see it satisfactorily carried out." The first
Administration of the Dominion of Canada consisted of:

Hon. JOHN A. MACDONALD, Premier and Minister of Justice.
Hon. GEORGE E. CARTIER, Minister of Militia.
Hon. ALEXANDER CAMPBELL, Postmaster-General.
Hon. A. T. GALT, Minister of Finance.

Hon. S. L. Tilley, Minister of Customs.
Hon. A. J. Fergusson-Blair, President of the Council.
Hon. H. L. Langevin, Secretary of State.
Hon. W. P. Howland, Minister of Inland Revenue.
Hon. Peter Mitchell, Minister of Marine and Fisheries.
Hon. A. G. Archibald, Secretary of State for the Provinces.
Hon. Edward Kenny, Receiver-General.
Hon. William McDougall, Minister of Public Works.
Hon. J. C. Chapais, Minister of Agriculture.

As the Ministry was composed of about equal numbers of Conservatives and Reformers, it was essentially a coalition Government and as such was opposed by that branch of the Reform party under the leadership of the Honourable George Brown.

On June 27, 1867, the Reform Convention met in Toronto, Mr. William Patrick, of Prescott, being chairman. The policy of the party was embodied in fifteen resolutions. These "accepted the new Constitution about to be inaugurated, with a determination to work it loyally and patiently, and to provide such amendments as experience from year to year may prove to be expedient," but condemned the composition of the Ministry in the following resolution.

" *Resolved*,—That coalitions of opposing political parties, for ordinary administrative purposes, inevitably result in the abandonment of principle by one or both parties to the compact, the lowering of public morality, lavish public expenditure and widespread corruption ; that the coalition of 1864 could only be justified on the ground of imperious necessity, as the only available mode of obtaining just representation for the people of Upper Canada, and on the ground that the compact then made was for a specific measure and for a stipulated period and was to come to an end as soon as a measure was attained ; and while the Convention is thoroughly satisfied that the Reform party has acted in the best interests of the country by sustaining the Government until the Confederation measure was secured, it deems it an imperative duty to declare that the temporary alliance between the Reform and Conservative parties should now cease, and that no Government will be satisfactory to the people of Upper Canada which is formed and maintained by a coalition of public men holding opposite political principles."

In the speeches which were made on the resolutions the conduct of those Reform members from Upper Canada who had accepted portfolios in the Cabinet, was strongly denounced. Replies were made by the Honourables W. P. Howland and William Macdougall, who stated that they had accepted office because they considered that the great Liberal party of Upper Canada should be represented in the first Cabinet of the Dominion, that they considered it their duty to work together with their Liberal friends from the Maritime Provinces, who had laboured so hard and sacrificed so much to bring about the Union, and finally that they were willing to submit their conduct to the decision of the electors of the country.

Many reasons may be adduced to prove that these gentlemen were right in the course which they pursued. Both parties had united upon a common principle—that of establishing the new Constitution upon a firm basis; of properly adjusting all its parts; and setting in motion the whole machinery. There was no occasion for a party fight; there were no grievances to redress; no old mismanagement to reform. No benefit could be derived from a quarrel; no good end could be subserved. No thirteen men could have come together for a nobler or more worthy purpose than that which induced Reformers and Conservatives to unite in the first Government of the Dominion of Canada, to establish the new Constitution which had been obtained by the sinking of party differences. Without a junction of parties in 1864, Confederation could not have been accomplished. Both parties were entitled to the honour of so splendid a result, and both had a right to share the triumphs and enjoy the rewards of so splendid an achievement. Mr. Brown had joined with these men on a former occasion; had worked with them; had participated in the festivities and honours enjoyed by them when delegates to England, and had praised them, both in public and in private, for the honourable manner in which they had acted with him in solving the problem of the Union. They were not

THE HON.
SIR H. L. LANGEVIN,
K.C.M.G., C.B.Q.C.,
P.C.
Minister of Public Works.

worse now than they were then, and to denounce members of his party for doing in 1867 what he had done in 1864 was most unreasonable.

The new Constitution had to be inaugurated under peculiar conditions, and harmony and union of parties were especially necessary to give it due *eclat* and effect ; party issues, which formerly existed, had been settled ; the object contemplated was not a party or sectional one, but national, and one in which all parties were interested. The men called upon to inaugurate the new order of things were peculiarly fitted for the task, because they had prepared it ; and a better guarantee was afforded to the country at large of the safety of the trust, when commended to the care of a coalition Government, than if in the hands of one which was strictly party. For these and other reasons which might be adduced, every reasonable man felt that the Administration was entitled to fair play, and to be judged by its policy and its acts, and that those Upper Canadian Reformers who gave it support and joined it as members, acted in a proper, patriotic and commendable manner.

Lord Monck was sworn in as Governor-General of the Dominion in the forenoon of July 1, 1867, and immediately announced that he had received Her Majesty's command to confer the title of K. C. B. on the Honourable John A. Macdonald, and the title of C. B. on the Honourables G. E. Cartier, S. L. Tilley, A. T. Galt, Charles Tupper, W. P. Howland, and William Macdougall.

Early in August writs for a new election were issued and preparations were made for a keen contest. Mr. Brown contested South Ontario with Mr. T. N. Gibbs, but was defeated by seventy-one votes. The Province of Ontario elected sixty-seven Ministerial supporters, and fifteen members of the Opposition. In the Province of Quebec all the constituencies but twelve were carried by the Government. In New Brunswick the Opposition only secured three seats. In Nova Scotia, however, Dr. Tupper was the only Government supporter who was returned.

The first Dominion Parliament opened on November 7th,

when the Honourable Joseph Cauchon was appointed Speaker of the Senate, and the Honourable James Cockburn was elected Speaker of the House of Commons. The Speech from the Throne foreshadowed a large amount of legislation respecting the currency, tariff, excise, and postal laws, the public works, management of the militia, care of the Indians, assimilation of the criminal laws, insolvency, the development of the fisheries, the building of the Intercolonial railway, etc. When the Bill for the construction of this railway was brought up, Mr. Dorion moved in amendment that the route should not be determined on without the consent of Parliament, which was rejected by a vote of 35 to 83, which may be taken as a fair indication of the relative strength of the Opposition and the Government. One of the most important events of the session was the adoption of a series of resolutions introduced by the Honourable Wm. Macdougall, with regard to the North-West, setting forth the reasons why Her Majesty should be graciously pleased to unite that country with Canada, and asking that authority should be granted to the Dominion Parliament to legislate on the subject. Mr. Macdougall's speech was able and exhaustive, the resolutions were all adopted, and a select committee appointed to draw up an address embodying them.

Parliament adjourned from December 21, 1867, to March 12, 1868. After being in session about three weeks the country was horror-stricken by the news of the assassination of the Honourable Thomas D'Arcy McGee. He had attended the House of Commons on the night of April 6th and made an eloquent speech on the subject of Dr. Tupper's mission to England. He left the Parliament Buildings about 2.30 on the morning of the 7th, accompanied by Mr. R. Macfarlane, M.P., and some messengers. They parted at the corner of Sparks and Metcalfe streets, he proceeding westward, along the former thoroughfare, to his boarding house. A few minutes later a son of Mrs. Trotter—the boarding-house keeper—who was a page in the House, and who was returning home after his duties, heard a pistol shot and, on arriving at his mother's door, found Mr. McGee lying dead, having been killed by a bullet which had struck the base of the skull in rear and passed through his mouth, carrying away several teeth. The cowardly murder was at once attributed to the Fenian brotherhood, in revenge for his outspoken denunciations of their unpatriotic schemes, and the most strenuous efforts were made to bring the assassin to justice. After a time the evidence pointed to Patrick James Whelan, a journeyman tailor, as the guilty one. He was accordingly arrested, tried, found guilty and hanged in the gaol at Ottawa on October 11, 1869.

Mr. McGee's tragic death caused the greatest sorrow to the whole country. He was a man beloved and esteemed for his qualities of head and heart and truly did Sir John Macdonald say of him " He might have lived a long and respected life had he chosen the easy path of popularity rather than the stern one of duty. He has lived a short life, respected and beloved, and has died a heroic death, a martyr to the cause of his country."

The Honourable Thomas D'Arcy McGee was known as a litterateur before he became a Canadian politician. He was an orator who had the art of making trifles graceful and brilliant, not that his speeches were wanting in the more sterling qualities of original thought and sound argument, but the utterance added grace and beauty to the matter and made it more pleasant to hear than to read. His countrymen were justly proud of his talents and regarded him as their especial representative. Genial, warm-hearted and impulsive, he had a host of friends amongst all classes of the population. He had represented Montreal West since 1857 and was several times elected by acclamation. He was descended from an old Ulster family and was born at Carlingford, County of Louth, Ireland, April 13, 1825, and educated at Wexford. Besides contributing largely to magazine literature in the United Kingdom and America, he had written the following works :—"Lives of Irish writers of the Seventh Century," "Life of Art," " Irish settlers in America," " Catholic history of America," " History of the Reformation in Ireland," " Canadian Ballads," and a " Popular history of Ireland."

Out of respect for Mr. McGee's memory, Parliament adjourned until April 14th. On re-assembling, the business was pushed through with all speed, and prorogation took place on May 22nd.

During the recess the attention of the Government was devoted to the pacification of Nova Scotia. Sir John Macdonald and some of his colleagues went to Halifax in August, but no immediate results followed. In October he again pressed the matter in a letter to Mr. Howe, expressing the willingness of the Government to consider all questions in a fair and equitable spirit, and offering Mr. Howe a seat in the Cabinet. Mr. Howe replied that he would still prefer a repeal of the Union Act but as there seemed little hope of that, he was disposed to enter into negotiations for better terms for his Province. The result was that documents were laid before the Ministry embodying the claims of Nova Scotia for better terms. These were carefully considered and an elaborate report thereon, drawn up by the Honourable John Rose, who had become Minister of Finance by the resignation of the Honourable A. T. Galt. He considered that it had been satisfactorily proved that the terms of Union were less favourable to Nova Scotia than to the other Provinces and, therefore, the Province was entitled to better terms. These terms having been embodied in an Order in Council and it having been agreed that a Bill embodying them should be submitted to Parliament, Mr. Howe abandoned all further opposition and entered the Cabinet as President of the Council, in the place of the Honourable Fergusson-Blair, deceased.

Lord Monck sailed from Quebec on December 14th and was succeeded by Sir John Young, who arrived at Ottawa on November 27th and was sworn in on December 1st.

The second session was opened on April 15, 1869. The date was unusually late, but was necessitated by the absence in England of Sir George Cartier and Honourable Wm. Macdougall, who were arranging for the transfer to the Dominion of the North-West Territory, and also by a change in the manner of keeping the Public Accounts, consequent on Confederation.

The session only lasted until June 23rd, but was productive of many interesting debates. One of these referred to the Intercolonial Railway, and Mr. Mackenzie expressed the views of the Opposition in the following resolutions :—

" That in the construction of the Intercolonial Railway it is of the highest importance for commercial and economical reasons, to have the shortest and cheapest line selected, which, in addition to the main object, will afford access to the best and nearest part on the Bay of Fundy.

" That the Bay of Chaleurs route selected by the Government is not one which will best promote the commercial interests of the Dominion, or best secure the settlement of the remote portions of the provinces through which the road will pass, and that, while it gives the smallest commercial advantage, it will entail the largest expenditure in its construction, and afterwards in its maintenance and working expenses.

" That in view of the serious effect to the finances of the Dominion, and the permanent and continuous loss to the commerce of the country, consequent on the adoption of a long and expensive route to the sea, it is desirable not to proceed with work on those portions of the line not common to the central or southern routes, with a view to the adoption of a route which will give access to the shortest and cheapest line, without interfering with the distance to Halifax as the ultimate terminus."

Mr. R. J. Cartwright moved an amendment setting forth the provisions of the Imperial and Dominion Acts, and concluding as follows :

" That under these circumstances the House considers that any discussion as to the route of the Intercolonial Railway would not answer any good purpose, and would greatly prejudice the credit of the Dominion at home and abroad."

The amendment was seconded by the Honourable Dr. Tupper. Both mover and seconder made very able speeches, pointing out that, in the negotiations with the Imperial Government, it had always been agreed that the latter should select the route. They had guaranteed the loan to build the line upon this express condition, and it would now be a breach of faith to pass Mr. Mackenzie's motion. The House concurred in this view, and the amendment was carried by a vote of 114 to 28.

When Mr. Howe made his motion, on June 11th, to go into committee on the resolutions fixing the amount at which the debt of Nova Scotia was to be taken, and granting an increased subsidy, Mr. Blake took exception to them as being unconstitutional, and moved an amendment to the effect that the liabilities of Canada and each province were settled by the British North American Act, that the Parliament of Canada could not change such basis of settlement, that the unauthorized assumption of such power would be injurious to the union, and therefore it was inexpedient to go into committee on the resolutions. A long debate ensued, in which part was taken by Messrs. Mackenzie, J. H. Cameron, Harrison, Tupper, Gray, Smith, Cartier, and Howe. On a vote being taken, the amendment was lost by 57 to 96. Mr. E. B. Wood offered another amendment declaring that it was inexpedient to disturb the financial arrangements with Nova Scotia, unless the other provinces were granted a corresponding advantage, which also was lost, the vote standing 46 to 88. Mr. Holton moved another amendment requiring the consent of all the other provinces to the arrangement, which was also lost on division by a vote of 52 to 97.

After prorogation Mr. Rose visited Washington with reference to a new Reciprocity Treaty, but was unsuccessful, and a short time afterwards acquired an interest in a banking concern, and sailed for England as the representative of the firm of Morton, Rose & Co. The position of Finance Minister was tendered to Sir A. T. Galt, but declined. It was then offered to Sir Francis Hincks, who accepted. He had been absent from Canada for fourteen years, during which period he had acted as Governor of Barbadoes and the Windward Islands, and as Governor of British Guiana. He offered himself for his old constituency, North Renfrew, and was elected by a majority of 120 over Mr. Findlay. A re-construction of the Cabinet took place, some new men being brought in, and some of the old Ministers changing portfolios. As re-constructed, the Ministry stood as follows :

SIR JOHN A. MACDONALD, Premier and Minister of Justice.
SIR GEORGE E. CARTIER, Minister of Militia.
SIR FRANCIS HINCKS, Minister of Finance.
SIR EDWARD KENNY, President of Privy Council.
HON. S. L. TILLEY, Minister of Customs.
HON. HECTOR L. LANGEVIN, Minister of Public Works.
HON. ALEXANDER MORRIS, Minister of Inland Revenue.
HON. JOSEPH HOWE, Secretary of State for the Provinces.
HON. PETER MITCHELL, Minister of Marine and Fisheries.
HON. ALEXANDER CAMPBELL, Postmaster-General.
HON. CHRISTOPHER DUNKIN, Minister of Agriculture.
HON. J. C. CHAPAIS, Receiver-General.
HON. J. C. AIKINS, Secretary of State and Registrar-General.

The Honourable William Macdougall resigned his place in the Administration to accept the position of Lieutenant-Governor of the North-West Territories, which had been acquired by the purchase of the rights of the Hudson's Bay Company, for the sum of £300,000. He arrived at Pembina on October 30th, but was prevented by an armed party of half-breeds from entering the country, and was obliged to return. The insurgents formed a provisional government of which Louis Riel was President, and proceeded to draw up a Bill of Rights. Many of those who disapproved of their conduct were cast into prison, and one of them, Thomas Scott, was murdered in the most cold-blooded and brutal manner. To quiet the fears of the half-breeds, and to inspire confidence as to the fairness of the treatment likely to be received from the Dominion Government, Bishop Tache was telegraphed to return from Rome. He did so, and left Ottawa on February 16, 1870, being empowered to invite delegates to Ottawa, and to offer amnesty for past offences. The arrival of a body of troops some months later under Colonel Wosley put an end to the insurrection, and the demands of the half-breeds were presented by delegates to the Dominion Government.

The third session of Parliament opened on February 15, 1870. The debate on the Address lasted for six days, and the whole policy of the Government was reviewed and critic-

ized. Sir A. T. Galt announced his inability to give the
Government any further support, and Sir Francis Hincks was
made the subject of a general attack, during which his past
political life was freely commented upon. Mr. Macdougall
also charged Mr. Howe with not having given him a proper
idea of the state of affairs at Fort Garry, and with having
failed to use his influence, during his recent visit to the Red
River country, in a proper manner. The Address was,
however, carried without any amendment being offered.

Mr. L. S. Huntingdon, a leading member of the Opposition, made a hot attack on the commercial policy of the
Government, and moved the following resolutions in favour of
freer intercourse with the United States.

"That an Address be presented, representing that the
increasing population and production of this Dominion
demand more extended markets, and a more unrestricted
interchange of commodities with other countries.

"That a continental system of free commercial intercourse, bringing under one general customs union with this
Dominion, countries chiefly interested in its trade, would lead
to the expansion of our commerce, and develop our resources
and our products.

"That such a system should place in a position of commercial equality and reciprocity all countries becoming parties
thereto.

"That a great advantage would result from placing the
Government of the Dominion in direct communication with
the several states which might be willing to negotiate for such
a customs' union.

"That it is expedient to obtain from the Imperial Government all necessary powers to enable the Government of the
Dominion to enter into direct communication with such
foreign states as would be disposed, upon terms advantageous
to Canada, to negotiate for such commercial regulations.

"That in all cases treaties enacting such proposed
customs, union should be submitted to the approval of Her
Majesty."

Mr. Huntingdon supported his resolutions in the strongest

possible manner, and was backed up by the Honourable A. A. Dorion, who declared himself warmly in favour of the proposed zollvereign, and argued that it did not involve discriminating duties against Great Britain.   He also urged that permission should be obtained from the Imperial Government to negotiate our own treaties.

Sir John Macdonald vigorously opposed the resolutions, urging that the course advocated really meant a separation from the mother country, and that it was much better for Canada to work in harmony with Great Britain than to attempt to act for herself, and sue *in forma pauperis* for commercial treaties with other countries.   He concluded an able and patriotic speech by moving in amendment

"That this House, while desirous of obtaining for this Dominion the freest access to the markets of the world, and thus augmenting its external prosperity, is satisfied that that object can best be obtained by the concurrent action of the Imperial and Canadian Governments.

"That any attempt to enter into treaties with foreign powers, without the strongest direct support of the mother country as a principal party, must fail, and that a customs' union with the United States, now so heavily taxed, would be unfair to the Empire, and injurious to the Dominion, and would weaken the ties now happily existing between them."

Many other speeches were made, but it was quite evident the House was in harmony with Sir John's views against union with the United States or separation from the Empire, and his amendment was carried by a vote of 100 to 58.

After passing many important measures, amongst which were the Manitoba, Banking, and Tariff Acts, Parliament was prorogued on May 12th.

On June 21st Honourable Charles Tupper, C. B., entered the Cabinet as successor to Sir Edward Kenny appointed Administrator of the Province of Nova Scotia.   On appealing to his constituents he was re-elected by acclamation.

On October 8th, Sir John Young was raised to the peerage under the title of Baron Lisgar.

The fourth session of the Dominion Parliament opened on

January 15, 1871. Amongst the subjects referred to in the Speech from the Throne were two very important ones, namely the reception of British Columbia into the Confederation, and the appointment of a Joint High Commission to consider the question of the fisheries and other matters.

Sir George E. Cartier introduced the resolutions, with respect to the former, and explained the policy of the Government. He said that the terms agreed to were in the nature of a treaty, and did not admit of alteration. They must be accepted or rejected as a whole. The clause which caused most debate was that which referred to the Pacific Railway and, on this point, he explained the policy of the Administration to be, to build the road by the aid of private companies, to whom would be granted a certain amount of land and, perhaps, a small money subsidy. He estimated the length of the road at 2,500 miles, and the land it was proposed to give would amount to about 64,000,000 acres. He forcibly commended the scheme to the consideration of the House, urging that union with British Columbia would give Canada a maritime position that, in time, would be second only to that of England. He was ably and eloquently supported by Mr. (now Sir Leonard) Tilley, Dr. (now Sir James) Grant, Mr. Masson, Colonel Gray, Sir Francis Hincks and others.

Mr. Mackenzie, on the part of the Opposition, said that "he looked upon the acquisition of British Columbia as a political necessity, but thought two much haste ought not to be made or mistakes would occur. He differed entirely with the Government on their railway policy. He did not think that the right way to build the railway was to give away all the best lands. These should be kept as free grants for immigrants. He was totally opposed to undertaking such an immense burden as guaranteeing to build this gigantic railway in ten years. He did not consider it capable of accomplishment, and it was improper to delude the people of British Columbia with the idea that it was." He concluded by moving in amendment :

" That all the words after 'that' be struck out, and the following inserted, ' the proposed terms of union with British

Columbia pledge the Dominion to commence within two years, and complete within ten years the Pacific Railway, the route for which has not been surveyed or its expenses calculated. The said terms also pledge the Government of Canada to a yearly payment to British Columbia of the sum of $100,000 in perpetuity, equal to a capital sum of $2,000,000, for the cession of a tract of waste land on the route of the Pacific Railway, to aid its construction, which British Columbia ought to cede without charge, in like manner as the lands of Canada are proposed to be ceded for the same purpose. The House is of opinion that Canada should not be pledged to do more than proceed at once with the necessary surveys, and, after the route is determined, to prosecute the work at as early a period as the state of the finances will justify."

Mr. Jones (Halifax) moved in amendment to the amendment :

"That the following words be added, 'The proposed engagement respecting the said Pacific Railway would, in the opinion of the House, press too heavily on the resources of Canada.'"

This was lost by a vote of 63 to 98.

Mr. Ross (Dundas) then moved in amendment :

"That, in the opinion of this House, the further consideration of the question be postponed for the present session of Parliament, in order that greater and more careful consideration may be given to a question of such magnitude and importance to the people of this Dominion."

This also failed to carry, the vote standing 75 to 85.

The vote was then taken on Mr. Mackenzie's amendment which was defeated by a vote of 67 to 94.

Honourable Mr. Dorion then moved in amendment :

"That it be resolved, in view of the engagements already entered into since Confederation, and the large expenditure urgently required for canal and railway purposes, this House would not be justified in imposing upon the people of this Dominion the enormous burdens required to construct within ten years a railway to the Pacific, as proposed by the resolutions submitted to the House."

This was also lost on division, the vote standing 70 to 91. The main motion was then carried on the same division.

On the motion for the second reading of the Address, in accordance with the resolutions, Mr. Mackenzie offered another amendment, as follows :

" That this House, while willing to give its best considera- tion to any reasonable terms of union with British Columbia, is of opinion that the terms embodied in the Address are so unreasonable and so unjust to Canada, that this House should not agree thereto."

After considerable further debate the amendment was lost by a vote of 68 to 86.

The Joint High Commission was the result of the action of the Canadian Ministry in 1870. The Fenian raids, which were apparently encouraged by the people of the United States, and the continual encroachments of their fishermen upon Canadian waters, gave rise to a feeling of dissatisfaction and irritation in Canada, and it was felt that something definite should be done about it. Accordingly, on June 9th of that year, an Order-in-Council was passed, appointing the Honourable Alexander Campbell a Commissioner to proceed to England and consult with the Imperial Government res- pecting " the proposed withdrawal of troops from Canada ; the question of fortifications ; the recent invasions of Canadian territory by citizens of the United States, and the previous threats and hostile preparations which compelled the Govern- ment to call out the militia, and to obtain the consent of Par- liament to the suspension of the Habeas Corpus Act ; the systematic trespasses on Canadian fishing grounds by United States fishermen, and the unsettled question as to the limits within which foreigners can fish under the Treaty of 1818."

Mr. Campbell succeeded in arriving at an understanding with Lord Kimberley, the Colonial Secretary, the result of which was that on January 26, 1871, Sir Edward Thornton, British Minister at Washington, addressed a letter to the Honourable Hamilton Fish, United States Secretary of State, proposing the appointment of a Joint High Commission to " treat and discuss the mode of settling the different questions which have arisen out of the fisheries, as well as all those which affect the relations of the United States towards Her Majesty's possessions in North America."

Mr. Fish replied "that the President approved of the proposal, but was of opinion that the removal of the differences which arose during the rebellion in the United States, and which have existed since then, growing out of the acts committed by the several armed vessels which have given rise to the claims generaly known as the 'Alabama claims,' will also be essential to the restoration of cordial and amicable relations between the two Governments, and he therefore proposed that this subject should also be treated by the Commission."

This was accepted "provided that all other claims, both of British subjects and citizens of the United States, arising out of acts committed during the recent civil war in this country are similarly referred to the same Commission."

This being agreed to, both sides proceeded at once to appoint Commissioners. Those who represented Great Britain were Earl de Grey and Ripon, President of the Privy Council; Sir Stafford Northcote, M.P., Sir Edward Thornton, British Minister at Washington; Sir John A. Macdonald, Premier of Canada; and Bernard Montague, Esq., Professor of International Law in the University of Oxford.

The American Commissioners were Messrs. Hamilton Fish, Secretary of State; Robert C. Schenck, United States Minister to Great Britain; Samuel Nelson, Judge of the United States Supreme Court; Ex-Judge E. R. Hoar, of Massachusetts, and George H. Williams, of Oregon.

Lord Tenterden acted as secretary to the British Commissioners, and Mr. J. C. Bancroft Davis as secretary to the Americans. The Commission was appointed after the Dominion Parliament had met, and Sir A. T. Galt, with, no doubt, the best intentions, thought it advisable to place on record the views of the House as to the stand which should be taken at the Conference, and accordingly moved a series of resolutions as to the claims of Canada. Finding that they were considered inopportune he withdrew them, but they brought from the *Globe* a manly editorial of which the following is an extract:

"The spirit and temper of the people of Canada, with respect to their fisheries, is perfectly well understood. The action taken by the Government last year was a direct recognition of the popular sentiment. A formal declaration on that point, therefore, by Parliament, is altogether superogatory, and to suggest by implication that any proposal will be made to alter or diminish the just rights of the Dominion, without our consent, is even more objectionable. We certainly fail to see the propriety of imputing to Great Britain an intention to sacrifice Canada, in any respect, to a desire for peace and friendly relations with the United States. We look upon the interests of Great Britain and Canada as identical and inseparable. We believe that our strength and safety consist in throwing upon Great Britain, and making her ministers feel the sole responsibility of ensuring the harmony of our relations with, and protecting our rights against, foreign powers. To hint broadly, and in the face of our watchful and greedy neighbour, that Great Britain may barter away the rights of her dependency, is surely a very strange mode of rendering support to Great Britain's or Canada's representatives on the Commission. Any eagerness to offer terms is pretty certain to encourage the Americans by whatever means they possess to secure what they desire without making any return for it. The Commission, as we understand it, is to act merely as a deliberative body. It will be time enough for us to protest when we find that its deliberations have resulted in any decision likely to compromise our national rights—an event not at all likely to arise. Public men who have been connected for years with the politics of this country, and who have had experience of the questions that have arisen between Canada and the United States, should know the temper of the Americans better than to suppose that their Commissioners are at all more likely to recognize the justice of the position assumed by Canada because we publicly register a string of inuendoes suggestive of our own weakness and a want of confidence in the Imperial Government."

The first meeting of the Commission was held February 27, 1881, and was adjourned from time to time until May 8th, when the Treaty of Washington was signed. The proceedings at these meetings, the decisions arrived at and the reasons therefor, the stand taken by Canada's representatives, and the provisions of the treaty itself, are so full and so exhaustively given in the speech made by Sir John Macdonald, in introducing the Bill to give effect to the treaty, on May 3, 1872, that we will quote it in full as the best possible explanation that can be given.

Sir John's position on the Commission was a most difficult one. The British members thought he took too strong a stand for Canadian interests, while the Reform party of Canada charged him with having sacrificed them. A careful perusal of his speech, which was a masterpiece of exposition, clear, logical and concise, will demonstrate that he acted in accordance with one central idea : that the full right of Canada to the in-shore fisheries should be acknowledged by England and that, whatever the Joint High Commission might decide, regarding them, such decision should be of no effect unless ratified by the Canadian Parliament. He took the precaution not to accept the appointment until an explicit declaration of our right to the in-shore fisheries had been given by the Imperial Parliament. And though he could not have refused to sign any treaty that might have been made, if he continued a member of the Commission to the last, he would have sent in his resignation as a member of that body, if he had not been able to exact the condition that the fishing articles should depend for their ratification on the Parliament of Canada. Carrying both these points, he secured the full admission of our rights of property and the right of our Parliament to guard them. Although the question was fiercely fought out in both branches of the Legislature, and his conduct strongly denounced by his opponents, time has fully justified the wisdom of his conduct, and those who opposed him then will now endorse his actions in Canada's interest.

CHAPTER XXVIII.

" MR. Speaker, I move for leave to bring in a Bill to carry into effect certain clauses of the treaty negotiated between the United States and Great Britain in 1871. The object of the Bill is stated in the title. It is to give validity, as far as Canada is concerned, to the treaty which was framed last year in the manner so well known to the House and country. The Bill in itself, as I proposed to introduce it the other day, was simply a Bill to suspend those clauses of the Fishery Acts which prevent fishermen of the United States from fishing in the in-shore waters of Canada, such suspension to continue during the existence of the treaty. I confined it to that object at the time, because the question really before this House, was whether the fishery articles of the treaty should receive sanction of Parliament or not. As, however, a desire was expressed on the other side that I should enter into the subject fully on asking leave to bring in the Bill, and as, on examining the cognate Act, which has been laid before Congress at Washington, I find that all the subjects—even those subjects which do not require legislation—have been repeated in that Act, in order, one would suppose, to make the Act in the nature of a contract to be obligatory during the existence of the treaty, so that in good faith it could not be repealed during that time, I propose to follow the same course.

"The Act I ask leave to bring in provides, in the first clause, for the suspension of the fishery laws of Canada, so far as they prevent citizens of the United States from fishing in our inshore waters. The Bill also provides that, during the existence of the treaty, fish and fish oil (except fish of the inland lakes of the United States and the rivers emptying into those lakes, and fish preserved in oil), being the produce of the fisheries of the United States, shall be admitted into Canada free of duty. The third clause provides for the continuance of the bonding system during the twelve years, or longer period, provided by the treaty, and the fourth clause provides that the right of transhipment contained in the 30th clause of the treaty shall, in like manner, be secured to citizens of the United States during the existence of the treaty. The last clause of the Bill provides that it shall come into effect whenever, upon an Order-in-Council, a proclamation of the Governor-General is issued, giving effect to the Act.

"In submitting the Act in this form, I am aware that objections might be taken to some of the clauses on the ground that, having relation to questions of trade and money, they should be commenced by resolution adopted in Committee of the Whole. That objection does not apply to the whole of the Bill—to those clauses which suspend the action of our Fishery Act ; but it would affect, according to the general principle, the clause which provides that there shall be no duty on fish and fish oil, and also the clauses respecting the bonding system and transhipment. I do not, however, anticipate that that objection will be taken, because in presenting the Bill in this form, I have followed the precedent established in 1854, when the measure relating to the Reciprocity Treaty was introduced in Parliament. It was then held that the Act, having been introduced as based upon a treaty which was submitted by a message from the Crown, became a matter of public and general policy, and ceased to be merely a matter of trade, and although those honourable gentlemen who interested themselves in parliamentary and political matters at that date will remember that the Act which was introduced by the Attorney-General for Lower Canada in 1854, Mr. Drummond, was simply an Act declaring that various articles, being the produce of the United

States, should, during the existence of the treaty, be received
free into Canada, and that Act repealed the tariff *pro tanto*,
it was not introduced by resolution, but after the treaty had
been submitted and laid on the table, and after a formal
message had been brought down by Mr. Morin, the leader
of the Government in the House, to the effect that the Bill
was introduced with the sanction of the Governor-General.
I do not, therefore, anticipate that objection will be taken by
any honourable member, and I suppose the precedent so
solemnly laid down at that time, will be held to be binding
now.   Should objection, however, be taken, the clauses of
the Bill respecting the suspension of the Fishery Act and
transhipment, are sufficient to be proceeded with in this
manner.   The other portions may be printed in italics and
can be brought up as parts of the Bill or separately as resolutions, as may be thought best.   The journals of the House
stated that on September 21, 1854, Mr. Chauveau submitted
a copy of the treaty, which was set out on the face of the
journals.   On the same day Mr. Drummond asked leave of
the House to bring in a Bill to give effect to a certain treaty
between Her Majesty and the United States of America;
and on the 22nd, on the order of the day, for the second reading of the Bill, Mr. Morin, by command, brought down a
message from the Governor-General signifying that it was
by His Excellency's sanction it had been introduced, where-
upon the House proceeded to the second reading.   That Bill
was a simple one declaring that various articles mentioned
in the treaty should, during the existence of the treaty, be
admitted into this country free of duty.   The House now,
Mr. Speaker, if they give leave that this Bill shall be introduced and read a first time will be in the possession of all
those portions of the Treaty of Washington that in any way
come within the action of the Legislature.

"Although the debate upon this subject will, as a matter
of course, take a wide range and will properly include all
the subjects connected with the treaty in which Canada has
any interest, yet it must not be forgotten that the treaty, as
a whole, is in force, with the particular exceptions I have

mentioned ; and the decision of this House will, after all, be simply whether the articles of the treaty, extending from the 18th to the 25th, shall receive the sanction of Parliament, or whether those portions of the treaty shall be a dead letter. This subject has excited a great deal of interest, as was natural in Canada, ever since May 8, 1871, when the treaty was signed at Washington. It has been largely discussed in the public prints, and opinions of various kinds have been expressed upon it—some altogether favourable, some altogether opposed, and many others of intermediate shades of opinion—and among other parts of the discussion has not been forgotten, the personal question relating to myself—the position I held as a member of this Government, and as one of the High Commissioners at Washington. Upon that question I shall have to speak by-and-bye, yet it is one that has lost much of its interest, from the fact that by the introduction of this Bill the House and country will see that the policy of the Government, of which I am a member, is to carry out or try to carry out the treaty, which I signed as a plenipotentiary of Her Majesty.

"Under the reservation made in the treaty, this House and the Legislature of Prince Edward Island have full power to accept the fishery articles or reject them. In that matter this House and Parliament have full and complete control. (Hear, hear). No matter what may be the consequences of the action of this Parliament, no matter what may be the consequences with respect to future relations between Canada and England, or between Canada and the United States, or between England and the United States, no matter what may be the consequences as to the existence of the present Government of Canada, it must not be forgotten that the House has full power to reject the clauses of the treaty if they please, and maintain the right of Canada to exclude Americans from in-shore fisheries, as if the treaty had never been made. (Hear, hear). That reservation was fully provided for in the treaty. It was made a portion of it—an essential portion, and, if it had not been so made, the name of the Minister of Justice of

Canada would not have been attached to it. (Hear, hear).
That right has been reserved, and this Parliament has full
power to deal with the whole question. I will by-and-bye
speak more at length as to the part I took in the negotiations,
but I feel that I performed my duty—a grave and serious
duty, but still my duty—in attaching my signature to the
treaty as one of Her Majesty's representatives and servants.
(Hear, hear).

"Now, sir, let me enter into a short retrospect of occurrences which transpired for some years before arrangements
were entered into for negotiating the treaty. The Reciprocity Treaty with the United States existed from 1854 to
1866, in which latter year it expired. Great exertions were
made by the Government of Canada, and a great desire was
expressed by the Parliament and people of Canada for a
renewal of that treaty. It was felt to have worked very
beneficially for Canada. It was felt to have worked also
to the advantage of the United States : and there was a
desire and a feeling that those growing interests which had
been constantly developing and increasing themselves during
the existence of the treaty would be greatly aided if it
were renewed and continued. I was a member of the Government at that time with some of my honourable friends who
are still my colleagues, and we took every step in our power,
we spared no effort, we left no stone unturned, in order to gain
that object. The House will remember that for the purpose
of either effecting a renewal of the treaty, or, if we could not
obtain that, of arriving at the same object by means of concurrent legislation, my honourable friend the member for Sherbrooke, at that time Finance Minister, and the present Lieutenant-Governor of Ontario went to Washington on behalf of
the Government of Canada. It is a matter of history that all
their exertions failed, and after their failure, by the general
consent—a consent in which I believe the people of Canada
were as one man—we came to the conclusion that it would be
humiliating to Canada to make any further exertions at
Washington or to do anything more in the way of pressing
for the renewal of that instrument, and the people of this

THE RESIDENCE OF REV. DR. WILLIAMSON, IN KINGSTON.

(Sir John's Headquarters during his recent Election.)

country, with great energy, addressed themselves to find other channels of trade, other means of developing and sustaining our various industries, in which, I am happy to say, they have been completely successful.

" Immediately on the expiration of the treaty our right to the exclusive use of the in-shore fisheries returned to us, and it will be in remembrance of the House, that Her Majesty's Government desired us not to resume, at least for a year, that right to the exclusion of American fishermen, and that the prohibition of Americans fishing in those waters should not be put in force either by Canada or the Maritime Provinces. All the provinces, I believe, desired to accede to the suggestion, and was pressed strongly on behalf of the late Province of Canada, that it would be against our interests if, for a moment after the treaty ceased, we allowed it to be supposed that American fishermen had a right to come into our waters as before ; and it was only because of the pressure of Her Majesty's Government and our desire to be in accord with that Government, as well as because of our desire to carry with us the moral support of Great Britain and the material assistance of her fleet, that we assented, with great reluctance, to the introduction of a system of licenses, for one year, at a nominal fee or rate. This was done avowedly by us for the purpose of asserting our right. No greater or stronger mode of asserting a right, and obtaining the acknowledgement of it by those who desire to enter our waters for the purpose of fishing could be devised than by exacting payment for the permission, and therefore it was that we assented to the licensing system. (Hear, hear).

" Although, in 1866, that system was commenced, it did not come immediately into force. We had not then fitted out a marine police force, for we were not altogether without expectation that the mind of the Government of the United States might take a different direction, and that there was a probability of negotiations being renewed respecting the revival of the Reciprocity Treaty ; and, therefore, although the system was established, it was not rigidly put in force, and no great exertion was made to seize trespassers who had not taken out licenses. In the first year, however, a great number of licenses were taken out, but when the fee was increased, so as to render it a substantial recognition of our rights, the payments became fewer and fewer, until at last it was found that the vessels who took out licenses were the exception, and that the great bulk of fishermen who entered our waters were trespassers ; and in addition to the fact that our fisheries were invaded, that we were receiving no consideration for the liberty, and that our rights were invaded boldly and aggressively, it was now stated by the American Government, or members of the American Cabinet, that the renewal of the Reciprocity Treaty was not only inexpedient, but unconstitutional, and that no such renewal could or would be made.

"The Government of Canada then, in 1870, after conference with the Imperial Government, and after receiving the promises of the Imperial Government that we should have the support of their fleet in the protection of our just rights— a promise which was faithfully carried out—prepared and fitted out a sufficient force of marine police vessels to protect our rights, and I am glad to believe that that policy was perfectly successful. Great firmness was used, but, at the same time, great discretion ; there was no harshness, and no seizures were made of a doubtful character. No desire to harass the foreign fishermen was evidenced, but, on the contrary, in any case in which there was doubt, the officers in command of the seizing vessels reported to the head of their department, and when the papers were laid before Government, they, in all cases, gave the offending parties the benefit of the doubt. Still, as it would be remembered, some of the fishermen made complaints, which complaints, although unjust, I am sorry to say were in some instances made and supported on oath, of harshness on the part of the cruisers, and an attempt was made to agitate the public mind of the United States against the people of Canada, and there was at that time a feeling on the part of a large portion of the people of the United States, which feeling, I am, however, happy to say, has since disappeared, that the action of Canada was unfriendly. Her Majesty's Government were of course appealed to by the authorities of the United States on all these subjects, and the complaints were bandied from one Government to the other, and proved a source of great irritation. While this feeling was being raised in the United States there was, on the other hand, a feeling among our fisherman that our rights were, to a very great degree, invaded.

" In order to avoid the possibility of dispute ; in order to avoid any appearance of harshness ; in order, while we were supporting our fishery rights, to prevent any case of collision between the Imperial Government and the United States, or between the Canadian authorities and the United States, we avoided making seizures within the bays, or in any way bringing up the 'headland question.' This is very unsatisfactory, because, as it was said by the fishermen, ' if we have these rights, we should be protected in the exercise of them.' And it was, therefore, well that that question should be settled at once and for ever. In addition, however, to the question of headlands, a new one had arisen of an exceedingly unpleasant nature. By the wording of the Convention of 1818, foreign fishermen were only allowed to enter our waters for the purpose of procuring wood, water and shelter ; but they claimed that they had a right, although fishing vessels, to enter our ports for trading purposes ; and it was alleged by our own fishermen that under pretence of trading, American fishermen were in the habit of invading our fishing grounds, and fishing in our waters. The Canadian Government thought it, therefore, well to press, not only by correspondence, but by a delegate who was a member of the Government, upon Her Majesty's Government the propriety of having that question settled with the United States, and consequently my friend and colleague, the Postmaster-General, went to England to deal with that subject. The results of his mission are before Parliament.

" At the same time that he dealt with the question I have just mentioned, he pressed upon the consideration of Her Majesty's Government the propriety of England making on our behalf a demand on the United States Government for reparation for the wrongs known as ' the Fenian Raids.'

England agreed to press upon the United States both these matters, and to ask that all the disputed questions relating to the in-shore fisheries under the Convention of 1818 should be settled in some mode to be agreed upon between the two nations, and also to press upon the United States the wrong sustained by Canada at the hands of citizens of the United States who had invaded our country.

'Before Her Majesty's Government had actually, in compliance with their promise, made any representation on these two subjects to the United States Government, England had been engaged in her own behalf in a controversy of a very grave character. It was known that what was commonly known as 'the Alabama claims' was a subject of dispute between the two countries, involving the gravest consequences, and that, hitherto, the results had been most unsatisfactory. An attempt had been made to settle the question by what was known as the Johnson-Clarendon Treaty, but that treaty had been rejected by the United States authorities. So long as this question remained unsettled between the two nations there was no possibility of the old friendly relations that had so long existed between them being restored, and England felt that it was of the first importance to her that those amicable relations should be restored. It was not only her desire to be in the most friendly position towards a country which was so closely associated with her by every tie, by common origin, by common interest, by common language, but it was also her interest to have every cloud removed between the two nations, because she had reason to feel that her position with respect to the other great powers of the world was greatly affected, by the knowledge which those other nations had of the position of affairs between the United States and herself. The prestige of Great Britain as a great power was affected most seriously by the absence of an *entente cordiale* between the two nations. Two years ago, England was, as a matter of course greatly interested in the great and serious questions which were then convulsing Europe, and was in danger of being drawn by some complication into hostile relations with some of the conflicting powers, and she felt—and I speak merely what must be obvious to every honourable member in the House—that she could not press or assert her opinion, with the same freedom of action, so long as she was aware, and so long as other nations were aware, that in case she should be unfortunately placed in a state of hostility towards any nation whatever, the United States Government would be forced by the United States people to press at that very time, when she might be engaged in mortal coflict with another nation, for a settlement of those Alabama claims. Hence, Mr. Speaker, the great desire of England, in my opinion, that that great question should be settled, and hence, also, the intermingling of the particular questions relating to Canada with the larger Imperial questions. And, sir, in my opinion, it was of greater consequence to Canada than to England, at least of as great consequence, that the Alabama question should be settled. (Cheers).

" Sir, England has promised to us, and we have all faith in that promise, that in case of war, the whole force of the Empire should be exerted in our defence. (Cheers). What would have been the position of England, and what would have been the position of Canada, if she had been called upon to use her whole force to defend us, when engaged in conflict elsewhere? Canada would, as a matter of course, in case of war between England and the United States, be the battle ground. We should be the sufferers, our country would be devastated, our people slaughtered, and our property destroyed, and while England would, I believe, under all circumstances, faithfully perform her promise to the utmost (cheers), she would be greatly impeded in carrying out her desire, if engaged elsewhere. It was, therefore, as much the interest of this Dominion as of England, that the Alabama and all other questions that in any way threatened the disturbance of the peaceful relations between the two countries should be settled and adjusted ; and therefore, although to a considerable extent I agree with the remarks that fell from the Minister of Finance when he made his Budget speech, that looking at the subject in a commercial point of view, it might have been better, in the interest of Canada, that the fishery and Fenian questions should have been settled free and apart from the Imperial question.

"I am pleased, and I was pleased, that the fact of Canada having asked England to make these demands upon the United States, gave an opportunity for re-opening the negotiations with respect to the Alabama and other matters. It was fortunate that we made that demand, for England could not, with due self-respect, have initiated or re-opened the Alabama question. She had concluded a treaty in London with the representative of the United States, and this treaty having been rejected by the Supreme Executive of the United States, could not herself have re-opened negotiations on the subject. And, therefore, it was fortunate, I say, for the peace of the Empire, and for the peace of Canada, that we asked England to make these demands upon the United States as it afforded the opportunity of all these questions being made again the subject of negotiation. The correspondence which is before the House, between the Secretary of State of the United States and the British Ambassador, Sir Edward Thornton, has shown how that result was arrived at. The invitation was made by the British Ambassador to consider the Fishery Question. The United States Government, I have no doubt, though, I do not know it as matter of fact, by a quiet and friendly understanding between the two powers, replied acceding to the request, on condition that the larger and graver matters of dispute were also made a matter of negotiation. Hence, it was sir, that the arrangements were made under which the Treaty of Washington was affected.

"Sir, I have said that it was of the greatest consequence to Canada, and to the future peace and prosperity of Canada, that every cloud which threatened the peace of England and the United States should be dispelled. I was struck with an expression that was used to me by a distinguished English statesman, that those powers in Europe who are not so friendly to England heard, with dismay, that the *entente cordiale* between the two nations was to be renewed (hear, hear), and you have seen mentioned in the public press the active exertions that were made by one power, or by the representative of one power, for the purpose of preventing that happy result (hear, hear), and although Mr. Catacazy has been disavowed by the Government of Russia, in the same way as poor Vicovich was on a previous occasion when he was the organ of Russia in the East. I cannot but feel that he was punished only because his zeal outran his discretion. I can vouch for his active exertions for the purpose of preventing this Treaty of Washington receiving the sanction of the Senate of the United States. (Hear, hear). While England, therefore, was strongly interested in the settlement of these questions both for herself and for Canada, the United States were also interested and made overtures in a most friendly spirit. I believe that there was a real desire among the people of the United States to be friendly towards England. I believe that the feeling of irritation, which had been caused by the unhappy events of the war, and by the escape of the Alabama had almost entirely disappeared, and I hope and believe that the people of the United States were then, and are now strongly in favour of establishing permanently a friendly feeling between the two nations.

"Then, besides, they had a further interest in settling all matters in dispute. So long as the United States and England were not on friendly terms, so long as they were standing aloof from each other, it affected very considerably the credit of the United States securities in Europe. Not only the funds of the United States as a whole, but the securities of every State of the Union, and of all American enterprises seeking the markets of the world were injuriously affected by the unsatisfactory relations between the two countries. They were, therefore, prepared to meet each other in this negotiation.

"To proceed with the history of the circumstances immediately preceding the formation of the Joint High Commission at Washington, I will state that on February 1, 1871, a communication was made to me by His Excellency, the Governor-General, on behalf of Her Majesty's Government, asking me, in case there was going to be a

Joint Commission to settle all questions between England and the United States, whether I would act as a member of that Commission. I give the date because it has been asked for. The communication was verbal, and founded upon a telegraphic communication to His Excellency which cannot be printed, being of a nature which the House can readily understand, ought not properly to be laid before this House. This communication was, in the first place, for myself alone, I was not allowed to mention it for the time to any one else. My reply was that I would be greatly embarrassed by any injunction of secrecy as regards my colleagues, and that under no circumstances would I accept the position without their consent. I subsequently received permission to communicate it to them, and I received their consent to act upon the Commission. Before accepting, however, I took occasion, for my own information and satisfaction, to ask through His Excellency what points of agreement and of difference existed between England and Canada with regard to the Fisheries. The answer was a very short one, by cable, and it was satisfactory to myself. It was afterwards extended in the despatch of February 16, 1871. It shortly stated that, of course, it was impossible for Her Majesty's Government to pledge themselves to any forgone conclusion ; that, as it was a matter of negotiation, it was, of course, out of the question on the part of either Government to give cast iron instructions to their representatives, because that would do away with every idea of a negotiation. But the despatch went on to say that Her Majesty's Government conidered our right to the in-shore fisheries beyond dispute ; that they also believed that our claims as to the headlands were just, but that those claims might properly be a matter of compromise. It went on further to state that Her Majesty's Government believed that, as a matter of strict right we could exclude the American fishermen entering our ports for purposes of trade and commerce, and that they could only enter our waters, in the language of the treaty, for wood, water and shelter ; but that this, in the opinion of Her Majesty's Government, would be a harsh construction of the treaty and might properly be a subject for compromise. On reading that despatch, I could have no difficulty, as a member of the Canadian Government, in accepting the position, to which my colleagues assented, of plenipotentiary to Washington, because, as a matter of law, our view of those three points was acknowledged to be correct, and the subject was therefore devoid of any embarrassment, from the fact of Canadians setting up pretensions which Her Majesty's Government could not support. (Hear, hear).

"When the proposition was first made to me, I must say that I felt considerable embarrassment and great reluctance to become a member of the Commission. I pointed out to my colleagues that I was to be one only of five, that I was in a position of being over-ruled continually in our discussions, and that I could not by any possibility bring due weight from my isolated position. I felt also that I would not receive from those who were politically opposed to me in Canada, that support which an officer going abroad on behalf of his country generally received, and had a right to expect. (Hear, hear). I knew that I would be made a mark of attack, and this House well knows that my anticipations have been verified. I knew that I would not get fair play. (Hear, hear). I knew that the same policy that had been carried out towards me for years and years would continue, and therefore it was a matter of grave consideration for myself, whether to accept the appointment or not. Sir, a sense of duty prevailed (cheers), and my colleagues pressed upon me also that I would be wanting in my duty to my country if I declined the appointment; that, if from a fear of the consequences, from a fear that I would sacrifice the position I held in the opinions of the people of Canada, I should shirk the duty, I would be unworthy of the confidence that I had received so long from a large portion of the people of Canada. (Cheers). What, said my colleagues, would be said if, in consequence of your refusal, Canada was not represented, and her interests in these matters allowed to go by default? England, after having offered that position to the first minister, and it having been refused by him, would have been quite at liberty to have proceeded with the commission and the settlement of all these questions without Canada being represented on the commission, and those very men who attack me now for having been there and taken a certain course, would have been just as loud in their complaints, and just as bitter in their attacks, because I had neglected the interests of Canada and refused the responsibility of asserting the rights of Canada at Washington. (Cheers). Sir, knowing, as I said before, what the consequences would be to myself of accepting that office, and foreseeing the attacks that would be made upon me, I addressed a letter to His Excellency the Governor-General, informing him of the great difficulties of my position, and that it was only from a sense of duty that I accepted the position. (Cheers).

"On proceeding to Washington I found a general desire among the two branches into which the Joint High Commission divided itself, an equal desire, I should say, on the part of the United States Commissioners as well as of the British Commissioners, that all questions should be settled so far as the two Governments could do so. There was a special desire that there should be a settlement. It was very easy for the commissioners, or the Government through their representatives, to make a treaty, but in the United States there is a power above and beyond the Government, the Senate of the United States, which had to be considered. It was felt that a second rejection of the treaty would be most disastrous for the future of both nations; that it would be a solemn declaration that there was no peaceable solution of the question between the two nations. An American statesman said to me, 'the rejection of the treaty now means war.' Not war to-morrow or at any given period, but war whenever England happened to be engaged in other troubles, and attacked from other sources. (Hear, hear).

"You may therefore imagine, Mr. Speaker, and this House may well imagine, the solemn considerations pressing upon my mind, as well as upon the minds of my colleagues in Canada, with whom I was in daily communication, if by any unwise course, or from any rigid or pre-conceived opinions, we should risk the destruction for ever of all hope of a peaceable solution of the difficulties between the two kindred nations. (Cheers). Still, sir, I did not forget that I was their chosen representative. I could not ignore the fact that I was selected a member of that commission from my acquaintance with Canadian politics. I had continually before me, not only the Imperial question, but the interests of the Dominion of Canada, which I was there especially to represent, and the difficulty of my position was, that if I gave undue prominence to the interests of Canada, I might justly be held, in England, to be taking a purely colonial and selfish view, regardless of the interests of the Empire as a whole, and the interests of Canada as a portion of the Empire, and, on the other hand, if I kept my eye solely on Imperial considerations, I might be held as neglecting my especial duty towards this my country, Canada. It was a difficult position, as the House will believe, a position that pressed upon me with great weight and severity at the time, and it has not been diminished in any way since I have returned, except by the cordial support of my colleagues, and I believe also my friends in this House. (Cheers).

"In order to show that I did not for a moment forget that I was there to represent the interests of Canada, I must ask you to look at the despatch of February 16, 1871, which reached me at Washington a few days after I arrived there—it will be seen that Lord Kimberly used this expression, ' as at present advised Her Majesty's Government are of opinion that the right of Canada to exclude Americans from fishing in the waters within the limits of three marine miles of the coast, is beyond dispute, and can only be ceded for an adequate consideration. Should this consideration take the form of a money payment, it appears to Her Majesty's Government that such an arrangement would be more likely to work well than if any conditions were annexed to the exercise of the privilege of fishing within the Canadian waters.' Having read that despatch, and the suggestion that an arrangement might be made on the basis of a money payment, and there being an absence of any statement that such an arrangement would only be made with the consent of Canada,

I thought it well to communicate with my colleagues at Ottawa, and although we had received again and again, assurances from Her Majesty's Government that those rights would not be affected, given away, or ceded, without our consent, it was thought advisable, in consequence of the omission of all reference to the necessity of Canada's assent being obtained to any monetary arrangement, to communicate by cable that Canada considered the Canadian Fisheries to be her property, and they could not be sold without her consent.

"That communication was made by the Canadian Government on March 10th, and of that Government I was a member, and not only did that communication proceed from the Canadian Government to England, giving them fair notice that the Canadian Government, of which I was a member, would insist upon the right of dealing with her own fisheries, but I took occasion to press upon the head of the British Commission at Washington, that my own individual opinion, as representing Canada, should be laid before Her Majesty's Government. The answer that came back at once by cable was extended in full in the despatch of March 17, 1871 ; and it was most satisfactory, as it stated that Her Majesty's Government had never any intention of advising Her Majesty to part with those fisheries without the consent of Canada. Armed with this I felt that I was relieved of a considerable amount of my embarrassment. I felt that no matter what arrangements might be made, no matter whether I was out-voted by my colleagues on the Commission, or what instructions might be given by Her Majesty's Government, the interests of Canada were safe, because they were in her own hands, and reserved for her own decision.

"Now, Mr. Speaker, it must not be supposed that this was not a substantial concession on the part of Her Majesty's Government. It is true that Lord Kimberley stated in his despatch of March 17th, that 'when the reciprocity treaty was concluded, the Acts of the Nova Scotia and New Brunswick Legislatures, relating to the Fisheries were suspended by Acts of those Legislatures, and the Fishery rights of Canada are now under the protection of a Canadian Act of Parliament, the repeal of which would be necessary in case of the cession of those rights to any foreign powers.' It is true, in one sense of the word, but it is also true that if Her Majesty, in the exercise of her power, had chosen to make a treaty with the United States, ceding not only those rights, but ceding the very land over which those waters flow, that treaty between England and the United States would have been binding, and the United States would have held England to it. No matter how unjust to Canada, after all her previous promises, still that treaty would be a valid and obligatory treaty between England and the United States, and the latter would have had the right to enforce its provisions, override any provincial laws and ordinances, and take possession of our waters and rights. It would have been a great wrong, but the consequences would have been the loss, practically, of our rights for ever, and so it was satisfactory that it should be settled, as it has been settled, without a doubt appearing upon the records of the conference at Washington. Now the recognition of the proprietary right of Canada in her fisheries forms a portion of the State papers of both countries. Now the rights of Canada to those fisheries are beyond dispute, and it is finally established that England cannot, and will not, under any circumstances whatever, cede those fisheries without the consent of Canada. So that in any future arrangement between Canada and England, or England and the United States, the rights of Canada will be respected, as it is conceded beyond dispute, that England has not the power to deprive Canada of them. We may now rest certain that for all time to come England will not, without our consent, make any cession of these interests.

"To come to the various subjects which interest Canada more particularly. I will address myself to them in detail, and first, I will consider the question of most importance to us, the one on which we are now specially asked to legislate, that which interests Canada as a whole most particularly, and which interests the Maritime provinces especially. I mean the articles of the treaty with respect to our fishery rights. I would in the first place say that the protocols which accompany the treaty, and which are in the hands of every member do not give chronologically an every day account of the transactions of the Conference, although as a general rule, I believe, the protocols of such Conferences are kept from day to day, but it was thought better to depart from the rule on this occasion, and only to record the conclusions arrived at; therefore, while the protocols substantially contain the result of the negotiations ended in the treaty, they must not be looked upon as chronological details of facts and incidents as they occurred. I say so because the protocol which relates more especially to the fisheries would lead one to suppose that at the first meeting, and without previous discussion the British Commissioners stated ' that they were prepared to discuss the question of the fisheries, either in detail or generally, so as either to enter into an examination of the respective rights of the two countries under the treaty of 1818, and the general law of nations, or to approach at once the settlement of the question on a comprehensive basis.' Now the fact is, that it was found by the British Commissioners when they arrived at Washington and had an opportunity of ascertaining the feeling that prevailed at that time, not only among the United States Commissioners, but among the public men of the United States whom they met there, and from their communications with other sources of information, that the feeling was universal that all questions should be settled beyond the possibility of dispute in the future, and more especially that if, by any possibility, a solution of the difficulty respecting the fisheries could be arrived at, or a satisfactory arrangement made by which the fishery question could be placed in abeyance as in 1854, it would be to the advantage of both nations.

" It must be remembered that the Commission sat in 1871, that the exclusion of American fishermen from our waters was enforced and kept up during the whole of 1870, and that great and loud, though I believe unfounded, complaints had been made that American fishing vessels had been illegally seized, although they had not trespassed upon our waters. Persons interested had been using every effort to arouse and stimulate

the minds of the people of the United States against Canada
and the Canadian authorities, and it was felt and expressed
that it would be a great bar to the chance of the treaty being
accepted by the United States, if one of the causes of irritation, which had been occurring a few months before should be
allowed to remain unsettled ; collisions would occur between
American fishermen claiming certain rights, and Canadians
resisting those claims, that thereby unfriendly feelings would
be aroused, and all the good which might be effected by the
treaty would be destroyed, by quarrels between man and man
engaged on the fishing grounds.

" This feeling prevailed, and I, as a Canadian, knowing
that the people of Canada desired, and had always expressed
a wish to enter into the most cordial reciprocal trade arrangements with the United States, so stated to the British Commissioners, and they had no hesitation, on being invited to do
so, in stating that they would desire by all means to remove
every cause of dissension respecting these fisheries by the
restoration of the old Reciprocity Treaty of 1854. An attempt
was made in 1865 by the honourable member for Sherbrooke
(Sir A. T. Galt) and Mr. Howland, on behalf of Canada, to
renew that treaty, but failed, because the circumstances of the
United States in 1865 were very different from what they were
in 1854, and it appeared out of the question, and impossible,
for the United States to agree to a treaty with exactly the
same provisions and of exactly the same nature as that of
1854. So the British Commissioners, believing that a treaty
similar in detail to that of 1854 could not be obtained, urged
that one conceived in the same spirit, but adapted to the
altered circumstances of the two countries, should be adopted,
and this view was strongly pressed upon the Joint Commission. This will appear from the protocol referring to this
branch of the treaty. It will also appear from the protocol
that the United States Commissioners stated that the
Reciprocity Treaty was out of the question, that it could not
be accepted without being submitted to both branches of
Congress, and there was not the slightest possibility of
Congress passing such an Act, and that the agreement by the

two Governments to a treaty, including provisions similar in
spirit to the treaty of 1854, would only ensure the rejection of
the treaty by the Senate, and, therefore, that some other
solution must be found.   I believe that the United States
Commissioners were candid and were accurate in their view of
the situation.   I believe that had the treaty contained all the
provisions, or the essential provisions of the treaty of 1854,
they would have ensured its rejection by the Senate.

   " When I speak of the conferences that were held on the
fisheries I would state, for the information of those members
of the House who may be unacquainted with the usage in such
matters, that the Commissioners did not act at the discussions
individually.   The conference was composed of two units, the
British Commission and the United States Commission.   If a
question arose in conference, on which either of the two parties,
the British or American branch, desired to consult together,
they retired, and on their return expressed their views as
a whole, without reference to the individual opinions of the
Commissioners.   As an individual member of the British
Commission, and on behalf of Canada, when it was found that
we could not obtain a renewal of the Reciprocity Treaty, I
urged upon my English coleagues that the Canadians should
be allowed to retain the exclusive enjoyment of the in-shore
fisheries, and that means should be used to arrive in some
way or other at a settlement of the disputed questions in
relation to the fisheries, so as to settle the headland question
and the other one relating to trading in our ports by American fishermen, and I would have been well satisfied, acting on
behalf of the Canadian Government, if that course had been
adopted by the Imperial Government ; but Her Majesty's
Government felt and so instructed her Commissioners, and it
was so felt by the United States Commissioners, that the
leaving of the chance of collision between the American
fishermen and the Canadian fishermen a matter of possibility,
would destroy or greatly prejudice the great object of the
negotiations that were to restore the amicable relations and
friendly feelings between the two nations, and therefore Her
Majesty's Government pressed that these questions should be

allowed to remain in abeyance, and that some other settlement in the way of compensation to Canada should be found.

"The protocol shows, Mr. Speaker, that the United States
Government, through their Commissioners, made a considerable advance, or at least some advance, in the direction of
Reciprocity, because they offered to exchange for our in-shore
fisheries in the first place, the right to fish in their waters
whatever that might be worth, and they offered to admit
Canadian coal, salt, fish, and—after 1874 lumber. They
offered Reciprocity in these articles. On behalf of Canada
the British Commissioners said that they did not consider
that that was a fair equivalent. (Hear, hear). It is not
necessary that I should enter into all the discussions and
arguments on that point, but it was pointed out by the British
Commissioners that already a measure had passed one branch
of the Legislature of the United States, making coal and
salt free, and stood ready to be passed by the other branch,
the Senate. It was believed at that time that the American
Congress for its own purpose, and in the interest of the American people, was about to take the duty off these articles,
and therefore the remission could not be considered as in
any way a compensation, as Congress was going to take off
the duty whether there was a treaty or not. Then as regards
the duty on lumber which was offered to be taken off in 1874
was pointed out that nearly a third of the whole of the time
for which the treaty was proposed to exist would expire
before the duty would be taken off our lumber. The British
Commissioners urged that under those circumstances the
offer could not be considered as a fair one, and that Canada
had a fair right to demand compensation over and above
these proposed reciprocal arrangements.

"Before that proposition was made I was in communication with my colleagues. The Canadian Government were
exceedingly anxious that the original object should be carried
out, that if we could not get reciprocity as it was in 1854
that we should be allowed to retain our fisheries and that
the questions in dispute should be settled ; but Her Majesty's
Government taking the strong ground that their acceding to

our wishes would be equivalent to an abandonment of carrying the treaty into effect, the Canadian Government reluct-
antly said that from a desire to meet Her Majesty's Government's views as much as possible, and not to allow it to be
felt in England, that from a selfish desire to obtain all we
desired we had frustrated the efforts of Her Majesty's Government to secure peace, we consented that the proposition I
have mentioned should be made, and so that proposition
was made to the United States.

"Although I do not know it as a matter of certainty, I
have reason to believe that, if it had not been for the action of
this Legislature last session, we would now be passing an Act
for the purpose of ratifying a treaty in which coal, salt, and
lumber from Canada would be received into the United States
free of duty. (Hear, hear). I have reason to believe that,
had it not been for the interposition of this Legislature, and I
speak now of political friends as well as foes, those terms
which were offered by the United States would have been a
portion of the treaty instead of its standing as it does now.
(Applause). I will tell the House why I say so. The offer
was made early by the United States Government. The
answer made by the British Commissioners was that, under
the circumstances, it was not a fair and adequate compensation for the privileges that were asked, and the British Commissioners, at the suggestion of the Canadian Government,
referred the question to Her Majesty's Government, whether
they had not a right, in addition to this offer of the United
States, to expect a pecuniary compensation; that pecuniary
compensation to be settled in some way or other. That took
place on March 25, 1871. On March 25th, I think the final
proposition was made by the United States Government, and
on March 22nd, only three days before, the resolution carried in
this House by which the duty was taken off coal and salt and
the other articles mentioned. Before that resolution was
carried here no feeling was expressed in the United States
against the taking off the duty on Canadian coal and salt imported into the United States; no one raised any difficulty
about it. I am as well satisfied as I can be of any thing which

I did not see occur, that the admission of Canadian coal and salt into the United States would have been placed in the treaty if it had not been for the action of this Legislature.

"On March 25th that offer was made, and it was referred to England. The English Government stated that they quite agreed in the opinion that, in addition to that offer, there should be compensation in money, and then, on April 17th, the American Commissioners withdrew, as they had a right to do, their offer altogether. And why did they withdraw the offer altogether? One of the commissioners in conversation said to me : ' I am quite surprised to find the opposition that has sprung up to the admission of Canadian coal and salt into our market. I was quite unprepared for the feeling that is exhibited.' I knew right well what the reason was. The monopolists having the control of American coal in Pennsylvania, and salt in New York, so long as the treaty would open to them the markets in Canada for their products, were willing that it should carry, because they would have the advantage of both markets, but when the duty was taken off in Canada, when you had opened our market to them, when they had the whole control of their own market, and free access to ours, whether for coal or salt, the monopolists brought down all their energies upon their friends in Congress, and through them a pressure on the American Government for the purpose of preventing the admission of Canadian coal and salt into the American market, and from that, I have no doubt, came the withdrawal by the American Commissioners of their offer. When my honourable friend from Bothwell (Mr. Mills) said last session, ' there goes the Canadian National Policy,' he was little aware of the consequences of the reckless course he had taken. (Hear, hear). Honourable gentlemen may laugh, but they will find it no laughing matter. The people of Canada, both east and west, will hold to strict account those who acted so unpatriotically in this matter.

"Under these circumstances, Mr. Speaker, I felt myself powerless, and when the American Commissioners made their last offer, which is now in the treaty, offering reciprocity in fisheries, that Canadians should fish in American waters, and

that Americans should fish in Canadian waters, and that fish
and fish oil should be reciprocally free, and that if on arbitration it were found that the bargain was an unjust one to
Canada, and Canada did not receive sufficient compensation
for her fisheries by that arrangement, it was remitted to Her
Majesty's Government to say what should be done, and as
will be seen by the the last sentence of the protocol : ' The
subject was further discussed in the Conferences of April 18th
and 19th, and the British Commissioners having referred the
last proposal to the Government, and received instructions
to accept it, the treaty articles, 18 to 25, were agreed to at the
Conference on April 23rd.' Thus then it occurred that these
articles from 18 to 25 are portions of the treaty. One of these
articles reserves to Canada the right of adoption or rejection
and it is for this Parliament now to say whether under all the
circumstances it should ratify or reject them.

" The papers that have been laid before the House show
what was the opinion of the Canadian Government. Under
present circumstances of that question, the Canadian Government believe that it is for the interest of Canada to accept the
treaty, to ratify it by legislation. (Hear, hear). They believe it is for the interest of Canada to accept it, and they
are more inclined to believe it from the fact which I must
say has surprised me, and surprised my colleagues, and has
surprised the country—that the portion of the treaty which
was supposed to be most unpopular and most prejudicial to
the interests of the Maritime Provinces has proved to
be the least unpopular. (Hear, hear). Sir, I could not
have anticipated that the American fishermen, who were
offered the advantages of fishing in our waters would be to a
man, opposed to the treaty as inflicting upon them a great
injury. I could not have anticipated that the fishermen of
the Maritime Provinces, who, at first expressed hostility,
would now, with a few exceptions, be anxious for its adoption.
(Hear, hear).

" In viewing these articles of the treaty, I would call the
consideration of the House to the fact that their scope and
aim have been greatly misrepresented by that portion of the

Canadian press which is opposed to the present Government. It has been alleged to be an ignominious sale of the property of Canada, a bartering away of the territorial rights of this country for money. Sir, no allegation could be more utterly unfounded than this. (Hear, hear). It is no more a transfer and sale of the territorial rights of Canada than was the treaty of 1854. The very basis of this treaty is reciprocity. (Hear, hear). To be sure it does not go as far and embrace as many articles as the treaty of 1852. I am sorry for it. I fought hard that it should be so, but the terms of this treaty are terms of reciprocity, and the very first clause ought to be sufficient evidence upon that point, for it declares that Canadians shall have the same right to fish in American waters, that Americans will have under the treaty to fish in Canadian waters. True it may be said that our fisheries are more valuable than theirs, but that does not effect the principle. The principle is this—that we were trying to make a reciprocity arrangement and going as far in the direction of reciprocity as possible. The principle is the same in each case, and as regards the treaty that has been negotiated it is not confined to reciprocity in the use of the in-shore fisheries of the two countries. It provides that the products of the fisheries of the two nations, fish oil as well as fish, shall be interchanged free. The only departure from the principle of reciprocity in the present treaty is the provision, that if it shall be found that Canada had made a bad bargain and had not received a fair compensation for what she gave ; if it shall be found that while there was reciprocity as to the enjoyment of rights and privileges, there was not true reciprocity in value, then the difference in value should be ascertained and paid to this country. (Hear, hear). Now, if there is anything approaching to the dishonourable and the degrading in these proposals I do not know the meaning of those terms. (Hear, hear). This provision may not be one that will meet the acceptance of the country, but I say that the manner in which it has been characterized, is a wilful and deliberate use of language which the parties employing it did not believe at the time to be accurate, and

to which they resorted for political reasons, and in order
to create misapprehensions in the country. Sir, there was
no humiliation. Canada would not tolerate an act of humiliation on the part of its Government. England would neither
advise nor permit one of her faithful colonies to be degraded
and cast down. (Cheers).

"But it is said that the American fisheries are of no
value to us. They are not as valuable as ours it is true, but
still they have a substantial value for us in this way—that
the exclusion of Canadian fishermen from the American coast
fisheries would have been a loss to the fishing interests of
the Maritime Provinces, and I will tell you why. It is quite
true that the mackerel fishery, which is the most valuable
fishery on these coasts, belongs chiefly to Canada, and that
the mackerel of the American coast is far inferior in every
respect to the Canadian fish, but it is also true that in
American waters, the favourite bait to catch the mackerel
with, known as the menhadden is found, and it is so much
the favourite bait that, one fishing vessel having this bait
on board, will draw a whole school of mackerel in the very
face of vessels having an inferior bait. Now the value of
the privilege of entering American waters for catching that
bait is very great. If Canadian fishermen were excluded
from American waters, by any combination among American
fishermen or by any Act of Congress, they might be deprived
of getting a single ounce of the bait. American fishermen
might combine for that object, or a law might be passed by
Congress forbidding the exportation of menhadden ; but by
the provision made in the treaty, Canadian fishermen are
allowed to enter into American waters to procure the bait,
and the consequences of that is, that no such combination can
exist and Canadians can purchase the bait and be able to fish
on equal terms with the Americans. (Hear, hear).

"It is thus seen, sir, that this Reciprocity Treaty is not a
mere matter of sentiment—it is a most valuable privilege,
which is not to be neglected, despised, or sneered at. With
respect to the language of these articles some questions have
been raised and placed on the paper, and I have asked the

THE RIGHT HONOURABLE THE MARQUIS OF LORNE, K.T., G.C.M.G.

Governor-General of Canada, November 1878, to October, 1883.

honourable gentlemen who were about to put them, to postpone doing so; and I now warn honourable members, and I do it with the most sincere desire to protect the interests of Canada, if this treaty becomes a treaty, and we ratify the fishery articles—I warn them not to raise questions which otherwise might not be raised. I think, Mr. Speaker, there is no greater instance in which a wise discretion can be used, than in not suggesting any doubts. With respect, however, to the question which was put by the honourable member for the county of Charlotte—and it is a question which might well be put, and which requires some answer—I would state to that honourable gentleman, and I think he will be satisfied with the answer, that the Treaty of 1871, in the matter his questions refers to, is larger and wider in its provisions in favour of Canada than was the Treaty of 1854, and that under the Treaty of 1854, no question was raised as to the exact locality of the catch, but all fish brought to the United States market by Canadian vessels were free. I say this advisedly, and I will discuss it with the honourable gentleman whenever he may choose to give me the opportunity. The same practice will, I have no doubt, be continued under the Treaty of 1871, unless the people of Canada themselves raise the objection. The warning I have just now expressed, I am sure the House will take in the spirit in which it is intended. No honourable member will, of course, be prevented from exercising his own discretion, but I felt it my duty to call the attention of the House to the necessity of great prudence in not raising needlessly, doubts as to the terms of the Treaty.

" It will be remembered that we have not given all our fisheries away, the treaty only applies to the fisheries of the old Province of Canada, and in order that the area should not be widened, it is provided that it shall only apply to the fisheries of Quebec, Nova Scotia, New Brunswick and Prince Edward Island, so that the treaty does not allow the Americans to have access to the Pacific coast fisheries, nor yet to the inexhaustible and priceless fisheries of the Hudson's Bay. Those are great sources of revenue yet undeveloped, but after the treaty is ratified, they will develop rapidly, and in twelve years from now, when the two nations sit down to reconsider the circumstances, and readjust the treaty, it will be found that other and great wealth will be at the disposal of the Dominion.

"I may be asked, though I have not seen that the point has excited any observation, why were not the products of the lake fisheries laid open to both nations, and in reply I may say that these fisheries were excepted at my instance. The Canadian fisheries on the north shores of the great lakes are most valuable. By a judicious system of preservation and protection we have greatly increased that source of. wealth. It is also known that from a concurrence of circumstances and from situation the fisheries on the south shores are not nearly so valuable as ours, and it therefore appeared that if we once allowed the American fishermen to have admission to our waters, with their various engines of destruction, all the care taken for many years to cultivate that source of wealth would be disturbed, injured, and prejudiced, and there would be no end of quarrels and dissatisfaction in our narrow waters, and no real reciprocity, and, therefore, that Canada would be much better off by preserving her own Inland Lake Fisheries to her herself, and have no right to enter the American market with the products of those fisheries. This was the reason why the lake fisheries were not included in this arrangement.

"Now, sir, under the present circumstances of the case, the Canadian Government have decided to press upon this House the policy of accepting this treaty and ratifying the Fishery Articles. I may be liable to the charge of injuring our case in discussing the advantages of the arrangement, because every word used by me may be quoted and used as evidence against us hereafter. The statement has been so thrown broadcast that the arrangement is a bad one for Canada, that in order to show to this House and the country that it is one that can be accepted, one is obliged to run the risk of his language being used before the Commissioners to settle the amount of compensation as an evidence of the value of the treaty to us.

"It seems to me that in looking at the treaty in a commercial point of view, and looking at the question whether it is right to accept the articles, we have to consider that interest which is most peculiarly first affected. Now, unless I am greatly misinformed the fishing interests with one or two exceptions for local reasons in Nova Scotia, are altogether in favour of the treaty. (Hear, hear). They are anxious to get admission of their fish into the American market ; they would view with sorrow any action of this House which would exclude them from that market ; they look forward with increasing confidence to a large development of their trade, and of that great industry, and I say that being the case, if it be to the interest of the fishermen, and for the advantage of that branch of the national industry, setting aside all other considerations, we ought not wilfully to injure that interest. What is the fact of the case as it stands now ? The only market in the world for the Canadian number one mackerel is the United States. That is their only market, and they are practically excluded from it by the present duty. The consequence of that duty is that they are at the mercy of the American fishermen ; they are made the hewers of wood and drawers of water for the Americans. They are obliged to sell their fish at the American's own price. The American fisher-men purchase their fish at a nominal value, and control the American market. The great profits of the trade are handed over to the American fishermen or the American merchants engaged in the trade, and they profit to the loss of our own people. Let any one go down the St. Lawrence on a summer trip, as many of us do, and call from the deck of the steamer to a fisherman in his boat and see for what a nominal price you can secure the whole of his catch, and that is from the absence of a market, and from the fact of the Canadian fishermen being completely under the control of the foreigner.

" With the duty off Canadian fish, the Canadian fisherman may send his fish at the right time, when he can obtain the best price, to the American market, and thus be the means of opening a profitable trade with the United States, in exchange. If, therefore, it is for the advantage of the Maritime Provinces, including that portion of Quebec, which is also largely interested in the fisheries, that this treaty should be ratified, and that this great market should be opened to them, on what ground should we deprive them of this right ? Is it not a selfish argument, that the fisheries can be used as a lever in order to gain reciprocity in flour, wheat and other cereals ? Are you to shut them off from this great market in order that you may coerce the United States into giving you an extension of the reciprocal principle ? Why, Mr. Speaker, if it were a valid argument, it would be a selfish one. What would be said by the people of Ontario if the United States had offered, for their own purposes, to admit Canadian grains free, and Nova Scotia had objected, saying, ' No, you shall not have that market ; you must be deprived of that market for ever, unless we can take in our fish also ; you must lose all that great advantage until we can get a market for our fish ' ? Apply the argument in this way and you will see how selfish it is.

"But the argument has no foundation, no basis of fact, and I will show this House how. In 1854, by a strict and rigid observance of the principle of exclusion, the American fishermen were driven out of those waters. At that time the United States was free from debt, and from taxation, and they · had large capital invested in their fisheries. Our fisheries were then in their infancy. They were a ' feeble ' people just beginning as fishermen, with little capital and little skill, and their operations were very restricted. I do not speak disparagingly, but in comparison with the fishermen of the United States there was an absence of capital and skill. The United States were free from taxation, they had this capital and skill, and all they wanted was our Canadian waters in which to invest that capital and exercise that skill, but how is it altered now ? Our fisheries are now no lever by which to obtain reciprocity in grain. What do the United States care for our fisheries ? The American fishermen are opposed to the treaty. Those interested in the fisheries are sending petition after petition to the United States Government and Congress praying that the treaty may be rejected. They say they do not want to come into our waters. The United States Government have gone into this treaty with every desire to settle all possible sources of difficulty, their fishermen complain that they will suffer by it, but the United States Government desire to meet us face to face, hand to hand, heart to heart, and to have an amicable settlement of all disputes. They know that they are not making political friends or gaining political strength because nearly the whole of the interest most affected by the fishery articles is against the treaty. But they desire that the ill feelings which arose during the civil war, and from the Alabama case, should be forgotten. A feeling of friendship has grown up between the nations, and it can be no other desire than to foster and encourage that feeling which dictates the agreeing to these particular articles. The United States Government will simply say—well, if you do not like these arrangements reject them—and the consequence will be on your own head if this friendship so auspiciously commenced is at any time broken by unhappy collisions in your waters."

" I AM afraid I must apologize to the House for the uninteresting manner in which I have laid the subject before the House so far. I was showing as well as I could my opinion, and my reasons for that opinion, that under the circumstances the treaty, although it is not what we desired, and although it is not what I pressed for, ought to be accepted. I shall not pursue that branch of the subject to greater length, as during the discussion of the measure I have no doubt that I shall have again an opportunity to reurge these and further views on the same subject as they may occur to me, or as they may be elicited.

" I shall, however, call the serious attention of the House, and especially of those members of the House who have given attention to the question in dispute as regards the validity of the several treaties between the United States and England, to the importance of this treaty in this respect, that it sets at rest now and for ever the disputed question as to whether the Convention of 1818 was not repealed, and obliterated by the treaty of 1854. This question, Mr. Speaker, is one that has occupied the attention of the United States Jurists and has been the subject of serious and elaborate discussions. From my point of view the pretension of the United States is erroneous, but it has been pressed, and we know the pertinacity with which such views are pressed by the United States. We have an example in the case of the navigation of the river St. Lawrence, which, while it was discussed from 1822 to 1828, and was apparently settled then for ever between the two nations, was revived by the President of the United States in his address of 1870, and the difference between the point of view as pressed in 1828, by the United States and that pressed in 1870, was shewn by the result of the treaty (Honourable Mr. Blake, 'hear, hear'). And, sir, it was of great importance in my point of view that this question, which has been so pressed by American jurists, and considering also the pertinacity with which such views are urged, should be set at rest for ever.

"The question has been strongly put in the American Law Review of April 1871, in an article understood to have been written by Judge Pomeroy, a jurist of standing in the United States, and that paper, I believe, expresses the real opinion of the writer—erroneous though I hold it to be—and his candour is shown by this fact, as well as from the known standing of the man, that in one portion of the article he demolishes the claim of the American fishermen to the right to trade in our water. He proves in an able argument that the claim of American fishermen to enter our harbours for any purpose other than wood, water, and shelter, is without foundation. The view taken by that writer and others—and among others by a writer whose name I do not know, but whose papers are very valuable from their ability, they appeared in the N.Y. *Nation*, is this : The treaty of 1783 was a treaty of peace, a settlement of boundary, and a division of country between two nations. The United States contended that that treaty was in force, and is now in force, as it was a treaty respecting boundary, and was not abrogated or affected by the war of 1812. Under the treaty of 1783, and by the terms of that treaty, the fishermen of the United States had the unrestrained right to enter into all our waters up to our shores, and to every part of British North America. After 1815 England contended that that permission was abrogated by the war and was not renewed by the Treaty of Peace of 1814. The two nations were thus at issue on that very grave point, and those who look back to the history of that day will find that the difference on that point threatened the renewal of war, and it was only settled by the compromise known as the Convention of 1818, by which the claim of the Americans to fish within three miles of our

shores, was renounced. The argument is, however, of a
nature too technical to be of interest to the House, and
requires to be very carefully studied before it can be understood, I will not, therefore, trouble the House, with that
argument but I will read one or two passages to show the
general statement of the case.

"'We shall now enquire whether the convention of 1818,
is an existing compact, and if not, what are the rights of
American fishermen under the Treaty of Peace of 1783.

"'Since the expiration of the Reciprocity Treaty in 1866,
the British Government, both at home and in the provinces,
has, in its statutes, its official instructions, and its diplomatic
correspondence, quietly assumed that the convention of 1818
is again operative in all its provisions. That the State
Department at Washington should, by its silence, have admitted the correctness of this assumption, which is equally
opposed to principle and to authority, is remarkable. We
shall maintain the proposition that the treaty of peace of 1783
is now in full force, that all limitations upon its efficiency
have been removed, and that it is the only source and foundation of American fishing rights within the North Eastern
Territorial waters. In pursuing the discussions we shall
show, first, that the renunciatory clauses of the convention
of 1818 have been removed ; and secondly, that article III,
of the treaty of 1783 thus left free from the restrictions of
the subsequent compact, was not abrogated by the war of
1812.'

The writer thus concludes :—

"'Article III of the treaty of 1783 is, therefore, in the
nature of an executed grant. It created and conferred at
one blow rights of property, perfect in their nature, and as
permanent as the dominion over the national soil. These
rights are held by the inhabitants of the United States, and
are to be exercised in British territorial waters. Unaffected
by the war of 1812, they still exist in full force and vigour.
Under the provisions of this treaty, American citizens are
now entitled to take fish on such parts of the coasts of Newfoundland as British fishermen use, and also on all the coasts,

bays, and creeks, of all other His Britannic Majesty's dominions in America, and to dry and cure fish in any of the unsettled bays, harbours, and creeks of Nova Scotia, the Magdalen Islands and Labrador.

"'The final conclusion thus reached is sustained by principle and by authority. We submit that it should be adopted by the Government of the United States, and made the basis of any further negotiations with Great Britain.'

"I quote this for the purpose of showing that the pretension was formally set up and elaborated by jurists of no mean standing or reputation, and therefore it is one of the merits of this treaty that it forever sets the dispute at rest. The writers on this subject, the very writers of whom I have spoken, admit that under this treaty the claim is gone, because it is a formal admission by the United States Government that, under the convention of 1818, we had, on May 8, 1871, the property of these in-shore fisheries, and this was so admitted after the question had been raised in the United States, that the ratification of the treaty of 1854 was equal, in its effect, to an abrogation of the convention of 1818. They agree by this treaty to buy their entry into our waters, and this is the strongest possible proof that their argument could be no longer maintained. Just as the payment of rent by a tenant is the strongest proof of his admission of the right of the landlord, so is the agreement to pay to Canada a fair sum as an equivalent for the use of our fisheries, an acknowledgment of the permanent continuance of our right. So much, sir, for that portion of the treaty which affects the fisheries.

"I alluded a minute ago to the St. Lawrence. The surrender of the free navigation of the River St. Lawrence in its natural state, was resisted by England up to 1828. The claim was renewed by the present Government of the United States, and asserted in a message to Congress by the present President of the United States. Her Majesty's Government, in the instructions sent to Her Commissioners, took the power and responsibility of the matter into her own hands. It was a matter which we could not control. Being a matter of boundary between two nations, and affecting a river which forms the boundary between the limits of the Empire and the limits of the United States, it is solely within the control of Her Majesty's Government, and in the instructions to the plenipotentiaries, this language is used : ' Her Majesty's Government are now willing to grant the free navigation of the St. Lawrence to the citizens of the United States, on the same conditions and tolls as imposed on British subjects.'

"I need not say, sir, that, as a matter of sentiment, I regretted this, but it was a matter of sentiment only. However, there could be no practical good to Canada in resisting the concession, and there was no possible evil inflicted on Canada by the concession of the privilege of navigating that small piece of broken water between St. Regis and Montreal. In no way could it affect, prejudicially, the interests of Canada, her trade, or her commerce. Without the use of our canals, the river was useless. Up to Montreal the St. Lawrence is open not only to the vessels of the United States, but to the vessels of the world. Canada courts the trade and the ships of the world, and it would have been most absurd to suppose that the ports of Quebec and Montreal should be closed to American shipping. No greater evidence of unfriendly relations short of actual war can be adduced, than the fact of the ports of a country being closed to the commerce of another. It never entered into the minds of any that our ports should be closed to the trade of the world in general, or the United States in particular, no more than it would enter into the minds of the English to close the ports of London or Liverpool—those ports whither the flags of every nation are invited and welcomed. (Cheers). From the source of the St. Lawrence to St. Regis the United States are part owners of the banks of the rivers, and by a well-known principle of international law the water flowing between the two banks is common to both, and not only is that a principle of law, but it is a matter of actual treaty. The only question then was whether, as the American people had set their hearts upon it, and as it could do no harm to Canada or to England, it would not be well to set this question at rest with the others, and make the concession. This was the line taken by Her

Majesty's Government, and which they had a right to take ; and when some one writes my biography—if I am ever thought worthy of having such an interesting document prepared—and when, as a matter of history, the questions connected with this treaty are upheld, it will be found that upon this, as well as upon every other point, I did all I could to protect the rights and claims of the Dominion. (Cheers).

" With respect to the right itself, I would call the attention of the House to the remarks of a distinguished English jurist upon the point. I have read from the work of an American jurist, and I will now read some remarks of Mr. Phillimore, a standard English writer on international law. What I am about to read was written under the idea that the Americans were claiming what would be of practical use to them. He was not aware that the difficulties of navigation were such that the concession would be of no practical use. He writes as follows :

" ' Great Britain possessed the northern shores of the lakes, and of the river in its whole extent to the sea, and also the southern bank of the river from the latitude forty-five degrees north to its mouth. The United States possessed the southern shores of the lakes, and of the St. Lawrence, to the point where their northern boundary touched the river. These two governments were therefore placed pretty much in the same attitude towards each other, with respect to the navigation of the St. Lawrence, as the United States and Spain had been in with respect to the navigation of the Mississippi, before the acquisitions of Louisiana and Florida.

" ' The argument on the part of the United States was much the same as that which they had employed with respect to the navigation of the Mississippi. They referred to the dispute about the opening of the Scheldt in 1874, and contended that, in the case of that river, the fact of the banks having been the creation of *artificial* labour was a much stronger reason, than could be said to exist in the case of the Mississippi for closing the mouths of the sea adjoining the Dutch Canals of the Sas and the Swin, and that this peculiarity probably caused the insertion of the stipulation in the Treaty of Westphalia ; that

the case of the St. Lawrence differed materially from that of
the Scheldt, and fell directly under the principle of free navigation embodied in the Treaty of Vienna respecting the
Rhine, the Neckar, the Mayne, the Moselle, the Meuse and
the Scheldt.   But especially it was urged, and with a force
which it must have been difficult to parry, that the present
claim of the United States with respect to the navigation of
the St. Lawrence, was precisely of the same nature as that
which Great Britain had put forward with respect to the navigation of the Mississippi when the mouth and lower shores of
that river were in the possession of another State, and of
which claim Great Britain had procured the recognition by the
Treaty of Paris in 1763.

"'The principle argument contained in the reply of Great
Britain was, that the liberty of passage by one nation through
the dominions of another was, according to the doctrine of the
most eminent writers upon International Law, a qualified
occasional exception to the paramount rights of property ;
that it was what these writers called an imperfect, and not a
perfect right ; that the Treaty of Vienna did not sanction this
notion of a natural right to the free passage over rivers, but,
on the contrary, the inference was that, not being a natural
right, it required to be established by a convention ; that the
right of passage once conceded must hold good for other
purposes besides those of trade in peace, for hostile purposes
in time of war ; that the United States could not consistently
urge their claim on principle without being prepared to apply
that principle by way of reciprocity, in favour of British
subjects, to the navigation of the Mississippi and the Hudson,
to which access might be had from Canada by land carriage
or by the canals of New York and Ohio.

"'The United States replied, that practically the St. Lawrence was a strait, and was subject to the same principles of
law ; and that as straits are accessory to the seas which they
unite and therefore the right of navigating them is common to
all nations, so the St. Lawrence connects with the ocean those
great inland lakes, on the shores of which the subjects of the
United States and Great Britain both dwell ; and, on the

same principle, the natural link of the river, like the natural link of the strait, must be equally available for the purpose of passage by both.   The passage over land, which was always pressing upon the minds of the writers on international law, is intrinsically different from a passage over water ; in the latter instance, no detriment or inconvenience can be sustained by the country to which it belongs.   The track of the ship is effaced as soon as made ; the track of an army may leave serious and lasting injury behind.   The United States would not shrink from the application of the analogy with respect to the navigation of the Mississippi, and whenever a connection was effected between it and Upper Canada, similar to that existing between the United States and the St. Lawrence, the same principle should be applied.   It was, however, to be recollected, that the case of rivers which both rise and disembogue themselves within the limits of the same nation is very distinguishable, upon principle, from that of rivers which, having their sources and navigable positions of their streams in States above, discharge themselves within the limits of other States below.

"'Lastly, the fact, that the free navigation of rivers had been made a matter of convention did not disprove that this navigation was a matter of natural right restored to its proper position by treaty.

"'The result of this controversy has hitherto produced no effect.   Great Britain has maintained her exclusive right.   The United States still remain debarred from the use of this great highway, and are not permitted to carry over it the produce of the vast and rich territories which border on the lakes above to the Atlantic ocean.

"'It seems difficult to deny that Great Britain may ground her refusal upon strict law ; but it is at least equally difficult to deny, first, that in so doing she exercises harshly an extreme and hard law ; secondly, that her conduct with respect to the navigation of the St. Lawrence is in glaring and discreditable inconsistency with her conduct with respect to the navigation of the Mississippi.   On the ground that she possessed a small tract of domain in which the Mississippi took its rise, she insisted on her right to navigate the entire volume of its waters ; on the ground that she possesses both banks of the St. Lawrence, where it disembogues itself into the sea, she denies to the United States the right of navigation, though about one half of the waters of Lakes Ontario, Erie, Huron and Superior, and the whole of Lake Michigan, through which the river flows, are the property of the United States.

"'An English writer upon International Law cannot but express a hope that this *summum jus*, which, in this case, approaches to *summa injuria*, may be voluntarily abandoned by his country. Since the late revolution in the South American Provinces, by which the dominion of Rosas was overthrown, there appears to be good reason to hope that the States of Paraguay, Bolivia, Buenos Ayres, and Brazil, will open the River Parana, to the navigation of the world.'"

" On reading a report of a speech of my honourable friend, the member for Lambton, on this subject—a very able and interesting speech, if he will allow me so to characterize it—I find that in speaking of the navigation of Lake Michigan, he stated that that lake was as much a portion of the St. Lawrence as the river itself. I do not know under what principle my honourable friend made that statement, but those inland seas are seas as much as the Black Sea is a sea and not a river. The lake is enclosed on all sides by the United States territory ; no portion of its shores belongs to Canada, and England has no right by International Law to claim its navigation. Sir, she never has claimed it, for if my honourable friend will look into the matter, he will find that these great lakes have ever been treated as inland seas, and as far as magnitude is concerned, are worthy of being so treated. Although Her Majesty's Commissioners pressed that the navigation of Lake Michigan should be granted as an equivalent for the navigation of the St. Lawrence, the argument could not be based on the same footing, and we did not and could not pretend to have the same grounds. It is, however, of little moment whether Canada has a grant by treaty of the free navigation of Lake Michigan or not, for the cities on the shores of that lake would never consent to have their ports closed, and there is no fear in the world of our vessels being excluded from those ports. The Western States, and especially those bordering on the Great Lakes, would resist this to the death. I would like to see a Congress that would venture to close the ports of Lake Michigan to the shipping of England, or of Canada, or of the world. The small portion of the St. Lawrence which lies between the two points I have mentioned, would be of no use, as there is no advantage to be obtained therefrom as a lever to obtain reciprocity.

Honourable Mr. Mackenzie : " Hear, hear."

Honourable Sir John A. Macdonald : " My honourable friend says ' Hear, hear,' but I will tell him that the only lever for obtaining reciprocity is the sole control of our canals. So long as we have the control of these canals we are the masters, and can do just as we please. American vessels on the down trip can run the rapids, if they get a strong Indian to steer, but they will never come back again unless Canada chooses. (Hear,. The keel drives through those waters, and then the mark disappears forever, and that vessel will be forever absent from the place that once knew it, unless by the consent of Canada. Therefore, as I pointed out before the recess, as we have no lever in our fisheries to get reciprocity, so we had none in the navigation of the St. Lawrence in its natural course. The real substantial means to obtain reciprocal trade with the United States is in the canals, and is expressly stated in the treaty ; and when the treaty, in clause 27, which relates to the canals, uses the words : ' The Government of Her Britannic Majesty engages to urge upon the Government of the Dominion of Canada to secure to the citizens of the United States the use of the Welland and St. Lawrence and other canals in the Dominion, on terms of equality, etc.,' it contains an admission by the United States, and it is of some advantage to have that admission, that the canals are our own property, which we can open to the United States as we please. The reason why this admission is important is this : article 26 provides that ' the navigation of the River St. Lawrence, ascending and descending from the 45th parallel of north latitude, where it ceases to form the boundary between the two countries, from, to and into the sea, shall forever remain free and open for the purposes of commerce to the citizens of the United States, subject to any laws and regulations of Great Britain or of the Dominion of Canada not inconsistent with such privileges of free navigation.' Therefore, lest it might be argued that, as at the time the treaty was made, it was known that, for the purpose of ascent, the river could not be overcome in its natural course, the provision granting the right of ascent must be held to include the navigation of the canals, through which alone the ascent could be made, the next clause provides and specifies that these canals are especially within the control of Canada and the Canadian Government, and prevents any inference being drawn from the language of the preceding article. I know, sir, that there has been, in some of the newspapers, a sneer cast upon the latter paragraph of that article, which gives the United States the free use of the St. Lawrence,—I refer to that part of the article which gives to Canadians the free navigation of the rivers Yukon, Porcupine and Stikine.

Honourable Mr. Mackenzie —" Hear, hear."

Honourable Sir John A. Macdonald—" My honourable friend again says 'hear, hear.' I hope that he will hear, and perhaps he will hear something he does not know. (Hear, hear). I may tell my honourable friend that the navigation of the River Yukon is a growing trade, and that the Americans are now sending vessels and are fitting out steamers for the navigation of the Yukon. I will tell my honourable friend that at this moment United States vessels are going up that river and are underselling the Hudson's Bay people in their own country, (hear, hear), and it is a matter of the very greatest importance to the Western country that the navigation of these rivers should be open to the commerce of British subjects, and that access should be had by means of these rivers, so that there is no necessity at all for the ironical cheer of my honourable friend. Sir, I am not unaware that under an old treaty entered into between Russia and England, the former granted to the latter the free navigation of these streams, and the free navigation of all the streams in Alaska. But that was a treaty between Russia and England, and although it may be argued, and would be argued by England, that when the United States took that country from Russia it took it with all its obligations ; yet, Mr. Speaker, there are two sides to that question. The United States, I venture to say, would hang an argument upon it, and I can only tell my honourable friend that the officers of the United States have exercised authority in the way of prohibition or obstruction, and have offered the pretext that that was a matter which had been settled between Russia and England, that the United States now had that country, and would deal with it as they chose, and, therefore, as this was a treaty to settle all old questions, and not to raise new ones, it was well that the free navigation of the rivers I have mentioned, should be settled at once between England and the United States, as before it had been between England and Russia.

" Before leaving the question of the St. Lawrence, I will make one remark, and will then proceed to another topic, and that is, that the article in question does not in any way hand over or divide any proprietary rights on the river St. Lawrence, or give any sovereignty over it, or confer any right whatever, except that of free navigation. Both banks belong to Canada—the management, the regulation, the tolls, the improvement, all belong to Canada. The only stipulation made in the treaty is that the United States vessels may use the St. Lawrence on as free terms as those of Canadian subjects. It is not a transfer of territorial rights—it is simply a permission to navigate the river by American vessels, that the navigation shall ever remain free and open for the purpose of commerce (and only for the purpose of commerce) 'to citizens of the United States, subject to any laws and regulations of Great Britain, or of the Dominion of Canada, not inconsistent with the privilege of free navigation.'

" Mr. Speaker, I shall now allude to one of the subjects included in the treaty, which relate to the navigation of our waters, although it was not contemplated in the instructions given to the British Commissioners by Her Majesty's Government, in fact the subject was scarcely known in England, and that is what is known as the St. Clair Flats question. It is known that the waters of the River St. Clair and the waters of Lake St. Clair divide the two countries ; that the boundary line which divides them is provided by treaty ; that the treaty of 1842 provides that all the channels and passages between the islands lying near the junction of the River St. Clair with the Lake, shall be equally free to both nations, so that all those channels were made common to both nations, and are so now. Canada has made appropriations for the purpose of improvement of these waters. There were also appropriations made—I forget whether by the United States or by the State of Michigan, or by private individuals—for the purpose of improving the waters, and the United States made a canal in and through the St. Clair Flats. The question then arose whether that canal was in Canadian territory, or within that of the United States. I have no doubt that the engineering officers appointed by the United States to choose the site of the canal and to construct it, acted in good faith in choosing the site, believing that it was in the United States, and from all I can learn, subsequent observations proved that to be the case.

Honourable Mr. Mackenzie : " Hear, hear."

Honourable Sir John A. Macdonald : " My honourable friend says ' hear, hear,' and I have no doubt he will give us an argument, and an able one, too, as he is quite competent to do, to show that under the treaty this canal is in Canada. An argument might be founded in favour of that view from the language of the report of the International Commissioners appointed to determine the boundary between the two countries, that is, if we looked at the language alone and combined with that language the evidence of those accustomed of old to navigate those waters. I admit that an argument might be based on the language of the report, when it speaks of the old ship channel, and that the evidence and statements that have been made as to the position of that channel, might have left it a matter of doubt whether the canal, or a portion of it, was within the boundary of Canada, but the Commissioners not only made a report, but they added to it a map, to which they placed their signatures, and any one reading the report with the map, and holding the map as a portion of the report, will see that this canal is in the United States. It might, but for the Treaty of Washington, have been unfortunate that it is so, because it might, perhaps, have impeded the navigation of the flats by Canadian vessels.

"But the question is whether, under the old treaty, and the report and map made according to its provisions (which report and map form, in fact, a portion of such treaty) the canal is within the United States boundary or not. When the point was raised that the map was inconsistent with the report, Her Majesty's Government, I have no doubt under the advice of Her Majesty's legal advisers, said it was a point that would not admit of argument, that the two must be taken together, and that the map explained and defined the meaning of the language of the report. But, sir, ' out of the nettle danger we pluck the flower safety.' The House will see by looking at the clause I referred to, that it is a matter of no consequence whether the canal is in the United States or Canada, because for all time to come that canal is to be used by the people of Canada on equal terms with the people of the United States. In the speech of my honourable friend to which I have referred, that canal, he says, is only secured to Canada during the ten years mentioned with reference to the fishery articles of the treaty. I say it is secured for all time, just as the navigation of the St. Lawrence is given for all time. The United States have gone to the expense of building the canal, and now we have the free use of it. If the United States put on a toll there we pay no greater toll than United States citizens, and it is of the first and last advantage to the commerce of both nations that the deepening of these channels should be gone on with; and I can tell my honourable friend, moreover, that in this present Congress there is a measure to spend a large additional sum of money on this canal out of the revenues of the United States for that object. So much for the St. Clair Flats.

"Now, sir, as to some of the advantages to be gained by the treaty, I would call the attention of the House to the 29th article, which ensures for the whole time of the existence of the treaty, for twelve years at least, the continuance of 'the bonding system.' We know how valuable that has been to us, how valuable, during the winter months, when we are deprived of the use of our own seaports on the St. Lawrence. The fact that the American press had occasionally called for the abolition of the system is a proof of the boon which they considered it to be. They have said at times, when they thought an unfriendly feeling existed towards them in Canada, that if Canadians would be so bumptious, they should be deprived of this system, and allowed to remain cooped up in their frozen country. If the United States should ever commit the folly of injuring their carrying trade by adopting a hostile policy in that respect, and they have occasionally, as we know, adopted a policy towards us adverse to their commercial interest, they could have done so before this treaty was ratified—they cannot do so now. For twelve years we have a right to the bonding system from the United States over all their avenues of trade, and long before that time expires, I hope we shall have the Canadian Pacific Railway reaching to the Pacific Ocean, and with the Intercolonial Railway reaching to Halifax, we shall have an uninterrupted line from one seaboard to the other. (Cheers). This is one of the substantial advantages that Canada has gained by this treaty.

"Then, sir, the 30th article conveys a most valuable privilege to the railways of Canada that are running from one part of the country to another, and I must take the occasion to say that if this has been pressed upon the consideration of the American Government and American Commissioners at Washington, during the negotiation, much of the merit is due to the honourable member for Lincoln (Mr. Merritt). He it was who supplied me with the facts; he it was who called attention to the great wrong to our trade by the Act of 1866 and impressed by him with the great importance of the subject, I was enabled to urge the adoption of this article and

to have it made a portion of the treaty. Now, sir, that this is
of importance you can see by reading the Buffalo papers.
Sometime ago they were crying out that the entrance had
been made by this wedge, which was to ruin their coasting
trade, and that the whole coasting trade of the lakes was being
handed over to Canada. Under this clause, if we choose to
accept it, Canadian vessels can go to Chicago; can take
American produce from American ports, and can carry it to
Windsor or Collingwood, or the Welland Railway. That
same American produce can be sent in bond from those and
other points along our railways, giving the traffic to our vessels
by water, and our railways by land, to Lake Ontario, and can
then be reshipped by Canadian vessels to Oswego, Ogdensburg, or Rochester, or other American ports; so that this clause
gives us, in some degree, a relaxation of the extreme, almost
harsh, exclusive coasting system of the United States (hear),
and I am quite sure that in this age of railways, and when the
votes and proceedings show that so many new railway undertakings are about to start, this will prove a substantial improvement on the former state of affairs. There is a provision that
if, in the exercise of our discretion, we choose to put a differential scale of tolls on American vessels passing through our
canals, and if New Brunswick should continue her export
duties on lumber passing down the River St. John, the United
States may withdraw from this arrangement, so that it will be
hereafter, if the treaty be adopted, and this Act passed, a
matter for the consideration of the Government of Canada in
the first place, and of the Legislature in the next, to determine
whether it is expedient for them to take advantage of this
boon that is offered to them. As to the expediency of their
doing so, I have no doubt, and I have no doubt Parliament
will eagerly seek to gain and establish those rights for our
ships and railways. (Hear, hear).

" The only other subject of peculiar interest to Canada in
connection with the treaty—the whole of it of course is interesting to Canada as a part of the Empire, but speaking of
Canada as such, and of the interest taken in the treaty locally
—the only other subject is the manner of disposing of the

San Juan boundary question. That is settled in a way that no one can object to. I do not know whether many honourable members have ever studied that question. It is a most interesting one, and has long been a cause of controversy between the two countries. I am bound to uphold, and I do uphold, the British view respecting the channel which forms the boundary as the correct one. The United States Government were, I believe, as sincerely convinced of the justice of their own case. Both believed they were in the right, both were firmly grounded in that opinion ; and such being the case, there was only one way out of it, and that was to leave it to be settled by impartial arbitration. I think the House will admit that no more distinguished arbiter could have been selected than the Emperor of Germany.* In the examination and decision of the question he will have the assistance of as able and eminent jurists as any in the world, for there is nowhere a more distinguished body than the jurists of Germany, who are especially familiar with the principles and practice of international law. Whatever the decision may be, whether for England or against it, you may be satisfied that you will get a most learned and careful judgment in the matter, to which we must bow if it is against us, and to which I am sure the United States will bow if it is against them. (Hear, hear).

"I think I have now gone through all the articles of interest connected with Canada, I shall now allude to one omission from it, and then I shall have done ; and that is the omission of all allusion to the settlement of the Fenian claims. That Canada was deeply wronged by those outrages known as the Fenian raids is indisputable. England has admitted it, and we all feel it. We felt deeply grieved when those raids were committed, and the belief was general, in which I must say I share, that sufficient vigilance and due diligence were not exercised by the American Government to prevent the organization, within their territory, of bands of armed men openly hostile to a peaceful country, and to put an end to incursions by men who carried war over our borders, slew our people and destroyed our property. It was therefore proper for us to

press upon England to seek compensation at the hands of the American Government for these great wrongs. As a consequence of our position, as a dependency, we could only do it through England. We had no means or authority to do it directly ourselves ; and consequently we urged our case upon the attention of England and she consented to open negotiations with the United States upon the subject. In the instructions it is stated that Canada had been invited to send in a statement of her claims to England and that it had not done so ; and I dare say it will be charged— indeed, I have seen it so stated in some of the newspapers— that that was an instance of Canadian neglect. Now, it is not an instance of Canadian neglect, but an instance of Canadian caution. (Hear, hear). Canada had a right to press for the payment of those claims, whatever the amount ; for all the money spent to repel those incursions had been taken out of the public treasury of Canada and had to be raised by the taxation of the country. Not only had they the right to press for that amount, but every individual Canadian who suffered in person or property because of those raids had a right to compensation.

"It was not for Canada, however, to put a limit to those claims, and to state what amount of money would be considered as a satisfactory liquidation of them. It has never been the case when commissions have been appointed for the settlement of such claims to hand in those claims in detail before the sitting of the commission. What Canada pressed for was that the principle should be established, that the demand should be made by England upon the United States, that that demand should be acquiesced in, that the question of damages should be referred to a tribunal like that now sitting at Washington for the investigation of claims connected with the civil war in the South, that time should be given within which the Canadian Government, as a Government, and every individual Canadian who suffered by those outrages, should have an opportunity of filing their claims, of putting in an account and of offering proof to establish their right to an indemnity. The Canadian Government

carefully avoided, by any statement of their views, the placing
of a limit upon those claims in advance of examination by
such a commission ; and I think the House and country will
agree that we acted with due discretion in that respect.
(Hear, hear). Now, one of the protocols will show the result
of the demand for indemnity. The demand was made by
the British Commissioners that this question should be discussed and considered by the commission, but the United
States Commissioners objected, taking the ground that the
consideration of these claims was not included in the correspondence and reference. In doing that they took the same
ground that my honourable friend the member for Sherbrooke, with his usual acuteness and appreciation of the value
of language, took when the matter was discussed in this
House before my departure for Washington. He said then
that he greatly doubted whether, under the correspondence
which led to the appointment of the High Commission, it
could be held that the Fenian claims were to be considered ;
and although my honourable friend the Minister of Militia
thought it might fairly be held that those claims were included, I myself could not help feeling the strength of the
argument advanced by the honourable member for Sherbrooke, and I stated at the time that I thought there was
great weight in the objection which he pointed out.

"The American Commissioners, as the event proved,
raised that objection, maintaining that the point was not
included in the correspondence in which the subjects of deliberation were stated, and when it was proposed to them by the
British Commissioners, the American Commissioners declined
to ask their Government for fresh instructions to enlarge the
scope of their duty in that respect. Now, we could not help
that. There was the correspondence to speak for itself, and
it was matter of considerable doubt whether those claims were
included in it. The British ambassador represented that he
had always thought that the correspondence did include them,
and he was struck with surprise—perhaps I ought not to say
surprise, for that was not the expression he used—but he
was certainly under the impression that it had been regarded

by all parties that they were covered by the correspondence. Still, let any one read these letters, and he will find it very doubtful. As it was doubtful, and as objection was raised on that ground, the British Commissioners had no power to compel the American Commissioners to determine the doubt in their favour, and force these claims upon their consideration. The consequence was that they were omitted from the deliberations of the commission. Whose fault was that? Certainly not ours. It was the fault of Her Majesty's Government in not demanding in clear language, in terms which could not be misunderstood, that the investigation of these claims should be one of the matters dealt with by the commission. (Hear, hear).

"It was a great disappointment to my colleagues in Canada, that the objection was taken, and that all hope of getting redress for the injury done by those Fenian raids was destroyed, so far as the commission at Washington was concerned, in consequence of the defective language of the correspondence, and the defective nature of the submission to the commissioners. Now, England was responsible for that error. England had promised to make the demand, and England had failed to make it. Not only that, but her Majesty's Government took the responsibility of withdrawing the claims altogether, and Mr. Gladstone fully assumed all the responsibility of this step, and relieved the Canadian Government from any share in it, when he stated openly in the House of Commons that the Imperial Government had seen fit to withdraw the claims, but that they had done so with great reluctance and sorrow for the manner in which Canada had been treated. Canada, therefore, had every right to look to England for that satisfaction which she failed to receive through the inadequacy of the correspondence to cover the question. England, by taking the responsibility of declining to push the claims, put herself in the position of the United States, and we had a fair and reasonable right to look to her to assume the responsibility of settling them. She did not decline that responsibility, and the consequence has been that, although we failed to obtain redress from the United States for those wrongs, we have had an opportunity of securing compensation from England, which would not have been offered to us if it had not been for the steps taken by this Government. (Hear, hear).

"But, sir, we are told that it is a great humiliation for Canada to take this money, or rather this money's worth. Why, it is our due. We are entitled to it, and we must have it from some one. England refused to ask it for us from the United States, and she accepted all the responsibility which that refusal involved. She was wise in accepting that responsibility ; she must take the consequences, and she is willing to do so. But the Canadian Government, on the other hand, were unwilling that the compensation which England thus acknowledged was due to us by her should take a direct pecuniary form. We were unwilling that it should be the payment of a certain amount of money, and there were several strong reasons why we should prefer not to accept reparation in that shape. In the first place, if a proposal of that kind were made, it would cause a discussion as to the amount to be paid by England, of a most unseemly character. We would have the spectacle of a judge appointed to examine the claims in detail, with Canada pressing her case upon his attention, and England probably resisting in some cases, and putting herself in an antagonistic position, which should not be allowed to occur between the mother country and the colony. It was, therefore, in the last degree unadvisable that the relations between Canada and the mother country, which throughout have been of so friendly and pleasant a character, should be placed in jeopardy in that way ; and, accordingly, a suggestion was made by us which, without causing England to expend a sixpence, or putting the least additional burden upon her people, would, if acted upon, do us more good, and prove of infinitely greater advantage than any amount of mere money compensation we could reasonably expect. This was a mode of disposing of the question in the highest degree satisfactory to both countries, and one which does not in the least compromise our dignity or our self-respect. (Hear, hear).

"The credit of Canada, thank God, is well-established ; her good faith is known wherever she has had financial dealings. Her Majesty's Government can go to the House of Commons and ask for authority to guarantee a Canadian loan with a well-grounded assurance that the people of England will never be called upon to put their hands in their pockets or tax themselves one farthing to pay it. (Cheers). At the same time the Imperial Government, by giving us this guarantee, grants us a boon the value of which, in enabling us to construct the great works of public improvement we have undertaken, was explained the other day so ably and in a manner that I would not attempt to imitate, by my honourable friend the Finance Minister. Besides the double advantage to ourselves in getting the endorsement of England without disadvantage to the English people, there is to be considered the great, the enormous benefit that accrues to Canada from this open avowal on the part of England of the interest she takes in the success of our great public enterprises. (Cheers). No one can say now when she is sending out one of her distinguished statesmen to take the place of the nobleman who now so worthily represents Her Majesty in the Dominion; no one can say when England is aiding us by endorsing a loan, spreading over so many years, and which will not be finally extinguished till most of us now here will have been gathered to our fathers; no one can say under these circumstances, she has any idea of separating herself from us and giving up the colonies. (Cheers .

"The solid substantial advantage of being able to obtain money on better terms than we could on our own credit alone, is not the only benefit this guarantee will confer upon us; for it will put a finish at once to the hopes of all dreamers or speculators who desire or believe in the alienation and separation of the colonies from the mother country. That is a more incalculable benefit than the mere advantage of England's guarantee of our financial stability, great and important as that is. (Loud cheers). Aye, but it is said that it is a humiliation to make a bargain of this kind. Why, sir, it was no humiliation in 1841 to obtain an Imperial guarantee for the loan necessary to construct the canals originally. It was not considered a humiliation to accept a guarantee for £1,400,000 in 1865 for the purpose of building fortifications, nor was it a humiliation to obtain £4,000,000 upon a similar guarantee to construct the Inter-colonial Railway.   Why is it a humiliation then, in this case, to accept the guarantee when England voluntarily comes forward and accepts the responsibility for withdrawing our claims in respect to the Fenian raids?   It was by no prompting from us that that responsibility was assumed, for Mr. Gladstone rose of his own motion in the House of Commons, and by accepting the responsibility admitted that it should take a tangible shape.   It did take such a shape, and I say a most satisfactory shape in the guarantee of £2,500,000 immediately, and we may say £4,000,000 in all, ultimately. (Cheers).

"But I hear it objected that Canada ought not to have made a bargain at all.   She should have allowed the Fenian claims to go, and dealt with the treaty separately, accepting or rejecting it on its merits.   Sir, Canada did not make a bargain of that kind, but she went fairly and openly to Her Majesty's Government and said : 'Here is a treaty that has been negotiated through your influence, and which affects important commercial interests in this country.   It is unpopular in Canada in its commercial aspect, but it is urged on us for Imperial causes, and for the sake of the peace of the Empire; but the pecuniary interests of Canada should, in the opinion of the Canadian Government, be considered, and the undoubted claim of Canada for compensation for these Fenian outrages has been set aside.   We may well, therefore, call upon you to strengthen our hands by showing that you are unwilling to sacrifice Canada altogether for Imperial purposes solely.'   Sir, we asked that for Canada, and the response was immediate and gratifying, except that England did not accept the whole of our proposition to guarantee a loan of £4,000,000. But I am as certain as I am standing in this House, and I am not speaking without book, that had it not been for the unfortunate cloud that arose between the United States and England, which threatened to interrupt the friendly settlement of all questions between them, but which, I am now happy to say, is passing away, the difficulty would have been removed by England permitting us to add to the £2,500,000, £1,400,000 which she guaranteed some years since to be expended on fortifications and other defensive preparations. That money had not been expended, and there would now have been no object in applying it for the construction of works which would have been a standing menace to the United States, and which would have been altogether out of place immediately after signing a treaty of peace and amity.

" I do not hesitate to say, and I repeat I am not speaking without book, that I believe a proposition of that kind would have been acceptable to Her Majesty's Government, but when the cloud arose ; when there was a possibility of this treaty being held as a nullity, and when there was danger of the relations between the two countries returning to the unfortunate position in which they were before—then was not the time for England to ask us, or for us to propose to give up the idea of fortifying our frontier, and defending our territory. Then was not the time either for the Canadian Government to show an unwillingness to spend money upon these works, or to defend and retain the Dominion as a dependency of the Sovereign of England (cheers). I say, therefore, that while we are actually receiving a guarantee of £2,500,000, if the relations of England and the United States are again brought into harmony, and the lowering cloud which recently sprung up is removed, and removed in such a way as never to appear again, then it may fairly be thought, it may reasonably be calculated upon, that we will have a guarantee of the full amount of £4,000,000, in order to carry out the great improvements we have entered upon. The Finance Minister has shewn you the advantages which will flow from that arrangement, and it would be presumption in me to add a word to what he so well said upon that point which was in the highest degree satisfactory to this House and in the highest degree also satisfactory to the people of the country.

" I shall now move the first reading of this Bill, and I shall simply sum up my remarks by saying that with respect

to the treaty I consider that every portion of it is unobjection-
able to the country, unless the articles connected with the
fisheries may be considered objectionable. With respect to
those articles, I ask this House fully and calmly to consider
the circumstances, and I believe, if they fully consider the
situation, that they will say it is for the good of Canada
that those articles should be ratified. Reject the treaty, and
you do not get reciprocity ; reject the treaty, and you leave
the fishermen of the Maritime Provinces at the mercy of the
Americans ; reject the treaty, and you will cut off the merchants
engaged in that trade from the American market. Reject
the treaty and you will have a large annual expenditure in
keeping up a marine police force to protect those fisheries,
amounting to about $84,000 per annum. Reject the treaty,
and you will have to call upon England to send her fleet and
give you both her moral and physical support, although you
will not adopt her policy ; reject the treaty, and you will find
that the bad feeling which formerly and until lately existed
in the United States against England will be transferred to
Canada : that the United States will say, and say justly,
' Here, when two nations like England and the United States
have settled all their differences and all their quarrels upon
a perpetual basis, these happy results are to be frustrated and
endangered by the Canadian people, because they have not
got the value of their fish for ten years.' (Cheers).

"It has been said by the honourable gentleman on my
left (Mr. Howe) in his speech to the Young Men's Christian
Association, that England had sacrificed the interests of
Canada. If England has sacrificed the interests of Canada,
what sacrifice has she not made in the cause of peace between
those two great nations, rendered herself liable, leaving out
all indirect claims, to pay millions out of her own treasury?
Has she not made all this sacrifice, which only Englishmen
and English statesmen can know, for the sake of peace—
and for whose sake has she made it ? Has she not made
it principally for the sake of Canada ? (Loud cheers). Let
Canada be severed from England—let England not be responsible to us, and for us, and what could the United States

do to England? Let England withdraw herself into her shell, and what can the United States do? England has got the supremacy of the sea—she is impregnable in every point but one, and that point is Canada ; and if England does call upon us to make a financial sacrifice ; does find it for the good of the Empire that we, England's first colony, should sacrifice something, I say that we would be unworthy of our proud position if we were not prepared to do so. (Cheers). I hope to live to see the day, and, if I do not, that my son may be spared to see Canada the right arm of England, (cheers) to see Canada a powerful auxilliary to the Empire, not as now a cause of anxiety and a source of danger. And I think that if we are worthy to hold that position as the right arm of England, we should not object to a sacrifice of this kind when so great an object is attained, and the object is a great and lasting one.

" It is said that amities between nations cannot be perpetual. But I say that this treaty which has gone through so many difficulties and dangers, if it is carried into effect, removes almost all possibility of war. If ever there was an irritating cause of war, it was from the occurrences arising out of the escape of those vessels, and when we see the United States people and Government forget this irritation, forget those occurrences, and submit such a question to arbitration, to the arbitration of a disinterested tribunal, they have established a principle which can never be forgotten in this world. No future question is ever likely to arise that will cause such irritation as the escape of the Alabama did, and if they could be got to agree to leave such a matter to the peaceful arbitrament of a friendly power, what future cause of quarrel can, in the imagination of man, occur that will not bear the same pacific solution that is sought for in this. I believe that this treaty is an epoch in the history of civilization, that it will set an example to the wide world that must be followed ; and with the growth of the great Anglo-Saxon family, and with the development of that mighty nation to the south of us, I believe that the principle of arbitration will be advocated and adopted as the sole principle of settlement of differences between the English speaking peoples, and that it will have a moral influence in the world. And although it may be opposed to the antecedents of other nations that great moral principle which has now been established among the Anglo-Saxon family, will spread itself over all the civilized world (Cheers). It is not too much to say that it is a great advance in the history of mankind, and I should be sorry if it were recorded that it was stopped for a moment by a selfish consideration of the interests of Canada.

"Had the Government of Canada taken the course, which was quite open to them, to recommend Parliament to reject those articles, it might have been a matter of some interest, as to what my position would have been. I am here at all events advocating the ratification of the treaty, and, I may say, notwithstanding the taunts of the honourable gentlemen opposite, that although I was chosen for the position of a Commissioner certainly because I was a Canadian, and presumably because I was a member of the Canadian Government, yet my commission was given to me as a British subject, as it was to Sir Stafford Northcote and other members of the Commission. I went to Washington as a Plenipotentiary, as Her Majesty's servant, and was bound by Her Majesty's instructions, and I would have been guilty of dereliction of duty if I had not carried out those instructions. And, sir, when I readily joined, under the circumstances, in every word of that treaty with the exception of the fishery articles, and when I succeeded in having inserted in the treaty a reservation to the Government and the people of Canada of the full right to accept or refuse that portion of it, I had no difficulty as to my course. (Cheers). I did not hesitate to state that if that clause had not been put in, I would have felt it necessary to resign my commission.

"I was perfectly aware in taking the course I did in signing the treaty, that I should be subject to reproach. I wrote to my friends in Canada from Washington that well I knew the storm of obloquy that would meet me on my return, and before even I crossed the border I was complimented with the names of Judas Iscariot, Benedict Arnold, etc. The whole vocabulary of Billingsgate was opened against me, but here I am, thank God, to-day, with the conviction that what I did was for the best interests of Canada ; and after all the benefits I have received at the hands of my countrymen, and after the confidence that has been accorded me for so many years, I would have been unworthy of that position and that confidence if I were not able to meet reproach for the sake of my countrymen. (Cheers). I have met that reproach, and I have met it in silence. I knew that a premature discussion would only exasperate still more the feelings of those who were arrayed against me, and of those who think more of their party than their country. (Loud cheers). I do not speak particularly of the honourable gentlemen opposite, but I say that the policy of the Opposition is regulated by a power behind the throne, which dictates what that policy must be. (Cheers). No one ever saw a patriotic policy emanate from that source, except on one occasion, and that was when that source was induced by myself to forget party struggles and party feelings for the common good of the country. (Cheers).

"I have not said a word for twelve months ; I have kept silence to this day, thinking better that the subject should be discussed on its own merits. How eagerly was I watched! If the Government should come out in favour of the treaty, then it was to be taken as being a betrayal of the people of Canada. If the Government should come out against the treaty, then the first Minister was to be charged with opposing the interests of the Empire. Which ever course we might take, they were lying in wait, ready with some mode of attack. But 'silence is golden,' Mr. Speaker, and I kept silence. I believe the sober second thought of this country accords with the sober second thought of the Government, and we come down here and ask the people of Canada, through their representatives, to accept this treaty, to accept it with all its imperfections, to accept it for the sake of peace, and for the sake of the great Empire of which we form a part. I now beg leave to introduce the Bill, and to state that I have the permission of His Excellency to do so."

Sir John Macdonald resumed his seat at 9.45 p.m., after hav-

ing spoken for four hours and a quarter, amid loud and continued applause from all parts of the House.

The debate in the Commons lasted until the morning of
the 17th, during which time forty-six members of the House
delivered speeches, and Mr. Blake and Mr. Bodwell proposed
amendments.   Both were voted down, and Sir John's motion
for the second reading of the Bill was carried, the division
lists showing 121 for and 55 against.   The Government policy
was nobly sustained, each province of the Confederation showing a majority in its favour.

CHAPTER XXX

The Pacific Railway—Sir George Cartier's Resolutions, April, 1872—Mr. Mac-
Kenzie's Opposition—Arrival of Lord Dufferin—Dissolution of Parliament—
General Election—Admission of Prince Edward Island- The Pacific Railway
Slander—Mr. Huntingdon's Resolutions—Sir John Macdonald's Motion for a
Special Committee—Reports of the Committee—The Oath's Bill—Publication
of Letters—Sir Hugh Allan's Affidavit—Adjournment to August 13th
Memorial of the Opposition Lord Dufferin's reply—Prorogation—Sir John
Macdonald's position—The Royal Commission—Meeting of Parliament—Mr.
Mackenzie's Amendment to the Address—Sir John's Speech -Resignation of
the Ministry—The Stolen Letters—Character of the Witnesses against the
Ministry—The Mackenzie Government—Dissolution of Parliament—General
Elections—Meeting of new Parliament, March 1874—Pacific Railway Reso-
lutions—Other Bills—Prorogation.

THE principal subject of discussion during the session
was the building of the Pacific Railway. During the
year 1871 two companies were formed for this purpose, one
called the Canada Pacific Railway Company, being under the
presidency of Sir Hugh Allan ; the other called the Inter-
Oceanic Railway Company, being under the presidency of
Honourable David Macpherson. The former was essentially
a Quebec company, the latter an Ontario company, and an
intense rivalry ensued. Each company obtained a charter,
the terms being the same, namely, that the capital should be
$10,000,000 in $100 shares, and that the company should not
be considered organized until $1,000,000 had been paid in.

" Under the circumstances it was a difficult matter for the
Government to deal with either, and therefore it was determined to pass a general Act, giving the Governor in Council
power to treat with one or the other, or with the two amalgamated, or failing a satisfactory arrangement, to grant a charter
to a new company.

On April 26, 1872, Sir George Cartier moved the House
into Committee of the Whole on the question. He explained
that the terms of Union with British Columbia required that
the road should be commenced within two years, and finished
within ten. That the Government desired power to enter into
an agreement with a company to construct the road, or, if one

company could not undertake the whole road, then with several companies for different parts. As the company could not be expected to build without assistance, it was proposed to give them 50,000,000 acres of land in alternate blocks, twenty miles square on each side of the line—the alternate blocks reserved being held for sale by the Government—and a cash subsidy of about $30,000,000.

Mr. Alexander Mackenzie objected to the proposition stating his conviction that it was impossible to construct the road within the time mentioned, and that the two companies were merely " rings " looking for plunder. On the authority of persons he considered competent to judge, he maintained that there were not more than 45,000,000 to 65,000,000 acres of good land in the North-West, and that after the proposed quantity had been given to the company, there would be little left for settlement. The powers proposed to be conferred on the Government he considered extravagant and dangerous, and that, if the resolutions were passed, the House would be abdicating its functions, and leaving to the Government matters over which it should retain control. He moved amendments embodying his views as also did other members of the Opposition, but the resolutions, with some slight changes, were carried by a large majority.

On the second reading of the Bill, Mr. Mackenzie said that he desired to get an expression of opinion from the House on the subject of the land policy therein expressed. He considered that actual settlers ought to be allowed to enter upon any of the blocks of land along the railway whether they were reserved for the company or for the Government, and moved, seconded by Mr. Dorion:

" That the Bill be referred back to the Committee of the Whole, with instructions so to amend the same as to provide that actual settlers may enter upon any sold or unsold lands, belonging either to the company to be entrusted with the construction of the railway, or to the Government in the alternate blocks reserved, on terms and conditions to be made ; which terms and conditions should be subject to the approval of Parliament ; and, further to provide that nothing therein contained shall prevent provision being made for setting apart a portion of the land reserved by the Government, in the alternate blocks or elsewhere, as free grants to actual settlers."

In reply, Sir John Macdonald said that Mr. Mackenzie had first objected to the road, because the country was not able to afford it, and now wanted to take away the best security the country had to offer for the building of the road. It was all nonsense to suppose that the people of Canada were going to build the road for the comfort and convenience of emigrants from the old country; there was plenty of land outside the twenty-mile belt which could be given free to settlers, but this belt was looked on as the principal means of paying for the construction of the road, and it was ridiculous to propose to give it away.

The amendment was lost on division. Yeas, 33; nays, 101. Other amendments were also lost, and the Bill passed through its second and third readings.

The last session of the first Parliament closed on June 14, 1872, when Lord Lisgar bade farewell to Canada and was succeeded by the Earl of Dufferin, who arrived on the 25th.

Lord Dufferin belongs to an old Irish family, and was born at Florence on June 21, 1826. He was educated at Eton and Oxford, and succeeded to the title in 1841, when only fifteen years of age. In 1849 he was appointed a Lord in Waiting to the Queen, which he held under Lord John Russell's Administration until 1852, and again filled the same office from 1854 to 1858, on the return of his party to power. In 1850 he was created an English baron, and took his seat in the House of Lords as Lord Clandeboye. In 1855 he accompanied Lord John Russell, as an *attaché*, to his special mission to Vienna, and displayed such administrative ability, that, in 1860, he was appointed by Lord Palmerston, British Commissioner to Syria, to enquire into the massacres of Christians which had been taking place, a task which he accomplished with so much satisfaction to the Government that he was made K.C.B. for his services. In 1864 he was made Lord Lieutenant of the County Down, and the same year took the position of Under-Secretary of State for India, which he held until 1866, when he became Under-Secretary of State for War. In the same year he was offered the Governorship of Bombay, but declined. On the return of the Liberal party to power, in December, 1868, he was appointed Chancellor of the Duchy of Lancaster and Paymaster, which he retained until his appointment as Governor-General of Canada.

Shortly after the close of the session the Honourable Alex. Morris was appointed Chief Justice of Manitoba, and was succeeded as Minister of Inland Revenue by the Honourable Charles Tupper, whose place as President of the Council was filled by the appointment of Honourable John O'Connor, M.P. for Essex.

Parliament was dissolved by proclamation on July 15th and writs for a new election issued, returnable on September 2nd.

In Kingston Sir John Macdonald was opposed by Mr. John Carruthers, a wealthy retired merchant, who was regarded as the strongest man the Reform party could bring forward. The contest was waged with great energy and bitterness, and on polling day the excitement was intense. In spite of the most strenuous efforts of his opponents, Sir John was returned by a majority of 131.

In other parts of the Dominion, elections were carried on with great vigour, the result being that the Government lost strength in Ontario, gained in the Maritime Provinces, and remained about the same in Quebec.

Sir Francis Hincks having retired on account of failing health, was succeeded as Finance Minister by the Honourable S. L. Tilley.

The first session of the second Parliament opened on March 5, 1873, when the Honourable P. J. O. Chauveau was appointed Speaker of the Senate, and Honourable James Cockburn was elected without opposition as Speaker of the House of Commons.

On May 16th, a message was received from His Excellency forwarding the papers in connection with the proposed admission of Prince Edward Island into the Union ; and, on the 20th, Honourable Mr. Tilley introduced a series of resolutions on which to base addresses to Her Majesty, praying for the union of the island with the Dominion. He explained that the total expense would be about $480,000, and the receipts, calculated upon those of the preceeding year, about $441,000. The Address was adopted and a Bill, providing for the admission of the island, introduced and passed.

But the momentous event that occurred during the session was that in connection with what is now known as the Pacific Railway Scandal. After the close of the session of 1872 an effort had been made to form an amalagamation between the two companies, known as the Canada Pacific and the Oceanic Railway Companies. A difficulty arose, however, as to the presidency, which Sir Hugh Allan wished to have guaranteed to himself, and the other company would not yield, desiring it to be left to the directors to decide. The Government did not care to favour one more than the other, and thereupon a new company was formed called the Canadian Pacific Railway Company, to which a charter was granted by letters patent on February 5, 1873, the promoters being Sir Hugh Allan, Montreal ; Honourable A. G. Archibald, Halifax ; Honourable J. C. Beaubien, Quebec ; J. B. Beaudry, Montreal ; E. R. Burpee, St. John ; F. W. Cumberland, Toronto ; Sandford Fleming, Ottawa ; R. N. Hall, Sherbrooke ; Honourable J. S. Helmcken, Victoria ; A. McDermot, Winnipeg ; D. McInnes, Hamilton ; Walter Shanly, Montreal ; John Walker, London.

The capital of the new company was fixed at $10,000,000, in $100 shares, which was not transferable for six years without the consent of the Dominion Government and the directors. Ten per cent. was to be at once paid up and deposited with the Receiver-General. Work was to be commenced at both ends simultaneously by July 20, 1873, and completed by 1881. The land grant was to be 50,000,000 acres, in alternate blocks of the same size, as reserved by the Government. The land thus retained by the Government to be held for twenty years at an upset price of $2.50 per acre. The money subsidy to be $30,000,000 less any expense the Government had been put to for surveys.

The terms were generally considered as satisfactory, and much gratification was felt at the manner in which the stock had been distributed all over the Dominion, and the provision that it was not transferable for six years, which prevented the possibility of the road falling into the hands of capitalists in the United States.

On April 2nd, Mr. Huntingdon, from his place in Parliament, made the following charges against the Ministry :

" That in anticipation of the legislation of last session as to the Pacific Railway, an agreement was made between Sir Hugh Allan, acting for himself and certain other Canadian promoters, and G. W. McMullen, acting for certain United States capitalists, whereby the latter agreed to furnish all the funds necessary for the construction of the contemplated railway, and to give the former a certain percentage of interest, in consideration of their interest and position, the scheme agreed on being ostensibly that of a Canadian company, with Sir Hugh Allan at its head.

" That the Government were aware that negotiations were pending between these parties.

" That subsequently an understanding was come to between the Government and Sir Hugh Allan and Mr. Abbott, M.P., that Sir Hugh Allan and his friends should advance a large sum of money for the purpose of aiding the elections of Ministers and their supporters at the ensuing general election, and that he and his friends should receive the contract for the construction of the railway.

" That, accordingly, Sir Hugh Allan did advance a large sum of money for the purpose mentioned, and at the solicitation, and under the pressing instances of Ministers.

" That part of the monies expended by Sir Hugh Allan in connection with the obtaining of the Act of Incorporation and Charter, were paid to him by the said United States capitalists under the agreement with him ; it is

" Ordered, that a committee of seven **members** be appointed to enquire into all the circumstances connected with the negotiations for the construction of the Pacific Railway, with the legislation of last session on the subject, and with the granting of the charter to Sir Hugh Allan and others ; with power to send for persons, papers, and records ; and with instructions to report in full the evidence taken before, and all proceedings of, said committee."

The motion was read by Mr. Huntingdon without any preface or remarks, and was received by the House in dead silence. A division was called for, and the motion was lost by a vote of 76 to 107.

The charges, however, made a profound sensation in the House and in the country, and Sir John Macdonald, recognizing the necessity of meeting them at once, on the following day addressed the House in these words :

" Mr. Speaker, I beg to give notice that I will, on Tuesday next, ask that the House shall appoint a Special Committee of five, to be selected by the House for the purpose of considering the subjects mentioned in the motion of the honourable member for Shefford, yesterday. The Committee shall be drawn by the House, and, if need be, shall have special power given to them to sit in recess, and, if need be, a Royal Commission shall be issued for the purpose of giving them additional powers."

On April 8th, Sir John Macdonald made the motion, of which he had given notice, and, in doing so, explained that the Government had voted down the motion of Mr. Huntingdon, not because they were afraid of enquiry, but because they took the motion as one of want of confidence. The Government courted the fullest enquiry, and were prepared to do anything in their power to facilitate the work of the Committee. The members of the Committee appointed by the House were Messrs. Blanchet, Blake, Dorion, McDonald (Pictou), Cameron (Cardwell).

On April 17th, the Honourable J. H. Cameron, Chairman of the Committee, presented the first report of the Committee, recommending that a Bill be introduced empowering the Committee to examine witnesses under oath. This Bill passed the House on the 21st, the Senate on the 29th, and received His Excellency's assent on May 3rd. On May 5th Mr. Cameron presented another report, covering a series of resolutions, to the effect that, owing to the absence in England of Sir George Cartier and Mr. J. J. C. Abbott—both material witnesses to the investigation—the Committee should adjourn until July 2nd, if Parliament should then be in session ; that the proceedings of the meeting should be secret ; that the Committee should be empowered to sit at such place or places as may be found expedient.   That part respecting the secrecy of the meetings was not pressed, and the balance came up for discussion on May 6th, on the motion of Mr. Cameron to adopt the resolutions.   The debate that ensued was very acrimonious, and resulted in an amendment being moved by the Honourable A. A. Dorion, which, after reciting the original motion of Mr. Huntingdon, went on as follows :

"That since the appointment of the Committee, when the unanimous feeling of the House was, that the enquiry should be actively prosecuted during the present session, nothing had occurred to justify the proposed adjournment of the Committee to July 2nd ; but, on the contrary, the interests of the country imperatively demand that the enquiry should be prosecuted without further delay."

Lost on division—yeas 76 ; nays 107.

On May 15th Mr. Huntingdon made some further statements and attempted to read extracts from some letters, but was ruled out of order by the Speaker.   He then moved that inasmuch as he was credibly informed that certain original documents, of the utmost importance in proving the charges made by him, were in the hands of a trustee under circumstances which rendered it exceedingly doubtful whether they might not be placed beyond the reach of the Committee before it met again on July 2nd, the Committee be ordered to meet at eleven o'clock next morning, when he (Mr. Huntingdon) would disclose the name of the trustee with a view to having him summoned to produce all documents in his possession relating to the enquiry.   The motion was adopted.

The next day, Mr. Cameron's motion to permit the Committee to sit, even though the House was not sitting, was carried by a vote of 101 to 66.

It being the rule that when Parliament is prorogued all

committees expire with it, to overcome the difficulty, on May 21st, Sir John Macdonald moved "That when the House adjourns on Friday next, it do stand adjourned until Wednesday, August 13th, next," which was carried without discussion. On the 23rd His Excellency gave assent to all the Bills passed during the session, and Parliament adjourned. Before doing so, Sir John replied to a question from Mr. Mackenzie that the meeting would only be *pro forma* to receive the report of the Committee, which could then be printed and distributed during recess, and that he did not think it would be necessary for any more than the two Speakers to be present as no business would be transacted. Mr. Holton thought that it would be necessary for a quorum of the House to be present, to which Sir John answered that if so, a sufficient number could be got in the neighbourhood of Ottawa without bringing members from a distance.

When the Bill, giving the Committee power to take evidence under oath, came before the Imperial Government, they decided that it was beyond the power of the Canadian Parliament to enact such a measure, and it was accordingly disallowed. This was made known on July 1st by an extra of the *Canada Gazette*. On the Committee assembling next day Mr. Cameron announced this fact, and a motion by Mr. McDonald (Picton), to the effect "that, inasmuch as the House had instructed the Committee to take evidence on oath and the Bill authorizing them to do so had been disallowed, the Committee could not proceed without further instructions from the House," was carried. Immediately after the adjournment Mr. Cameron read a letter addressed to him, as chairman of the Committee, by Sir John Macdonald, offering to issue a Royal Commission to the members of the Committee if they would continue their labours, the Commission being instructed to report to the House. This offer was declined by Messrs. Dorion and Blake, and the Committee adjourned until August 13th.

On the morning of July 4th a profound sensation was created in the country by the simultaneous publication in the Toronto *Globe* and Montreal *Herald* of seventeen letters and three telegrams addressed by Sir Hugh Allan to Messrs. C. M. Smith, G. W. McMullen and other American capitalists, which disclosed the fact that, in spite of the opposition of the Government, he had for a long time retained his connection with these men and was most anxious to continue to do so, and had spent a large sum of money in the furtherance of the interests of his company and proposed giving away the enormous amount of $850,000 of stock to certain gentlemen mentioned in his letter, and spending the further sum of $100,000 in cash in a manner not disclosed, but for which he " cou'd not get receipts." The letters were evidently intended as confidential and were written in that free and unrestrained manner that men may be expected to adopt when communicating with others in whom they repose unlimited confidence as men of honour.

The letters were commented upon by the *Globe* in very strong language, and the extreme view given " that the man who occupies the position of First Minister is hopelessly involved in an infamous and corrupt conspiracy." So far from any such fact being disclosed by the letters, the very contrary opinion would be formed by any person reading them in an impartial and judicial manner. In the whole seventeen letters his name appears but three times, once with regard to an appointment to meet him, a second time with regard to a coolness which Sir Hugh thought had sprung up between him and Sir George Cartier, and a third time when Sir Hugh informed Mr. McMullen that Sir John and Sir George Cartier had long ago made up their minds not to give the charter either to his company or to Mr. D. L. Macpherson's, but to form another company and have the work done under Government control.

Sir Hugh Allan lost no time in meeting these letters, and in the Montreal *Gazette* of the following morning (May 5th) there appeared a very long and exhaustive affidavit made by him. In this he gives a short history of the formation and progress of his company, the negotiations with the Inter-Oceanic and his connection with American capitalists. As Mr. Huntingdon's charges against the Government were in connection with the latter, we will give such extracts as will explain Sir Hugh's position and views.

"That notwithstanding that the Bill, which was so introduced, contemplated by its terms the exclusion of foreigners, I did not feel, by any means, convinced that the Government would insist upon any such condition, believing as I did, and do, that such a proposition was impolitic and unnecessary. I did not, therefore, feel justified in entirely breaking off my connection with the American associates, although I acquainted them with the difficulty which might arise if the Government took the same position which the majority of the people, with whom I conversed at Ottawa, appeared to do.　.　.　.　.　.　.　.

But, in point of fact, when the discussions as to the mode in which the company should be formed, were entered upon with the Government, late in the autumn, I came to understand decisively, that they could not be admitted, and I notified them of the fact, and that the negotiations must cease between us, by a letter which has not been published in the *Herald* to-day, but which was in the following terms :—

MONTREAL, *October* 24, 1872.

MY DEAR MR. McMULLEN.—No action has yet (as far as I know) been taken by the Government in the matter of the Pacific Railroad. The opposition of the Ontario party will, I think, have the effect of shutting out our American friends from any participation in the road and I apprehend that all negotiation is at an end. It is still uncertain how it (the contract) will be given, but in any case the Government seem inclined to exact a declaration that no foreigners will have, directly or indirectly, any interest in it. But everything is in a state of uncertainty, and I think it is unnecessary for you to visit New York on this business at present, or at all, till you hear what the result is likely to be. Public sentiment seems to be decided that the road shall be built by Canadians only. Yours truly.

(Signed)　　　HUGH ALLAN.

GEO McMULLEN, ESQ.,
　　PICTON, ONT.

"These sworn statements of Sir Hugh Allan are a perfect answer to Mr. Huntingdon's first two resolutions. Respecting the third and fourth which charged that an understanding was come to between the Government and Sir Hugh Allan, that the latter and his friends ' should advance a large sum of money for the purpose of aiding the elections of Ministers and their supporters at the ensuing general election, and that he and his friends should receive that contract for the construction of the railway. That, accordingly, Sir Hugh Allan did advance a large sum of money for the purpose mentioned and at the solicitation and under the pressing instance of Ministers.' Sir Hugh Allan swears :—

" ' From that time also, communication between myself and my former associates ceased, having finally been broken off by myself as soon as I ascertained the desire of the Government. And I state further, positively, that no money derived from any fund or from any of my former American associates was expended in assisting my friends or the friends of the Government at the recent general elections.

" ' That with regard to the construction which appears to be intended to be placed upon the statements in the letter referred to, as to the preliminary expenses, connected with the charter, I state most positively and explicitly that I never made any arangement or came to any understanding of any kind or description with the Government or any of its members, as to the payment of any sum to any one, or in any way whatever, in consideration of receiving the contract for the Canadian Pacific Railway.' "

Sir Hugh Allan then states that he had expended sums approaching those mentioned in his letters, as he conceived he had a perfect right to do, and repeats his denial that any portion of those sums of money were paid to the members of the Government, or were received by them or on their behalf, directly or indirectly, as a consideration in any form for any advantage to him in connection with the Pacific Railway.

The statement in the fifth resolution is only a repetition of that made in the second and is positively denied by the affidavit.

Sir Hugh's sworn statement was considered satisfactory, and public interest in the matter became much abated. It was revived and increased, however, a fortnight later, by a letter published by Mr. McMullen, which contained copies of some letters and telegrams from Sir George Cartier and Sir John Macdonald which indicated that Sir Hugh Allan had advanced large sums of money for election purposes. The conclusion sought to be drawn from these documents was that they covered an agreement with the Government to grant the charter of the Pacific Railway to Sir Hugh Allan in compensation for the assistance thus given. This conclusion was denied on the authority of the Ministry, in an editorial of the Montreal *Gazette*, published July 21st, which promised also " that at the earliest possible moment the whole of the facts and circumstances will be laid before a tribunal competent to receive evidence respecting them under oath."

As August 13th approached, it became evident that the Opposition were determined to prevent the meeting of Parliament being a formal one for the purpose of receiving the report of the Special Committee, and then being prorogued according to the well-understood arrangement made at the time of adjournment in May. They were anxious to proceed with the investigation without any further delay, but it was urged in reply that in a matter so nearly concerning the honour of Ministers, it would be most unjust to admit testimony which was not given under the sanctity of an oath, and with the fear of punishment for perjury before the eyes of the witnesses.

On the appointed day His Excellency proceeded to the Senate Chamber for the purpose of proroguing Parliament, but previously received a deputation of members who, through their chairman, Mr. R. J. Cartwright, presented the following memorial :

" The undersigned members of the House of Commons of Canada desire respectfully to approach your Excellency and humbly to represent that more than four months have elapsed since the Honourable Mr. Huntingdon made, from his place in the House, grave charges of corruption against your Excellency's constitutional advisers in reference to the Pacific Railway contract ; that although the House has appointed a

Committee to inquire into the said charges, the proceedings of this Committee have on various grounds, been postponed, and the enquiry has not yet taken place ; that the honour of the country imperatively requires that no further delay should take place in the investigation of charges of so grave a character, and which it is the duty and undoubted right and privilege of the Commons to prosecute.

" The undersigned are deeply impressed with the conviction that any attempt to postpone this enquiry, or to remove it from the jurisdiction of the Commons, would create the most intense dissatisfaction, and they, therefore, pray your Excellency not to prorogue Parliament until the House of Commons shall have an opportunity of taking such steps as it may deem necessary and expedient with reference to this important matter."

His Excellency in reply stated that he regretted as much as any one the delay which had taken place, and mentioned the causes which had contributed to this, especially the Oath's Bill which had been disallowed by the Imperial Government, and thereby prevented the evidence being taken in the solemn manner contemplated.   He then continued : " You then proceed to urge me, on grounds which are very fairly and forcibly stated, to decline the advice which has been unanimously tendered me by my responsible Ministers, and to refuse to prorogue Parliament, in other words you require me to dismiss them from my Councils, for, gentlemen, you must be aware that this would be the necessary result of my assenting to your recommendation.   Upon what grounds would I be justified in taking so grave a step?   What guarantee can you afford me that the Parliament of the Dominion would endorse such an act of personal interference on my part?   You, yourselves, gentlemen, do not form an actual moiety of the House of Commons, and I have no means therefore, of ascertaining that the majority of that body subscribe to the opinion you have enounced.   Again, to what should I have to appeal in justification of my conduct ?   It is true grave charges have been preferred against these gentlemen, charges which I admit require the most searching investigation, but, as you yourselves remark in your memorandum, the truth of these accusations still remains untested. One of the authors of this correspondence which has made so painful an impression on the public, has admitted that many of his statements were hasty and inaccurate, and has denied on oath the correctness of the deductions drawn from them. Various assertions contained in the narrative of the other have been positively contradicted. Is the Governor-General, upon the strength of such evidence as this, to drive from his presence gentlemen who for years have filled the highest offices of state, and in whom, during the recent session, Parliament has repeatedly declared its continued confidence? It is true certain documents of grave significance have lately been published in the newspapers in connection with these matters, in regard to which the fullest explanation must be given, but no proof has yet been adduced which necessarily connects them with the culpable transactions of which it is asserted they formed a part, however questionable they may appear, as placed in juxtaposition with the correspondence to which they have been appended by the person who has possessed himself of them. Under these circumstances what right has the Governor-General, on his personal responsibility, to proclaim to Canada—nay, not only to Canada, but to America and Europe, as such a proceeding on his part must necessarily do, that he believes his Ministers guilty of the crimes alleged against them?" He then referred to the understanding under which Parliament had adjourned, and announced his intention of issuing a Royal Commission, and that Parliament would be summoned in about ten weeks to receive the report.

When the Commons met, Mr. Mackenzie read a motion declaring that it was the imperative duty of the House to have a full investigation into the charges; that the assumption of the duty by any tribunal appointed by the Ministry would be a gross breach of the privileges of the House, and that it was highly reprehensible for any person to presume to advise His Excellency to prorogue Parliament until it had taken action in the matter of enquiry. Before he had proceeded far, Black Rod appeared and was greeted by strong marks of disappro-

bation from the Opposition. The Speaker at once arose and
was followed to the Senate Chamber by the Conservative
members, the Liberals retaining their seats. Subsequently
they organized a meeting in the Railway Committee room,
and passed resolutions similar in effect to the memorial presented to His Excellency.

The position in which Sir John Macdonald and his Government were placed was most embarrassing. Upon the
charges being made he had at once moved for a Committee of
Enquiry, which Committee was appointed by the House and
not by the Ministry. It had met and asked for power to take
evidence under oath which was at once granted. Then finding
that the two principal witnesses were in England, it had with
the consent of the House, adjourned to a time at which they
might be expected to return. On re-assembling they found
that the " Oath's Bill " had been disallowed and again adjourned for new instructions from the House. When Parliament re-assembled it was in accordance with an understanding
that it should be *pro forma*, and but few of the Government
supporters were present. The Opposition on the other hand
had assembled in full strength, and if the Ministry had advised
His Excellency to depart from the understanding as to prorogation and meet for business, they would have been met by
an adverse majority and any motion of condemnation or want
of confidence could have been carried. If, on the other hand,
they had summoned the full strength of their supporters, and
the House had proceeded to business, power to take evidence
on oath could not have been granted to the Committee, for
that had already been declared *ultra vires*, and if the enquiry
had gone on it must have been without the protection of
solemnly sworn testimony, and the act of the House in passing
the Oath's Bill, and the utterances of His Excellency show,
beyond dispute, that on all sides it was considered that in
so grave a matter the Ministry were entitled to this. The
course adopted in advising the issue of a Royal Commission
would therefore seem a very proper one, and had it been
accepted by the Opposition a thorough investigation could
have been made, and a judgment given which would have

either cleared the Ministry or for ever driven out of public life
those who were found guilty. The report was directed to be
made to the House, and if there had been any suspicion of
an undue leaning towards the accused Ministers, it was in the
power of Parliament to have refused to accept it, and to have
taken such other steps as the maintenance of its dignity might
seem to require.

On the day following prorogation (August 14th), His
Excellency the Governor-General issued a Royal Commission
to Judges Polette and Gowan and ex-Judge Day, three gentlemen of unblemished reputation and high legal knowledge.
Lord Dufferin thus speaks of them in his despatch to the
Colonial Secretary : Only one of them is personally known to
me, viz : Judge Day, who, as Chancellor of McGill University,
received me on my visit to that institution. Since that we
have improved our acquaintance, and I have no hesitation
in stating, both from what I know and have learned, that I
have every confidence in Judge Day's high sense of honour,
capacity and firmness. I have also considered it my duty to
satisfy myself as to the qualifications of the other two gentlemen with whom he is associated, and I am in a position
to inform your lordship that they are generally regarded as
persons of unblemished integrity, sound judgment, and professional ability, while the length of time all three have been
removed from politics frees them from the suspicion of
political partizanship."

The Commission assembled at Ottawa on August 18th,
and commenced the examination of witnesses on September
4th. Mr. Huntingdon refused to recognize, or to appear
before them, and would not furnish the names of witnesses.
Following his example the following also failed to obey the
summons to attend : G. W. McMullen, C. M. Smith, Honourable A. B. Foster, Honourable Thomas McGreevy, John A.
Perkins and George Norris, jr. Thirty-six witnesses appeared
and gave testimony. Sir John Macdonald, Sir Francis
Hincks, Mr. Langevin, and other members of the Government
were examined at length, and declared in the most positive
terms that the charge, that the Government, or any members

of it, had made a contract with Sir Hugh Allan, or any one else, with regard to the Pacific Railway, in consideration of furnishing funds for election purposes, was absolutely false. That Sir Hugh Allan had contributed to the funds for election expenses was not denied, but he explained his reasons for doing so to be that he approved of the railway and canal policy of the Government, which was advantageous to his business, and desired to see them returned to power, in preference to the Liberals, whose policy, as indicated by their speeches, he found would be injurious to the country, and especially detrimental to his business. So far from the Government having sold him the contract, Sir John Macdonald had positively refused to sanction the terms of a letter written to him by Sir George Cartier, and which contained only an expression of opinion as to the probable course the Government would take with regard to the amalgamation of the two companies and the contract to be granted. This letter was as follows :

MONTREAL, *July* 30, 1872.

DEAR SIR HUGH :

I enclose you copies of telegrams received from Sir John A. Macdonald, and with reference to their contents I would say that, in my opinion, the Governor-in-Council will approve of the amalgamation of your company with the Inter-Oceanic Company, under the name of the Canadian Pacific Railway Company, the Provisional Board of the amalgamated company to be composed of seventeen members, of which four shall be named from the Province of Quebec by the Canada Pacific Railway Company ; four from the Province of Ontario by the Inter-Oceanic Railway Company ; and the remainder by the Government; the amalgamated company to have the power specified in the tenth section of the Act incorporating the Canada Pacific Railway Company, etc., the agreement of amalgamation to be executed between the companies, within two months from this date.

The Canada Pacific Company might take the initiative in procuring the amalgamation ; and if the Inter-Oceanic Company should not execute an agreement of amalgamation upon such terms, and within such limited time, I think the contemplated arrangements should be made with the Canada Pacific Railway under its charter.

Upon the subscription and payment on account of stock being made as required by the Act of last session respecting the Canada Pacific Railway Company, I have no doubt but that the Governor-in-Council will agree with the company for the construction and working of the Canadian Pacific Railway with such branches as shall be agreed upon, and will grant to the company all such subsidies and assistance as they are empowered to do by the Government Act. I believe all the advantages which the Government Act empowers the Government to confer upon any company, will be required to enable the works contemplated to be successfully carried through, and I am convinced that they will be accorded to the company to be formed by amalgamation, or to the Canada Pacific Company, as the case may be. I would add that, as I approve of the measures to which I have referred in this letter, I shall use my best endeavours to have them carried into effect.

Very truly yours,

(Sgd.)   GEO. E. CARTIER.

Sir John's views as to this letter having been communicated to Sir Hugh Allan, it was immediately returned by that gentleman to Sir George Cartier.

Parliament re-assembled on October 23rd, when Sir John Macdonald at once laid upon the table messages from His Excellency the Governor-General, transmitting all the papers connected with the case, and also the report of the Royal Commission. The great debate took place upon the second paragraph of the Address, which was as follows:

" That we thank His Excellency for his statement that, in accordance with the intimation given by him at the close of last session, he has caused Parliament to be summoned at the earliest moment after the receipt of the report of the Commissioners, appointed by His Excellency, to enquire into certain matters connected with the Canadian Pacific Railway."

As soon as it was read, Mr. Mackenzie rose, and in a lengthy and bitter speech reviewed the history of the railway and the policy of the Government in connection with it, and argued that the recent developments had clearly shewn that the Government were determined to carry the elections at all hazards, and had used the Pacific Railway contract as the means to obtain the money to gain their ends. He concluded by moving, seconded by Mr. Coffin :

" That the following words be added to the paragraph, ' And we have to acquaint His Excellency that by their course in reference to the investigation of the charges preferred by

Mr. Huntingdon, in his place in this House, and under the facts disclosed in the evidence laid before us, His Excellency's advisers have merited the censure of this House.'"

Mr. Mackenzie was followed by Dr. Tupper, Mr. Huntingdon, Sir Francis Hincks, Mr. James Macdonald and many others, until November 3rd, when Sir John Macdonald rose to speak. His speech lasted for five and a half hours, and covered every point that had been raised. It is too long to be given here in full, and much of its force would be lost by cutting it down, we will, therefore, only give the concluding portion.

"The Government never gave Sir Hugh Allan any contract that I am aware of. We never gave him any contract in which he had a controlling influence. We had formed a committee of thirteen men, chosen carefully and painfully, for the purpose of controlling Sir Hugh Allan, and preventing him from having any undue influence. We promised, we provided that not one of the Board should hold more than $100,000 of the stock; that not one single man should have any interest in the contract whatever. I put it to your own minds. There were thirteen gentlemen—Sir Hugh Allan and others—incorporated by that charter. That charter —study it, take it home with you. Is there any single power, privilege or advantage given to Sir Hugh Allan with that contract that has not been given equally to the other twelve? (Cheers). It is not pretended that any of the other twelve paid money for their positions. It is not contended that the gentlemen gave anything further than their own personal feelings, might dictate. (Cheers). You cannot name a man of these thirteen that has got any advantage over the other, except that Sir Hugh Allan has his name down first on the paper. (Cheers). Can anyone believe that the Government is guilty of the charges made against them? I call upon anyone who does to read that charter. Is there anything in that contract? If there is a word in that charter which derogates from the rights of Canada; if there is any undue privilege, or right, or preponderance, given to anyone of these thirteen directors, I say, Mr. Speaker, I am condemned. But,

sir, I commit myself, the Government commits itself to the
hands of this House ; and far beyond this House, it commits
itself to the country at large. (Loud cheers). We have faithfully done our duty. We have fought the battle of Confederation. We have fought the battle of Union. We have had
party strife setting province against province ; and more than
all, we have had, in the greatest province, the preponderating
province of the Dominion, every prejudice and sectional feeling that could be arrayed against us. I have been the victim
of that conduct to a great extent ; but I have fought the
battle of Confederation, the battle of Union, the battle of the
Dominion of Canada. I throw myself upon this House ; I
throw myself upon this country ; I throw myself upon
posterity ; and I know, that notwithstanding the many failings
of my life, I shall have the voice of this country and this
House rallying around me. (Cheers). And, sir, if I am
mistaken in that, I can confidently appeal to a higher court—
to the court of my own conscience, and to the court of
posterity. (Cheers). I leave it with this House with every
confidence. I am equal to either fortune. I can see past the
decision of this House, either for or against me ; but whether
if be for or against me, I know—and it is no vain boast for me
to say so, for even my enemies will admit that I am no boaster
—that there does not exist in Canada a man who has given
more of his time, more of his heart, more of his wealth, or
more of his intellect and power, such as they may be, for the
good of this Dominion of Canada." (Loud and prolonged
cheers).

Other speeches were made, but it soon became evident
that the strength of the Government was being sapped.
Whether or not there was any truth in the rumours with which
the air was filled, of promises to prominent men, or of other
human devices brought to bear on the weak-hearted and weak
kneed ; or that there had set in one of those irresistible tenden-
cies on the part of popular feeling to rush, unthinkingly and
unreasonably, on the spur of the moment, to hasty and unjust
conclusions without properly weighing the evidence, it is needless to enquire. The majority of Sir John's friends stood

nobly by him, but not all, and, when the party whips whispered
that, if a vote were taken, the amendment would probably be
carried by a majority of two, on November 5th, he placed
his resignation and that of his Ministry in the hands of the
Governor-General.   The unfairness and falsity of the charges
against him have long since been recognized.   Public opinion,
after mature deliberation, and on sober second thought,
pronounced him "not guilty," and not only restored him to
place and power, but established him so firmly that never
again during his lifetime was he disturbed.

In the above narrative of this very eventful period in Sir
John Macdonald's life we have confined ourselves to a mere
statement of facts, but, before leaving the subject, it is proper
that we should refer to the means by which it was sought to
obtain incriminating evidence against him and his Ministry.
Mr. Huntingdon was the accuser, and his right-hand man was
George W. McMullen, a person to whom the papers did not
hesitate to apply every epithet which could convey contempt,
as a man void of principle, and an unscrupulous adventurer.
It was with him that Sir Hugh Allan conducted the correspondence respecting the interests of the American capitalists
in his proposed company, and, when he thought that Sir
Hugh had committed himself in such a way that the
publication of his letters would damage him before the Canadian public, he went to him and demanded blackmail for their
return.   Sir Hugh, believing that his interests required Mr.
McMullen's silence, paid him a sum of money, and agreed to
pay him the further sum of $17,000 for the letters, after the
session was over.   But Mr. McMullen never got this $17,000,
and why?   Can there be any doubt of the story which was
accepted at the time, that he got a higher bid and, for
increased gold, betrayed Sir Hugh, and sold his letters to be
used against him?   In addition to the letters and telegrams
which appeared on July 4th, other documents were afterwards
published, and how were these obtained?   By paying $1,500
to Mr. Abbott's confidential clerk to steal them from his
desk.   Sir Hugh Allan's office was also entered at night time
and copies made of telegrams he had received, and even the

Post Office was not safe, for a letter from Sir John Macdonald to Mr. J. H. Pope was opened and published. No reference to these discreditable occurrences has been made in the statement given above of the Pacific Railway Slander, because it was desired to make the narrative as little heated as possible, but now they can be rightly brought in to emphasize the unfair treatment accorded to Sir John Macdonald on the strength of documents obtained in this dishonourable way, and in accepting the unsworn statement of one man of more than doubtful character, to the exclusion of the sworn testimony of thirty-six men of recognized high character and unquestioned honour.

The character of the men who were represented as American capitalists, and upon whose testimony Mr. Huntingdon and his friends relied to fix upon Sir John Macdonald and his Ministers a charge of selling a contract and dragging the honour of Canada in the dust, can best be gathered from an editorial article from the Chicago *Times* reproduced in the Toronto *Mail* of March 5, 1877.

"There is a notorious family in Chicago—the McMullens. They came here from Canada. They now teach the public morality, honesty, and piety in an unfortunate attempt at a newspaper called *The Post*. The public has some interest in these notorious persons at the present time because they are endeavouring to fasten themselves upon the city treasury.

"These men have a history which is interesting, even to persons not much concerned as to who gets the city printing.

"George W. McMullen, the brass and brains of the family is the man who achieved distinction in connection with the Canadian Pacific *Credit Mobilier*. This was a gigantic swindle. Its purpose was identical with that of Oakes Ames in the swindle of the same name in the United States. McMullen did considerable work in the Canadian *Credit Mobilier* and was caught and exposed. He threatened libel suits upon several newspapers in Canada which characterized him in terms equivalent to perjurer and blackmailer, and when the newspapers challenged him to bring his case to action, he failed to appear. The charges remain on record.

They will never be brought to trial by McMullen. Sir Hugh Allen was also involved in this swindle. A number of letters passed between him and G. W. McMullen mutually compromising. Allan had a character to lose, but McMullen had the letters. The Toronto *Mail* asserted that McMullen blackmailed Sir Hugh as the condition of not making the damaging disclosures public. The anti-Allan faction knew that the letters existed, and they thought they knew the material McMullen was made of. Overtures for the purchase of the letters were quietly begun, and, after dallying between the crazed Sir Hugh, who is said to have offered all he was worth to get the letters, and the other faction who put the price up higher McMullen took the better bargain.

"The *Mail* characterized McMullen as an eavesdropper, a listener at key-holes, a loathsome spy who sat at men's tables, broke their bread and ate their meat, and then slunk away to sell the secrets obtained under cover of hospitality and pledge of confidential intercourse. That journal publicly branded him as a blackmailer and a perjurer, and McMullen, after a pretence of bringing a suit against the *Mail*, never faced it in court. In the investigation instituted by the Dominion Parliament into the *Credit Mobilier* swindle, McMullen was awarded immunity against conviction for alleged perjury on condition that he betrayed his associates in the conspiracy.

"Meanwhile this honest and industrious family were engaged in a dubious enterprise in Chicago. They ran a bank and the famous State Insurance Company. George C. Smith and the McMullens ran the bank. The McMullens and George C. Smith ran the State Insurance Company. After the fire, George W. McMullen, on behalf of the bank, hurried around to the policy-holders, told them the insurance company was 'bust,' and that they would be extremely lucky if they got ten cents on the dollar, and, being a generous man, he offered them ten cents on the dollar. Many of them accepted—poor workingmen, widows, washerwomen, and such other victims as had been entrapped into giving their money into the swindle in the first place. Then the managers of the insurance company—the McMullens and Smith—had a meeting, and ordered themselves to pay to the bank in full the 10 per cent. policies; and then the bank managers— Smith and the McMullens—put the 90 per cent. in their pockets. It was only a few days ago that the robbed and swindled policy-holders had their latest meeting, to hear their attorney's report as to the progress made in getting the money back.

"When the State Insurance swindle was brought into court, there was some extraordinary developments. The policy-holders insisted that the bank ledger should be produced, in order that the money stolen from them, while they were houseless and homeless, might be traced and recovered. The court gave the order. It was then alleged that the bank ledger was lost. The information was conveyed to the policy-holders that it was not lost, that it was in the bank the day the court sent for it, and that D. S. McMullen had the book. D. S. McMullen was examined. His story surpassed any of Munchausen's. He swore that one day, while riding alone, he left his buggy and went into a house. When he returned to his vehicle he found therein a package wrapped in paper and sealed. He admitted that it was of the form, and size, and style of the bank-ledger, and that it was sealed with the seal of the bank. An anonymous note laid upon it requested him to take charge of the package for a friend who would some time call for it. He did not know the writing, did not save the note, even to identify the friend when he should call again. Some time subsequently he received another anonymous note requesting him to bring the package in his buggy to a certain corner of the Court House square; to leave it in his buggy, go away from the vehicle, and the owner of the package would get it during his absence. He complied with the request. Didn't look to see who took it away. Didn't know what became of it. Had no idea who the friend was, or whether it was the same person who had so impetuously deposited in his buggy the mysterious package, in the first place. The ledger was not found, and the victims of the State Insurance swindle know no more to-day

than they did then, what became of their money, except that
it passed into the pockets of thieves.   Judge Drummond
delivered some remarks concerning D. S. McMullen's truth-
fulness, which justify the suspicion that he is a worthy brother
of George W. McMullen.   In fact, Judge Drummond delivered a eulogy upon the McMullen family, which rarely falls
to the lot of members of the human race.   The unfortunate
policy-holders who sold out to George W. McMullen and his
agents for ten cents on the dollar thought they had fared
badly ; but the still more unfortunate policy-holders who
refused to sell, got less, and none of them are likely to recover
a cent, even with the aid of the court."

It is unnecessary to give the balance of the article, which
deals with other members of the family, showing that another
brother had been indicted for perjury and fraud against the
United States, while occupying the position of gauger, and that
still another one had been before the grand jury in connection with an attempt to obtain the city printing by bribery.

It is not to be wondered at that when the big-hearted
Canadian public learned all these facts and came to know
the true inwardness of the plot against Sir John Macdonald,
that they should hasten to restore him to that place in their
hearts, which he had previously enjoyed, and by their votes
at the polls, testify to the renewal of their confidence.

On November 7th, the new Ministry was sworn in as
follows :

Hon. Alex. Mackenzie, Premier and Minister of Public Works.

Hon. Antoine A. Dorion, Minister of Justice.

Hon. Albert J. Smith, Minister of Marine and Fisheries.

Hon. Luc Letellier de St. Just, Minister of Agriculture.

Hon. Richard John Cartwright, Minister of Finance.

Hon. David Laird, Minister of the Interior.

Hon. David Christie, Secretary of State.

Hon. Isaac Burpee, Minister of Customs.

Hon. Donald A. Macdonald, Postmaster-General.

Hon. Thomas Coffin, Receiver-General.

Hon. Telesphore Fournier, Minister of Inland Revenue.

Hon. William Ross, Minister of Militia.

Hon. Edward Blake, without portfolio.

Hon. Richard W. Scott, without portfolio.

On January 9, 1874, Honourable David Christie was appointed Speaker of the Senate, and was succeeded as Secretary of State by the Honourable R. W. Scott. On January 20th, Honourable L. S. Huntingdon was appointed President of the Council.

Mr. Mackenzie, probably feeling that he could not rely with certainty upon a Parliament elected under a Conservative Government, and which had given that Government a large majority up to the time of their resignation, resolved upon advising a dissolution, which the Governor-General conceded, and on January 2nd writs for a new election were issued. The result was that he completely swept the country, and came back with a majority of about eighty.

The new Parliament met on March 26th, when Honourable T. W. Anglin was unanimously elected Speaker of the Commons.

On May 12th Mr. Mackenzie moved the House into Committee of the Whole on his Pacific Railway Resolutions, the main points about which were, that the road was to be divided into four sections, viz : *First*, from Lake Nipissing to the west end of Lake Superior ; *Second*, from No. 1 to Red River ; *Third*, from Red River to a point between Fort Edmonton and the foot of the Rocky Mountains ; *Fourth*, thence to the Pacific. A line of telegraph to be constructed in advance of the railway. The road to be constructed under the Department of Public Works. The land grant to consist of 20,000 acres per mile in alternate sections, two-thirds to be sold by the Government at prices agreed upon, and the proceeds paid to the contractors as the work went on. The Government to have power, if found more advantageous, to contract and work the railway as a public work. The money grant to be $10,000 per mile for construction and rolling stock, and 4 per cent. on a sum per mile to be fixed by contract, for running the road.

In introducing the Bill, Mr. Mackenzie reviewed the past history of the road, and said that he had not at all changed his mind as to the impossibility of completing the road within the period mentioned in the agreement with British Columbia.

He considered that the road would have to be built by the country, but it need not all be built at once. He favoured the construction of short lines of railway to connect the magnificent water stretches of the continent, which would afford a summer route to the foot of the Rockies, and be quite sufficient for many years to come. He did not consider it at all necessary to build at present the 557 miles from Nipissing to Nipigon. With regard to the section west of the Rocky Mountains, he said : "The British Columbia section will, of course, have to be proceeded with as fast as we can do it, as it is essential to keep faith with the spirit and, as far as possible, with the letter of the agreement."

Honourable Dr. Tupper took exception to the Government scheme, claiming that, if carried out, it would impose an unbearable amount of taxation upon the country. The Bill, however, passed its third reading without amendment.

Parliament was prorogued on May 26th, after passing one hundred and seventeen Bills, amongst the most important of which were an Act authorizing a loan of £8,000,000 sterling, and an Act to take the construction of the Intercolonial Railway out of the hands of Commissioners, and place it under the control of the Public Works Department.

I T would, no doubt, make these pages more complete were
we to follow the course of the Mackenzie Government
during the five years they were in power. Their policy, with
respect to the building of the Pacific Railway, the trouble
with British Columbia, the Carnarvon terms, Lord Dufferin's
visit and speech at Victoria, are all necessary to a complete
history of our great national highway, but it would be inconsistent with the task we have undertaken, to refer to them
except from the stand-point from which they were viewed
by Sir John Macdonald. For the same reason we shall omit
all reference to the trade policy pursued during these years,
and pass on to the time when he brought before Parliament
his resolutions in favour of a protective or national policy,
merely remarking of the period that had elapsed between this
and his resignation of office, that Sir John Macdonald was
unanimously elected leader of the Canadian Liberal-Conservative Opposition on November 6, 1873, and, in that capacity,
not only refrained from offering any factious opposition to
the Government, but on several occasions, gave them the
benefit of his ability and long experience in perfecting some
of their most important measures, notably, the Insolvent Act
and the Act constituting the Supreme Court of the Dominion.
He disagreed with them entirely, however, on their trade
policy and on March 10, 1876, on the motion to go into
Committee of Supply, moved the following amendment :

" That this House regrets His Excellency the Governor-General has not been advised to recommend to Parliament a measure for the re-adjustment of the tariff, which would not only aid in alleviating the stagnation of business deplored in the gracious Speech from the Throne, but would also afford fitting encouragement and protection to the struggling manufacturers and industries, as well as to the agricultural products of this country."

Sir John made an elaborate speech in support of his motion and from that time forth, in Parliament and out of Parliament, lost no opportunity of advocating his scheme. It was already apparent that the tide of popular opinion was turning in his favour and during the succeeding summer, warm invitations were extended to him to visit different parts of the country and address the people at open air meetings. These picnics were attended by thousands of the electors, accompanied by their wives and families, and proved an admirable medium for bringing before the great body of the people, the arguments he had to advance in favour of his policy. He was invariably attended by some of the most skilful debaters of his party who, by their able and exhaustive speeches, materially assisted his efforts. As an example of one of these, we will take the Norfolk demonstration, held at the town of Simcoe, on September 27, 1876. He was accompanied by the Honourable William McDougall, and on arrival, was greeted with the utmost enthusiasm by a vast number of people. An address, embodying the feelings of affection and admiration entertained towards him by his numerous friends in both Ridings of the County, was presented, after which speeches were made first by prominent local men, and then by their guests. That of Mr. McDougall was a brilliant retrospect of occurrences since Confederation, and a forcible defence of his own conduct and that of his fellow Reformers who had joined hands with the Conservatives in bringing about this event, and afterwards assisted in perfecting the arrangements then made, and who did not conceive it to be their duty to desert the Ministry and follow Mr.

Brown. His effort met with great appreciation and he was warmly cheered throughout.

The following is a copy of the Address which was read to Sir John Macdonald by Mr. Livingstone, the Secretary of the Liberal-Conservative Association of the North Riding of Norfolk :

To the Right Honourable Sir John Macdonald, K.C.B :

The Conservatives of Norfolk hail with pleasure your visit to their county, and earnestly hope that your life will be prolonged, and that your health will enable you for years to continue their chief. Many of those present to-day to greet you with a loyal welcome, have been your admirers and steadfast friends since you first entered political life, and have watched with intense interest the career of the distinguished leader who, by his kindness of heart and urbanity of manner, has endeared himself to his followers; who, for more than a quarter of a century, led his party in triumph from one victory to another; and all hold in high esteem the great statesman who, on obtaining position, found this country a number of separate provinces, but who, upon retiring from the helm of state, left it a vast Dominion extending from the Atlantic to the Pacific, with its people peaceful, prosperous and contented—a statesman who, by his eminent abilities, has won for himself an illustrious name, and a fame as imperishable as the history of his country.

It is not because you are deemed faultless that this large Assembly has met to do you honour ; it is because Conservatives believe that if you erred in the administration of affairs your errors were of judgment and not of intention, and they have ever been proud of you because your slanderers, although they have been both numerous and malignant, have never succeeded in connecting your name with any act by which the interest or honour of your country was sacrificed; or with having used your position to enrich or aggrandize yourself or your friends by dishonourable means.

The ovations you receive wherever you go prove that you still possess the fullest confidence of Conservatives—and, we believe, of a vast majority of the Canadian people—and are omens that you are soon to be restored to the power which was wrested from you by dishonest means, and by oft repeated charges of wrong doing, which were unsustained by evidence, and which were false, but which, for a time, so blinded the electors to your real worth, and to the true merits of the case, that your party was defeated at the polls.

Conservatives believe that your restoration to power will be a blessing to your country, and that the country will witness one of your greatest triumphs, when, by wise legislation, you will have brought prosperity back to the Dominion, and will have swept away the great depression which at present overwhelms the Canadian industries.

On behalf of the Conservatives of Norfolk we bid you welcome, and have the honour to present you with this Address.

JOHN WILSON,
President, North Norfolk Conservative Association.
W. DAWSON,
President, South Norfolk Conservative Association.
W. WILSON LIVINGSTONE,
Secretary, North Norfolk Conservative Association.
J. WESLEY RYERSON
Secretary, South Norfolk Conservative Association.
SIMCOE, *September 27, 1876.*

The following is but a small portion of the Speech made by Sir John Macdonald.   Its great length prevents our giving it in full :

" Mr. Chairman, Ladies and Gentlemen—If I have for thirty years been in public life ; if I have for nearly twenty years been a member of the Government ; and if, during the greater part of that period, I have been the most reviled, calumniated and abused man in Canada, I have my compensation here.   I have my reward, my exceeding great reward, when I find that such an Assembly as this, in the glorious old county of Norfolk, comes here to do honour to myself.   It is a reward of which any statesman should be proud.   It is a testimony which I feel at the very bottom of my heart, and I would, indeed, be insensible to your kindness if I did not accept it, not only as a reward for my long services, and for all the toil and trouble that have fallen upon me for many years, but as a verdict of acquittal at your hands, from all the charges against me of wilful wrong doing.   No man is more conscious than I am of my faults.   Looking back at my history, and at the history of Canada, I freely admit that, guided by the light of experience, there are many things in my political career that I now could wish had been otherwise. There are acts of omission and commission which I regret ; but your testimony, and the testimony of my own conscience, alike show that, as you believe, and as I know, whether I was right or wrong in any political act at the time, I was acting according to the best of my judgment for the interest of our

President Canadian Pacific Railways.

common country. (Hear, hear). I want no more impartial
jury than you. I want no other verdict than from your hands
and from men like you in this Dominion, and especially in
this Province of Ontario—my own Province—and wherever I
have gone during this summer, I have been received kindly
by friends and political foes, listened to with respect by the
latter, and by my friends greeted with enthusiasm. These
meetings are of the very greatest importance. Public men in
meeting their countrymen as I have been doing this summer,
have only been copying the example of public men in the
mother country. The public men of England, who are
members of the House of Commons, are in the habit of visiting
their constituents, and entering fully into a discussion of the
political questions of the day. And yet when we commenced
these meetings—and I tell you that in no one case did I
suggest an invitation, the meetings through the country being
free and spontaneous expressions of feeling towards me—
they were laughed and jeered at and belittled. (Cheers).

"When we were forced to go out of office we left this
country in a happy and contented state. (Cheers). In
November, 1873, the credit of this country was greater than
it ever was before. We left you a country in which there was
peace and prosperity, where the people were satisfied with the
state of affairs, where there was confidence in business, a pride
in the future of the country, and a feeling of certainty that we
were going forward, and as we had risen from being four
provinces to be one great Dominion, so it was felt we had a
great future before us in its development. There was universal
confidence and satisfaction throughout Canada, and there was
peace and contentment. What do you find now? Is there
peace and contentment now? Is there confidence—('No, no,')
—is there confidence in any branch of public affairs? Is there
confidence in any branch of the industries of this country?
Are not our manufacturers suffering all over the Dominion in
consequence of the injudicious action of the Government in
meddling and muddling with our tariff? Have they not
shaken our credit? Are not our manufacturers closing or
working at half time? Are not our mechanics working at

half wages, and is there any prospect that things will be better ? There is universal discontent, universal dissatisfaction, and a well-grounded belief that the present men in power, no matter how patriotic their intentions may be, do not possess the capacity to govern this country wisely and well.

" Gentlemen, there is another issue between the present Government and the Opposition. We are in favour of a tariff that will incidentally give (protection to our manufacturers, that will develop our manufacturing industries. We believe that that can be done, and if done it will give a home market to our farmers.) The farmers will be satisfied when they know that large bodies of operatives are working in the mills and manufactories in every village and town in the country. They know that every man of them is a consumer, and that he must have pork and flour, beef and all that the farmers raise, and they know that instead of being obliged to send their grain to a foreign and uncertain market they will have a market at their own door. And the careful housewife, every farmer's wife, will know that everything that is produced under her care—the poultry, the eggs, the butter, and the garden stuff—will find a ready and profitable market in the neighbouring town or village.

(' No country is great with only one industry. Agriculture is our most important, but it cannot be our only staple. All men are not fit to be farmers ; there are men with mechanical and manufacturing genius who desire to become operatives or manufacturers of some kind,)and we must have the means to employ them, and when there is a large body of successful and prosperous farmers and a large body of successful and prosperous manufacturers, the farmer will have a home market for his produce, and the manufacturer a home market for his goods, and we shall have nothing to fear. And, therefore, I have been urging upon my friends—I have told them that we must lay aside all old party quarrels about old party doings. (Cheers). Those old matters are matters before the flood— (cheers)—which have gone by and are settled forever—many of them settled by the Governments of which I have been a member. Why should parties divide on these old quarrels? Let us divide on questions affecting the present and future interest of the country.

("The question of the day is that of the protection of our farmers from the unfair competition of foreign produce, and the protection of our manufacturers. I am in favour of reciprocal free trade if it can be obtained, but so long as the policy of the United States closes their markets to our products we should have a policy of our own as well, and consult only our own interests.) That subject wisely and vigorously dealt with, you will see confidence restored, the present depression dispelled, and the country prosperous and contented. The whole country is now dissatisfied, even the political partizans of the Government own that these men are incapable, and the whole country knows it. I have said that the agriculturists and the manufacturers must not divide their interests. They must act together. In 1870 the Government, of which I was a member, began the National Policy and put small duties on flour, coal, salt, etc. I then told the manufacturers that they could not expect to get protection from the farmers unless their interests were also protected. They must make a common interest of it; unless you manufacturers will protect the farmers they will not protect you. (Cheers).

"When I went to Washington in 1871, that policy was repealed in my absence, and it had a prejudicial effect upon the negotiations we were making at that time, But Mr. Mackenzie says we had a majority in the House at that time. True, but the whole of the Opposition voted for the repeal of this National Policy, and some of our friends, who were Free Traders, from the Lower Provinces voted with them. The majority of our friends voted to support the measure. But there was a sufficient minority of our friends who voted with the whole body of the Opposition, and the Act of 1870 was repealed. I told the manufacturers who favoured the repeal how selfish and unwise it was, because some few articles might be got cheaper for their purposes, to thwart the wishes of the farmers when they would probably be applying shortly for protection for themselves. Gentlemen, they will not make

the mistake again ; they see the error now, and are anxious
to act with the farmers. And, gentlemen, if now you act
together as one man, I promise you you will see your manufactures flourish, and you will get a home market. Then the
depression will disappear, but it will not disappear until
another very lamentable thing happens—the present Ministry
must disappear too. (Cheers and laughter). Great as the
calamity will be, it must happen, or the present depression will
continue. You must do it or you will remain a slaughter -
market. ✱ (The Americans have the whole control of your
markets, and when they at any time produce too much for
their own markets, they send their surplus goods over here to
sell them off at a sacrifice and bring down the price of every
article in Canada, and thus our manufactures are obliged
to close their establishments or employ their workmen on half
or quarter time. Why, it has not been denied that, according
to the statement of Mr. W. P. Howland, President of the
Dominion Board of Trade, 400,000 workingmen have been
obliged to leave Canada to find employment in the United
States.) Mr. Mackenzie attempts to deny it, and he takes
credit that some had found work on the Welland Canal, work
which they would never have got if we had not carried the
measure for enlarging that work, and commenced its construction.

 ("Gentlemen, our workmen can be fully employed if we
encourage our manufactures ; they need not go over to
the States to add strength and wealth to a foreign country and
to deprive us of that strength and wealth. If we have work
here, at home, our country will be prosperous and happy, and,
gentlemen, it is a consummation devoutly to be wished
for, and I pray you to take the lesson to heart and cast aside
all factious and partizan feelings which may have been
imbibed for the purpose of supporting designing politicians
like Mr. Mackenzie or myself. (Laughter). It has been said
that party is the madness of many for the gain of a few. It
may be so when it is a mere question between the ins and the
outs, but when the people divide on living questions we shall
have parties of earnest men, who will select the best men

to carry out their views in Parliament. Speaking as I do, and feeling as I do that our views are correct, I invite the calm consideration of the people of Canada, of the electors of this county, at the next general election to (return men who will see that their interests are protected.) It will not be by taking those who say they will vote protection, but who, like Mr. Charlton, when the question is put before the House, speak one way and vote the other. That kind of thing is a humbug, and you must not elect a man because he merely promises to vote for protection.

"You know very well there can be no alteration in the tariff unless it is brought down by the Government. No independent member can move a rise in the tariff; it must be introduced by the Government. So you must not support a man unless he pledges himself to vote, not only for protection, but against any Government which will not bring down a measure for the purpose.

" No, no, you must get the Government out, and put in a Government that will carry it. Mr. Mackenzie is trying to frighten his own discontented friends by asserting that if they go out Sir John Macdonald and his bad men will come in. Now that does not at all follow. This is a free country and the people will choose for themselves; the elector can, by calm and deliberate action, elect men who are pledged to carry out this great policy intelligently, and who will only give their confidence to a Government worthy of it. There are many good men in public life besides Mr. Mackenzie and myself; if Mr. Mackenzie died—and what a loss that would be to the country—(laughter)—and if I died—I have no doubt that the country would flourish as it does now—only better, if not under the present Government. (Hear, hear). All this cry is a bugaboo to keep themselves in. No, put them out if they are unfit and put other and better men in their places.

" Ladies and gentlemen, I have to thank you for the kindness and enthusiasm shown by you in this magnificent demonstration; I have to thank you from the bottom of my heart. I should be deeply insensible if I did not feel your kindness, confidence, and aid ; and the consolation it will give to my friends, my wife, and my children, after all that I have borne with, when they see and read how you, my fellow-countrymen, rally round me, and how my friends in other parts of the country have rallied round me.   I have suffered, and my family have suffered still more, from the continued abuse that has been poured upon me, but that is all wiped away, that is all forgotten.   (Hear, hear).   If, perhaps, I am more popular than I have been in Ontario, and I believe I am —(hear, hear)—a good deal of my popularity is to be attributed to the feeling of the generous people of this country that it is unfair to heap such obloquy on a man who has worked so hard for his country."

Of the many able addresses made during this period, on the question of Protection vs. Free Trade, there was probably none that attracted greater attention than that delivered by Mr. Thomas White, Jr., in the City Hall, London, at the invitation of the Board of Trade, on January 12, 1877.   The audience was composed of merchants, manufacturers and business men generally, from the city and surrounding towns and villages and numbered about six hundred.   The meeting was presided over by Mr. George Moorhead, President of the Board of Trade, and on the platform were the Mayor and a full representation of the banking and mercantile community, the clergy, etc.   The Chairman introduced Mr. White in flattering terms, who, on rising, was received with loud applause.   His address was so well arranged, so able, so logical, so convincing, and so clearly expounded the policy of Sir John Macdonald and the Conservative party that, after a lapse of a quarter of a century, it is as appropriate and as interesting as when delivered, and may be read with pleasure and profit.   We, therefore give the following voluminous extracts :—

" When the Board of Trade of the city of London did me the honour to invite me to this city to deliver an address upon so important a subject as the relations of the question of Free Trade and Protection to the interests of Canada, I confess to you I had a great deal of hesitation about the propriety of my accepting that invitation. I have no doubt whatever in my own mind as to the importance of this question. I have no doubt in my own mind that it arises, in its relation to the real interests of this Dominion, far above any other question that is prominent in the discussions of the country. But I am a strong party man—I am tolerably known as such ; and my only fear in accepting this invitation was that some persons might be ill-natured enough to suppose that I had some party or sinister motive in accepting it. This question, I think, may fairly be discussed without relation to party to-night. (Hear, hear). I think it may fairly be thus discussed, for this reason : That there are in all the political parties of this country considerable diversity of opinion upon the subject. (Hear, hear). Among both parties will be found those who are strong free-traders, and those who are strong protectionists. And I propose, therefore, in discussing it with you here this evening, to deal with it not in its relation to party at all. I desire that we all should, as I hope to be able to, forget that we are party men in any sense whatever, and remember only that we are Canadians, deeply interested in the prosperity of this country. (Loud applause).

"You will allow me, before I enter upon the discussion itself, to refer somewhat briefly to the tariff legislation of Canada. You will remember that in 1855-56, and 1856 particularly, we had great prosperity in Canada. The Grand Trunk Railway was being built. Enormous sums of English capital were introduced and were being expended in the country. Employment was given to the people ; numerous people were brought over from the Old World, some of whom are now to be found among the most prosperous farmers in this and other sections of the Dominion of Canada—men who came here as navvies to work upon the Grand Trunk Railway. Upon the completion of that work the crisis of 1857 came upon us. The prosperity which we had enjoyed for a short time, and which we had all hoped might be permanent, passed away, together with the magnificent schemes of future riches which many a man had built up on the strength of having purchased a lot where a station was going to be built, and had got the geographer to draw him plans of the future city with its magnificent churches and town hall, and other prominent buildings. But they were compelled to realize that the country was not prosperous because of the temporary introduction of capital into it, and the mere temporary expenditure of that capital. Then came the most important act in our tariff legislation. I refer to the Act of 1858, when Mr. Galt, now Sir Alexander Galt, for the first time in Canada introduced the protection principle, and I think you will agree with me that that had an important influence upon the interests of this country. Those of you who look back and remember that period will agree with me that the industries which sprang up, almost as if by magic, in different parts of the country as the result of the protective duties, compensate us to a very considerable extent for the cessation of those large expenditures in capital which we had had in consequence of the construction of the Grand Trunk Railway. That was the first protectionist, and, I say, the most important Act in the tariff legislation of old Canada ; and it had an influence upon the prosperity of the country, such as no one can for a moment question.

" Our next most important Act—it was important because it was apparently in direct reversal of the policy of 1858—was the tariff of 1866, when the same Finance Minister, Mr. Galt, then a member of the Coalition Government, introduced a Bill which, on the average, reduced the duty on the unenumerated list to fifteen per cent. It is important for a moment to understand the reasons which justified, and the circumstances which rendered possible, that act of legislation. We were at that time discussing the question of Confederation. All parties in Canada had united together to 'ground arms' in relation to the old party disputes which had separated them before that time. They had agreed, I say, to 'ground arms,' and to build up a great Confederation, which would extend from the Atlantic to the Pacific, and to secure for the future of this country that prosperity which seemed almost impossible in the existing state of things. Our friends in the Maritime Provinces were strong free traders ; that is, strong free traders in the sense that they desired a low import duty ; their duties averaged not more than twelve and a-half per cent. And one of the strongest arguments used against going into Confederation was the high duties of the old Provinces of Canada. The object, therefore, of that reduction was to assist those friends of Confederation in the Lower Provinces in bringing about that union, the effect of which would be to add a million consumers for the producers of Canada, and would secure for the whole the greater prosperity which all desired.

" Now, what were the circumstances which rendered that possible ? The United States had just emerged from a great war, and that war had paralysed all their industries. That war had enforced a system of internal taxation which had increased enormously the cost of everything ; they produced a system of high duties which increased the cost of everything they imported. They were in that condition which afforded to us, lying alongside of them, and free from these unfortunate circumstances, a higher protection than any possible duty which could have been put on by the Canadian Government. It was fortunate for us, it was fortunate for those who look upon the prosperity of Canada as largely dependent upon a fiscal policy, at that time, when it was necessary—in order to secure this Confederation—to yield somewhat to the views of the Maritime Provinces, that we should, at the same time, be so situated in relation to the neighbouring Republic, that we had a state of affairs which secured us absolute, entire, and complete protection for all the industries of this country. You will remember, gentlemen, looking back at that time, that, down to 1873, the people of Canada suffered nothing from the reduction of the duties to fifteen per cent. The industries of Canada suffered nothing in consequence of the change of tariff. On the contrary, prosperity prevailed in every part of the Dominion, and the industries which had been established under the tariff of 1858 continued and flourished. We were saved from that (undue, that unfair competition which has since done so much to injure and paralyse our industries.) We were saved from that during these years.

" Now, gentlemen, I am aware that there is a general

opinion prevailing that the high prices of articles in the United States at that time were due entirely to high import duties. I am aware that it is alleged as one of the reasons why we should avoid a protective policy, that the protective system at that time was a serious burden of taxes upon the people of the neighbouring Republic. No fallacy could be greater. What caused the high price of goods—as I shall be able to show to your entire satisfaction, I think, before I have done—was not the import duties, but the internal revenue duties which had nothing to do with protection—that internal system of taxation which, instead of being in favour, was directly against any idea of protection, because it is perfectly clear that if you put a duty, say of twenty-five per cent., on an article, in order that you may have it manufactured in the country, and then put on an internal revenue duty of twenty per cent., in order to raise a revenue, it is clear, I say, that the actual protection is reduced to five per cent., and not twenty-five per cent. It was, therefore, I say, the internal revenue system in the United States which at that time caused high prices for every thing purchased in that country. In 1873 a change again took place. The revenue system of the country was fast returning to its normal condition. The ordinary industries of the United States were fast resuming their old state, in consequence of the removal of one duty after another in the internal revenue system, and things began to change so that from that time down to the present, under a steadily increasing ratio, cheapness became the rule instead of dearness for articles in the United States.

"You will remember, at least those living in large cities and I suppose some of you know in London, that it was not, an uncommon thing for American travellers and tourists to come to Canadian cities to purchase large supplies of what they required, and by a system of 'underground railway,' take them to the United States, and thus save, by the difference of the prices here and there, enough to pay for a pleasant summer tour—which, therefore, cost them nothing. What is the fact to-day? In the city of Montreal and in the city of Toronto, and I daresay in the city of London, Americans no longer come to buy articles; but I know people in the city of Montreal who go to New York and there purchase goods—just as New Yorkers did in Montreal, four or five years ago, and they can purchase them cheaper than they can purchase them here, and by the same system of 'underground railway' they bring them to this side of the line, and make a large profit.   This is a change recognized everywhere, and has done much to provoke the discussion and to revive the interest in the question of free trade and protection—which is the most marked feature of the discussions in the country during the last three or four years.

"I am compelled to refer to these discussions in dealing with the question which I have before me.   I shall be compelled to refer to the utterances of public men ; I propose especially to take the utterances of the Finance Minister in his budget speech last session, not in a party sense, gentlemen, but simply in the sense that in that speech we have the most authoritative statement of the arguments of those who believe that the true policy of this country will be found in assimilating our system as nearly as possible to that of England, and avoiding as far as we possibly can, that of the United States. It is in that sense, and in that sense only, that I propose to refer to the very able speech—admitted to be able by all parties—of Mr. Cartwright, during the last session of Parliament.   He put the case very practically.   He stated a plain issue between one side and the other—it could hardly have been more distinctly put.   What Mr. Cartwright said upon that point was as follows : 'It becomes us to consider the various remedies proposed for this unfortunate state of affairs.' He was describing the depression and the demand for a revision of the tariff, to which it had given rise.   'In the first place I desire to expend a few words on the general impression which prevails, even in quarters where we would hardly expect to find it, that it is in the power of this Government, of any Government, this Legislature or any Legislature, to make a country prosperous by the mere stroke of a pen or the enactment of Acts of Parliament.   I would like honourable gentlemen in this house and out of it, who entertain that illusion, as

I consider it, to think to what such a course would lead, and I
ask them if they are prepared to pay the price. You cannot
have at one and the same time, a free Government and a
paternal Government.' I say, gentlemen, it is impossible to
put the case of the two phases of the opinion on this question
more strongly than it is here put. That is, whether a country
can be rendered prosperous by a policy of a Government or
Legislature.

"We are fortunate, in dealing with this question, in having
the practical experience of those who have studied the question in both its phases in the neighbouring republic. I propose, therefore, rather than give my own opinions, to give you
the opinion of some of those gentlemen ; and first I shall call
your attention to an extract from a speech delivered by Mr.
Granger on the Tariff Bill of New York, introduced into the
House of Representatives at Washington in the year 1857.
The subject then being discussed was that with which we are
dealing to-night. A Protection Bill had been introduced, a
strong agitation existed on the subject, although the agitation
was only successful in 1861, when the Act came into force
before the war broke out. Here is Mr. Granger's opinion of
the tariff legislation, and its effects on the country. He says :
—'Since the war of 1812, we have at three different times
resorted to a protective tariff, to relieve us from financial
distress. From 1818 to 1824, with a mere revenue tariff, the
balance of trade was against us, and, during that term of
six years, our exports of specie exceeded our imports
$10,000,000. This caused the protective tariff of 1824, and the
effect of the change was soon felt. Confidence and activity
returned, and, instead of exporting specie, we imported specie
to a large amount. The effect was so obvious and gratifying
that the still higher tariff of 1828 was enacted—the highest we
ever had. Under these two protective tariffs of 1824 and
1828 up to 1834, ten years, the whole country was blessed
with a prosperity perhaps never before equalled in this or
any other country. In these ten years of protection, from
1824 to 1834, we imported thirty millions of specie more than
we exported and paid off the debts of two wars—that of

the revolution, and of 1812—in all, principal and interest, $100,000,000. Next came the descending compromise tariff of Mr. Clay, reluctantly conceded to the opponents of protection. By a sliding scale this tariff brought us down to a horizontal tariff of 20 per cent. The result was the Government soon found itself out of funds and out of credit. The tariff of 1842 was arranged for protection and revenue incidentally. It justified the expectations of the most sanguine friends, but it was allowed only a brief existence. It was said in high places that the principle of Protection was wrong, and in an evil hour Congress adopted the maxim, and the tariff of 1842 was repealed, and that of 1846, the present one, substituted. Sir, unless we have a radical change in our tariff laws, we shall surely have another financial crash. We must manufacture more and import less, and keep our specie at home. We have a foreign debt of nearly $250,000,000. Protection is vastly more important to us now than revenue, but we can have them both at once if we will.' That, gentlemen, is the opinion of Mr. Granger on the tariff, in its relation to its effect on the country. He contended that if a change were not made in the tariff of the country, they would have a financial crash. Whether in consequence of the tariff not being altered, I do not pretend to say, but certainly the crash did come.

"I will give you another opinion—the opinion of an eminent United States public man—of a man who, however much one might differ from his political opinions, was respected by all, and who was deeply concerned for the prosperity of the whole people of the United States. I refer to the late Horace Greeley. He said :—' It is within my own recollection that, after the last war we carried on against Great Britain, there was a universal collapse ; foreign goods crowded our markets and American factories were shut up ; then was labour without employment and agriculture without recompense, which created a feeling that agitated the country. After eight years of commotion the tariff was enacted expressly for Protection. This was enhanced in 1828, and the country arose out of its misery and bankruptcy and collapse into prosperity and thrift. That I know, for I saw it.' That was the confession of Mr. Greeley as to the power of the Government or Legislature, by the enactment of wise laws, at such times as it was deemed advisable, to affect the prosperity of the people.

" I will quote one other extract from the speech of another great man in the neighbouring Republic—a man whose name is honoured as that of a great man, not only in his own country, but wherever the English language is spoken— Mr. Henry Clay. He thus discusses the two periods of the country's existence, under a Protective policy, and under a policy of Free Trade :—' Eight years ago it was my painful duty to present to the other House of Congress an unexaggerated picture of the general distress pervading the whole land. We must all yet remember some of its frightful features. We all know that the people were then oppressed and borne down by an enormous load of debt ; that the value of property was at the lowest point of depression ; that ruinous sales and sacrifices were everywhere made of real estate ; that stop laws, and relief laws, and paper money, were adopted to save the people from impending destruction ; that a deficit in the public revenue existed, which compelled the Government to seize upon and divert from its legitimate object the appropriations to the Sinking Fund to redeem the national debt, and that our commerce and navigation were threatened with a complete paralysis. In short, sir, if I were to select any term of years since the adoption of the present constitution which exhibited a scene of the most widespread dismay and desolation, it would be exactly that term of seven years which immediately preceded the establishment of the tariff of 1824.' That was a sufficiently gloomy picture of national distress ; but he had a brighter picture to present as its counterpart. ' I have now to perform the more pleasing task of exhibiting an imperfect sketch of the existing state of the unparalleled prosperity of the country. On a general survey, we behold cultivation extended, the arts flourishing, the face of the country improved, our people fully and profitably employed, and the public countenance exhibiting tranquility, contentment, and happiness. And, if we descend into particulars, we have the agreeable contemplation of a people out of debt; land rising slowly in value, but in a secure and salutary degree; a ready, though not extravagant, market for all the surplus productions of our industry; innumerable flocks and herds browsing and gamboling on ten thousand hills, and plains covered with rich and verdant grasses; our cities expanded, and whole villages springing up, as it were, by enchantment; our tonnage, foreign and coast-wise, swelling and fully occupied; the rivers of our interior animated by the perpetual thunder and lightning of countless steamboats; the currency sound and abundant; the public debt of two wars nearly redeemed; and, to crown all, the public treasury overflowing, embarassing Congress not to find subjects of taxation, but to select the objects which shall be liberated from the impost. If the term of seven years were to be selected of the greatest prosperity which this people have enjoyed since the establishment of their present constitution, it would be exactly that period of seven years which immediately followed the passage of the tariff of 1824, This transformation of the conditions of the country from gloom and distress to lightness and prosperity, has been mainly the work of American legislation fostering American industry, instead of allowing it to be controlled by foreign legislation cherishing foreign industry.' That, gentlemen, is the opinion of Henry Clay, a great man, all will admit— a man fully competent to give an opinion on the effect of legislation upon the people, and it must be admitted by all parties that the inference which he drew, and the strong opinion which he gave utterance to, was contrary to the opinion of Mr. Cartwright, Mr. Clay being clearly of opinion that, under certain conditions, the Legislature could pass such measures as, under certain conditions, would improve and enhance the prosperity of the people. (Applause).

" But, gentlemen, we are able to prove that Mr. Clay was right by our own experience in Canada. I have already referred to the effect of the tariff passed in 1858. Every one will admit that the effect of that tariff was to increase the prosperity of our country by the building up of manufactures. It did more. By its adoption of the *ad valorem* as opposed to the specific system of duties a direct trade was built up, the effect of which has been to produce this magnificent result —that Canada to-day stands fourth amongst the maritime nations of the world. (Applause). You will remember that in 1872, the American Government took the duty off tea. Sir Francis Hincks, then Financial Minister in Canada, recognizing the fact that it would be well for Canada to adopt a similar policy, took the duty off tea imported into Canada. But after he had passed the Bill taking off the duty, he discovered that the American people (following the course they generally adopt) considering their own interests as opposed to the interests of Great Britain and this country, had a clause in their law by which a duty of 10 per cent. was charged on all tea imported from countries west of the Cape of Good Hope. There was nothing said in this clause about Canada or Great Britain ; but they were (as they were really meant to be) alone included ; and, of course 10 per cent., special duty, was charged on all tea exported by way of Canada to the United States. Sir Francis Hincks, with that acuteness which all parties admit he possesses, with that instinct in relation to the interests of the people which is peculiarly his own ; said that if we permitted Free Trade with the United States, and allowed them to charge 10 per cent. duty, the effect would be the transfer of the entire tea trade to the United States. Sir Francis, therefore, passed an Act in the same session, providing that the Governor in Council might, by Order in Council, impose a duty on all tea coming from the United States, equal to the duty charged by the United States on tea imported into that country from Canada, and that Act had preserved to Canada its own tea trade, and we enjoyed all its advantages.

" A direct trade was fast springing up, and was becoming one of the great factors of the country's prosperity when, in 1874, Mr. Cartwright proposed again to alter the duties. He did not put on the 10 per cent., and what was the result ? It was that the direct tea trade of Canada was destroyed by a stroke of the pen embodied in an Act of the Legislature. Many men in the City of Montreal, prominent tea men, had actually been compelled to leave that city and go to the United States, from whence they are issuing circulars to the trade all over the Dominion of Canada, hoping from that point to do the business which they formerly did from the Canadian city. And the same from all our cities as the result of that simple matter of 10 per cent. I am aware that it is said that there never was 10 per cent. before Sir Francis Hincks put it on ; and that, therefore, Mr. Cartwright did simply what had always been done by previous Governments. Let me show that that argument is not strictly a fair one. When we had tea duties before, they were part *ad valorem* and part specific. To the extent that they were *ad valorem*, they were a direct premium upon a direct trade—that this, a duty charged upon the article at the point of export (in China, for instance) coming here. To the extent the duty was *ad valorem*, it was a direct incentive to direct trade. Men going to the city of New York to purchase a quantity of tea would be compelled to pay duty on the charges of getting it to New York, as well as on the actual cost of the tea ; but if he got it direct from China he had only to pay *ad valorem* rate upon the prices in China. So that, practically, we had what was equivalent to the 10 per cent. differential duty in this understanding. But by the system of to-day that has been taken away.

"Then, gentlemen, you remember the effect in connection with the sugar duties. Owing to the American ' drawback ' which is simply a bounty concealed as a ' drawback '—our refineries in Canada have actually been compelled to close up. I am not going to discuss that question in all its bearings. As Dundreary says : ' It is one of those questions which no fellow can understand.' But the prominent fact we know is that 400 heads of families have been thrown out of employment ; the refineries have been shut up, and a direct incentive to West India trade, as I shall show further on, has been destroyed, simply for want of legislation, for want of 'a stroke of the pen embodied in legislation,' which would meet the policy of the United States in giving their heavy ' drawback ' to

American refiners, by which they are able to glut this market. Indeed, Mr. Cartwright practically admits that the action of the Government may materially affect the condition of the people, for here let me give another extract from that speech: ' Any man who carefully examines the working of their system,' that is the American system, 'will find that their high tariff had tended most materially to enrich a very few and seriously impoverish the great masses of the people. I believe the creation of collossal fortunes, such as has taken place there (in the United States), and perhaps in other countries, does threaten serious mischief. I have no objection to the accumulation of reasonable independence, nor do I indulge any hope of enacting sumptuary laws to limit the amount which any man should accumulate in a life-time ; but I do say that anything which overrides the ordinary natural laws, and operates in the direction of large accumulations in a few hands, is dangerous and ought to be discouraged.' Now, gentlemen, without for a moment arguing that point at this time, I think you will agree with me that it cannot be said in one and the same speech, or at any rate it ought not, that it is not in the power of Legislature by a stroke of the pen, or by any mere Act of Parliament, to affect the prosperity of the people, while at the same time you may so far effect them as to allow the building up of colossal fortunes in the hands of the few, and seriously to impoverish the many. (Loud applause).

"There is, however, a great deal of difficulty in keeping our free trade friends to any direct line of argument. I have shown you that Mr. Cartwright's views—and his views are those of a great many others—are that the effect of protection is to build up colossal fortunes in the hands of the few, to the prejudice of the great mass of the people. Now, what does David Wells say as to this—and this statement of Mr. Wells' is quoted by Mr. Cartwright, and I take the quotation from the speech of that gentleman : ' Every prophecy so confidently made in the past as to the results of protection in inducing national prosperity has been falsified, and one has only to pick out the separate industries which have been especially protected to find out the ones which are more especially unprofitable and dependent.

"It is sufficient to say that the existing depression and stagnation is without parallel, eight of the principal mills of the country having been sold, on compulsion, within a comparatively recent period, for much less than fifty per cent. of their cost of construction ; the Glendham mills in particular —one of the largest and best equipped woollen establishments in the United States, advantageously located on the Hudson, about fifty miles above New York, and representing over one million of dollars paid in—having changed hands since April 1st, last, for a consideration of less than two hundred thousand dollars. Here, then, we have Mr. Wells' assurance that 'one has only to pick out separate industries especially protected to find out those unprofitable.'

"Now, gentlemen, that statement may be right, or it may be wrong. I am not going to say whether it is right or wrong ; but what I am going to say is this : that if the effect of protection has been to destroy the industries which were protected, and that they have been unprofitable and dependent just in proportion as they have been protected, then it cannot be true that the effect of protection is to build up colossal fortunes in the hands of a few to the prejudice of the many. (Applause). If, however—and I think that is an important statement to consider—if it be true that the effect of protection is to build up colossal fortunes in the hands of the few, and to seriously impoverish the great masses of the people —then, gentlemen, I say that is a good argument against protection, and no really true-hearted, honest, patriotic man ought, for one moment, to advocate it. The principle should be, undoubtedly, 'the greatest good for the greatest number.' If the effect of protection is simply to benefit the few to the injury of the many, then, I say, let the few perish, but give us prosperity for the many. (Hear, hear). That, undoubtedly, is what every honest, patriotic man would say. But what are the facts ?

"Let us look at them, and in the light of them judge whether the effect of protection is 'to build colossal fortunes in the hands of the few, and seriously to impoverish the masses of the people.' Now, we have two countries which may fairly be taken as illustrations of the two systems. We have England on the one side—which, however, is not a fair illustration of the free trade system as applied to the world over, for the reason that the peculiar position of England, her immense wealth, her tremendous accumulations of coal and iron lying together ; her insular position, her command of an enormous mercantile marine, many of which advantages were built up by a system of protection and restriction as great as that which ever prevailed in any other country—I say these advantages give her a position which renders it impossible to cite her for illustration for a country like Canada, or the United States twenty-five or fifty years ago. We are urged to adopt England's policy, I presume, because the policy there does not, it would seem, build up colossal fortunes in the hands of the few, and does not seriously impoverish the great masses of the people. The United States is cited as an example which should deter us, because its system does build up colossal fortunes in the hands of the few, and seriously impoverishes the many. I have no desire to say one word against the dear old mother land, but we are dealing with practical questions, and we must deal with them as facts present themselves to us. I say, what is the position ? There is one fact in relation to the United States and Canada of which I think we may be proud, both Americans and Canadians—that is, in no country on the face of the earth is the distribution of the wealth, and the comforts which produce wealth, so general and universal as on this North American continent, both sides of the lines. (Hear, hear).

" Look at one fact I will give you as an illustration of the distribution of the wealth among the masses of the people in the United States. According to the report of the Imperial Commissioners on Emigration—and that is an authority which ought to be accepted without cavil—in one year, in 1870, there were sent from America in amounts to pay the passages of immigrants to come to the United States—and these were sent by people who had themselves come out, and were com-

Wilfrid Laurier

paratively poor—the enormous sum of £727,408 sterling, or in round figures $3,627,040; while in the twenty-three years from 1848 to 1870 inclusive, the amount they sent over was £16,334,000 sterling, or an average, annually, of $3,550,870. These are the evidences of the condition of the great masses of the people in the United States. What is the condition of the poor in England? On this point I will not cite hostile testimony, but I will quote English opinions. Mr. John Bright should be taken as a correct exponent on this question, if any man may be. He says : ' There are one million people who are paupers on the parish in England, and another million are perpetually lingering on the very verge of pauperism.' What does Sir Morton Peto say : ' It is an awful consideration that in England, abounding as it does with wealth and prosperity, there are nearly a million of human beings receiving indoor and outdoor relief as paupers in the different unions, besides the still greater number dependent upon the hand of charity. As the population of England and Wales, by the late census, were 20,205,504, it follows that nearly one-twentieth part of our people are subsisting upon charity.'

" Then I will quote Mr. Joseph Kay, a Cambridge man, in a work on the condition of British workmen: ' The poor of England are more depressed, more pauperized, more numerous in comparison to the other classes, more irreligious, and very much worse educated than the poor of any other European nation, solely excepting Russia, Turkey, South Italy, Portugal and Spain.' Lord Napier says, and his statement, it will be seen, has direct reference to the point urged by Mr. Cartwright : ' The proportion of those who possess, to those who possess nothing, is probably smaller in some parts of England at this moment, than it ever was in any settled community, except in some of the republics of antiquity, where the business of mechanical industry was delegated to slaves.' Judge Byles, another English authority, writes as follows:— ' In the fierce struggle of universal competition, those whom the climate enables, or misery forces, or slavery compels, to live worse and produce cheapest, will necessarily beat out

of the market and starve those whose wages are better.   It is
a struggle between the working classes of all nations, which
shall descend first and nearest to the condition of brutes.'
That is a very hard sentence, but unfortunately I am afraid
that, under free trade conditions, it is only too accurate a
statement of conditions of labour and successful competition.
The City Chamberlain of Glasgow reports that : 'By the
census of 1861 more than 28,000 houses in Glasgow were
found to consist of but a single apartment each, and above
32,000 of but two, so that of the whole 82,000 families comprising the city, upwards of 60,000 were housed in dwellings
of one or two apartments each.

   " Now, gentlemen, having given you these English authorities as to the condition of the masses in England, let me give
you an extract from an English authority, concerning the condition of the masses in the United States, under a system,
which, according to Mr. Cartwright, ought to seriously
impoverish the great masses of the people while creating
colossal fortunes in the hands of a few.   Let me give you the
opinion of Mr. Archibald, British Consul at New York—I find
it in a blue book which has been compiled from the reports of
different consuls on the conditions of labour in all parts of the
world, and submitted to the Imperial Parliament in 1872—and
what does he say : ' The value of intelligent labour has never
been so much appreciated in the United States as during
the last twelve years.   A completion of railway facilities
linking the new States of the North-West to the eastern sea-
board ; a rapid development of the agricultural resources of
these States by the vast crowds of immigrants brought over
by the transatlantic steamships, which, in return, convey into
their holds the cereal and other agricultural products of the
labour they have borne to these shores ; a protective tariff
stimulating for the last ten years the industries of the older
States ; the social condition and political institutions of the
country, promising advantages to the immigrant and his
children, not so fully enjoyed in their native lands ; have all
combined in presenting inducements to the working classes of
Europe, of which they have not been slow to avail themselves,

as is shown by the statistics of immigration. . . There is probably no country in the world, which, outside of the immigration ports, offers equal advantages to the operators or farm labourers.' That is the testimony of Mr. Archibald in relation to the people in that country, under whose system, according to those who argue in favour of Free Trade, colossal fortunes should have been built up by a few, and the great masses impoverished. (Applause).

" Now, there is another argument used by those who call themselves free traders—I again quote from the speech of Mr. Cartwright in the same sense as before—and this is, that —' The effect of a high tariff is not to add to any extent to the population of the country, but to promote an artificial transference from the rural districts to the towns and cities at the expense of the agricultural interests. If you discriminate against the agricultural interests, if you enact that they shall receive less from the results of their labour than they would without your interference, then you undoubtedly promote an artificial transference from the country to the town. . .
There is not the slightest doubt that this has been one—although I will not say a very great—cause of the commercial depression in this country. I say the *onus* is now thrown upon those who advocate a high protective tariff. Let them consider what they ask this country to do. They ask us to tax nineteen-twentieths of the population for the sake of the one-twentieth.'

" I agree that there is no justice in assisting to build up one class at the expense of another. If that fact could be established—and it was almost a shibboleth of free traders—I would give up my advocacy of protection. The question is, does protection discriminate? In regard to this point I will give a quaint illustration advanced by Mr. Horace Greeley in 1873, as to the mutual interests of the people in this system. He says: ' I am a printer of news-papers, and I have no other product to sell; and whatever I buy must be bought from the proceeds of the sale of news-papers. Now, I am a consumer of iron, and in my business, probably, have 100 tons of iron in the basement only of the building in which I work.   I want to buy it cheaper ; but, in order to do so, I must consider, not merely what the price is in dollars, but how I shall get the dollars.   Now, I say, give me iron makers who will buy my newspapers off me, and I can afford to give them more for the iron I need than I can give to the iron-workers who cannot, in the nature of things, and will not, purchase my paper.   This is a very simple proposition, but it covers the whole ground.'   Mr. Greely, by using American iron, secured employment for a large number of people, who bought his paper.   They made him more prosperous, though he paid more for his iron, and thus the mutual interest is admirably established.

"Then we have another statement by another man, whose name had doubtless been heard of—General Jackson.   He was arguing in favour of Protection in the interest of the agriculturist, he being a representative of an agricultural county, and what does he say : ' I will ask what is the real situation of the agriculturist ?   Where has the American farmer a market for his surplus products ?   Except for cotton he has neither a foreign nor a home market.   Does not this clearly prove, when there is no market at home or abroad, that there is too much labour employed in agriculture, and that the channels of labour should be multiplied?   Common sense points out at once the remedy.   Draw from agriculture the superabundant labour, employ it in mechanism and manufactures, thereby creating a home market for your bread-stuffs, and distributing labour to a most profitable account, and benefits to the country will result.   Take from agriculture in the United States six hundred thousand men, women and children, and you at once give a home market for more bread-stuffs than all Europe now furnishes.   In short, sir, we have been too long subject to the policy of British merchants.   It is time we should become a little more Americanized, and instead of feeding the paupers and labourers of Europe, feed our own, or else, in a short time, by continuing our present policy, we shall be paupers ourselves.   It is, therefore, my opinion that a careful tariff is much wanted to pay our national debt and afford us the means of that defence within

ourselves on which the safety and liberty of our country
depend, and last, though not least, give a proper distribution
to our labour, which must prove beneficial to the happiness,
independence and wealth of the community.'

"This was written in 1823, if I remember rightly. Now,
I think it must be admitted that the argument was fairly
put, and accorded with experience. Look at our own experience. What was the value of great centres of trade and
industry? Take London and the farms around it. What
renders the farms here more valuable and the farmers
more wealthy than they would be if they were in Mus-
koka? You say at once, because they have a home
market. There is a large number of people here that require
their products ; and the fact is seen that the advantage of the
farmer is in the building of these centres of population.
Protection does not discriminate against the farmers.
It is a most remarkable doctrine that the farmers are
injured by the people becoming consumers rather than
producers of agricultural products." Mr. White then
proceeded to point out "that the measure of taxation of
the people is the requirement of the Government. If
they require $23,000,000 they must raise it, no matter how ;
if no more, they do not require to raise it ; and if in raising it
they so distribute it as to enhance large industries, he maintained it was for the benefit of the country, and did not add
to the taxes of the people. But if the effect of protection
is to enhance the price of certain articles, then there is a
taxation of one interest for the benefit of another. But I
contend that protection does not necessarily and permanently increase the cost of the articles protected, and in support
of that proposition I will give two or three instances from the
States.

"The first extract would be from a publication recently
made on the iron trade of America : 'Before axes were made
in this country, except by country blacksmiths, English axes,
cost our farmers and others from $2 to $4 each. By the tariff
of 1828, a protective duty of thirty-five per cent. was levied
upon imported axes. Under this protection the Collins Com-

pany of Hartford, introduced labor-saving machinery, much of which was invented, patented, and constructed by themselves. In 1836 foreign and home made axes were selling side by side in the American market at $15 and $16 per dozen, at which time foreign producers withdrew their competition, abandoning the entire market to American manufacturers. Then home rivalry and improved methods continued the decline in prices. Axes were selling in 1838 at $13 to $15.25 per dozen; in 1840 at $13 to $14; in 1843 at $11 to $12; in 1845 at $10.50 to $11; in 1849 at $8 to $10. In 1876 the price of the best American axes in the market is $9.50 per dozen, currency, and the country exports large quantities to foreign markets.' Now, that is the effect of protection upon one article—that of axes.

" Then, in the same publication, we have this extract : ' A list of the wholesale prices at New York of fifty-seven leading articles of hardware and cutlery, prepared for us by Mr. David Williams, publisher of *The Iron Age*, shows that more than half of them are cheaper in currency in 1876 than gold in 1860, with two exceptions; the remainder are as cheap now as in 1860.'

" But, strangely enough, I have Mr. Cartwright's own admission that the effect will not be to increase the price. He says : ' As to the curious allegations made by the protectionists that if our manufacturing friends are sufficiently protected it will not increase the cost to the consumer, as sufficient competition will arise to cut down prices so low that we shall be just as well off as under the present tariff, I have simply this to say, that I think in time that result would be produced, but I also think it would take time, and during that period a few gentlemen would make large fortunes, while the rest of the community would have to pay an enormous price for that benefit. But I may add, sir, if that is to be the result, if the desire of the protectionists is by internal competition to cut down the standard of prices, I would strongly recommend the gentlemen to begin now, and by these means defy competition.' I think the latter statement unworthy of any public man. Mr. Cartwright knows—and every intelligent man must know—that the condition for building up industries is to accumulate capital around them. And how can capital be best accumulated ? By the protection of young industries, that they may be able to grow up in our midst. And to tell manufacturers that they are to invest their capital, and start their enterprises, and then to be subjected to the unfair 'slaughtering' of a neighbouring nation, is simply to insult the intelligence of every manufacturer in the land. (Applause).

" And now I come to a question which has recently, and with considerable cause, too, given rise to a great deal of discussion in this country. I refer to the fact of Canada being made a slaughter market for the United States. Mr. Cartwright admits this when he says : ' I don't propose at this moment to enter fully into the discussion raised as to Canada being a sacrifice or slaughter market. But I must admit, candidly and honestly, that I have no doubt that the distress of the manufacturers has been aggravated—though I will not say to what extent—by this cause.' That is a fair admission of Mr. Cartwright, and every one knows it is only too true—that Canada has been made a slaughter market for the United States. And the United States is not an exceptional case to this rule. It is the object of all large manufacturing communities to kill off small manufacturing communities, first by opposing a high tariff, and then by flooding the markets of its less able competitor. Here is a statement made by Lord Brougham in the House of Lords in 1816: ' It is well worth while to incur a loss upon the first exportation, in order by the glut to stifle in the cradle those rising manufactures in the United States which the war has forced into existence contrary to the natural course of things.' Lord Brougham's opinion of the ' natural state of things' was that the people of this country should be hewers of wood and drawers of water to the manufacturers of the mother land. With all due respect to the memory of Lord Brougham, I think the people of this country will differ from him. (Applause).

" Not only that, but in 1854 an English Royal Parliamentary Commission reported : ' The labouring classes, generally in the manufacturing districts of this country, and especially in the iron and coal districts, are very little aware of the extent to which they are often indebted for their being employed at all, to the immense losses which their employers voluntarily incur in bad times in order to destroy foreign competition, and to gain and keep possession of foreign markets. The large capital of this country is the great instrument of warfare against the competing capital of foreign countries, and the most essential instruments now remaining by which our manufacturing supremacy can be maintained.' The great object which they had in view was even to the extent of sacrifice, to kill off whatever manufactures appeared to be springing up in other countries, in order that they might secure the market for themselves.

" While that process is going on, it is quite true you may have cheap goods, while industries are being destroyed, while capital is being driven from the country, while men who were employed among you are compelled to 'take up stakes' and, with their families, seek in a more prosperous place the employment denied them here—while all these things are going on you may have goods cheaper ; but the moment rival manufactories are put out of sight, the instant the object is attained, there is no longer any sacrifice of the goods, and you have to pay the price the manufacturer chooses to exact. (Hear, hear).

" Now, I am aware that it is said in answer to what I have just been saying, that it is an inevitable rule of political economy that consumers always pay the duty. On tea in this country, that is true, because we do not produce tea ; on rice, that is true, because we do not produce rice ; on whatever we cannot produce that is quite true—that the consumer must pay the duty on the cost of the article. But that is not true in relation to articles which we do produce ; and I can give you two illustrations. When Mr. Galt brought in his tariff of 1858 the Sheffield manufacturers petitioned the Imperial Government to disallow the Act. To them it was horrible that colonists like us should be guilty of establishing manufactories and competing with their mightinesses in Sheffield, and they implored the Government of that day to say, as Lord Brougham put it, that 'the natural condition of things should be restored.' While they furnished the articles, it should be matter of no moment to them what the duties were if the consumer paid the duty. But it was because they knew that we did not pay the duty, and because we were competing with them, and compelling them to reduce the prices that they petitioned the Imperial Government.

"But I will notice for a moment a question put by my friend, Mr. Mills, a short time ago, when he addressed the Chamber of Commerce in this city, and I notice it because a question put by him assumes an importance which it would not otherwise have. The question is, 'if protection was good, why did not England adopt it?' Well, that does seem a 'poser' for protectionists. But, gentlemen, I will just show you two English authorities, giving one of the reasons why England adopted free trade in the first instance, and inferentially why it continues free trade. Mr. Robertson, M.P., during the discussion on Free Trade said : ' It was idle for us to endeavour to persuade other nations to join with us in adopting the principles of what was called Free Trade. Other nations knew, as well as the noble lord opposite and those who acted with him, what we meant by Free Trade was nothing more or less than, by means of the great advantages we enjoyed, to get monopoly of all their markets for our manufacturers, and to prevent them, one and all, from ever becoming manufacturing nations.' In this extract and in others that I have quoted, you have the answer to Mr. Mills' question. Possessing the numerous advantages which England possesses, she can afford to become the apostle of Free Trade, in order that the prevalence of her opinions may secure the uninterrupted control of foreign markets for her manufacturers. (Applause). I will refer once more to the speech by Mr. Mills, delivered here. I accept his challenge, and I assert that the following grounds are true in respect to protection : It increases capital ; it increases labour ; it stimulates trade ; it improves appliances.

"And now, gentlemen, I have a word to say in reference to whether this policy is appropriate to Canada. We are a

16

colony of the British Empire, and God grant that we may long remain so. (Hear, hear, and applause). We have had discussions as to whether it is advisable to have independence for this country ; and we have had discussions whether it would be better to have Canada annexed to the United States ; and there have been proposals to establish an American Zollverein. The independence cry is dead, and we will bury it out of sight. So far as an American Zollverein is concerned, I had the pleasure of being appointed one of the delegates of the Dominion Board of Trade to the meeting of the National Board of Trade at St. Louis. We went there with the instructions to try and have a reciprocity in trade established. They were anxious to have Free Trade with us, but they wanted a deal more than reciprocity. They proposed to abolish the entire Custom Houses along the line, and that Canada and the United States should impose equal duties on all articles coming from other countries. That was simply to cut connection with Great Britain—'hear, hear) —because to combine with another power to discriminate against the mother land was simply to declare separation from her. And the honest course would be to separate at once. (Applause).

" We, of course, did not accede to the proposal. But the National Board passed a resolution—I am afraid as a mere matter of courtesy to the Canadian delegates—which they have repeated at every meeting since then, without any influence on the Government, that it was desirable to have reciprocity with this country. Our greatest competitor is the United States. They slaughter in this country because of its proximity. Everyone must see that when a nation has manufacturing power for 40,000,000 people, it can as easily, and with scarcely any additional cost, manufacture for 44,000,000. They are thus enabled, during certain seasons, to sell their goods in this country at a mere nothing rather than force them into their own market, during a dull season, and thus bring down the price there. By slaughtering their goods in this country, they are enabled not only to keep up their own prices but to kill off our manufactures. (Applause).

"And what we have to complain of is, that this advantage is given to the United States, whose trade regulations are hostile to us, and whose whole fiscal policy has been against us. (Hear, hear, and applause). And the only policy you are met with by the United States, when you wish a change, is inimical to your interests ; not a policy to your advantage, but one which they consider will have the ultimate effect of driving us into annexation. We propose a policy to put a stop to this feeling, which every Canadian must dislike. It is said we cannot adopt a differential duty. Mr. Irving, during the debate in the House of Commons last year, made some very appropriate remarks on this subject. He cited a clause of the Convention of Commerce, in 1815, which is commonly said to show that we cannot adopt these differential duties. Here is the clause : ' No higher or other duties shall be imposed on the importations into the territories of his Britannic Majesty in Europe, of any articles the growth, produce, or manufacture of the United States, and no higher or other duties shall be imposed on the importation into the United States of any articles, the growth, produce, or manufacture of His Britannic Majesty's territories in Europe, than are or shall be payable on like articles being the growth, produce, or manufacture of any other foreign country.' It is quite clear from that clause that England cannot adopt a system of differential duties, as against the United States. But the next clause goes on to say : ' The intercourse between the United States and His Britannic Majesty's possessions in the West Indies, or on the continent of North America, shall not be affected by any of the provisions of this article, but each party shall remain in the complete possession of his rights.' Not only, therefore, is there nothing in that treaty which prevents us from adopting differential duties, but there is an express provisions in it that we shall not be so prevented. And we have had differential duties as late as 1847. Not only that, but the tea duty of Sir Francis Hincks was a differential tariff. It was placed on your statute book, and there was not any attempt by the United States or England to prevent it. That is a system of differential duties which may be fairly placed on articles at the present time.

"Many people say we should have reciprocity. No doubt for a great many people it would be well to have reciprocity. No doubt the farmer, living on the frontier would feel it to be an advantage. No doubt he must feel a hardship in the farmer of the United States being allowed to bring his produce to sell in the Canadian market without being charged a duty, and he (the Canadian) unable to take his produce over to the United States without paying a heavy duty. Reciprocity in the natural products of the country would be a good thing. But I do not believe that reciprocity, in regard to manufactured goods, is possible. If we took off the duty on goods imported from the United States, we could not, as loyal subjects, impose duties on goods brought from the mother country. If we have free interchange with the United States, we must have the same with Britain. (Applause. All protection against the mother country would thus be gone. We would find ourselves in this position : We would have the country free to the United States and to Britain, and would be unable to maintain, much less to increase, our present manufactures, while the United States would be protected from all the countries of the world.

"There is another argument I wish to advance in favour of protection. It promotes immigration. Emigrants from the mother land, on arriving in this country, do not all want to be sent into the woods to earn a livelihood ; do not all desire to leave the occupations taught them at home, in order to become agriculturists here. They want a diversity of employment, and unless we have legislation of the kind I have mentioned, legislation which will permit the skilled workman to continue his calling in this country, they will most assuredly wend their way to the United States, and seek there that employment which, through a narrowsighted policy, is denied them here. We have vast territories to fill up in the North-West and British Columbia, that glorious land which Lord Dufferin so lately visited, and spoke so approvingly of. It is our duty to fill up these vast territories, to develop their wonderful resources, and we can best assist in doing so by the adoption of a policy which will tend to improve the condition of the manufacturer, and in the nature of things materially benefit all classes of the community. We don't want to be hewers of wood and drawers of water for our neighbours for all time to come. That is not our object. Our aim should be to legislate to build up Canadian interests, that capital may find profitable investment, labour diversified employment, and the people prosperous and contented homes.'

Mr. White resumed his seat amid loud and long continued applause.

Mr. Carling said "he had great pleasure indeed in moving the thanks of the citizens of London to Mr. White for his very able and instructive lecture. Mr. White had come to this city at great inconvenience to himself, at the request of the Board of Trade, and he was quite sure that the citizens of London would highly appreciate his able lecture. It was not a ques- of politics he had come amongst us to discuss. It was a vital question, and deeply affected the commercial interests of the Dominion. It was to determine whether a policy should be adopted calculated to induce parties to live amongst us, or to deter them from assisting us in building up the new Dominion. If Free Trade was better calculated to do that, then let us have it. If protection was deemed the best policy for Canada, then let us pin our faith to it. It was our duty to weigh well the views advanced by representative men of both people, and then decide which is the best for the country. Let us adopt a national policy. In concluding he spoke of his friend, Mr. White, whom he had known personally and politically for over twenty years, as a gentleman who was certain to hold a high position in this country, and who had worked his way up from a small beginning at Peterboro' to be one of the leading thinkers in the commercial metropolis of Canada. (Applause. Mr. White was highly respected as a man of talent and ability, and he (the speaker) was acquainted with no man whose judgment he would sooner rely upon for a sound opinion than Mr. Thomas White." (Loud applause).

A day or two later Mr. White tested the question at a

meeting of the Dominion Board of Trade by moving the following resolution :

" That in the opinion of this Board the principle of Protection to the manufactures of the country is of vital importance to its prosperity, and that, in any revision of the tariff, this principle should be embodied, especially in the case of such articles as the unfair and unequal competition has pressed most heavily upon." He called attention to the fact that the figures quoted by Col. Walker were taken from the Trade and Navigation returns for the period ending July 1, 1875, and did not give any idea of the condition of affairs during the last eighteen months, the very period in which the slaughtering complained of had been carried on most extensively. He also called attention to the fact that the import trade of the United States had largely increased under a Protective tariff, having more than doubled since 1861. He pointed out that in Free Trade England, when Commissioners met in 1865 to agree upon a system of sugar duties with other countries, a rule was adopted that in case any one of the nations represented at the Convention should offer bounties, any or all the others should be permitted to increase the tax to an equivalent extent. He denied that Canadian consumers got the benefit of the bounty to refiners in the United States, and the action of the British Commissioners in providing against such a contingency proved this. The fact was our fiscal policy was driving the consumer out of the country, and diminishing the trade of the Dominion. While we were proposing to subsidize steamers to carry the mails to the West Indies, we were by our sugar duties destroying the trade with that country. He agreed with Mr. Wood, of Quebec, that the prosperity of the United States was largely due to the Free Trade between the several States. But suppose any one of those States found itself surrounded by high tariffs, while it had no protection itself? What would be the result ? It would drive manufactures from the unprotected State. That was precisely the position in which Canada stood. It was against such a condition of affairs that his amendment was directed, and he asked the Board to adopt it.

The amendment was seconded by Mr. Sanford.

Mr. Lyman said of late years he had observed a great increase in the numbers of those favourable to Protection. It had always amazed him to see Montreal importers vote against Protection, for the most important thing for an importer is to have consumers. Without manufactories there could be no employment for emigrants and artizans, and they had to drift off to the United States to find it. There could be no doubt of the intention of the United States manufacturers slaughtering their goods in this country in order to secure it as a market. They had been told that the United States had suffered from Protection. He would like very much to see Canada suffer in the same way, as they had all seen the extraordinary growth of the Republic during the last century. As for over-production in this country crowding our own markets, there was no such thing. The over-production arose not from the produce of our manufacturers, but from the heavy importation of foreign goods on a low tariff. Importation governed the price of the whole quantity in the market, as home manufacturers had to conform to the prices quoted in the trade lists of the agents of foreign houses. When capitalists preferred to invest their money in the United States instead of Canada, it was a sure indication that they favoured a protective tariff.

Mr. Thomson called attention to the boot and shoe trade of Canada, which was prospering under a $17\frac{1}{2}$ per cent. tariff, and he would like to know why it was that other industries did not prosper also. He was opposed to any great increase in the tariff, and especially to a 25 per cent. tariff, which, he thought, would be a limit that would increase the industries to their own ruin.

The amendment was then carried—yeas 24 ; nays 14.

Ayes—Messrs. Clemow, Dobson, Farrell, Fraser, Gillespie, Howland, Hannan, Kirkpatrick, Lyman, Long, McLennan, McKechnie, Oille, Ogilvie, Paterson, Perley, Rees, Rowland, Rosamond, Robinson, Sanford, Thomson, White, Woods. Total ayes—24.

Nays—Messrs. Brown, Bronson, Cameron, Corcoran, Fry,

Joseph, Kerry, McMaster, Pennock, Skead, Stairs, Shahyn Walker, Wood. Total nays—14.

The Protectionists received the announcement of the victory with loud applause.

Other speeches were made, both for protection and Free Trade, from which we select the following :

Mr. McKechnie was pleased to find a growing sentiment in favour of Protection. He advocated the imposition of increased duties on refined sugars. He denied that Protection would increase the cost of living, and contended that the opposite would be the result. Experience had proved that the establishment of home industries had invariably benefited the consumer. He argued against the policy which opened our markets to the manufacturers of the United States, while theirs were closed to us. He pointed to the example of our neighbours to show the benefits of Protection. A protective tariff, instead of cutting off revenue, had yielded enough to pay the interest on the national debt and some of the principal, while the want of it had driven our workingmen to the neighbouring country to look for employment. Every one wanted a Reciprocity Treaty, but we could never get it until we had something to give. Our farming population were becoming alive to the importance of protecting their industries. They saw that home competition would keep down prices, while it would improve their markets.

Mr. Clemow did not wish the Board to suppose that the Ottawa district favoured Free Trade. The lumber trade were looking for Protection. They felt the competition of Western timber merchants at Quebec and the effects of the hostile tariff of the United States. It was all very well to talk of Free Trade cheapening living, but what was the good of cheap articles if the people had nothing to buy them with ? Ottawa was suffering from the low tariff. The mechanics had gone to the United States. Lumbermen found workmen going to Michigan and Wisconsin for employment, while the great iron mines near the city were undeveloped for want of Protection. A policy was needed which would keep our people at home. (Cheers).

Mr Woods (Quebec) said if the tariff was the cause of the commercial depression that was an argument in favour of Free Trade, for we had more Protection now than for many years past. He maintained that the depression of trade in the United States was greater than in Canada. The shipping trade had been almost obliterated by Protection. There was nothing in the United States to encourage us to take the retrograde step of adopting Protection. The internal Free Trade of the United States gave them what prosperity they enjoyed. Their foreign trade was well nigh obliterated. His strong conviction was that the proper policy for Canada was the one now followed, a tariff for revenue purposes, so framed as to levy the largest duties on luxuries and the next on articles which we can manufacture ourselves. He argued against the imposition of Protective duties on sugar. If the United States Government were desirous of giving a bounty to the refiners for the benefit of consumers, our people had nothing to complain of. If the proposition of the refiners were adopted, it would be simply giving a bonus of $500,000 per annum to keep 6,000 working people in Canada.

"Mr Sandford (Hamilton) said all that Protectionists wanted was internal Free Trade, such as Mr. Woods admitted had built up the prosperity of the United States. That was just what was denied to us by the existing tariff.

Dr. Oille, (St. Catharines), in reply to Major Walker's remarks, wished to know if we were benefited by practical Free Trade in pig iron, steel rails, and bar iron. The fact was, that notwithstanding the high protective tariff on those articles in the United States, we paid as much for ours. The difference was that we had to buy ours abroad, while the United States consumer had his manufactured at the same price at home. When steel rails were first manufactured, they were imported into the United States at high prices. A heavy duty was put on them, and home industries at once sprang into existence. The result was that they manufactured their own rails, and the railway companies got them as cheaply as they could get abroad. By our policy we paid as much for such articles as our neighbours, while we were without the large manufacturing industries which were flourishing in the neighbouring country. We had the humiliating spectacle of Americans coming to Ottawa and taking ore from our mines, carrying it to the United States, smelting it, and sending back to us our own iron manufactured. We import to day 250,000 barrels of flour. Under a proper policy, we would import the grain, manufacture it and the barrels, and send it to the Lower Provinces, while we would bring back in return cargoes of their products. Under a proper policy our Maritime Provinces would be the Great Britain of America.

Mr. Howland contended that Canada never had but one satisfactory tariff, that of Galt's of twenty per cent. Under that tariff manufactures had thrived. Nothing but fanaticism prevented free traders from seeing that Canada was placed at a disadvantage in her relations with the United States. He contended that the duties of the neighbouring country were differential against the Dominion. He did not advocate the imposition of the same duties on our side, because a lower tariff would answer our purpose.

At this point the Premier and Messrs. Vail, Smith and Burpee entered, and were received with cheers. They were introduced to the United States delegates, and seated with them near the President.

Mr. Howland continued his argument in favour of Protection. He contended that our home industries were dying out from the extreme competition of our neighbours, and furnished several illustrations in proof of the assertion. The farmers were beginning to feel the same competition in their line. The Grangers had recently passed a resolution in favour of Protection to agricultural industries. Without a re-adjusted and increased tariff, Confederation would never be accomplished. The inter-Provincial trade which it would stimulate would draw us closer together, develop our immense natural resources, and restore the prosperity which this country should enjoy. This was a national policy which would make us feel we were all Canadians, and interested in the prosperity of every section of the country.

Mr. White lived to see his views carried into practical

effect, and, as a Minister of the Crown, had many opportunities of raising his voice in defence of Canadian interests.   In the prime of life, and at the zenith of his usefulness, he was suddenly stricken down, and passed away on April 21, 1888. He was a close friend of Sir John Macdonald who, in endeavouring to announce his death to the House, completely broke down, and laying his head on his desk, burst into deep sobs.   The whole House was deeply affected, and few could keep back their rising tears, for Mr. White had hosts of friends and no enemies.

CHAPTER XXXII

General election September 17, 1878—Defeat of the Mackenzie Government—Sir
John Macdonald forms a new Government—Departure of Lord Dufferin—
Lord Lorne and H. R. H. the Princess Louise—The National Policy resolutions March 14, 1879—Sir Leonard Tilley's speech—A short summary
of his political history—Death of the Honourable George Brown—A
memorial statue erected in Queen's Park—Tributes to his memory by
Honourable Oliver Mowat and Honourable George Allan.

IN the autumn of 1878 Parliament was dissolved and a
general election held on September 17th. The issue before
the people was whether or not they desired protection to home
industries, and they pronounced in favour of the policy in a
manner that even the most sanguine of its advocates had
never hoped for. The electors also, doubtless, felt that an
injustice had been done to Sir John Macdonald and his Ministry in 1873 in pronouncing them guilty on such utter want of
evidence, and were anxious to make atonement. The Opposition swept the country even more completely than Mr.
Mackenzie had done in 1874, and, finding himself left in such
a hopeless minority, that gentleman handed in the resignations
of his Cabinet to His Excellency the Governor-General. For
the first time since 1844, Sir John was defeated in his old
constituency, Kingston, but was elected for Marquette, Manitoba. He was entrusted with the task of forming a new
Government, which he succeeded in doing as follows :

RIGHT HON. SIR JOHN A. MACDONALD, Premier and Minister of the
Interior.

HON. S. L. TILLEY, Minister of Finance.

HON. CHARLES TUPPER, Minister of Public Works.

HON. J. H. POPE, Minister of Agriculture.

HON. JAMES MACDONALD, Minister of Justice.

HON. L. F. R. MASSON, Minister of Militia.

HON. J. C. POPE, Minister of Marine and Fisheries.

HON. L. F. G. BABY, Minister of Inland Revenue.

HON. MACKENZIE BOWELL, Minister of Customs.

HON. ALEXANDER CAMPBELL, Receiver-General.

HON. H. L. LANGEVIN, Postmaster-General

HON. J. C. AIKEN, Secretary of State.

HON. JOHN O'CONNOR, President of the Council.

HON. R. D. WILMOT, Speaker of the Senate.

HON. CHARLES H. TUPPER.
LL.B., P.C.
Minister of Marine and Fisheries.

HON. JOHN COSTIGAN.
J.P., P.C.
Minister of Inland Revenue.

HON. GEORGE E. FOSTER.
B.A., D.C.L., P.C.
Minister of Finance.

Shortly afterwards, Lord Dufferin having completed his term of six years, sailed for England. During his stay in Canada he had won the respect, admiration and affection of the people of Canada and his departure was deeply regretted. The warm feeling entertained was shown by the large number of addresses presented to him, one of which was joined in by nearly every municipal body in Canada. He was succeeded by the Marquis of Lorne, who, accompanied by H. R. H. the Princess Louise, arrived in Halifax on November 23rd and were received with all possible honour.

It would be a congenial task to present to our readers some of the very eloquent speeches made by Lord Dufferin during the period he presided over the destinies of the country, and to try and convey some idea of the popularity of both himself and Lady Dufferin amongst the Canadian people, but it would be impossible to do justice to the subject within a limited space, and the story has already been told so fully and clearly by Mr. Leggo and Mr. Stewart, that the better course is not to touch upon ground which has already been so ably occupied.

The Marquis of Lorne is descended from one of the most illustrious and ancient families in Scottish history, the annals of whose ancestors are traced back until they become dim in the twilight of tradition. But since Gillespie Campbell, in the eleventh century, acquired by marriage the lordship of Lochow, in Argyleshire, the records of the family may be plainly followed. From him descended Sir Colin Campbell, of Lochow, who became distinguished both in war and in peace, and who received the surname of "Mohr" or "Great." From him the chief of the house is to this day styled, in Gaelic, "MacCailean Mohr" or "The Great Colin." In 1280, he was knighted by Alexander III., and eleven years later he was slain in a contest with his powerful neighbour, the Lord of Lorne. This event occasioned bitter feud between the two families, which existed for many years, but was finally terminated, romantically, by the marriage of the first ' of Argyle to the heiress of Lorne. For hundreds of ye. after this time the history of the family is inseparably inwoven with the

history of Scotland.   The first and also the last Marquis of
Argyle was Gillespie Grumach, or Archibald the Grim, who
was beheaded during the reign of Charles II.   His son, taking
part against the reigning power, escaped to the Continent, but
subsequently returned to Scotland to invade that kingdom
simultaneously with the Duke of Monmouth's unlucky rising
in the south.   His small force was defeated while marching on
Glasgow, and he was captured and suffered the same fate as
his father.   The estates were confiscated, and the family
seemed doomed to extinction ; but the revolution of 1688
brought it once more into prominence, and its representative
was created the Duke of Argyle and Marquis of Lorne.   The
next successor to the titles played a very conspicuous part in
the history of his time, and has been immortalized in verse by
Pope, and in prose by Sir Walter Scott.   The head of the
family at the present time is the eighth Duke of Argyle, a
celebrated statesman who has filled several important offices
under different Administrations, and who has achieved considerable reputation as a man of science and of letters.   Upon the
formation of Mr. Gladstone's Cabinet in December, 1868, he
became Secretary of State for India, and conducted its affairs
with marked ability until the Liberal Government was deposed
in February, 1874.   The late General Grant said that the Duke
of Argyle inspired in him a higher respect than any other man
in Europe.   This, from the ex-President of the United States,
whose discriminating sense and judgment in observing men
was unsurpassed, and who had met nearly all the distinguished
men in the world, is a rare compliment, but doubtless as
deserving as true.   In 1844, the Duke married Lady Elizabeth
Georgina Sutherland Leveson-Gower, eldest daughter of the
second Duke of Sutherland, and late Mistress of the Royal
Robes.   By this union he has twelve children, the eldest
of whom, the Right Honourable Sir John George Edward
Henry Douglas Sutherland Campbell, K. T., G. C. M. G., Marquis of Lorne, was born at the Stafford House, St. James'
Park, London, on August 6, 1845.   He was educated at Eton,
and afterwards passed successively to the University of St.
Andrew's and Trinity College, Cambridge.   In 1866 he

became connected with the military, by appointment as Captain of the London Scottish Volunteers, and in 1868 was commissioned Lieut.-Colonel of the Argyle and Bute Volunteer Artillery Brigade. For literary and artistic pursuits the Marquis possesses much natural ability as well as a cultivated taste, the result of study, observation and experience. His first published work was "A Tour in the Tropics," the result of his observations during a trip through the West Indies and the eastern part of North America in 1866. Although the author was very young at this time, the appearance of this work displayed to the public the keen sense of observation and discriminating judgment which he inherits from his father. During this trip he made his first visit to Canada, and conceived a very favourable impression of this country. His next publication was "Guida and Lita, a Tale of the Rivieta," a poem which attracted much interest, not so much on account of its titled author, as because of the genuine worth and beauty of its composition. In 1877 appeared from his pen "The Book of Psalms, literally rendered in verse," which is doubtless the best of his literary productions. It called forth much praise, and is a work of great merit.

In 1868 he became a member of the House of Commons, representing the constituency of Argyleshire, and was re-elected by acclamation in two subsequent general elections, and continued in Parliament until his appointment to Canada. During part of the Duke of Argyle's term of office in Mr. Gladstone's Cabinet, the Marquis acted as his private secretary, displaying much aptitude for affairs of state.

On March 21, 1871, he was united in marriage to Her Royal Highness, the Princess Louise Caroline Alberta, Duchess of Saxony, the sixth child and fourth daughter of Her Majesty Queen Victoria, who was born on March 18, 1848. Since her marriage brought her prominently before the public, she has been regarded with much affectionate interest by the people ; and her personal qualities, independilently of her high rank, are such as to have earned for her the love and respect of all with whom she had been brought in contact.

As we are now dealing with a period within the memory of every one and it is necessary to hurry on to the concluding portions of the work, we will not attempt to follow the remainder of Sir John Macdonald's career in the detailed manner that was necessary in the earlier chapters. It, consequently, becomes impossible to dwell upon the acts or characteristics of any of the Governor's-General, under whom he had the honour of serving in his later years. Therefore, while proposing to return for a while, to deal with the National Policy and the Pacific Railway, we will, at this point anticipate a little and say that Lord Lorne remained in Canada as Governor-General, until October 23, 1883, when his successor, Lord Lansdowne, was sworn into office. He proved to be a worthy successor to Lord Dufferin, and both he and H.R.H. the Princess Louise won warm places in the hearts of the Canadian people. The sentiments of the nation were fitly voiced in the speeches of Sir John Macdonald and Mr. Blake in moving and seconding the adoption of an address to him, upon his retirement from office. Sir John Macdonald said : " When we heard that Lord Lorne was appointed to hold the great office of representative of Her Majesty in Canada, we rejoiced that the selection had fallen on the scion of so illustrious a race as that of Argyle ; and I, with every countryman of mine, rejoiced that the son of McCallum More should be here to represent the Queen. That pleasure was increased by the knowledge that he was to be accompanied by Her Royal Highness the daughter of our Sovereign. Though our expectations were high, I am glad to believe that the country and this House, as the representative of the country, believe our expectations to have been fulfilled. From the time he first assumed office until now, he has devoted himself with great industry, energy, and ability, and, I am glad to say, with great success, to forwarding all the interests of Canada, not in a mere *dilettante* perfunctory way, but in a searching manner, earnestly enquiring into the position of the country, its capabilities and resources and the best way of advancing all its interests, material, intellectual, moral, and artistic. He has not spared himself. He

has visited every Province of the Dominion, not as a mere
traveller, but as one anxious to make all enquiries fully to
inform himself of our wants, wishes, and aspirations. Now
that he is leaving us, we must express our regret at his departure. We regret extremely to lose, also, as a matter of
course, his illustrious consort. During the short time her
health has enabled her to be with us, she has endeared herself
to every one with whom she has come into contact by the
kindly and sympathetic manner with which she has viewed
both men and things in Canada. We must not forget that,
although we have been deprived of much of her presence,
and of the light such a presence casts around the metropolis,
the accident which caused her absence was occasioned by
her attending to her duties as the wife of the Governor-
General, in coming to be present at one of the official cere-
monies, the duty of presiding at which was cast upon Lord
Lorne and herself as his consort."

Mr. Blake, in seconding the resolution, as leader of the
Opposition, said : " Honourable gentlemen opposite, of course
have, from their connection with His Excellency as his
responsible advisers, the opportunity of speaking with a
greater knowledge as to the discharge of his political duties,
than those who have not that opportunity. But, viewing His
Excellency's conduct from the position we occupy, we can
cordially concur in the sentiment that he has been a good
constitutional Governor, and that, so far as his public conduct
has enabled us to judge, he has fully realized and acted upon
those great principles of responsible Government which are
so dear, equally in this and the mother country, and which
form, in the opinion of both, the vital element of their system
of Government. The Governor of Canada has, as this
Address indicates, many important duties to perform. Those
duties His Excellency has assiduously attended to ; and, in
the spirit the honourable gentleman has expressed, we have
every reason to believe that he has devoted his time, his
energies, his ability, his intellect, to the thorough understanding and comprehension of the situation of this country, to an
attention to its physical and moral position, and to enabling

himself, as far as his high position would permit, to give fit expression to what our wishes, wants, and aspirations are, here, during the discharge of his high duty, and hereafter in the councils of his country, to which he will, no doubt, shortly be called ; that expression which will be of great use to us—not an expression of indiscriminate praise, which we do not want, but the judicious expression of such a measure of praise and approbation as may convince the public whom he addresses, that they are the sentiments of his heart, based upon a thorough comprehension of all the circumstances of this country. The honourable gentleman has alluded to His Excellency's illustrious consort, and the representative of the Queen by office and by birth, her illustrious daughter. We are glad to send this message back. We are here in a democratic country, where the Throne is not supported by the arrangements of society, which are supposed, in other lands, to be essential to a monarchy ; but there exists here in the minds of the people, a firm, thorough, and fervent—because a reasonable—loyalty to that system under which, if they do not entirely regulate their affairs, at any rate they have the most perfect measure of self-control and of self-government.

The following is the joint address which was adopted by both Houses :

To His Excellency the Right Honourable Sir John Douglas Sutherland Campbell (commonly called the Marquis of Lorne), Knight of the Most Ancient and Most Noble Order of the Thistle ; Knight Grand Cross of the Most Distinguished Order of St. Michael and St. George, Governor-General of Canada, and Vice-Admiral of the same, etc., etc.

MAY IT PLEASE YOUR EXCELLENCY :

We, Her Majesty's dutiful subjects, the Senate and House of Commons of Canada in Parliament assembled, desire, on behalf of those whom we represent, as well as on our own, to give expression to the general feeling of regret with which the country has learned, that Your Excellency's official connection with Canada is soon about to cease.

We are happy, however, to believe that in the Councils of the Empire in the future, and wherever opportunity enables you to render her service, Canada will ever find in Your Excellency a steadfast friend, with knowledge of her wants and aspirations, and an earnest desire to forward her interests.

Your Excellency's zealous endeavours to inform yourself by personal observation of the character, capabilities and requirements of every section of the Dominion, have been highly appreciated by its people, and we feel that the country is under deep obligations to you for your untiring efforts to make its resources widely and favourably known.

The warm personal interest which Your Excellency has taken in everything calculated to stimulate and encourage intellectual energy among us, and to advance science and art, will long be gratefully remembered ; the success of Your Excellency's efforts has fortified us in the belief that a full development of our national life is perfectly consistent with the closest and most loyal connection with the Empire.

The presence of your illustrious consort in Canada seems to have drawn us closer to our beloved Sovereign, and in saying farewell to Your Excellency and to Her Royal Highness, whose kindly and gracious sympathies, manifested on so many occasions, have endeared her to all hearts, we humbly beg that you will personally convey to Her Majesty the declaration of our loyal attachment, and our determination to maintain firm, and abiding our connection with the great Empire over which she rules.   (Signed).

D. L. MACPHERSON,
Speaker of the Senate.

J. G. BLANCHET,
Speaker of the House of Commons.

On May 25th, the members of the House of Commons went in a body to the Senate Chamber where, together with the members of the Upper House, they were received by the Governor-General and the Princess Louise. The address adopted by both Houses was then presented to His Excellency by the Privy Councillors who were in attendance, and the Marquis of Lorne made the following reply :

" Honourable Gentlemen—No higher personal honour can be received by a public man than that which, by this Address, you have been pleased to accord to me. In asking you to accept my gratitude, I thank you, also, for your words regarding the Princess, whose affection for Canada fully equals mine. It will be my pride and duty to aid you in the future to the utmost of my power.

" Now that the pre-arranged term of our residence among you draws to its end, and the happiest five years I have ever known are nearly spent, it is my fortune to look back on a time during which all domestic discord has been avoided, our friendship with the great neighbouring republic has been sustained, and an uninterrupted prosperity has marked the advance of the Dominion.

" In no other land have the last seventeen years—the space of time which has elapsed since your Federation—witnessed such progress.   Other countries have had their territories enlarged, and their destines determined by trouble and war, but no blood has stained the bonds which have knit together your free and order-loving populations.   And yet, in this period, so brief in the life of a nation, you have attained to a union whose characteristics, from sea to sea, are the same.

" A judicature above suspicion ; self-governing communities entrusting to a strong central Government all national interests ; the toleration of all faiths, with favour to none ; a franchise recognizing the rights of labour by the exclusion only of the idlers ; the maintenance of a Government not privileged to exist for any fixed term, but ever susceptible to the change of public opinion, and ever open through a responsible Ministry to the scrutiny of the people ; these are the features of your rising power.

" Finally, you present the spectacle of a nation, already possessing the means to make its position respected by its resources in men available at sea or on land.   May these never be required except to gather the harvests, the bounty that God has so lavishly bestowed upon you.   The spirit, however, which made your fathers resist encroachments on your soil and liberties, is with you now, and it is as certain to-day as it was formerly, that you are ready to take on yourselves the necessary burden to ensure the permanence of your laws and institutions.

" You have the power to make treaties on your own responsibility with foreign nations, and your High Commissioner is associated for purposes of negotiation with the foreign office.

" You are not the subjects, but the free allies of the great country which gave you birth, and is ready with all its energy to be the champion of your interests.   Standing side by side,

Canada and Great Britain work together for the commercial advancement of each other. It is the recognition of this which makes such an occasion as the present significant, personalities, however dear to individuals, are of no possible moment. These may be happy or unhappy accidents, but the satisfaction experienced from the condition of the connection now subsisting between the old and new lands, can be affected by no personal accident.

" I therefore rejoice that again it has been your determination to show that Canada remains as firmly rooted as ever in love to that free union which ensures to you and to Great Britain equal advantages. Without it, the maintenance of your institutions and national autonomy would not be allowed to endure for a twelvemonth, while the loss of the alliance of the communities which were once the dependencies of England, would be a heavy blow to her commerce and renown.

" I thank you once more for your words, which shall be dear treasures to me forever, and may the end of the term of each public servant who fills with you the office which constitutes him at once your chief magistrate and the representative of a united empire, be a day for pronouncing in favour of a free national Government, defended by such Imperial alliance."

On March 14, 1879, the Honourable S. L. Tilley made his Budget Speech introducing the National Policy. Much of it was of course of a statistical nature and would be uninteresting to the general reader, we will, therefore, only give those parts which deal with the principle upon which the new tariff was formed.

" Mr. Chairman,—It is only recently that I have quite realized the great changes that have taken place throughout the Dominion of Canada since I last had the honour of a seat in Parliament. To-day I fully realize them, and the increased difficulties devolving upon me, as Finance Minister, compared with the position of affairs when I submitted my financial statement in 1873. Then my work was a very easy one indeed. Honourable Ministers on the opposite benches were pleased, on that occasion, to compliment me on that statement, but I felt that I had earned no compliment, that if that speech was acceptable to the House, it was because of the satisfactory statements I was able to make with reference to the condition of the Dominion and also of the finances of the Dominion. Then, sir, I was able to point to steady and increasing surplusses and revenue, and that, too, in the face of a steady reduction of taxation. Then I was able to point with some degree of confidence to the prospective expenditures of the Dominion, extending over ten years. To-day I cannot speak of it with the same confidence. Then the construction of the Pacific Railway was under regulations that confined and limited the liabilities of the Dominion to $30,000,000. To-day I am not in a position to say what expenditure or responsibilities we may incur with reference to that great undertaking. There has been a change in the policy. But it will become the duty of the Government and of Parliament to consider, while we have not the limit to our liabilities that we had, whether we cannot, by some means, construct that great work largely out of the 200,000,000 acres of land lying within the wheat area of that magnificent country.

"Then, sir, I could point with pride and with satisfaction to the increased capital of our banks and the large dividend they paid. To-day I regret to say that we must point to deprecated values and to small dividends. Then I could point to the general prosperity of the country. To-day we must all admit that it is greatly depressed. Then I could point with satisfaction to the various manufacturing industries that were in operation throughout the length and breadth of the Dominion, remunerative to the men who had invested their capital in them, and giving employment to tens of thousands. To-day many of the furnaces are cold, the machinery in many cases is idle, and those establishments that are in operation are only employed half time and are scarcely paying the interest on the money invested. Then, sir, we could point to the agricultural interest as most prosperous, with a satisfactory home market and satisfactory prices abroad. To-day they have a limited market with low prices, and anything but a satisfactory market abroad. Then, sir, we could point to a very valuable and extensive West India trade ; to-day it does not exist. Then, sir, we could point to a profitable and direct tea trade, that has been demoralized and destroyed. Then everything appeared to be prosperous ; to-day, though it looks gloomy, I hope there is a silver lining to the cloud, that we may yet see illuminating the whole of the Dominion, and changing our present position to one of happiness and prosperity. /

"Mr. Chairman, there has been, and very naturally so, a good deal of interest and anxiety manifested on the part of the friends of the National Policy, as it is called, in regard to its early introduction. I can quite understand that, because, believing as they do, and as a majority of this House do, that that policy is calculated to bring prosperity to the country, it was but natural that they should be anxious for its introduction, and that not a day should be lost. And it is satisfactory to know that, great and difficult as is the responsibility which rests upon me here, I may trust that the proposition I am about to submit will be sustained, not only by a majority of this House, but by an overwhelming majority in the country. It was natural, therefore, Mr. Chairman, that the friends of this policy should be anxious for its introduction, and it was pleasing and satisfactory to see that even the Opposition vied with the friends of the Government in that anxiety. It is most encouraging to me, because, of course, all Oppositions are patriotic, and certainly a patriotic Opposition, anxious for the introduction of this measure, could not have desired that a bad measure, and one not calculated to benefit the country should be forced hastily upon it. Therefore, I take it for granted that, in addition to the support from the gentlemen behind me, we shall have the support of gentlemen opposite to our policy and the propositions we are about to submit.

"But, perhaps, it will not be out of place for me to offer a few remarks in justification of the apparent delay that has taken place. It will be remembered that the Government was only formed on October 19th. Some delay took place in awaiting the arrival in Canada of an honourable member, who, I am satisfied, is one whom, whatever the political opinions of gentlemen of this House may be, all would have been anxious to see consulted before the Government was formed—I mean the Minister of Militia. The Government, therefore, was not completed till October 19th. The members of the Government had to return for re-election, and those elections, though they were hastened with all possible rapidity, because we felt there was a great deal of work to be done, were not over until the early part of November, when we returned to the city of Ottawa. And what did we find? As Minister of Finance, I cannot say I found the finances in the most satisfactory condition. I found, sir, that we had maturing in London, between the early part of November and January 1st, an indebtedness of $15,500,000 with nothing to meet it but the prospective payment of the Fishery Award. On this side of the Atlantic we had in the various banks of the Dominion something like $5,000,000, and between that date and January 1st, with the subsidy of the provinces and payments to contractors who were constructing public works, something like $3,000,000 had to be paid ; and then, considering the position the banks were in all over the Dominion, the uncertainty as to what might transpire, it was just possible that a reduction in the reserves might take place, and that meant a demand on the Dominion Treasury. Every dollar we found it necessary to take from the banks at the time was embarrassing, and was reluctantly withdrawn. But it was inevitable that the Finance Minister should proceed to London, with the least possible delay, that arrangements might be made to sustain the credit and the honour of the Dominion. Well, sir, in order to avoid that, feeling the importance of every member of the Government being at his post in order to prepare measures for the meeting of Parliament, a cable message was sent to our agents on the other side to ask if the visit of the Finance Minister to London could not be avoided. The answer was " No; his presence here is absolutely necessary." Under these circumstances I proceeded to London, and I placed a loan of £3,000,000 sterling upon the market there.

" Then sir, after my return to Canada, it became necessary that we should consider the whole question of the tariff. It is not a question that can be settled in a day. It is not a question that can be settled intelligently in weeks, indeed it would have been well if we could have had more time to consider it than we have had, considering the magnitude and importance of the work. I can appeal to other Finance Ministers, and especially to my immediate predecessor, who, in 1874, made several changes in the tariff of that day, to speak of the difficulties there are in making even as few changes as were then made. But, if we undertake, as the present Government have undertaken, to re-adjust and re-organize, and, I may say, make an entirely new tariff, having for its object not only the realization of $2,000,000 more revenue than will be collected this year, but, in addition to providing for that deficiency, to adjust the tariff with a view of giving effect to what has been, and is to-day declared to be the policy of the majority of this House —I mean the protection of the industries of the country—the magnitude of the undertaking will be the better appreciated. Sir, we have invited gentlemen from all parts of the Dominion, and representing all interests in the Dominion, to assist us in the re-adjustment of the tariff, because we did not feel— though perhaps we possess an average intelligence in ordinary Government matters—we did not feel that we knew every-thing. We did not feel that we were prepared, without advice and assistance from men of experience with reference to these matters, to re-adjust and make a judicious tariff. We, there-fore, invited those who were interested in the general interests of the country, or interested in any special interests. Gentle-men who took an opposite view, met us and discussed these questions, and I may say that, down to as late a period as yesterday, though the propositions are submitted to-day, we were favoured with the co-operation and opinion of gentlemen who represent their particular or general views with reference to the great questions we have under consideration. We have laboured zealously and arduously, and I trust it will be found successfully ; and we are now about to submit our views for the consideration of this House. I think we may appeal with some degree of confidence to gentlemen in opposition, in approval of the early period at which this tariff is being intro-duced, when I call to the mind of these honourable gentlemen that their Government was formed on November 7, 1873; ours on October 19th; that my predecessor did not submit his tariff and budget speech until April 14th, this being March 14th.   When we submit to this House the result of our deliberations you will all understand the nature and extent of the consideration that must necessarily have been given to them.   I trust that this House and the country will feel that we have presented our views at as early a period as possible, taking all these facts into consideration.

"Let me refer to some circumstances that led to the present depression in the revenue.   During and after the war in the United States it is well understood that that country lost a large portion of its export trade, and its manufacturing industries were to a certain extent paralyzed; and it was only about 1872 or 1873 that they really commenced to restore their manufacturing industries, and endeavoured to find an extended market elsewhere for the manufactures of their country. Lying as we do alongside that great country, we were looked upon as a desirable market for their surplus products, and our American neighbours, always competent to judge of their own interests and act wisely in regard to them, put forth every effort to obtain access to our market.   It is well known by the term slaughter-market what they have been doing for the last four or five years in Canada; that, in order to find an outlet for their surplus manufactures, they have been willing to send them into this country at any price that would be a little below that of the Canadian manufacturer.   It is well known also that they had their agents in every part of the Dominion seeking purchasers for their surplus, and that those agents have been enabled, under our existing laws, to enter those goods at a price much lower than they ought to have paid, which was their value in the place of purchase.   It is well-known, moreover, that the United States Government, in order to encourage special interests in that country, granted a bounty upon certain manufactures, and so gave to them the exclusive market of the Dominion, and, under those circumstances, we have lost a very important trade, possessed previous to 1873.   In addition to the loss of the West India trade, by the repeal of the 10 per cent. duty on tea, we lost the direct tea trade, and all the advantages resulting from it, by its transfer from the Dominion to New York and Boston. Under all those circumstances, and with the high duty imposed by the United States on the agricultural products of the Dominion, by which we are, to a great extent, excluded from them, while the manufactures of that country are forced into our market, we could not expect prosperity or success in the Dominion, so long as that state of things continued. These are some of the difficulties which have led to our present state of affairs.

"Now after having made these few remarks on that head, I desire to call the attention of the House to the remedy. I know this is a difficult question—that it is the opinion of some honourable members, that no matter what proposition you may make, or what legislation you introduce, it cannot improve or increase the prosperity of the country. The Government entertain a different opinion. I may say, at the outset, it would have been much more agreeable if we could have met the House without the necessity of increased taxation. But in the imposition of the duties we are now about to ask the House to impose, it may be said we shall receive from the imports from foreign countries a larger portion of the $2,000,000 we require than we shall receive from the mother country. I believe such will be the effect, but I think that in making such a statement to this House, belonging, as we do to, and forming a part of that great country—a country that receives our natural products without any taxation, everything we have to send to her—apart from our national feelings, I think this House will not object if, in the propositions before me, they touch more heavily the imports from foreign countries than from our fatherland. I have this to say to our American friends: In 1865 they abrogated the reciprocity treaty, and, from that day to the present, a large portion of the imports from that country into the Dominion have been admitted free. We have hoped, and hoped in vain, that by the adoption of that policy we would lead our American friends to treat us in a more liberal spirit with regard to the same articles. / Well, after having waited twelve years for the consideration of this subject, the Government, requiring more revenue, have determined to ask this House to impose upon the products of the United States that have been free, such a duty as may seem consistent with our position. But the Government couple with the proposal, in order to show that we approach this question with no unfriendly spirit, a resolution that will be laid on the table containing a proposition to this effect : That as to articles named, which are the natural products of the country, including lumber, if the United States take off the duties in part or in whole, we are prepared to meet them with equal concessions. The Government believe in a reciprocity tariff, yet may discuss free trade or protection, but the question of to-day is : Shall we have a reciprocity tariff, or a one-sided tariff?

"We found, as I stated before, that it was important to encourage the exportation of our manufactures to foreign countries, and we are prepared now to say that the policy of the Government is to give every manufacturer in the Dominion of Canada a drawback on the duties they may pay upon goods used in the manufactures of the Dominion exported. We found, also, sir, as I have already pointed out, that under the bounty system of some foreign countries, our sugar-refining trade, and other interests, were materially affected. Well, sir, the Government have decided to ask this House to impose countervailing duties under such circumstances. I trust that this proposition will receive the support of both sides of the House, because some six months since, when the deputation of sugar refiners in London waited upon Mr. Gladstone and Sir Stafford Northcote, both of them being gentlemen representing Free Trade views, they declared, in the most emphatic terms, that when a Government came in and thus interfered with the legitimate trade of the country, they were prepared to impose countervailing duties. To make this matter plain, and place it beyond dispute, the Government propose to ask the House for authority to collect on all such articles an *ad valorem* duty on their value, irrespective of drawbacks. My colleagues say, explain it. For instance, a cent and a quarter drawback per pound is granted on cut nails exported to the Dominion of Canada; the duty will be calculated on the value of the nails, irrespective of that drawback.   Now, a bounty is given on sugar in excess of the duty which is paid by the sugar refiners; the Government will exact an *ad valorem* duty on the value of that sugar irrespective of the drawback. I may also state, Mr. Chairman, that another reason why I think our American neighbours should not object to the imposition of the duties we propose, is this : It is a fact, though not generally known, that the average percentage of revenue that is imposed on all imports into the Dominion of Canada, at the present time, taking the returns for last year as our criterion, is $13\frac{3}{4}$ per cent.   The amount of duty collected on the imports from Great Britain is a fraction under $17\frac{1}{2}$ per cent. ; while the amount of duty collected on the imports from the United States is a fraction under 10 per cent."

After dealing minutely with the changes which would be effected by the new tariff, Mr. Tilley concluded as follows :

" It appears to me, Mr. Chairman, and I think the House will agree with me, that the Government have endeavoured— whether successfully or not—to carry out the policy that we were pledged to inaugurate.   We have endeavoured to meet every possible interest—the mining, the manufacturing, and the agricultural interests.   We have endeavoured to assist our shipping and ship-building interest, which is in a very depressed condition.   We have endeavoured not to injure the lumber interest, because they now have a very important article used by their people at about the same rate of duty they had it before—I refer to pork.   They have tea at a cheaper price than before ; they have molasses cheaper. These articles enter largely into consumption with them. They have, as have every other class of exporters in the Dominion, many advantages, under the propositions that we are about to submit, that they did not enjoy before.   In the interest of lumbermen and of commerce generally, the present Government, as well as our predecessors, have expended large sums of money for the improvement of the navigation of our rivers and of our coast, by the erection of lighthouses, and in their maintenance. This, of course, is an advantage to the shipping interests as well. A proposition is also to be submitted to the House, which you will find in the estimates, to extend a telegraph down the St. Lawrence. This proposition was submitted to the people of the Dominion by an able and experienced gentleman, a member of the House. I need not name him, because the interest he has taken is well known. This proposition is in the interest of commerce, and of our shipping, and of humanity. It is in the interest of every industry that exports any article from this country to the old world, because an expenditure of this kind will reduce the rate of charges in the shape of insurance and other charges on the shipping, and that is more absolutely in the interest of the exporter than in the interest of the owner of the ship.

"In our policy, as just propounded, we have dealt with the agricultural interest, the mining interest, the shipping interest, indirectly with the lumbering interest, and with very many other interests, and it does appear to me that we have now arrived at a time when it becomes necessary for this country, for this Parliament, to decide whether we are to remain in the position we now occupy, with a certainty that within two years, with the existing laws upon our statute-book, almost every manufacturing industry in the country will be closed up, and the money invested in it lost. The time has arrived, I think, when it becomes our duty to decide whether the thousands of men throughout the length and breadth of this country who are unemployed, shall seek employment in another country, or shall find it in this Dominion; the time has arrived when we are to decide whether we will be simply hewers of wood and drawers of water; whether we will be simply agriculturists raising wheat, and lumbermen producing more lumber than we can use, or Great Britain and the United States will take from us at remunerative prices; whether we will confine our attention to the fisheries and certain other small industries, and cease to be what we have been, and not rise to be what I believe we are destined to be, under wise and judicious legislation,—or whether we will inaugurate a policy that will, by its provisions, say to the industries of the country, we will give you sufficient protection ; we will give you a market for what you can produce ; we will say that, while our neighbours build up a Chinese wall, we will impose a reasonable duty on their products coming into this country ; at all events, we will maintain for our agricultural and other productions, largely the market of our own Dominion.   The time has certainly arrived when we must consider whether we will allow matters to remain as they are, with the result of being an unimportant and uninteresting portion of Her Majesty's Dominions, or will rise to the position, which, I believe Providence has destined us to occupy, by means which, I believe, though I may be over sanguine ; which my colleagues believe, though they may be over sanguine ; which the country believes, are calculated to bring prosperity and happiness to the people, to give employment to the thousands who are (unemployed,) and to make this a great and prosperous country, as we all desire and hope it will be."

This would seem to be an appropriate place to give some particulars of the history of Sir Leonard Tilley, who, if not the father of the National Policy, is entitled to all the credit for putting it in shape and working out the details.   The following account of his life, previous to Confederation, is taken from a newspaper article that appeared at the time of the meeting of the Conference in Quebec, to arrange the terms of union :

" This distinguished gentleman, who has made so high a mark in the politics of New Brunswick, was born on May 8, 1818, in Queen's County, in that province.   He was educated in the Queen's County Grammar School.   He was first elected to the Provincial Parliament in May, 1850, for the city of St. John, and sat as its representative during the session of 1851, when he resigned his seat.   He was again elected in 1854, and at the special session, in November of that year, he was appointed a member of the Executive Council and Provincial Secretary.   On returning to his constituents in the same month he was re-elected by acclamation.   In May,

1856, Parliament was dissolved by the Lieut-Governor of the Province, Mr. Manners Sutton, who rejected the advice of his Ministers on the prohibitory liquor law question. They resigned and gave place to a new Administration. At the general election which followed Mr. Tilley was defeated. A man of his great ability and usefulness could not, however, be long left out of public life with benefit to the country, and he was recalled to office in June, 1857, when the Liberal party of the province returned to power. On that occasion he was opposed before his constituents by Mr. J. W. Lawrence, but without success, Mr. Tilley being elected by a majority of over 200. Since that time he has continued in the Government as Provincial Secretary ; in April, 1861, becoming senior member of the Executive Council and Premier of the Government.

"As a politician, Mr. Tilley is shrewd and penetrating ; as a debater, ready, fluent and forcible ; as a man, genial and kind-hearted ; and as a citizen (to use the familiar word of the neighbouring States) he is scrupulously upright and honourable. In him are combined, perhaps, more of the qualities which go to make up a statesman than are possessed by any of the other delegates from the Maritime Provinces."

To which we will add, continuing the history down to 1891, that he entered the Dominion Government in 1867 as Minister of Customs, and became Minister of Finance in 1873, on the resignation of Sir Francis Hincks, and held that office until the Government resigned in November of that year. On the return to power of the Liberal-Conservative party in 1878, he again accepted the office of Finance Minister, and remained a member of the Cabinet until November, 1885, when he was compelled to resign his seat in Parliament and in the Cabinet, owing to failing health. On his return to office in 1878 he was intrusted by Sir John A. Macdonald with the preparation of the Protective Tariff. His propositions were generally affirmed by his colleagues, and were, with one exception, accepted by Parliament. He was a member of the Sub-Committee of Council to arrange the terms of union with the representatives for Prince Edward Island, British Columbia and Newfound-

LORD LANSDOWNE

land. He took an active part in the discussion of all financial questions submitted to Parliament. He was eleven years a member of the Government of the province of New Brunswick, and thirteen years a member of the Dominion Parliament. No man in Canada, except the late Sir John Macdonald, has served as long as a member of Local and Dominion Governments as has Sir Leonard Tilley, to which has to be added more than ten years service as Lieut.-Governor of his native province. He was created a Companion of the Bath (Civil) by Her Majesty in 1867, and a Knight Commander of the Order of St. Michael and St. George May 24, 1879.

On March 25, 1880, the country was horror-stricken at the news of the attempted assassination of the Honourable George Brown. He was sitting in his office in the *Globe* buildings when a printer named George Bennett came in and asked for a certificate as to character. He had been dismissed by the foreman for drunkenness and irregularity. Mr. Brown replied that he had nothing to do with these things and referred him to the foreman or paymaster who knew all about him. He replied that he had already done so and been refused. He then commenced fumbling at his hip pocket, and it struck Mr. Brown that he was trying to draw a pistol and he at once seized him. The weapon had meantime been withdrawn and Bennett discharged it, the ball passing through the fleshy part of Mr. Brown's leg. He, however, did not relax his hold, and, while calling for assistance, managed to disarm his assailant. He made light of his wound, but was conveyed to his residence and medical assistance sent for. No danger was anticipated, but, being a man of great energy, he could not quietly yield to the necessary restrictions and insisted upon transacting business and doing other imprudent things. The result was that violent inflammation set in and after some days he grew delirious. After that he gradually grew weaker and weaker, until the struggle finally ceased on May 9th.

It was felt by Mr. Brown's friends that his long public services should not be forgotten, or his name allowed to pass into oblivion, a subscription list was therefore started, and a

couple of years later a bronze statue was erected to his
memory in Queen's Park, Toronto. Many prominent men of
both political parties were present on the occasion of the
unveiling, and we have much pleasure in referring to the
tributes paid to his memory.

Honourable Mr. Mowat said : " In consequence of Mr.
Mackenzie's not having sufficiently recovered his health to
speak with safety, the office has devolved upon me of saying
something in regard to Mr. Brown from the standpoint of his
party and political friends. It is a great gratification to those
in whose name I speak to know that neither esteem nor admiration of our lamented friend is now confined to his political
allies. The incessant warfare in which for many years he was
engaged, and the uncompromising vigour with which that
warfare was, on his part, carried on, made for him many
enemies. Some of his enemies can see no good in him, but it
is pleasant to know that not a few Canadians of hostile political opinions and sympathies have, notwithstanding, a kindly
feeling towards their old opponent, and some appreciation also
of his merits. A distinguished Conservative, a fellow-Senator,
is here to-day to give expression to these sentiments (applause),
and I am glad to see that not a few other Conservatives have
come with him to do honour to the memory of our friend.

" Mr. Brown is the first public man in Ontario in whose
memory a statue has been erected. Of our public men who
have passed away, not one had more friends than he had, and
I venture to say that not one was more generally lamented.
Those who mourned his death as a personal and public
calamity were to be found in every part of the Dominion,
and amongst Canadians of all classes and all creeds. The
place selected for erecting his statute is, with the approval
of all parties, the park of the University—an institution in
whose efficiency and prosperity he had, all his life, taken a
most lively interest. The springs of action which governed
his life, are, to a very great extent, to be found in his early
training and associations. He received his education in Edinburgh, he left Scotland and came to America with his father
and his father's family while yet a youth, and two-thirds of

his life were passed here. By parental example and early teaching he was, in religion, a strong Protestant and an earnest Presbyterian, and in politics a Liberal and a Loyalist. (Applause). The studies and observations of his mature years confirmed in him the principles in which he had been educated ; and all his life he stood by those principles.

" All his life he loved his Queen and the grand old Islands of the sea over which she has reigned so long and so happily. All his life he loved British connection and British institutions ; and all his life he did his part in maintaining like sentiments wherever his influence extended. He was proud of his British nationality, and was in no haste to discover, and had no disposition to assume, that the time was near when the interests of Canada required the severing of our political relation to the old land ; but he, at the same time, recognized a supreme duty to be owing to the land of his domicile, and was always zealous in promoting whatever in his judgment was for the true and permanent good of Canada. Nor had any loyal British subject, anywhere, a kinder and more appreciative feeling than he had towards the great American Republic on our borders, or towards its energetic and progressive people.

" All his life he was in heart and soul a Liberal, as Liberalism is understood in England, and as Liberalism is understood in Canada. He was always in harmony with the great majority of the Liberal party in the Province, and generally, though not always, with its other leaders. All his life his sympathies were with the masses everywhere. He loved freedom with the profoundest love, and sympathized with all oppressed or ill-governed people. Slavery he hated with intense hatred, whatever its locality was, or whatever the colour of the slave or the master. All his life the subject of the education of the people was dear to him. He desired to see the utmost practicable extension of education amongst all classes, and the greatest possible efficiency in our Public Schools, our High Schools, and our Colleges. In regard to our Public Schools he was an earnest advocate for making them free to all, both as a means of increasing their efficiency.

and in order to give to the poorest in the land the advantage of the best schools and on the same footing as others. So in respect to every other subject of public interest. Regarding agriculture as the basis of the country's wealth and prosperity, he took a warm and active interest from an early period in all things relating to the calling of the farmer. He saw the enormous difference which skill makes in the productiveness of the soil, and in the profits of the agriculturist.

"I have spoken of his religious position. All his life he continued to be attached to Protestantism, and to that form of it which Scotchmen have generally preferred to all others. He had no sympathy with skeptics or agnostics, or with heterodoxy of any kind within the pale of his own church. (Applause). But he appreciated with equal earnestness, and recognized heartily, the good which there is in all Christian Churches. He was zealous for the religious equality of all religious denominations. He desired for them equal rights as far as legislation or government had to do with these. He was against exclusive claims on the part of any Church, and was, therefore, for entire separation between Church and State as best for Canada, whatever might be the case elsewhere. For like reasons he was for the secularization of the Clergy Reserves, aud for the undenominationalizing of the Provincial University. Until these objects had been accomplished, he waged hot warfare against all claims which stood in the way. While the controversy for these objects was going on, he was necessarily in strong opposition to the Church of England ; but when the fight was over, and religious equality secured, his warfare against that Church ceased, and henceforward the Church of England had, outside of its own pale, no better friend than Mr. Brown was.

"So, when the Lower Canada Roman Catholic majority in the Legislature was found to be opposed to the secularization of the Upper Canada Clergy Reserves, and when measures, distasteful to Protestants, were forced through Parliament, or were threatened, he spoke out the thoughts and fears of his fellow Protestants on these subjects. But when the Reserves were secularized, and a constitution was secured which left

matters of education, and the other local affairs of each
province, to the exclusive jurisdiction of the Province, and all
danger of encroachment from outside influence had become
impossible, his warfare as a politician against Roman Catholics, their priests and professors, came to an end.   And before
his death this section of our fellow-citizens gradually resumed
the friendly political and personal relations towards him and
his party, which they had occupied before that warfare
arose.

"Apart from political questions, in regard to which there
was and will be the greatest possible difference of opinion, his
journal was recognized by all parties as maintaining a healthy
moral and religious tone. It ever took the moral and religious
side of all non-political subjects with which a public journal
has to deal ; and religious men of all denominations and
political parties felt that, as such, the *Globe* and its proprietor
was in sympathy with them, whatever many of them thought
of the politics of the paper, or of Mr. Brown's method of
dealing with his political opponents.

"In politics he was, for many years of his life, the
acknowledged leader of the Liberal Party in Upper Canada,
and, as such, his ambition was to have public confidence, not
by advocating political doctrines which he did not himself
hold, and by conforming to prejudices which he did not share ;
he desired the esteem and confidence of his fellows to come
from his championship of the policy he loved, and from the
sympathy which that championship should create.   He
desired the power which might come from sympathy with him
as a patriot and a Liberal, a friend of religious equality and of
popular rights.

"Political opponents have sometimes ascribed to him an
overweening desire for office, and have attempted to account
on that hypothesis now for one and now for another of the acts
of his public life ; but nothing could be more unfounded,
and nothing can be more easily disproved.   I was behind the
scenes for seven years before I retired from public life in 1864,
and I know that the general feeling of his associates and
followers was, that he was not anxious enough for office, that

the obtaining of office was not only no part of his policy, but that his desire was, that his party and himself should remain in opposition until the objects should be obtained which are identified with his name, and which, however important and desirable, not a few of his friends and his foes alike regarded as impracticable. But the political platform which he adopted at an early date, and never ceased to insist upon, is sufficient to demonstrate that office could not possible have been his object. Take, for example, one of the planks, representation by population. He insisted that the two sections of the Province, Upper and Lower Canada, should be represented in the United Legislature according to population, without reference to a dividing line between the two sections of the province. The law, as it stood, gave to each section the same number of representatives, and the population of Upper Canada greatly exceeded that of Lower Canada. Mr. Brown insisted that this was unjust, and in the resolutions which he from time to time moved in the Legislative Assembly, and in the speeches which he made there and elsewhere, his habit was to trace all political grievances to the absence of that representation in Parliament to which Upper Canada was entitled. This policy was calculated to unite, and did, to a large extent, unite Lower Canada in antagonism to him and his party, and enabled the Government to be carried on with a minority from Upper Canada. Other planks of his political platform alienated from him, for many years, a large section of the Roman Catholic electors of his own province who had previously belonged to the Liberal Party. His policy in regard to all these matters, it is plain, was the worst possible for a politician whose aim was office, and it did not require a tithe of Mr. Brown's foresight or sagacity to perceive this. Looking at his whole life, it is certain that either he was wholly wanting in desire for political office, or that the desire had less weight with him than with any other man in public life.

"The coalition of 1864 was an example of his boldness of character. It was a coalition with the men whom for years he had been attacking and denouncing. That coalition brought about the federation of all the provinces of British America except Newfoundland, and has brought about the incorporation into Canada of the immense territory then claimed or occupied by the Hudson Bay Company, a favourite project of Mr. Brown's, and settled the principal difficulties which had heretofore divided Canadian parties. These great issues could only have been accomplished by means of a coalition of parties. I do not purpose to suggest what share in the merit of the work belongs to each of the several parties to the coalition. But all agree that unless Mr. Brown had been a party to the undertaking, there could have been no coalition and no Confederation, and the necessity for the changes which the coalition accomplished arose from Mr. Brown's long-continued contention, that constitutional changes were absolutely necessary both in the public interest and as a matter of justice and right, and from the part which he had had in creating a public sentiment throughout Upper Canada in accordance with this view. He also took an active part in framing the Constitution which is now embodied in the British North American Act, and one important feature of it, the absence of any Legislative Council in this province, may be regarded as altogether due to him. In some of the other provinces the example of the Ontario Constitution has since, in this respect, been followed, and in all probability it will ultimately be followed in all the provinces of the Dominion.

" Attempts have sometimes been made to show that in this or the other act of his life there was inconsistency, and from the alleged inconsistency dishonesty has been inferred. But if consistency of opinion and policy is a cardinal virtue in a public man, it may confidently be said of Mr. Brown that no leading British or Canadian statesman of any party has ever pursued a more consistent course than he did. If there had been more ground than there is for an imputation of inconsistency it would be proper to remember that inconsistency may be honest or dishonest. Inconsistency may be the result of honest conviction, and apparent inconsistency may be the necessary consequence of a change of circumstances. Actual or apparent inconsistency may thus happen to be the duty of a good man and earnest patriot. Numerous instances have occurred in both English and Canadian history, with reference to which this doctrine has to be borne in mind by the friends of successful statesmen, politicians and political writers, of all parties.

"One of Mr. Brown's most remarkable qualities was the readiness with which he was able to throw off the enormous burdens of his business cares and public anxieties, as if they were nothing. He could turn away in a moment from any great subject of interest, and amidst all his cares could confine his attention to any subject of however little comparative moment, and appear to be the most care-free of men. In the social circle he was always a conversable and delightful companion, and in the domestic circle he was a loving, appreciative and attentive husband, an affectionate, considerate father.

"I do not profess to set forth Mr. Brown's faults and weaknesses. Everyone has these. But I claim for his memory that he was a man of wonderful power of intellect, wonderful energy and wonderful industry, an exceptionally vigorous writer and an exceptionally effective public speaker, and a man who had all his life many strong friends ; that he began public life with strong convictions, embracing almost the whole field of public questions, and that his policy on these questions was the result of these convictions. I claim for his memory that as a journalist and a politician, his influence on the whole was on the side of religion, morality and the public good. He was for thirty-seven years one of the most prominent public men in Canada, and during this period he exerted influence on our country so great that there are but one or two living men whose friends would claim for them an equal influence. From what he was, and what he did, his memory is precious, and will never cease to be precious to many thousands of the Canadian people. (Loud and prolonged applause).

Honourable G. W. Allan next came forward and said : " I have been honoured with the request to address a few words to you on this occasion, and I do so the more gladly because I was given to understand that it was the earnest desire of the friends of the great statesman whose statue has just been unveiled to-day, that the ceremony should be as far as possible divested of any party character, and thus enable all alike, Conservatives as well as Liberals, to offer fitting homage to the memory of one who, for nearly forty years, occupied so conspicuous a place in the political history of Canada. May I be permitted to say also that it is particularly grateful to me to be allowed an opportunity, by taking part in this day's proceedings, of testifying to the feelings of personal regard which more intimate acquaintance and intercourse with the late Mr. Brown during the latter years of his life led me to entertain for him, and it is a deep satisfaction to me to feel that I preserved his friendship unbroken and uninterrupted to the day of his death.

"To Mr. Brown's political career it is scarcely necessary that I should do more than allude, after the eloquent and enthusiastic address of the Attorney-General, who has naturally spoken of it with all the ardour and admiration of one who is in perfect sympathy with his subject, but that man's mind must indeed be miserably warped and prejudiced who does not cordially recognize (whatever may be his own political views) the wonderful ability, the enormous energy, the untiring zeal with which Mr. Brown originated and followed up, whether in his place in Parliament or through the paper he controlled, those measures which he believed to be for the best interests of his adopted country. Indomitable energy was, indeed, one of the most striking features in Mr. Brown's character, and it was that wonderful force and vigour which made him for so many years, whether in office or out of office, the one supreme leader of his party, whose authority none ventured to question, and gave him a power and influence which no single public man in this country, except it be his great Conservative rival, Sir John Macdonald, has ever attained to. I can testify also, from my personal knowledge of Mr. Brown, that he threw the same energy into matters which had no connection whatever with politics, and was at all times ready, with his vigorous assistance, in all undertakings which he thought might be useful to the country, or in any way beneficial to his fellow-citizens.

" The Attorney-General has dwelt upon one important event, perhaps the most important event in its consequences to this country, in which Mr. Brown bore a principal part. I need scarcely say that I allude to the Confederation of the British North American Provinces. In originating and carrying out that great scheme, Mr. Brown acted cordially with old political opponents as well as friends, and in a noble picture, lately painted, of the ' Fathers of Confederation,' the work of a Canadian artist, which now adorns the vestibule of the Houses of Parliament at Ottawa, there is, I rejoice to say, preserved an admirable likeness of the great Liberal chief, who patriotically joined hands with leading statesmen of all parties to carry through a measure which has made Canada a nation, and a power in the Empire, of which she forms a part. There were many other measures in which Mr. Brown took a leading part during his long political career, and which Mr. Mowat has touched upon, on which public men differed widely, and opposed each other with all the bitterness and violence of party strife, and yet, looking calmly back upon them, when time and experience have given better opportunity for forming an impartial judgment, even those who were most strongly opposed to Mr. Brown will now be ready to recognize all that was good and patriotic in his objects and motives, where before they could, perhaps, only see what appeared to them unwise or injurious. It will, indeed, be an evil day for Canada when party spirit shall become so rampant that we cease to appreciate all that is good and noble in a political opponent.

" Doubtless, on subjects of such vital interest amid the struggle and excitement of political warfare, it is not always easy to do justice to those who are opposed to us, but as it has been well and generously said in a leading journal of the day, ' after the din and smoke of the contest has passed away, then good and true men on either side should always be ready to do justice to their adversaries. And those who were his strongest opponents are now ready to admit the patriotism and fortitude which ran through George Brown's whole career.' There was one trait which shone conspicuously

ously through the whole of Mr. Brown's public life, and that was his unswerving loyalty to British connection. Like the veteran statesman who, this morning, performed what, I am sure, was to him the loving office of unveiling the statue of his old and valued friend, George Brown, while claiming for Canada the fullest political liberty and self-government, would as soon have cut off his right hand as to countenance or support anything which looked towards separation from the Empire. Canada, its interests and its prosperity, had a deep and abiding hold upon that great heart, but it did not displace the allegiance which he owed to his Sovereign, nor the patriotic pride of a loyal subject in the mightiest empire which the world has ever seen.

"While yet in the full vigour of life, with convictions as strong, and acted upon as vigorously as ever, but with many prejudices softened or removed, with a judgment ripened and matured by long and varied experience—no longer actively engaged in the thick of party warfare, but occupying a position which seemed to promise many long years of public usefulness as a member of a body of whose rights and constitutional position he was, to the last day of his life, a staunch defender, still recognized alike by friends and opponents as a power in the land—George Brown was suddenly stricken down, and after many weeks of suffering was carried to his grave, mourned by men of all parties, who alike acknowledged 'that a great man in Israel' had, indeed, been taken away. Fitting then it is that all should take a generous and loving part in this day's ceremony, and that noble statue, which has been given to-day to the people of Canada, speaks forth as it were, to all who gaze upon it—not only now, but in the generations to come—the true patriotic sentiment that Canadians, without distinction of party, will ever honour and respect the memory of all that is good and great in the public men of their common country." (Applause).

ON July 10, 1880, Sir John Macdonald, Sir Charles Tupper, and Mr. John Henry Pope proceeded to England for the purpose of interesting capitalists in the building of the Pacific railway and, if possible, making a contract. They succeeded in their mission so well that, on September 16th, they were able to announce that the preliminaries had been arranged, and then returned to Canada. They were followed by the representatives of the syndicate who, after a conference of a fortnight, signed a carefully prepared contract for the completion of the work. The terms of this agreement were not made known until after the meeting of Parliament, on December 9th. It was a long document of forty-one clauses, and too technical in its language to be of interest to the general reader. A better idea of its contents will be obtained from the following extracts, taken from the very able speech with which it was brought before the House by Sir Charles Tupper.

Sir Charles Tupper said : " Mr. Chairman, it affords me very much pleasure to rise for the purpose of submitting a motion to the House in relation to the most important question that has ever engaged the attention of this Parliament —a motion which submits for the approval of this House the means by which that great national work, the Pacific railway, shall be completed and operated hereafter in a way that has more than once obtained the approval of the House and the sanction of the people of this country, and upon terms more favourable than any that have ever previously been offered to the House. I shall be obliged, Mr. Chairman, to ask the indulgence of the House while, at some considerable length, I

place before it the grounds upon which I affirm that this resolution embodies the policy of the Parliament of Canada, as
expressed on more than one occasion, that these resolutions
present terms for the consideration of this Parliament for the
completion of this work more favourable than any previously
submitted. And, sir, I have the less hesitation in asking the
indulgence of the House, because I ask it mainly for the
purpose of repeating to the House statements made by gentlemen of much greater ability than myself, and occupying
positions in this House and country second to no other, and
but for what took place here yesterday, I would have felt
warranted in expressing the opinion that the resolutions, grave
and important as they are, would receive the unanimous
consent of this Parliament."

Mr. Blake—" Hear, hear."

Sir Charles Tupper—" I would, I say, have been warranted
in arriving at that conclusion but for the very significant
indications that were made from the other side of the House,
because these resolutions only ask honourable gentlemen on
both sides of the House to affirm a proposition to which they
have again and again, as public men, committed themselves.

"I need not remind the House that when my right
honourable friend, the leader of the Government, occupied in
1871 the same position which he now occupies, the policy of
constructing a great line that would connect the two great
oceans which form the eastern and western boundaries of the
Dominion of Canada received the approval of this House.
And not only did the policy of accomplishing that great work
receive the endorsation of a large majority in the Parliament
of this country, but in specific terms, the means by which that
work should be accomplished, were embodied in the form of a
resolution, and submitted for the consideration of Parliament.
It was moved by the late lamented Sir George Cartier : ' That
the railway referred to in the Address to Her Majesty concerning the union of British Columbia with Canada, adopted by
this House on Saturday, April 1st, should be constructed and
worked by private enterprise and not by the Dominion
Government, and that the public aid to be given to secure that

undertaking, should consist of such liberal grants of land and such subsidy, and any other aid not unduly pressing on the industry and resources of the country, as the Parliament of Canada shall hereafter determine.'"

Mr. Blake—"That was the resolution first brought down."

Sir Charles Tupper—"That was the first resolution, and it was amended to state more strongly that the work should not involve an increase in the existing rate of taxation. The honourable gentlemen will agree with me that it embodies the mode upon which the road should be constructed. Now, sir, although honourable gentlemen in this House, although the two great parties represented in this House, may entertain differences of opinion as to the construction of the railway, and the means that may be adequate to its accomplishment, the House was unanimous in that, because the honourable gentlemen representing the Opposition in this House supported a resolution introduced as an amendment to ours by the present Chief Justice Dorion, declaring that the road should be constructed in no other way, adding to the resolution the words 'and not otherwise.' The object of which was to make it impossible for any government to secure the construction of the road in any other mode than through the agency of a private company, or aided by a grant of lands and money. And while the resolution, moved by Sir George Cartier, declaring that the work should be constructed in that way, received the support of every gentleman on this side of the House, the still stronger affirmation moved by Mr. Dorion, that the work should not be done in any other way, received, I believe, the support of every gentleman on the other side of the House. Therefore, I think I may say that the policy of Parliament, not the policy of any one party, was distinctly affirmed in the resolution placed on the journals in 1871.

"In 1872 it became necessary to state in distinct terms what aid the Government proposed, under the authority of that resolution, to offer for the construction of the railway. The journals of 1872 will show that Parliament, by a deliberate vote and by a very large majority, placed at the service of the Government a sum of $30,000,000 in money, and a grant of 50,000,000 acres of land for the construction of the main line, and an additional amount of 20,000 acres of land per mile for the Pembina branch of eighty-five miles, and of 25,000 acres of land per mile for the Nipigon branch. At that time, sir, I may remind the House that it was expected, as possibly may prove to be the case yet, that the line of the Pacific railway from Nipissing westward would run to the north of Lake Nipigon ; and provision was therefore made for a branch, by a vote of 25,000 acres of land per mile for one hundred and twenty miles to secure connection between Lake Superior and the main line. Now, sir, these terms became the subject of very considerable discussion in this House and out of it ; and the Government having been sustained by a majority placing at their disposal that amount of money and that amount of lands to secure the construction of the railway, and the term of Parliament having expired, the House was dissolved and the country appealed to. And, sir, after that question was placed before the country, a very sufficient working majority was returned to support the Government and confirm the policy which the House had adopted, both as to the mode in which the work was to be constructed, and as to the public money and public lands which the Government were authorized to use for the purpose of securing the construction of this work.

" Under the authority of this House in 1872, and under the authority of the people of this country, the Government entered into a contract with a number of gentlemen, who subsequently selected Sir Hugh Allan as the president of the company, for the purpose of constructing the railway on the terms that I have now mentioned to the House. I need not, at this period, remind the House that that company, embracing a number of the most able, leading, and influential men in finance and commerce, proceeded to England, at that time at all events the great money market of the world - I might almost say that it was then the only market in the world. They proceeded to England, and exhausted every means in their power to obtain the support of financial men in such a way as to enable them to carry that contract to completion. If my recollection does not fail me, the honourable leader of the late Government on more than one occasion expressed the hope that that company would be successful. He always expressed his strong conviction that the means were altogether inadequate to secure the object in view ; but I think that on more than one occasion he expressed the patriotic hope that these gentlemen would succeed in obtaining the capital required, upon those terms. But, sir, they did not succeed as every person knows. After having exhausted every effort in their power, they were obliged to return and surrender the charter, under which they received authority to endeavour to obtain money for the construction of this great work.

"Well, sir, a very unpleasant result followed, and the then Government of this country met with a defeat. The means placed at their disposal to secure the construction of the great work which these gentlemen had in hand proved inadequate, and the Government also succumbed to the pressure from honourable gentlemen opposite. It is not a pleasant topic, and I will not dwell any longer upon it than is absolutely necessary to introduce the Administration which followed, led by the honourable member for Lambton. Now, sir, I have said on more than one occasion that in my judgment, inasmuch as the only authority which Parliament had given for the construction of the railway required that it should be done by a private company, aided by a grant of land and money, and inasmuch as the resolution embodying that statement, as the honourable leader of the Opposition has correctly reminded me, also embodied the statement that it should not increase the existing rate of taxation, and inasmuch as the Finance Minister of the Government at once announced to Parliament the fact that there was a great impending deficiency between the revenue and expenditure, it became patent that no progress could be made except in contravention of both these propositions. I have said before, and I repeat now, that in my judgment the honourable leader of the then Government would have been warranted in stating that he was obliged to leave the question of the construction of the railway in abeyance. But, sir, he did commit himself in the most formal and authentic manner to

the construction of the road, and notwithstanding the difficulties which had occurred, he appealed to the people of this
country in the most formal manner in which it is possible.

"The House will, perhaps, allow me to draw attention to
some very important statements contained in his manifesto.
The honourable gentleman said : ' We must meet the diffi-
' culty imposed on Canada by the reckless arrangements of the
' last Government, with reference to the Pacific railway, under
' which they pledged the land and resources of this country
' to the commencement of that gigantic work in July, 1873,
' and to its completion by July, 1880.' The honourable gentleman will see that the term ' reckless arrangement ' is confined and limited by the honourable gentlemen to the short
time which we had allowed ourselves for the construction of
the work, and not to the work itself. The honourable gentleman further said : ' That contract has already been broken.
' Over a million of dollars has now been spent in surveys and
' no particular line has as yet, been located. The bargain is
' as we always said, incapable of literal fulfilment. We must
' make arrangements with British Columbia for such a relaxa-
' tion of the terms as will give time for the completion of the
' surveys and subsequent prosecution of the work, with such
' speed as the resources of the country shall permit of, and
' without too largely increasing the burden of taxation upon
' the people.' The honourable gentlemen went on to say that
they must, in the meantime, obtain some means of communication across the continent, and that it would be their policy
to ' unite the enormous stretches of magnificent water com-
' munication with the lines of railway to the Rocky Moun-
' tains.'

"In 1874 the honourable gentleman introduced a Bill for
the purpose of providing for the construction of the railway,
and in the course of a very able and exhaustive speech he
placed very fully on record the opinions which he held, and
which embodied the opinions of the Government at that time.
He stated, as will be seen on reference to the *Hansard* of May
12, 1874, that ' the duty was imposed upon Parliament ' '
' providing a great scheme of carrying out the obliga'

imposed upon us by the solemn action of Parliament in this
'matter.   The original scheme was one that I opposed at the
' time of its passage here, as one that in my mind then seemed
' impracticable within the time that was proposed, and imprac-
' ticable also within the means proposed to be used to accom-
' plish it.'   I wish to invite the attention of the House to the
formal declaration made on the floor of Parliament by the
late Prime Minister, that the means that Parliament had
placed at the disposal of the late Government by their predecessors, $30,000,000 and 54,000,000 acres of land, was
utterly inadequate to secure the construction of the work.
Then the honourable gentleman continues, 'I have not changed
' that opinion, but being placed here in the Government, I am
' bound to endeavour, to the utmost of my ability, to devise
' such means as may seem within our reach to accomplish in
' the spirit, if not in not in the letter, the obligations imposed
' upon us by the treaty of union—for it was a treaty of union—
' with British Columbia.'   I am sure that British Columbia will
be very glad to be again reminded that the leader of the
Opposition maintained that this was an absolute treaty of
union with British Columbia.

    "In 1875 the honourable gentleman, having had an oppor-
tunity of considering the proposals which were embodied in
his Bill, to which I shall invite the attention of the House
more especially at a later period, obtained authority from this
House to go on with the immediate construction of the railway by the direct agency of the Government, for he could not
obtain it in any other way.   Having obtained power from this
House to give, not only $10,000 per mile for every mile
between Lake Nipissing and the shores of the Pacific, and
20,000 acres of land per mile, but also to give $10,000 in cash
per mile for the branch eighty-five miles long to Pembina,
and 20,000 acres ; and $10,000 and 20,000 acres per mile
for the Georgian Bay branch of eighty-five miles long ; and
also to give the further sum of four per cent. interest for
twenty-five years upon such sums as might be found necessary
in order to secure the construction of the work.

comfiIn 1876, after longer experience, after having found that the financial difficulties of the country had certainly not decreased, the honourable gentleman was still undismayed, for in 1876, from the high and authoritative position of a Prime Minister submitting the policy of his Government to the country, after full and deliberate consideration, he enunciated the following views : ' We have felt from the first that while it ' was utterly impossible to implement to the letter the engage- ' ments entered into by our predecessors, the good faith of the ' country demanded that the Administration should do every- ' thing that was reasonable, and in their power, to carry out the ' pledges made to British Columbia, if not the entire obligation, ' at least such parts of it as seemed to be within their power, ' and most conducive to the welfare of the whole Dominion, as ' well as to satisfy all reasonable men in the province of British ' Columbia, which province had fancied itself entitled to com- ' plain of an apparent want of good faith in carrying out these ' obligations. In endeavouring to accomplish this result we ' have had serious difficulties to contend with, to which I shall ' shortly allude. The Act of 1874 prescribes that the Govern- ' ment may build the road on contract in the ordinary way, or ' it may be built on the terms set forth in Section 8, which ' provides that the Government may pay $10,000 and grant ' 20,000 acres of land per mile, with four per cent. for twenty-five ' years upon any additional amount in the tenders, to a com- ' pany to construct portions of the line. The intention of the ' Government was, as soon as the surveys were in a sufficiently ' advanced state, to invite tenders for the construction of such ' portions of the work as in the judgment of Parliament it might ' be considered desirable to go on with, and that in the mean- ' time the money that had been spent in grading should be ' held to be a part of the $10,000 a mile referred to in Section ' 8. Whether the Government would be in a position during ' the coming season to have contracts obtained and submitted ' to Parliament for the whole line at its next session, is perhaps ' problematical.' So that the honourable gentleman in 1876 not only contemplated going on steadily with the prosecution of the work, or very important sections of the work, but had it in contemplation to invite tenders for the construction

of the whole railway on terms which, as I shall show specifically hereafter, were largely in excess of any authority we ever
obtained from Parliament, and terms that, as I have said
before, he himself held, and I suppose conscientiously held, to
be utterly inadequate.

"In 1877, after another year's experience, the honourable
gentleman again stated the policy that still was the policy of
his Administration in reference to this work. The late
Administration in entering into the agreement for bringing
British Columbia into the Confederation had an express obligation as to the building of the railway across the continent,
from Lake Nipissing on the east to the Pacific Ocean on the
west, within a specified number of years. 'When the present
'Administration,' he said, 'acceded to power, they felt that this
'like all treaty obligations, was one which imposed upon them
'certain duties of administration and government which they
'had no right to neglect, and that they were bound to carry the
'scheme practically into effect to the extent that I have indi-
'cated. The whole effort of the Administration from that day
'to this has been directed to the accomplishment of this object
'in the way that would seem to be most practicable and most
'available, considering the difficulties to be encountered and the
'cost to be incurred.' So that down to 1878, the House will see,
the honourable gentleman still remained true to the obligation
of the rapid construction of the railway, of its construction by
the agency of a private company, and a grant of land and
money. In 1878, the last occasion on which the honourable
gentleman, with the authority of Prime Minister, discussed the
question, he said, 'There can be no question of this, that it
'was in itself a desirable object to obtain railway communica-
'tion from one end of our Dominion to the other, traversing
'the continent from east to west. So far as the desirability of
'obtaining such a connection may be concerned, there can be
'no real difference of opinion between any two parties in this
'country, or amongst any class of our population.' So that I
am very glad, on this important question, in submitting resolutions of such magnitude for the consideration of this House,
to have the authority of the leader of the late Government,

HON. JOHN G. HAGGART, P.C.
Postmaster-General.

after years of close and careful examination of this question, given to the House and the country, that it was a matter, not only of vital importance to the country, but upon which both parties were agreed, not only in this House, but outside of it.

" In 1878 the honourable gentleman also said : ' I have to ' say in conclusion that nothing has given myself and the ' Government more concern than the matters connected with ' the Pacific railway. We are alive to this consideration—that ' it is of vast importance to the country that this road should ' be built as soon as the country is able to do it without impos- ' ing burdens upon the present ratepayers which would be ' intolerable.' I quite agree with the honourable gentleman in that statement, and I am proud to be able to stand here to-day and offer for the honourable gentleman's consideration, and I trust, after full consideration, for his support, a proposi- tion that will secure to this country the construction of that which he has declared to be not only a matter of honour to which the country was bound, but a matter of the deepest necessity to the development of the country, upon terms that will not impose any intolerable burdens on the ratepayers.

" In 1878 there was a general election, the result being that my right honourable friend (Sir John Macdonald) was again charged with the important duty of administering the public affairs of this country, and again brought face to face with this great work. We found ourselves then called upon to deal with a work upon which a large amount of public money had been expended, and in a way that would prove utterly useless to the country unless measures were taken promptly to carry, at all events, the work under construction to completion. We, there- fore, were not in a position to effect any change of policy, as honourable gentlemen opposite will see. But we came to Parliament to reaffirm the policy of utilizing the lands of the North-West for the purpose of obtaining the construction of that vast work. There was every reason in the world why we should adopt that policy in the first instance and return to it afterwards. Every person knows that the development of this great territory was concerned in this gigantic undertak- ing ; that, irrespective of the question of the connection of

British Columbia, the progress and prosperity of Canada were to be promoted by the construction of the railway. We were, therefore, compelled to take it up as we found it, and go on with it as a Government work. To make the work, upon which so much had already been expended, of use to the country, we asked the House to place at our disposal 100,000,-000 of acres for the purpose of covering the expenditure in connection with the railway. We felt that by that means we should obtain the means of recouping to the treasury every dollar expended on this work. Honourable gentlemen also know that we proposed to obtain the co-operation of the Imperial Government.

"Although we had not propounded the policy of carrying on this work by the Government, we took up the work as we found it. We placed under contract the 127 miles of the road which the leader of the late Government had announced it as his intention to build, which he had assured the people of British Columbia he intended to build, and which, under the terms of Lord Carnarvon, he was bound to place under contract. When we met Parliament with the statement that we were going on with this work, I think we scarcely met with the amount of aid and co-operation from gentlemen opposite to which we were entitled. As we were only carrying out what they proposed, we had a right to expect to be met in a manner different to that in which we were met by them. The leader of the Opposition moved—and in making this motion he submitted a resolution directly in antagonism to the policy of the Government which he supported, and to his own recorded utterances on the floor of this House—that we should break faith with British Columbia and with Lord Carnavon, and that we should give—I was going to say the lie—to Lord Dufferin, who stated on his honour as a man that every particle of the terms of agreement with British Columbia was in a state of literal fulfilment. The result of the moving of this resolution was to place on the records of Parliament a vote of 131 to 49 that good faith should be kept with British Columbia ; but we owed it to Canada to take up this work and prosecute it in such a way as we believed was absolutely necessary in order to bring it within such limits as would enable us to revert to the original policy of building the road by means of a company ; and had we not placed that section under contract in British Columbia, had we not vigorously prosecuted the one hundred and eighty-five miles wanted to complete the line between Lake Superior and Red River, we would not have been able to stand here, laying before the House the best proposal for the construction of the road which has ever been made to this Parliament. (Cheers).

" When the Government of Canada had to present themselves to capitalists, either in this country or in the United States or in England, and show how that year after year they had to meet Parliament with an alarming deficit and were unable to provide for it, and were adding from year to year to the accumulated indebtedness of the country, not for the prosecution of public works that were going to give an impetus to our industries, but merely to enable the ordinary expenditure of the country to be met, they failed. But when all this was changed, the aspect of affairs in relation to this work was also changed. Under the previous condition of things my honourable friend opposite could not obtain offers in response to the advertisements which he published all over the world. The honourable gentleman might fairly assume that we could not obtain any offers either. But as I say —when under a changed policy, and when the Government had successfully grappled with the most difficult portions of this great work, and shown to the capitalists of the world, under the authority of this House, that 100,000,000 acres of land were placed at our disposal for the prosecution of the undertaking that we were not afraid to go on with its construction, or afraid to show that the construction of the railway was a work capable of fulfilment ; when we proved to the capitalists of the world that we ourselves had some confidence in this country and in its development, and that we were prepared to grapple with this gigantic work, the aspect of affairs was wholly changed. Well, sir, under these circumstances the Government submitted their policy to Parliament, and they were met by obstruction. Last session they were met by a complete change of front on the part of the Opposition in this House and the country.

"The men who had for five years declared that they were prepared to construct the Canadian Pacific Railway as a public work, the men who had pledged themselves to British Columbia to construct it as a public work, and who had in this House, in every way that men could, bound themselves, called a halt in order to obstruct the Government, when we took the only means by which we could remove the difficulty which had prevented the honourable gentlemen obtaining any offers in reply to the advertisement that he had sent all over the country. I have the advertisement in my hand. It was published on May 29, 1876, and it says that 'they invite tenders to be sent in, on or before January, '1877, under the provision of the Canadian Pacific Railway 'Act of 1874, which enacts that the contractors for its construc- 'tion and working shall receive lands or the proceeds of lands.' 'Then it goes on to say that 'the proceeds of the lands at the 'rate of 20,000 acres, and cash at the rate of $10,000 for each 'mile of railway constructed, together with interest at the rate 'of four per cent. for twenty-five years from the completion of 'the work on any further sum which may be stipulated in the 'contract, shall be paid,' and that 'the Act requires persons 'tendering to state in their offer the lowest sum, if any, per 'mile, upon which such interest will be required.' That adver- tisement was published all over the world, in Great Britain, in this country, and I presume in the United States, and to it no response was made. I believe, under the circumstances to which I have adverted, that the time had come when we might deal with this matter from a better position."

Sir Charles then went into calculations to show the cost of the road under the previous and present proposed plans to be as follows : 1873, $84,700,000 ; 1874, $106,387,300 ; 1880, $78,000,000 ; and dwelt at length on the value of the lands and the probable cost of the work. On the latter point we quote as follows :

"I will now give honourable gentlemen opposite an authority as to the cost of this work about to be undertaken that I think they will be compelled to accept. On May 12, 1874, the honourable gentleman (Mr. Mackenzie) said the cost from Lake Superior to Burrard Inlet would probably be $100,000,000, or something like that. This was an estimate from the leader of the late Government, the then Minister of Public Works, and submitted to Parliament on the authority of his own engineers, with all the judgment and experience that could be brought to bear upon it—that $100,-000,000 would be required for the road from Lake Superior at Thunder Bay to the Pacific ocean ; and yet the present proposition secures the construction of the entire road within ten years from the first of July next, from Lake Nipissing to Burrard Inlet, at a cost to the country, at the estimate honourable gentlemen opposite placed on the lands, of $78,000,-000." He continued : " We propose to give $10,000 per mile and a grant, the same as that proposed by the late Government, of 20,000 acres, and we invite intending competitors to state the amount for which they will require the guarantee at four per cent. in order to give them what they may deem a sufficient sum wherewith to build the road. We know that some think $10,000 per mile and 20,000 acres of land, supposing they realize on an average $1 an acre, will not build the road. It would more than build it in some parts, but from end to end it is evident it would not build it. The Intercolonial railway will cost $45,000 a mile, traversing on the whole a very favourable country. The Northern Pacific railway, in the accounts published by the company, has cost, so far as it has been carried, that is to Red River, $47,500, or $48,000 per mile in round numbers. That road traverses almost wholly a prairie region easily accessible, and where materials were easily found, and is altogether quite as favourable as the most favourable spot of any part of our territories —with this advantage, that it was much nearer to the producers of supplies than any portion of our line except that on the immediate borders of the lakes. The Central Pacific I will not touch, as the cost of that road was so enormous as not to afford any criterion at all, because of the extraordinary amount of jobbing connected with it. But, judging

from the cost of other railways, we have no reason to suppose
it will be possible to construct this line from end to end at
a less price than $40,000 per mile, and it may exceed that
by several thousands of dollars. Part of it will, of course,
exceed that very much, though on the whole of the sections
east of the Rocky Mountains, something in the neighbourhood of that figure will cover the outlay.'

"The leader of the late Government further stated that
the road could not be built as a commercial enterprise, and
expressed a desire that the gentlemen who undertook the
responsibility should show him how it was possible to construct a railway 2,500 miles long out of the pockets of a
population of four millions, passing, during almost its entire
length through an uninhabited country and for a still greater
portion of its length through a country of very rough character. I am glad the time has come when we can respond to
the honourable gentleman. We are in a position to show him
now that that gigantic work can be accomplished, and upon
terms more favourable than any the most sanguine person in
this country ventured to look for. And I ask the honourable
gentleman not to forget, now that he is sitting on the Opposition benches, that in estimating the cost as a Minister he felt
he would not be doing his duty if he did not draw the attention of the House to the fact that when the road was constructed the liability resting upon the country would not be
discharged, but just commencing.

"The honourable gentleman (Mr. Mackenzie) went on to
say : 'Supposing it only takes the minimum amount estim-
'ated by Mr. Sandford Fleming, viz., 100,000,000, you have
'a pretty good idea of what it must cost the country in the
'end. When you double the debt of the country you will not
'be able to accomplish the borrowing of the sum of money
'that would be required to build the road, paying the attend-
'ant expense of management and the debt, interest, and every-
'thing else connected with it.' The honourable gentleman
opposite last session also enforced very strongly upon our
attention the fact that if we went on with this work as a
Government work, and stood pledged in the face of the

country and of the financial world to an expenditure of eighty
to a hundred million dollars for the construction of the railway, we could hardly be surprised if it increased the cost
of the money we were obliged to borrow in the money
markets of the world. The honourable gentleman said : ' If
' you add six per cent. upon the minimum amount to the
' existing obligations of this country, you will have in addition
' to our present annual burdens, $6,000,000, which, added to
' the cost of management, would probably make a continuous
' drain of $12,000,000 before you would have a cent to apply to
' the ordinary business of the country.' A rather startling
ground for the honourable gentleman to take, but one which
commended itself to all those who listened to the honourable
gentleman's address.

"The honourable member for Lambton continued : ' Then
' we come to the consideration of what would be the
' position of the road after it was completed. We have it on
' Mr. Fleming's authority, that until at least 3,000,000 of
' people are drawn into that uninhabited territory, it is quite
' impossible to expect the road to pay its running expenses.
' Mr. Fleming estimates these at not less than $3,000,000 per
' annum, and they have still further to be supplemented by the
' proportion of money required each year to renew the road.
' First, we would pay $100,000,000 to build the road ; next,
' $8,000,000 to operate it, subject to the deduction of whatever
' traffic the road received ; and, thirdly, we would have to
' renew sleepers and rails every eight years unless we used steel
' rails.' This is the pleasant picture which the honourable
gentleman himself drew for the consideration of the House
and country. And now it appears he hesitates to secure the
construction and operation of this road for ever at a cost of
$78,000,000.

"My honourable friend, the leader of the Opposition (Mr.
Blake), no longer than a year ago, was good enough to give
the House his opinion as to the cost of this road, and the
liability that would be incurred, and I invite his attention to
his own estimate as he then gave it. He said : ' Again, of
' course, the through traffic depends on the road being first-

'class, and we must remember that after we have spent all the
'Minister proposes, we shall have, not a Pacific, but a coloniz-
'ation road. According to the old system of construction, the
'central section would cost, including the other items I have
'mentioned, altogether over $42,500,000, leaving out entirely
'both ends. What are the ends to cost? Forty-five million
'dollars is, as I have stated, the cost from Edmonton to Burrard
'Inlet on the west, and the cost from Fort William to Nipissing
'on the east the honourable member for Lambton estimates at
'$32,500,000. Thus the ends make up together $77,000,000,
'the centre and the past expenditure to $42,500,000, making a
'total of $120,000,000.' And yet the honourable gentleman is
startled and astounded, and exhibits the most wonderful
alarm, when he finds a proposal laid on the table of the House
to secure the construction of all that work which, at the
cheapest rate, was, according to him, to cost $120,000,000, for
$78,000,000.

"The honourable gentleman (Mr. Blake) proceeded to say,
that besides this enormous expenditure to which he had
referred, he did not know how many millions of interest there
would be. He said : ' Six millions a year they had to consider
'for running expenses, which Mr. Fleming estimated at
'$8,000,000, and which his (Mr. Blake's) honourable friend
'(Mr. Mackenzie) estimated at a gross sum of $6,750,000 a
'year for the whole line, or $4,500,000 a year from Fort William
'to the Pacific. Of course, against this sum was to be set the
'receipts which, in some sections, perhaps, would meet expendi-
'ture, but in the early days, if not for a long time, he (Mr.
'Blake) believed the road would have to be run at a loss.' I
know that this is an authority for which the honourable
leader of the Opposition has a most profound respect (cheers
and laughter), and I trust that in submitting such criticisms as
in the interests of the country every Government measure of
this kind ought to receive, the honourable gentleman will not
lose sight of the position he took in criticising our proposals
twelve months ago.

"I trust I have given to the House sufficient evidence to
show not only that the proposal which I have the honour to

submit to Parliament is entitled to the favourable consideration of the Opposition, not only that it is greatly within the
amount voted by this House in 1873, and subsequently in
1874, for the construction of the railway, but that it is a
contract based upon figures, which compared with those which
honourable gentlemen opposite, after all their experience in
connection with this work, regarded as altogether insufficient
for its construction, are exceedingly favourable to this country.
Now I am bound to say I never felt more grateful in Parliamentary life than when, notwithstanding the startling statements made by those honourable gentlemen, this House placed
100,000,000 acres at the disposal of the Government for the
purpose of constructing the railway.   I knew that every intelligent man in this House and out of it regarded that measure
as of vital importance to the country.   I knew they felt it was
a duty we owed to the country to grapple with this great
work, notwithstanding the enormous liability it involved. The
Government were sensible of this generous feeling on the part
of their supporters in this House in sustaining us, notwithstanding the fears and the alarm that was sought to be created
by honourable gentlemen opposite when they found themselves in Opposition.

" I say the House can understand the pleasure with which
we meet the people of Canada through their representatives
to-night, and are enabled to say that by the means which we
were authorized to use for the construction of this work, we
are in a position to state not only that the entire construction
from end to end, but that the responsibility of operating it
hereafter, are to be taken off the shoulders of Canada for the
insignificant consideration of something like the cost to the
country of $2,000,000 per annum.   That will be the ultimate
cost, assuming that we have to pay the interest on all the
money the syndicate will obtain under this contract.   We are
in a position not only to show that, but to show that out of
the 100,000,000 acres of land that Parliament placed two years
ago at our disposal we have 75,000,000 acres left with which
to meet the $2,000,000 of expenditure, and that expenditure
will be diminished until at no distant day we will not only

have the proud satisfaction of seeing Canada assume an advanced and triumphant position, but that she will be relieved from the expenditure of a single dollar in connection with the construction or operation of this railway.

"The gentlemen who have undertaken this work stand before the people of this country to-day in the strongest position that it is possible for gentlemen to occupy in relation to a great enterprise such as this. The Canadians engaged in the enterprise are men who are second to none in respect of commercial standing and capacity, and by their success in carrying out their own great railway enterprises they have afforded us the best possible guarantee for the manner in which they will fulfil their engagements with the Government and Parliament of Canada. This company embraces capitalists, both of our own and of other countries, who are men of the highest character, men whose names are the best guarantee that could be offered the people of Canada that any enterprise they may undertake will be successful. With regard to the terms of the contract, I do not hesitate to say that no greater injury could have been inflicted on the people of Canada than to have made the conditions of the engagement so onerous that instead of insuring their successful fulfilment, they would have led to failure. I say that everything that men could do for the purpose of obtaining the best terms in their power has been done, but our idea has been that we owed it to Canada to make a contract that was capable of fulfilment, to give those gentlemen a fair contract, and afford them a fair opportunity of grappling with this great, this gigantic enterprise that we were so anxious to transfer from our shoulders to theirs. Whether you look at the American, or the Canadian, or at the English, French or German gentlemen associated with this enterprise, I believe that Canada has been most fortunate, and the Government has been most fortunate, in having this work placed in their hands.

"It is stated that the security of $1,000,000 for the carrying out of the contract is too small. They say that a paid-up capital of $5,000,000 within two years, and a deposit of $1,000,000 is too small. My opinion of security is this—that provided you get the parties who are most likely to deal successfully with the matter, the less security you demand the better, because in proportion as you lock up the resources of the party, the more you decrease his power to carry on his work successfully.

"The syndicate intend tne road to be completed to the foot of the Rocky Mountains at the end of three years from the present time. If it be thought a gigantic work to build 300 miles of railway by this powerful syndicate in a year, I may tell honourable gentlemen, for their information, that within the last year a few of these gentlemen completed between 200 and 300 miles of railway themselves, through a somewhat similar country ; and therefore it is not an extravagant statement for them to make in stating that they intend to construct to the foot of the Rocky Mountains in three years and to build 300 miles of this road during the coming season. What does that involve ? It involves the expenditure of an enormous amount of capital at the outset. The very moment this contract is ratified by Parliament, these gentlemen have to put their hands in their pockets, and not only rake therefrom $1,000,000 to deposit with us as security, but they have to put their hands into another pocket the next hour, and take out another million to equip the road ; and that will be done within the course of the year. After reading the lachrymose statements of the honourable leader of the late Government about these lands and the difficulty of getting them sold, it is not unreasonable to suppose that with all their energy and industry it will take two or three years before they can make these lands to any large extent serviceable by a return of money from their sale.

"These gentlemen have, therefore, at the outset, to lay out an enormous sum of money for equipment and in providing the plant necessary to run that work during the coming three years ; and they have in the next place to wait for a considerable period before they can receive any return for the lands. At the end of the three years all that plant will, of course, be applicable to the other sections. I believe, therefore, the more it is examined, the more it will be found that in the division of

money no injustice has been done, and those who place confidence, not in us, but in the statement of the leader of the late
Government, have only to take his own statements, which
have been read to-night, and that was his estimate of $40,000
per mile for the portion to be constructed west of Red River,
to perceive the advantage of the proposed arrangement.
There is another million they have to put their hands into
their pockets to pay us, and that is for the work we have constructed west of the Red River, and the material we have on
hand applicable for the purposes of construction.

"Under these circumstances, honourable gentlemen's minds
will be relieved to know that we have made the very best
division of the money, if the enterprise is to prove anything
but a failure. There is a great expenditure of money to be
made, at the very outset, in bringing people to this country.
I regard this proposal to secure the construction of the Canada
Pacific Railway by the agency of this company, as of the most
vital importance from the point of view that, instead of having
to struggle with railway companies in competition for emigrants, we will have a gigantic railway company, with all its
ramifications in the United States, France, Germany, and the
British Islands, co-operating with the Government of Canada.
But all that will involve a present outlay of a very large sum
of money by these gentlemen. The only hope they can have
of having any means of sustaining the railway, if it is constructed, is by getting population as rapidly as possible into
the fertile valleys of the North-West, and thus furnish the
traffic which alone can support the operation of this railway.

"I am told that another very objectionable feature is the
exemption of the lands from taxation. I have no hesitation
in saying I would have been very glad if that was not in the
contract, if it were only to meet the strong prejudice that
exists in this country on that question. But there were two
things we had to consider. One was to make the best bargain
we could for Canada, and the other was not to impose terms,
that without being of any material advantage to the country
would be likely to lead to disaster in the money markets of the
world, when the prospectus was placed on those markets.

Every one will understand that the position in respect to the taxation is not changed in the slightest degree from that in which we stood last year. When we were constructing this road as a Government work, when my honourable friend was constructing it by direct Government agency, no taxation could have been raised on these lands until they were utilized, or until they were occupied. No province, municipality or corporation of any kind, at present or that could be created hereafter, could impose the slightest tax on those lands until they were sold or occupied; and when they are sold or occupied now, that moment they are liable to taxation.

" I will not stop to discuss the question of the road itself being exempt from taxation, because honourable gentlemen have only to turn to the laws of the United States. The policy of the Government of the United States has always been that the national lines of railway, the roadway, the road itself, the stations, everything embraced in the term railway, should be exempt from taxation. One of the judges of the courts of the United States declared that as these great lines of road were national works, were public easements; that as they were for the benefit and advancement of the whole country, they should not be subject to any taxation, state or municipal. We have, therefore, only followed the practice that has prevailed in the United States, and that which honourable gentlemen opposite will feel was incumbent upon us. What was our position? We were asking these gentlemen to come forward and take a position from which we shrank. I do not hesitate to say that, important as the enterprise was, the Government felt it was one of enormous magnitude, and trembled almost when they regarded the great cost of construction and operation of the road when constructed; and I ask when we were shifting from our shoulders to the shoulders of a private company all the responsibility, I ask this House, in candour, to tell me whether they do not think that, as far as we could, we ought to have put these gentlemen in as favourable a position for the construction of the road as we occupied ourselves? That is all we have done, and, as I have said before, the moment the lands are utilized and occupied they become liable to taxation.

" It is said that a great enormity has been committed by the prohibition to construct lines running in any other direction than a certain one—south-west and west by south-west. Well, sir, I am a little surprised to hear any such objection, and I shall listen with great interest to honourable gentlemen on the other side of the House if they have any objection of that kind to make. A year ago a company, with as strong claims to consideration as it would be possible for any company to have on the Parliament of Canada, came to us for permission to construct a railway. They asked for no money. They asked no aid. They only asked for permission to construct a railway of a certain kind. Why did we refuse it ? Why, sir, we were very sorry to refuse it, but the Government, having taken the subject into careful consideration, decided, inasmuch as Canada was dealing with the construction of the great Canadian Pacific Railway, and inasmuch as the only hope of maintaining this road, and of operating it after it was built, was to retain the traffic of the Canadian North-West by the trunk line, we came to the conclusion that it was not in the interests of the country, however greatly any section might demand and need it, to construct a line which would carry the traffic of the North-West out of our country, and leave our trunk line, which had cost the country such a great sum of money, denuded of the traffic necessary to sustain it.

" I am glad that I shall not be compelled to trespass further upon the attention of the House. When I rose I expressed the pride and pleasure it gave me to be able to propound to Parliament a measure which will secure in ten years the construction of the Pacific railway upon terms more favourable than the most enthusiastic friend of the railway had ventured to hope, and to which this Parliament will have the opportunity of putting its seal of ratification. I have the satisfaction of knowing that throughout this country every man breathed more freely when he learned that the great undertaking of constructing and operating the railway was to be lifted from the shoulders of the Government, and that the liability the country was going to incur was to be brought within, not only the limit which, in its present financial condition, it is prepared to meet, but within such limits that the proceeds from the sale of the lands granted for the construction of the line will wipe out all liabilities at no distant day.

" And I say we should be traitors to ourselves and to our children if we should hesitate to secure, on terms such as we have the pleasure of submitting to Parliament, the construction of the work which is going to develop all the enormous resources of the North-West, and to pour into that country a tide of population which will be a tower of strength to every part of Canada, a tide of industrious and intelligent men who will not only produce national, as well as individual, wealth in that section of the Dominion, but will create such a demand for the supplies which must come from the older provinces, as well as give new life and vitality to every industry in which those provinces are engaged.

" Under these circumstances we had a right to expect that support which, in justice to themselves and their position as statesmen, honourable gentlemen opposite should give us. I say, sir, that looking at this matter from a party point of view, the lowest point of view, I feel that these gentlemen, by following the course they propose, are promoting the interests of the party now in power, just as they promoted our interests when they placed themselves in antagonism to the National Policy, which the great mass of the people desired. Sir, I am disappointed at the course of the honourable gentlemen, but I hope, upon future reflection, at no distant day the results of this measure will be such as to compel these gentlemen candidly to admit that in taking the course which we have followed we have done what is calculated to promote the best interests of the country, and that it has been attended with a success exceeding our most sanguine expectations." (Loud and long continued applause).

CHAPTER XXXIV.

THE terms of the contract did not meet with the approval of the Opposition. Mr. Blake criticised it in a very able speech, examining every clause in the most minute manner and was followed by other members of his party. None of the conditions seemed to find favour in their eyes. They objected to the subsidy, to the time limit, the exemptions from taxations, the clause against competing roads, etc. Mr. Blake was so much opposed to the fulfilment of the bargain that, during the Christmas holidays, he organized public meetings at Toronto and elsewhere, to enable him better to present his views before the country and thus bring such pressure upon Parliament that the Government would not be able to carry their measure. On these occasions he presented his arguments in a clever and forcible manner which so impressed his audiences that anti-syndicate resolutions were passed. In his opening remarks in the St. Lawrence Hall, Toronto, he said : " I am very sorry that the circumstances are such as to require a meeting to be called at this time of the year. It is a time at which I am sure we would all very much rather be otherwise occupied than we are to be occupied to-night. It is a time of social and domestic enjoyment, of pleasant memories, and of peace and good fellowship, and I hope that although we are engaged from the necessity of the case in an occupation somewhat incongruous, yet that enough of the spirit of this time will prevail to render our discussion good-humoured and civil with one another. It is with this view that you have an opportunity to learn something of and to make up your minds upon the great question before its fate is irrevocably sealed. It is now only a few days since the

Pacific Railway bargain was made public, and within a very few days we will resume the discussion of it. It was intended by those who thought they could pass the measure that we should have closed the discussion before this time, and that already, before you had an opportunity of informing yourselves upon it, it should have been made into a law. That intention has not prevailed, but there is only a short breathing space before the period at which the peoples' representatives in Parliament will be called upon for their votes on this subject, and in the meantime it is of the highest consequence that the people themselves, whose interests, both in this generation and in generations yet unborn, are materially affected by this measure, should have an opportunity to speak their minds. Those of us who acted together as the Liberal party ten years ago, opposed the terms of union with British Columbia on the score of the obligations then entered into to construct the Canada Pacific Railway, commencing it within two years and finishing it within ten years, and we declared that a work of such gigantic magnitude, over an unknown country ought not to be stipulated for, either as to its commencement or its conclusion, by any time except that when it was possible to achieve it with the resources of the country. We were overruled then, as we may be overruled now, by the majority in Parliament, and the country was in some sort bound by obligations, the fatal effect of which is urged now as the excuse for this bargain to which your assent is sought."

The pecuniary result of the contract Mr. Blake estimated to be, that including the completed portions of the road, which were to be handed over to the syndicate, they would receive in cash, or its equivalent, $6,000,000, and 25,000,000 acres of land, which at $3.18 per acre, would be worth $79,500,000. The cost of the whole road still to be completed he placed at $50,000,000, less the Government subsidy of $25,000,000, so that all the money the syndicate would require to furnish would be $25,000,000, and for this amount they would get a completed road costing about $80,000,000, and the land grant valued as above. If, therefore, these lands only sold for $1.00 per acre the syndicate would get the railway free of cost. The policy which he proposed in place of that of the Government may be gathered from the following extracts :

"The true course is to go to work and build the railway where it is wanted now, to build it to complete the connection with Thunder Bay (applause), and continue it as the needs of the settlement of the country require. Railway facilities are required to settle the North-West. What is needed to pay for the unproductive ends of this line ? A productive middle portion. Make the middle, make the backbone, get in the population. Put the railroad there ; do what is necessary to give the lands value, and when you have the population and the sustaining power, then, if you please, proceed with the construction. They admit these lands will not have a value unless the railway goes there. You can put it there at the expenditure of a very few millions of dollars, or a very few millions of acres of land. You can put it through those very parts necessary in order to develop the North-West, and give value to the remainder of the lands and yet keep the bulk of these lands to acquire the additional value which the railway will give them. Don't part with them now when they have not this value, keep them until then, and when they are worth money, make their value build the rest of the road.

"I now want to show you how great economy might be effected at the eastern end of the road. This proposal to build the section north of Lake Superior is a new one, for it has hitherto been regarded by both Governments as a thing of the future. According to Sandford Fleming's estimate the road will cost $22,686,000, or eleven-twenty-fifths of the whole road. The subsidy in land and money divided so as to give this branch a fair share would give $11,000,000 and the same number of acres of land. At $3.18, average price laid down by Government, or at say $3.00, this land would be worth $33,000,000, in all equal to a cash subsidy of $44,000,000. All this is to be sunk in building the eastern link. My proposition is to establish communication with the West, and furnish a through line to seaboard at one-eleventh of the cost of this scheme, and within three instead of within ten years. But before I talk to you of the railway connection, let me show you what the country would be if you went no further than the Sault. If you get up to that point you get to the waters of Lake Superior, with a good harbour and a run of 300 miles to Thunder Bay. After which a connection of 460 miles by rail will take you to Selkirk. You have thus, for nine months in the year, the directest route that man can devise to the North-West, and I find that the grades and curves on the Thunder Bay line are so good that the cost per bushel for grain over this portion of the Lake Superior route should not exceed two cents per bushel. It would pay well at 2½c. per bushel. The only objections that can be urged against this route is the necessity for transhipment, and the fact that it is not open all the year. All that you get by building to the Sault ; but that is not all. That is the most insignificant part of the benefit. From the Sault to the Straits of Mackinaw is but thirty or forty miles. From this point westward a link of some sixty-three miles is already built, and from the Northern Pacific junction at Duluth the company is cutting out the road, so that within one or two years there will be complete railway communication between Duluth and the Sault. This means a present route to the North-West by this circuitous line fifty to eighty miles longer than is proposed to be built. It means as practicable a route as you can ever get to the North-West. It means that you would get for the expenditure of one-eleventh of what you propose to spend in the east, in less than one-third of the time, a road for all purposes equally good by way of all rail connection, and a first-class land and water route through our own territory. (Loud cheers).

" That is what it does for the North-West, and for you in connection with the North-West. But that is not all. That road is the key of the possession of the trans-continental trade of nearly 400 miles of the United States of America. The Northern Pacific Railway is stretching out towards the Sault, knowing that its shortest line to New York is through Canada by way of Brockville. Canada has in the Sault Ste. Marie the key of the position, and to an enormous trade ; a trade not simply in the future, though largely so, perhaps, but capable of enormous improvement in the present. These men offer in ten years, at an expense of from $20,000,-000 to $40,000,000 to give you an all-rail communication with the North-West.   I offer you for one-eleventh part of the sum to give you through railway connection with the North-West in three years on a first-class road, for the traffic of the north-western States will be such as to demand first-class accommo-dation.   I offer you in three years not merely the present small and prospectively large traffic, but also the present large and infinitely greater traffic of an immense portion of Ameri-can territory.   The shortest air line from San Francisco to Europe is by the Sault Ste. Marie.   Instead of groping for ten long years, and at infinite cost, through this new wilder-ness in which your children are asked to wander, I ask you to take in three years, at a fraction of the cost, the important traffic of the North-West and the prospective traffic of the South-West as well.   As to the eastern connection, when it is demanded let it be built."

Speaking of freight rates, Mr. Blake said : " Their first tariff will necessarily be high, for, as just pointed out by a gentleman in the audience in the case of the St. Paul, Minneapolis, and Manitoba, where the traffic is light the rates must be proportionally heavy.   Once that high tariff is fixed it never can be lowered until the happy day arrives when they can pay ten per cent. upon the whole of your money invested in its construction.   (Cheers and laughter).   Let us see how the North-West will be affected by this.   The middle will have to pay for the ends, for neither the eastern nor western sections can be made to pay.   So, that the man who has his grain carried over the prairie section will have to pay not only a fair price for the carriage, but also the losses upon the unproductive sections, and on top of all that a dividend upon the whole capital invested in the road.   The syndicate might sink a few millions of dollars in the road, though it would be made up to them from sales of land.   Suppose they invested $5,000,000, and the road cost $90,000,000, they would make

$9,000,000, a year. Wouldn't you like to belong to the syndicate?" (Loud cheers and laughter).

It is with no intention to do injustice to Mr. Blake's able effort that we do not quote more of it. From his point of view it was a masterly production and demanded an answer. This answer was given by Sir Charles Tupper at London and other places, and the speeches of these two great political gladiators will furnish to the careful reader the best view of the position taken by the Government and by the Opposition on this great question. We will, therefore, only add that Mr. Blake entirely disapproved of the conditions, and considered the contract a "monstrous abortion." We are quite safe in saying that even though no modification should have taken place in his views during the last ten years, a great change has taken place in the views of those who listened to him in 1880, and that the people of Canada to-day recognize the wisdom of the policy then inaugurated, and would not do without the Canadian Pacific Railway, and go back to the old condition of affairs under any circumstances whatever.

It was, of course, impossible that in a debate of so much importance, Sir John Macdonald should not take a leading part. The great scheme had originated in his brain, and it is a well understood fact that when he first promulgated the idea, he was considered so far in advance of the times that he had, not only to contend with his political foes, but even to persuade his most intimate friends, of the feasibility of the project. When, therefore, it was about to take a shape that would ensure its successful completion and the proposed contract was being fiercely attacked by the members of the Opposition, he joined with his Ministers in a vigorous defence. Parliament having re-assembled after the Christmas holidays, the debate was renewed with great earnestness. On January 17, 1881, Sir John made a most eloquent speech. We will not give it in full, but only such portions as will convey a fair idea of the arguments he advanced.

He said: " I intended on Friday night to have made some remarks on the amendment that was then in your hands, but unfortunately for myself, and perhaps fortunately for the House, I was too much indisposed to be able to do so, and I was obliged to leave the Chamber. That motion, however, disposed of, considerable discussion was carried on, but it was still supposed to be *en regle*, and with your permission, and the permission of the House, I shall offer a few remarks, and they will not be long, on the subject so brought up and involved in that resolution and the amendment, and on the discussion which arose upon it. Sir, in the first place I would like to speak of the position of the Government with respect to the whole question. It is true it has been treated *ad nauseam* in this House and in the country, but, holding the position that I do, I think it not improper or a waste of time if I recall the attention of the House to some of the facts connected with the present condition of this great enterprise, and in doing so I must offer my most humble and respectful apology to my colleague who sits next me, the Minister of Railways, because he has again and again gone over the whole ground in a manner which I may imitate, but which I cannot hope to emulate.

" It is known that from the time that British Columbia came into Confederation—and I need not read the journals of the House to prove the fact—the declared preference of both sides of the House of the then Parliament was in favour of the construction of the Pacific railway by an incorporated company. If we commence from that starting point, and if we look through the whole line of the discussion and the whole line of the policy of the two Governments which have had to deal with that question, we shall find that thread running through the whole subject, connecting it in such a manner that it could not, without complete severance of the thread, be altered. It was felt in the country, in the House, and by every thinking man, that if we should be fortunate enough, if Canada should have sufficient credit in the market where capitalists most do congregate, to induce capitalists to come forward and undertake this great work, we would have obtained for the Dominion a great advantage. Our legislation was based upon that idea in 1872. The legislation of the Government that succeeded us was based upon the same

Stanley of Preston

principle, that it was advisable to avoid all the trouble, responsibility and uncertainty, and all the danger to be apprehended of making a great work like this a political engine. It was thought by all parties that it was of the greatest consequence that all those obstructions to the successful prosecution of the work, to the carrying out of this great object, and connecting this country from sea to sea, and making it one in fact as well as in law, should be removed ; that it was of the greatest consequence that the work should be expedited, that it should not be carried on as a political work, that it should not be made a matter over which rival parties could or would fight ; that it should be undertaken on commercial principles, and be built by a body of capitalists like any other railway, with the hope and expectation that the capitalists would get a full, fair return for all their risk, for all their expenditure, and for all their responsibility.

" The whole country was in favour of that proposition, if it was possible to have it carried out. We tried, and we failed, although we made an effort —a strong and almost a successful effort—in 1872 to thus build the railway. I will not drag into this discussion, as far as I am concerned, and as far as my remarks are connected with the subject, any references to the political past. Allusions were made to it by those opposed to the Government, especially by those who desired to asperse myself, but, sir, there is the record ; there is the fruit of the appeal to the country, and I am Prime Minister of Canada. But whatever may have been the cause of the failure of Sir Hugh Allen and the first company that was organized for the purpose of building this road, I can see without reference to any political reason why that company was defeated. I can only say it was not from any want of the strongest opposition offered to the Government of which I was the head, but it was in consequence of the two things occurring together : the personal object in attacking the Government and the desire to overthrow the scheme.

" It has been urged in this House, and I say it has been proved, that the present scheme laid before the House for its approval is a more favourable scheme than that proposed in

1872. Whatever may be the merits of other offers or tenders, whatever may be the merits of the last offer that has just been laid on the table, I believe there is no man of candour and common sense, who understands figures but will see that the proposition which the Government on its responsibility entered into with the Syndicate in 1880, was more favourable to the country than the arrangement made with Sir Hugh Allan in 1872. And I would ask this House and this country if Canada would not have been a great gainer, if we had accepted and carried out that proposition of Sir Hugh Allan in 1872. Nine precious years have been lost since that time which can never be recovered, during the whole of which the road would have been in successful process of construction. The men engaged in that scheme, if they could have got the ear of the European capitalists, were strong enough to push that road across the country, and at the end of those nine years, instead of there being scarcely the footprint of a white man outside the Province of Manitoba, we would have had hundreds of thousands of people, who have gone from mere despair to the United States, crowding into our own North-West Territories ; that country, instead of having but a small settlement in the eastern end of it, would have been the happy home of hundreds of thousands—to use the smallest figure—of civilized men, of earnest, active labouring men, working for themselves and their families, and making that country, much sooner than it will be now, a populous and a prosperous country.

" But there is little use in regrets like these. We on this side of the House are not responsible for this delay, and we appeal confidently to the country and confidently to posterity ; we appeal confidently to every candid man to say if this Dominion of ours, of which we are so proud, about the future of which we are so anxious, and yet so certain, would not have been infinitely greater in our time, in the time of the oldest of us, if the future of that country would not have been opened out as a great branch of the Dominion, if the contract of 1872 had been carried out. Still, sir, it was not to be. Our efforts failed, and we fell in those efforts. We were succeeded by a

Government strong in numbers, strong in ability, and at the head of it a practical man. The fact of his being a practical man was a matter of boast, and of just boast, among those who gather around him. He had directed his best energies to the object ; he had at his back a body so strong that no opposition could effectively thwart him, oppose him or even obstruct him, and that honourable gentleman states himself that he was not obstructed, that he was not opposed, that he was not in any way impeded by the Opposition of the day, and he, sir, took up the same line of policy in essence that we initiated in 1872. And he, sir, served honestly and faithfully, I believe, to relieve his Government and relieve himself and his party from the responsibilities of his position, and of the pledges which were made, and which he and those who served under him were under obligations which could not, without dishonour, be broken, which could not be delayed, which could not, without disgrace and discredit be postponed.

" It was admitted that there was a sacred obligation ; it was admitted that there was a treaty made with British Columbia, with the people and the Government of British Columbia, and not only was it an agreement, a solemn bargain made between Canada and British Columbia, but it was formally sanctioned by Her Majesty's Government. It was a matter of Colonial policy and Imperial policy that that road should be constructed, and the late Government leader, my honourable friend from Lambton, who is absent from his place to-day, and who, I fear, is absent from the same cause which compelled my absence on Friday night, and I regret his absence very sincerely,—I say my honourable friend felt himself bound to that policy. Both the Government, of which I was the head, and the Government, of which he was the head, were bound by the original resolutions that were passed at the time that British Columbia came in, were bound to the policy that this road should be built with the aid of money and land, and built by an incorporated company if possible, and some went so far as to say, built in no other way. He was hampered by that obligation, but it hampered both Governments. The delegates from British Columbia came in when the motion was

carried ; they assented to it at the time; it became in fact the
law of the land, and when they went home there was not a
word of reproach from the delegates of British Columbia. All
they wanted was that the spirit of the resolution should
be carried out so far as men could carry on honestly and
fairly, and straight-forwardly, a solemn compact, an obligatory
pledge, a treaty not to be broken without dishonour.

" Both Governments felt themselves bound to make every
exertion to build the railway by means of the intervention of
a body of capitalists incorporated for that purpose. As we
had tried, so did the succeeding Government, and they
advertised in a manner which has been stated and explained,
and I need not go through the details again. Advertisements
were issued by the honourable member for Lambton, then
head of the Government, telling capitalists all over the world
to come forward and tender for the work, but tenders would
not come in. Whether it was that Canada had not the credit
it now has ; whether it was that the Government of the day
had not the credit that the present Government of Canada
has ; whether it was that the circumstances of the money
market were unpropitious at the time ; whether it was that
the country in the North-West was not so well known then as
now, I cannot say. Perhaps all those causes were conjoined
to prevent success, but, at all events, the call upon the
capitalists of the world by the late Government did not
succeed.

. . . .

" The Government, I say, had every right to use all their
exertions in order to relieve themselves and the country of the
obligation of building this road and the still greater obligation
of running it. Let any one consider for a moment what these
obligations are, and how they press upon the Government.
We see this in the Intercolonial and in every public work.
Why, sir, it is actually impossible, although my honourable
friend has overcome many obstacles with regard to the Intercolonial Railway, for the Government to run that railroad
satisfactorily. It is made a political cause of complaint in
every way ; the men that are put on the railroad from the

porter upwards become civil servants. If one of these men are put on from any cause whatever, he is said to be a political hack ; if he is removed, it is said his removal was on account of his political opinions ; if a cow is killed on the road, a motion is made in respect to it by the member of the House who has the owner's vote and support. The responsibility, the expense, the worry and the annoyance of a Government having charge of such a work are such that, for these causes alone, it was considered advisable to get out of the responsibility. We have had enough evidence of that in this House,

" Well, sir, we went to England, and, though in England, we occasionally saw what was going on. The Opposition —oh, how frightened they were lest we should succeed, and cablegram after cablegram came to Canada, informing the country, with an expression of regret, that we had miserably and wretchedly failed ; then they said it was an evidence of want of confidence of the people of England in the present Administration. How could any body of capitalists put any confidence or trust in a Government stamped with the Pacific Railway scandal ? It was said that if it had been another Government, having greater confidence and greater purity of character, and greater ability, the result would be different. There were tears (crocodile tears, perhaps) dropped upon the unhappy fate of Canada in having such an incompetent and criminal Government that could, within nine years from the original transaction, carry out a beneficial arrangement by which it was proposed to endeavour to get English capitalists to take their place and build that road.

" However, sir, we did, and in the speech at Hochelaga that I hear so much about, a speech that can hardly be dignified by the name of speech, I announced the fact that we had made the contract. I say so now—we made the contract firm.

" The pledges made to British Columbia and the pledges made in reference to the future of this Dominion will be carried out under the auspices of a Conservative Government and with the support of a Conservative majority. (Applause). That road will be constructed, and notwithstanding all the wiles of the Opposition and the flimsy arrangement which has

been concocted, the road is going to be built, and will be
proceeded with vigorously, continuously, systematically, and
successfully to completion. And the fate of Canada will then,
as a Dominion, be sealed. Then will the fate of Canada, as
one great body, be fixed beyond the possibility of honourable
gentlemen to unsettle. The emigrant from Europe will find
here a happy and comfortable home in the great west, secured
by the exertion of the Conservative party. (Applause).
But then, sir, comes the interjection after the arrangements
have been made, and the Government had made a contract,
that honourable gentlemen opposite three or four years ago
would have leaped at and bragged and boasted of as a wonderful proof of their superior administrative ability ; we now
have the assertion that the contract was made without due
authority.

"We have had tragedy, comedy and farce from the other
side. (Laughter and applause). Sir, it commenced with
tragedy (hear, hear) ; the contract was declared oppressive ;
the amount of money to be given was enormous ; we were
giving away the whole lands of the North-West ; not an acre
was to be left for the free and independent foot of the free and
independent settler ; there was to be a monopoly handed over
to this company ; we had painted the tyranny of this company
that was to override the people by raising a high tariff, and
the tyranny of a great monopoly who was to keep in their
control a large area of lands, out of which they expect to
build this railway, for some hundreds of years, in order that,
through the exertions of others, the value of their acreage
might be increased. This was the tragedy (hear, hear), and
the honourable gentlemen opposite played it so well that
if they did not affect the whole audience, we could see tears of
pity trickling down the cheeks of gentlemen sitting on that
side of the House. (Laughter). Then, sir, we had the
comedy. The comedy was that when every one of the
speeches of these honourable gentlemen was read to them, it
was proved last year, or the year before, or in previous years,
they had thought one way, and that now they spoke in another
way. (Hear, hear). Then it was the most amusing and comic

thing in the world. Every honourable gentleman got up and
said, ' I am not bound by that (hear, hear) ; it is true that I
said so two years ago, but circumstances are changed in two
years or one year, or in eight months in one case, but to what
I said eight months ago I am not bound now. (Cheers and
laughter). This was very comic (laughter) ; it amused us all ;
it amused the House, and the whole country chuckled on
a broad grin. (Laughter). These honourable gentlemen said
it was true we were fools eight months ago and two years
ago, but because we were fools in the past, you have no right,
being Ministers, to be fools too ; you have no right to advocate the follies we advocated.

" The honourable gentlemen opposite have not hidden
their lights under a bushel ; their words have not been spoken
in a corner. We know the governing policy of the Opposition,
enumerated on several occasions, and repeated in this House
during the present session by the leader of the Opposition
(Mr. Blake) ; we know he is opposed to the building of the
road through British Columbia ; that he has, from the time
the subject was brought before Parliament, protested against
it, using such language to that province as ' Erring sister,
depart in peace ;' we know he has ridiculed the idea of forc-
ing a railroad through an inhospitable region of mountains,
that would get no traffic, but, built at enormous expense,
would be no real value. The honourable gentleman has
adhered to that policy. Last session he moved that the
further construction of the road through British Columbia, in
allusion to the contract given out by the present Government
under advertisements published by the late Government, and
for the purpose of carrying out its policy, be postponed, as
also all action with that object, and I expressed my regret at
the unavoidable absence of my honourable friend from Lambton on this occasion, but greatly as I regret that, I still more
greatly regretted his humiliation at the time last session when
the honourable gentleman's motion was in our hands. If I
were his worst enemy, and wished to triumph over him, I
would not desire a greater humiliation or tragic fate, or a more
wretched ending of a statesman than that, at the whip of the

man who had deposed him, or the man who had removed
and supplanted him, he should be obliged to eat his own
words and vote in favour of postponing the construction of the
road through British Columbia, that he should have to belie—
I use not the word in an offensive sense—his own advertisements and all action of the Government in asking for tenders
for his building of the road.

"What did this advertisement mean and the calling for
tenders? Was it a sham, a fraud? Assuming, like those who
did not know, that the honourable gentleman went down to
the depths of degradation to use that argument himself, and
say that he did not mean anything by that advertisement, but
really wished to ascertain the probable cost of the work,
because it was stated in this House that that was the object
of issuing advertisements, so that contractors were called upon
to come from not only all parts of the Dominion, but San
Francisco, the United States and the world, to consider this
matter, and they had to go over the whole ground with their
surveyors and engineers, make their surveys and estimates at
the greatest trouble and expense, in order to ascertain the
character of this work, and that the Canadian Government
might be able to say to them afterward, 'Gentlemen, we are
very much obliged to you for the information you have given
us, gathered at your expense and not at that of the public.'
Not one of the gentlemen of the late Government could have
done that, I am sure, or have said that the advertisement was
not *bona fide*, was not for the purpose of giving out work,
otherwise it was a mockery, a delusion and a snare, an injury
to every man put to expense in connection with it and to all
the professional men and capitalists of the world.

"The policy of the leader of the Opposition, as avowed
and expressed, his policy as a Minister would be to stop all
work in British Columbia; not a mile would be built, not a
train would ever run through British Columbia if he could
help it; not a particle of trade or commerce would pass over
a line through that province to the east if he had his will, and
that province would be compelled to appeal to the paramount
power, to the justice of the British Government and Parlia-

ment, where justice is always rendered, to relieve her from connection with a people so devoid of honour, so devoid of character, so unworthy of a place among the nations, and Her Majesty's Government would see that justice was done to that long suffering people. That was the policy of the leader of the Opposition with regard to the west. Now, his policy with regard to the east was hostile to the construction of the road north of Lake Superior. He avows his predilection for the Sault Ste. Marie line, to draw off trade into the United States, to strengthen, to renew, to extend and develop our commerce with the United States, to the utter destruction of the great plain basis and policy of the Dominion, which is to connect the great countries composing the Dominion from sea to sea, by one vast iron chain, which cannot, and will never be broken.

"That was the policy of the honourable gentleman, and it was supported and would be supported by the whole party. It was supported by their organ also. I do not often read it, for I do not think it very wholesome reading, but I am told it goes in strongly for the Sault Ste. Marie road, yet we all remember, for I have heard it read many a time, the manner in which that organ in days of old denounced the building of the Sault road as hazardous to the best interests of Canada, and destructive to the future of the Dominion, as calculated to unite us, willy-nilly, with the States by a commercial connection which must be followed by a political connection a little later, and I am told that organ strongly supports the honourable leader of the Opposition, just as strongly as some years ago it vigorously and in a loyal British sense opposed him. The same men do not govern that paper now, and if the chief man who conducted that paper was now living, I do not believe he would so belie his whole life and all his interests as to surrender a great connecting principle which, whatever might be the subjects of contention across the floor, kept him always united with the party of which I am an humble member, always united in defending British interests, in defending monarchical institutions, and in trying, as far as possible, to keep us a people free and independent of all exter-

nal relations with any country in the world except our grand
old mother country, England.

"Yes, I am proud to say that if our scheme is carried out,
the steamer landing at Halifax will discharge its freight and
emigrants upon a British railway, which will go through
Quebec and through Ontario to the far west on British
territory, under the British flag, under Canadian laws, and
without any chance of either the immigrant being deluded or
seduced away from his allegiance or his proposed residence in
Canada, or the traffic coming from England or from Asia
being subjected to the possible prohibition or offensive
restrictive taxation or customs regulations of a foreign
power.

"I believe that the men who signed the contract are men
of honour and great wealth, who cannot afford to lose their
character, prestige and credit in the markets of the world by
breaking a contract, but we felt we had no right to take their
word for it, and therefore stipulated in the contract that the
company should commence from the beginning of the Canadian Pacific line, possibly at Callendar station, and proceed
vigorously and in such a manner that the annual progress shall
secure completion at the end of ten years. You must remember that this is one contract and not a separate contract to
build the eastern or the central section ; it is a contract to
build both, and if the company fail in performing their contract, in carrying out their obligations as to the Lake Superior
road, they have no right to claim a subsidy in land or money
because of having done so much work on the prairie. If they
fail on one section, although they may have built twice the
number of miles that they promised across the prairies, may
have finished them to our thorough satisfaction, when they
come to demand the land and the money, if they have not
worked vigorously and continuously on the Lake Superior section, achieving a rate of annual progress, assuring us that it will
be finished within the proper time, then we shall say, 'No you
don't ; you shall not have this money ; no, you have built the
prairie section, but you have left other parts of the roads which
must go on *pari passu*, and we will not give you a dollar or an

acre, because, though you have done the full amount on the
prairies, you have been a failure, to a great extent, elsewhere.'

" We desire, the country desires that the road, when built,
should be a Canadian road, the main channel for Canadian
traffic, for the carriage of the treasure and traffic of the west
to the seaboard through Canada. So far as we can we shall
not allow it to be built for the benefit of the United States,
and our North-West drained by the United States lines.
Then, again starting from the foot of the Rocky Mountains,
perhaps one of the most fertile, if not the most fertile, section
lies directly at the eastern slope of the Rocky Mountains.
The freight from British Columbia for the east we desire to
keep on our own railroad as long as we legitimately can.
We believe it will carry freight as cheaply and satisfy the
wants of the country as fairly as any American railway. But,
sir, we desire to have the trade kept on our own side, that not
one of the trains that passes over the Canadian Pacific Railway will run into the United States if we can help it, but may
instead pass through our own country, that we may build up
Montreal, Quebec, Toronto, Halifax and St. John by means of
a great Canadian line, carrying as much traffic as possible by
the course of trade through our own country.

" I do not mean to say we can prevent cheaper channels
being opened. There is no way to prevent other railroads
running across the continent through our own country. Our
Dominion is as big as all Europe, and we might as well say
that the railways running from Paris to Moscow might supply
the wants of all Europe as that this railway might supply the
wants of the whole North-West. There will be room for as
many railways in that country by-and-bye as there are in
Europe, and if there should be any attempt—and the attempt
would be futile—on the part of the Canadian Pacific Railway
to impose excessive prices and rates, it would be folly, and would
soon be exposed by the construction of rival lines east and west,
which would open up our country in all directions, and prove
amply sufficient to prevent the possibility of a monopoly,
which has been made such a bugbear of by honourable gentlemen opposite. I was going to say that a train starting from

the foot of the Rocky Mountains might obtain connections by a line running through in a south-easterly direction with roads in the United States. I was going to say that a train starting from the foot of the Rocky Mountains might be bled by a line from any southerly direction connected with the United States, and so much traffic would be carried off to the United States, and a few miles farther another line might connect with another American line, and so on, sir, until long before we got to Winnipeg or the Red River, the main portion of the trade would be carried off from our line into American channels. That magnificent river, the Rhine, starting with pride from its source, runs through the finest portions of Europe, and yet has a miserable, wretched end, being lost in the sands as it approaches the sea ; and such would be the fate of the Canada Pacific Railway if we allowed it to be bled by subsidiary lines, feeding foreign railways, adding to foreign wealth, and increasing foreign revenue by carrying off our trade, until before we arrived at the terminal points in Ontario and at Montreal, it would be so depleted that it would almost die of inanition.

Mr. Blake—(Hear, hear).

Sir John Macdonald—" No men in their senses would undertake to build the 450 miles through that stern country to the north of Lake Superior, and run it for ten long years, unless they knew that there was some check placed upon these lines. Not a pound of freight would go from our North-West; it would almost all go to the United States. (Hear, hear). Some of it would come to us, but the great portion of the trade would go through the United States by the favoured line of honourable gentlemen opposite, without any hope of getting it back to Canada at the Sault Ste. Marie. (Hear, hear). Sir, we know what a great amount, what an enormous amount of capital American capitalists possess who are connected with the railways of the United States. We have seen evidences of the mad rivalry which has existed occasionally between some great railway lines of that country. You have seen them run railways at ruinous rates in the hopes of breaking each other down. Sir, with our road backed by a country of scarcely four millions, with our infant country and with our infant capitalists, what chance would they have against the whole of the United States capitalists? What chance would they have? The Americans would offer to carry freight for nothing and pay shippers for sending freight that way. It would not all come by the Sault Ste. Marie. It would come to Duluth. It would come to Chicago. It would come through a hundred different channels. It would percolate through the United States to New York and Boston, and to the other ports, and, sir, after our railway was proved to be useless, they might perhaps come into the market and buy up our line as they have bought up other lines. (Hear, hear).

" Railway and telegraph lines are under no protection from foreign capitalists coming in and buying them up, and getting control of our markets, and cutting us off from the trade which should come from the great west and by Canadian railways to the River St. Lawrence. (Hear, hear). They could afford for a series of years, with their enormous wealth, with their enormous capital, exceeding the revenue of many first-class Governments in Europe, to put their rates for freight down to such a figure as would ruin our road, as would ruin the contractors, as would ruin the company and render it utterly impossible for them to continue in competition. And, sir, what can be more wretched or more miserable in any country than an insolvent railway. (Hear, hear). What could be more wretched and miserable, and destructive to the future of a country than the offering on the market of the stock of an insolvent railway. (Hear, hear). They cannot supply or renew the rails ; they cannot maintain the road-bed in repair ; they cannot keep the line supplied with railway stock. Sir, the road would become shrunken, shrunken, shrunken until it fell an easy prey to this ring. (Hear, hear.) We cannot afford to run such a risk. (Cheers). We saw what a wheat ring did in Chicago. They raised the price of the necessaries of life. The ring in Chicago raised the price of the poor man's loaf for a whole year in order to make a profit at the expense of the labouring poor of Europe and of all the rest of the world ; and a similar combination, but infinitely richer, with infinitely more capital, and infinitely more unscrupulous—and no men are so unscrupulous, and so reckless as the railway speculators and proprietors in the United States—would be formed in this case. (Applause).

" It was essentially as a matter of precaution and a matter of necessity, and a matter of self-defence, that we provided that this road should not be depleted of this traffic in the manner in which I have mentioned (cheers), and that the road should be allowed fair play for twenty years from now, and only ten years after construction (hear, hear, and cheers), and that it should be protected from the chance of being robbed of all the profits, robbed of all the gain, the legitimate gain which the company expects to get from this enterprise and the employment of their capital. (Cheers). This was done only to protect them for the first ten years of their infant traffic. (Applause). We know perfectly well it will take many years before that country is filled up with a large population, and that the first ten years will be most unprofitable. We know perfectly well that it will require all the exertion, and all the skill, and all the management of the company to make the eastern and western sections of this road fully compensate them, and fully compensate them for their responsibility and for their expenditure during these ten years. In order to give them a chance we have provided that the Dominion Parliament—mind you the Dominion Parliament, we cannot check any other Parliament ; we cannot check Ontario ; we cannot check Manitoba—shall, for the first ten years after the construction of the road, give their own road, into which they are putting so much money and so much land, a fair chance of existence.

" I know we can appeal to our countrymen. I know we can appeal to the patriotism of the people of Canada. We can tell them that we want a line that will connect Halifax with the Pacific ocean. We can tell them, even from the mouths of our enemies, that out of our lands we can pay off every single farthing, every cent taken out of the pockets of the people twenty fold, and we will have a great Pacific railway. This is what we will have. . . Mr. Speaker, the whole thing is an attempt to destroy the Pacific railway. . ''

The Government policy was supported by the House, the Act passed its third reading on February 14th, and received the Royal assent the following day.

Of the men who undertook the contract to build the Canadian Pacific Railway, those with whom we are most familiar are Lord Mount-Stephen, Mr. R. B. Angus, Mr. Duncan McIntyre and Sir Donald Smith.

Of these, Lord Mount-Stephen is a fellow-townsman of Thomas Carlyle, being a native of Dufftown, Banffshire, Scotland. He early displayed the ability and enterprise which have always characterized him as a man, and, dissatisfied with the narrow sphere afforded him in his native place, he went to London, where he entered the service of the great mercantile house of J. F. Pawson & Co., St. Paul's Churchyard. He came to Canada in the spring of 1850, at the instance of his cousin, the late Mr. William Stephen, senior member of the firm of W. Stephen & Co., St. Helen Street, Montreal, the predecessors of the present firm of Robertson, Linton & Co.

On the death of the head of the firm, in 1862, he purchased the latter's interest from his heirs, and after obtaining control of the business, entered extensively into the manufacture of Canadian tweeds and other stuffs. In this venture he succeeded so well that he soon withdrew from the wholesale business and devoted his attention exclusively to manufacturing. He became one of the directors of the Bank of Montreal, and when the late David Torrance died, he became President of the bank.

His railway operations have made his name familiar to Canadians. He formed one of a syndicate to purchase the interest of the Dutch bond-holders in the St. Paul and Pacific Railway, which was then projected to St. Vincent and partially constructed. Foreseeing the surpassing importance of this line, when connection should be established with the Canadian North-West by means of the Pembina branch of the Canadian Pacific, Mr. Stephen and his associates resolved to obtain possession of it, and were fortunate in being able to do so by purchasing at a heavy discount the bonds of the road. They at once pushed on the work of construction, and were soon in a position to enjoy an absolute monopoly of railway traffic, not only in the North-West of Canada, but also into a large area of Minnesota and Dakota. Their success enabled them to go on constructing their projected lines in various directions through the above-named States, so that they soon had a regular net-work of roads collecting the traffic of the North-West and pouring it into St. Paul. With an eye to the fitness of things they named their line the St. Paul and Manitoba Railway, for, until the completion of the C. P. R., it was the only winter outlet for the traffic of the Canadian North-West.

Lord Mount-Stephen is one of the most popular and kind-hearted men in the Dominion, and has given away immense sums of money to charitable and other deserving objects. In 1885 he joined his cousin, Sir Donald A. Smith, in founding in the Royal College of Music, London, the " Montreal Scholarship," tenable for three years, and open to the residents of Montreal and its neighbourhood.

Two years later the same gentlemen contributed the magnificent sum of $1,000,000 ($500,000 each), to build, at Montreal, a new hospital to be called the Victoria Hospital. In 1886 Her Majesty, the Queen, created him a baronet, in recognition of his great services in connection with the Canadian Pacific Railway, and in 1891 he was raised to the peerage, under the title of Lord Mount-Stephen. His adopted daughter was married to the son of Sir Stafford Northcote during the sittings of the Joint High Commission, which negotiated the Treaty of Washington, and, of which young Mr. Northcote was an *attaché*.

Sir Donald A. Smith was born and educated in Morayshire, Scotland. At an early age he went into the employment of the Hudson's Bay Company and remained there for many years, rising through all the grades of the service, until in 1888, he was elected governor of the corporation. He married Isabella, daughter of the late Richard Hardisty, one of the officers of the Company, and who had formerly been in the British Army. When the North-West Territories were purchased by the Canadian Government, they appointed the Honourable William McDougall as the first Lieutenant-Governor, but, on arriving at the boundary line, he was prevented by an armed force from proceeding farther, and was obliged to return to Ottawa. Sir Donald Smith was appointed a Special Commissioner to enquire into the causes of this obstruction, on account of his intimate knowledge of the country and the confidence reposed in him by the inhabitants as the result of his many years of intimate connection with them. In 1870 he was appointed a member of the Executive Council of the North-West Territories. He represented Winnipeg and St. John in the Manitoba Assembly, from the first meeting of that body in 1871 until January, 1874. When Manitoba was admitted to the Union in 1871, Sir Donald Smith was returned to the House of Commons as member for Selkirk. He was re-elected in 1872, 1874 and 1878, but the latter election was voided. In 1887 he was elected for Montreal West, and again in 1891. He is President of the Bank of Montreal and a Director of the Canadian Pacific Railway. For services in connection with this great national undertaking he was created a K.C.M.G. Sir Donald is one of the most liberal of our public men, and by a wise beneficence has done a world of good with his wealth. In his more munificent gifts he has been associated with his cousin Lord Mount-Stephen.

Mr. Duncan McIntyre was born in the Highlands of Scotland, not far north of Aberdeen. He came to Canada in 1849, and was a clerk for many years with Stewart & McIntyre, a well-known mercantile firm of Montreal. While in their employ he travelled a good deal in the Ottawa Valley, and thus became deeply impressed with its great natural advantages. He purchased a farm at Renfrew, on which some members of his family resided, and during leisure intervals Mr. McIntyre was wont, in company with business friends, to indulge in hunting excursions in various parts of the Ottawa district. In this way he acquired a minute knowledge of the topography of the country traversed by the Canada Central Railway, a work in which Mr. McIntyre learned to take a deep interest, and in the future of which he believed. Mr.

McIntyre, retired from mercantile business, after a very successful career of some eighteen years. The principals of the house with which he was connected, Messrs. Stuart & McIntyre, had retired some time previously, each withdrawing a considerable sum as his share, and leaving Mr. Duncan McIntyre to emulate their success. In the course of his trips up the Ottawa Valley he made the acquaintance of Mr. Foster, who was then President of the Canada Central, and soon became one of the directors. When Mr. Foster secured the contract for the construction of the Canada Central Extension, Mr. McIntyre took an interest in it along with him, and as the result of a succession of transactions and changes he came to the head of the road, and by repute, its virtual owner.

Mr. Robert B. Angus was born at Bathgate, near Edinburgh, Scotland, and was one of four exceedingly clever brothers ; with them he received his education in the Edinburgh schools, and seems to have made excellent use of his training. He left his native land when quite a lad, and was for a time employed in one of the Manchester banks. He came to this country in 1852 and entered the British Bank, where he remained a comparatively short time, accepting the post of a junior clerk in the Bank of Montreal. He continued to rise in the estimation of his employers, and was afterwards sent to Chicago to administer the affairs of the branch in that city. Mr. King, shortly after his accession to the position of General Manager, secured for Mr. Angus the post of Assistant-Manager, and when Mr. King became President, Mr. Angus was appointed General Manager in his place, a position he held until he went into the St. Paul and Manitoba Railway business. Mr. Angus, though a strict and keen man of business, is possessed of fine social qualities and has made himself very popular with all classes. As manager of a large monetary institution it was his duty to look strictly after its funds, and no man could do this better, but as a private citizen he was always very liberal.

Mr. William Cornelius Van Horne, the President of the Canadian Pacific Railway was born in Will County,

Illinois, February 3, 1843, and is of Dutch descent, springing from the old Knickerbocker stock. He commenced his railway career in 1856 as a telegraph operator in the office of the Illinois Central Railroad at Chicago, and afterwards, until 1864, served in various capacities on the Michigan Central railroad. From 1864 to 1872 he was connected with the Chicago and Alton Railway, filling successively the positions of train despatcher, superintendent of telegraphs, and divisional superintendent. In 1872 he became General Superintendent of the St. Louis, Kansas City and Northern Railway, and, in 1874, General Manager of the Southern Minnesota Railway, and in 1877 President of the Company. In October, 1878, he returned to the Chicago and Alton Railway as General Superintendent, but continued, until 1879, to hold the office of President of the Southern Minnesota Railway. In January, 1880, he became General Superintendent of the Chicago, Milwaukee and St. Paul Railway, resigning this office at the end of 1881, to become General Manager of the Canadian Pacific Railway, the construction of which, by the company, had recently been commenced. In 1884 he became Vice-President of the company, and in 1888, on the retirement of Sir George Stephen (now Lord Mount-Stephen) he was elected President, in which office he has since continued.

The phenomenal rate at which the road was constructed is largely due to his skill, indomitable perseverance and pluck. The Bill which gave effect to the contract received the royal assent, February 15, 1881, and ten years were given for the construction, but such was the energy with which the work was pushed forward that the last spike was driven by Sir Donald Smith at Eagle Pass on November 7, 1885, a record in railroad building which has never been equalled or even approached in any part of the world.

As an instance of the vigour shown in the construction of this great undertaking we may mention that in the year 1883 the extraordinary number of 918 miles was built, the average quantity of track laid in crossing the prairies being three and a-half miles per day, and, on two days, the astounding distance of over six miles per day was laid, the track being made from one end only, and being fully tied and spiked, the rails being laid continuously, and in no case drawn ahead by teams. The next two years the construction was proceeded with, with the same untiring energy, and the whole road was fully ballasted and ready for passenger traffic early in 1886. On June 28th of that year the first through train left Montreal for Vancouver, and on July 9th Sir John Macdonald realized the dream of his ambition by starting on a journey to the Pacific coast on the completed Canadian Pacific Railway.

Since its opening the line has been operated with so much ability, carefulness and attention to the wants of its patrons, that it has completely won the confidence of the travelling and commercial community.

But the energies of the company were not confined to the mere fulfilment of its contract with the Government. Much more was done in order that the railway might fully serve its purpose as a commercial enterprise. Independent connections with the Atlantic sea-board were secured by the purchase of lines leading eastward to Montreal and Quebec ; branch lines to the chief centres of trade in eastern Canada were provided by purchase and construction, to collect and distribute the traffic of the main line ; and other branch lines were built in the North-West for the development of the great prairies.

The close of 1885 found the company, not yet five years old, in possession of no less than 4,315 miles of railway including the longest continuous line in the world, extending from Quebec and Montreal all the way across the continent to the Pacific Ocean, a distance of 3,050 miles ; and by the midsummer of 1886 all this vast system was fully equipped and fairly working throughout. Villages and towns, and even cities followed close upon the heels of the line-builders ; the forests were cleared away, the prairie's soil was turned over, mines were opened, and even before the last rail was in place the completed sections were carrying a large and profitable traffic. The touch of this young giant of the north was felt upon the world's commerce almost before its existence was known ; and, not content with the trade of the golden shores of the Pacific from California to Alaska, its arms at once

reached out across that broad ocean and grasped the teas and silks of China and Japan to exchange them for the fabrics of Europe and North America.

The next three years were marked by an enormous development of traffic and by the addition of 800 more miles of railway to the company's system.   One line was extended eastward from Montreal across the State of Maine to a connection with the railway system of the Maritime Provinces of Canada, affording connections with the seaports of Halifax and St. John ; another was completed from Sudbury, on the company's main line, to Sault Ste. Marie, at the outlet of Lake Superior, where a long steel bridge carries the railway across to a connection with the two important American lines leading westward—one to St. Paul and Minneapolis and thence continuing across Dakota, the other through the numberless iron mines of the Marquette and Gogebic districts to Duluth, at the western extremity of Lake Superior ; still another, the latest built, continues the company's lines westward from Toronto to Detroit, connecting there with lines to Chicago, St. Louis, and all of the great Mississippi Valley.   And now, the company's lines spread out towards the west like the fingers of a gigantic hand, and the question " Will it pay ? " is answered with earnings for the past year of sixteen and a-half million dollars, and profits of six and a-quarter millions.

Canada's iron girdle has given a magnetic impulse to her fields, her mines, and her manufactories, and the modest colony of yesterday is to-day an energetic nation with great plans and hopes and aspirations.

PARLIAMENT was dissolved on May 18, 1882, and writs issued for a new election, returnable August 7th. The result proved that the policy pursued by the Government met the approval of the country, for they were again returned to power with a large body of supporters. The losses on the Opposition side were very heavy, some of their best men being defeated. The most prominent of these were Sir Richard Cartwright, Sir A. T. Smith, and Messrs. Huntingdon, Mills, Anglin, D. A. Macdonald, A. G. Jones, R. Laflamme and D. Laird.

On October 8, 1884, Sir John Macdonald sailed for England. He had not been well for some time and desired to avail himself of the skill of Sir Andrew Clarke, under whose care he had been on previous occasions. During his visit he received a great deal of attention and many honours. From November 22nd to 24th he was the guest of the Prince of Wales at Sandringham. On the latter date he was entertained at dinner by the Beaconsfield Club, the chair being taken by Sir Stafford Northcote. In the course of his speech the latter made the following appreciative remarks : " If the progress of Canada had been as great as it undoubtedly had been during the last forty years, if Canada now held so high a position in the estimation of the world, if the difficulties which from time to time had arisen in the development and organization of the great Canadian community had been so successfully overcome, there was one man to whom, above all others, that great progress was owing, and that man was Sir John Macdonald."

On the following day Sir John went to Windsor Castle accompanied by Mr. and Mrs. Gladstone, the Earl of Derby and Sir John McNeil, and had the distinguished honour of dining with the Queen and the Royal Family. Afterwards Her Majesty conferred upon him the Grand Cross of the Bath and herself invested him with the riband and star of the Order. He remained at Windsor Castle that night as the guest of the Queen, and on the following day returned to London, where he was entertained at a dinner given in his honour at the Empire Club. The chair was taken by the Marquis of Lorne, and amongst the distinguished men present were the Marquis of Salisbury, the Duke of Sutherland, the Earl of Kimberley, Secretary of State for India ; the Earl of Derby, Secretary of State for the Colonies ; the Earl of Carnarvon, ex-Colonial Secretary ; the Marquis of Normanby, Viscount Bury, Mr. W. H. Smith, Sir Thomas Brassey, Sir Charles Tupper and Sir John Rose.

In proposing the toast of the evening, the Marquis of Lorne spoke of Sir John Macdonald as "the most successful statesman in one of the most successful of the younger nations of the world ; as a Minister whose characteristics are breadth of views and largeness of heart, and hoped that he might long be able to take his part in the public life which, for forty years, he had led, illustrated and adorned." In reply, Sir John Macdonald expressed his gratification at having his health proposed by Lord Lorne, an ex-Governor-General of Canada, and one who had not only ruled wisely and well, but had endeared himself to the whole population. He accepted the compliment paid him not merely as a personal one, but as a recognition of the importance of Canada as a part of the Empire. The people of Canada, without regard to politics or party, would be proud of the demonstration. He then referred in eloquent terms to the marvellous change which had taken place in the country since he had first entered public life in 1844, and gave a sketch of the history of Canada during those forty years. He described the present position and prospects of the Dominion, and concluded by expressing a warm hope for a closer alliance of all the colonies with the mother country.   Lord Salisbury also gave expression to his "admiration for the distinguished career and the personal character of our honoured guest, and said that he could express no warmer wish for Canada than that, in her long future, she may have many statesmen who will shed as much lustre on her history, and will confer as many benefits on her people, as Sir John Macdonald has done."

His visit to England, and the honours paid him, attracted a great deal of attention, and the newspapers spoke of him and his speeches in the highest terms, the London *Standard* pointing out that "in advancing Sir John Macdonald to the dignity of a G. C. B., Her Majesty had conferred upon him what, according to Lord Beaconsfield, was practically the highest meritorious distinction it was in the power of the Sovereign to bestow."

Sir John returned to Canada on December 9th, and found that his friends and admirers had made extensive arrangements to celebrate in a fitting manner the conclusion of his fortieth year of public life.   Ten thousand delegates from the constituencies of Ontario were appointed to hold a Convention at Toronto on the 17th and 18th.   This Convention was held at the Grand Opera House, and the crowd was so great that hundreds were unable to obtain admission.   An address from those present was presented to Sir John, to which he made a reply that was received with great enthusiasm.   A Liberal-Conservative Association for the province was then formed, of which he was unanimously elected President, and Mr. W. R. Meredith, Vice-President.   In the evening a magnificent banquet was given in the Pavilion of the Horticultural Gardens, at which 1,200 persons sat down.   The speeches were numerous and interesting, and were listened to with great attention by a crowd of spectators, largely composed of ladies, who filled the galleries.

A similar demonstration took place in Montreal in the beginning of the new year—January 12 and 13, 1885.   The streets through which Sir John passed from the railway station were brilliantly illuminated.   Thousands of people with bands of music joined in the procession, and the respect and attachment felt towards him was testified by the vociferous cheering which greeted him along the whole route. On arrival at the drill hall, many addresses were presented to him, and speeches made by the leading men present. The next night a banquet was given him in the large dining-room of the Windsor Hotel, which was crowded to its utmost capacity. The speeches lasted until a late hour, the principal theme being the great services which the guest of the evening had rendered to his country, coupled with a hope that he might long be spared to guide the destinies of Canada.

Meanwhile the Marquis of Lorne had been succeeded as Governor-General by the Marquis of Lansdowne, who also bears the titles of Earl of Wycombe, Viscount Cain and Cainstine, Lord Wycombe, Baron of Chipping-Wycombe, Earl of Kerry and Earl of Shelburne, Viscount Clanmaurice and Fitzmaurice, Baron of Kerry, Lixnaw, and Dunkerron. He was born January 14, 1845, and succeeded to the title in 1866. He received his education at Eton and Balliol College, Oxford. In 1869 he married Lady Maud Evelyn Hamilton, youngest daughter of the first Duke of Abercorn. He was a Commissioner of the Exchequer of Great Britain, and of the Treasury of Ireland 1868-72; Under-Secretary of State for War 1872-74; and Under-Secretary for India 1880. He arrived in Canada on October 23, 1883, after a very stormy passage across the ocean. Addresses were presented to him to which he replied in a manner that charmed his hearers. The French were especially delighted by his replying to them in their own language, and remarked upon the purity of his accent. On the following day he proceeded to Ottawa. As, for many reasons, we are compelled to abstain from referring to the very pleasant subject of the acts and doings of our Governors since Confederation, we will now only add that after a sojourn in Canada of less than five years, Lord Lansdowne was called to the higher office of Viceroy of India. The news of his approaching departure was received with feelings of the deepest regret, and it was resolved to signify the appreciation felt of his efforts to promote the good of the country, and to testify to the warm feelings enter-

tained towards him and Lady Lansdowne, by a public entertainment.   This took place at the Russell House on May 15,
1888, and we give the proceedings as reported in the *Citizen* of
the following morning.   His speech on the occasion was
eloquent, practical and sympathetic, and his remarks respecting the Pacific railway, the Fisheries' question, the duties and
responsibilities of a Governor-General, Commercial Union with
the United States, and Imperial Federation, are worthy of the
most attentive perusal :

"When it was definitely announced that Lord Stanley of
Preston had been appointed to succeed Lord Lansdowne as
Governor-General of Canada, in consequence of the latter
having been chosen to succeed Lord Dufferin in the Governor-
Generalship of India, a general desire was expressed that His
Excellency should not be allowed to depart from Ottawa
without an opportunity being afforded of demonstrating to
him the high esteem in which he and the Marchioness of
Lansdowne are held by the citizens of the Capital of the
Dominion.   A meeting was called by His Worship the
Mayor for the purpose of considering the best means of
putting the public wish into practical shape, and it was finally
decided that a banquet should be tendered His Excellency,
which would afford him an opportunity of making a speech in
review of his administration of public affairs in the Dominion
during the last four and a-half years, and that, on the occasion
of his departure from the city, the popular sentiment should
find expression in a demonstrative display.   His Excellency
was pleased to intimate to the Mayor that a banquet would be
to him the most acceptable tribute of respect, as he was
desirous that his last public utterances in Canada should be
spoken in the city where he had spent the greater portion of
the time he has represented Her Majesty in the Dominion.

"The banquet took place at the Russell House and
proved in every respect an unqualified success.   It is safe
to say that it was the most brilliant and the most representative social entertainment ever witnessed in Ottawa.   The
chair was occupied by His Worship, the Mayor, and on his
right were His Excellency ; Sir Hector Langevin, Minister of

Public Works; Honourable Mackenzie Bowell, Minister of Customs; Honourable W. A. McLelan, Postmaster-General; Honourable John Costigan, Minister of Inland Revenue; Honourable J. A. Chapleau, Secretary of State; Honourable George E. Foster, Minister of Marine and Fisheries; Honourable G. W. Allan, Speaker of the Senate; Lieutenant-General Sir Fred Middleton, Sir Richard Cartwright, Honourable Mr. Justice Fournier, Honourable Wilfred Laurier, Honourable Alexander McFarlane, Honourable J. G. Ross, Honourable F. Clemow. On the left Right Honourable Sir John Macdonald, Premier and President of the Council; Honourable Sir Charles Tupper, Minister of Finance; Honourable Sir Adolphe Caron, Minister of Militia; Honourable Frank Smith; Honourable J. S. D. Thompson, Minister of Justice; Honourable J. J. C. Abbott; Honourable Sir William Ritchie, Chief Justice of the Supreme Court of Canada; Honourable William Macdougall, Honourable R. W. Scott, Honourable R. B. Dickey, Honourable Donald McInnes, Honourable Dr. Casgrain, the Honourable Speaker Ouimet, Sir James Grant, and the Honourable George A. Kirkpatrick. The vice chairs were occupied by Sheriff Sweetland and Mr. Charles Magee. Altogether about 240 gentlemen were present.

In proposing the toast of the evening the Mayor, Mr. McLeod Stewart said: "Gentlemen,—It is permitted to me to-night to discharge a most agreeable duty, one of the most agreeable of a lifetime, and that is to propose the health of our distinguished guest the Governor-General of Canada. (Cheers). Lord Lansdowne came to us four and a half years ago, with all the prestige of a noble lineage, and preceded by the reputation which always pertains to the cultured scholar and the distinguished statesman. He has proved himself a most able and constitutional representative of Her Majesty in this country. He has made for himself a most honourable record, and he now leaves us rich in the affections and dear to the hearts of the great mass of the Canadian people." (Cheers). Addressing the Governor-General, the Mayor said: "When Your Excellency reaches the shores of England, and you relinquish the great trust which has been confided to you, tell Her Majesty the Queen that the little Ottawa which she graciously designated as the seat of government has grown into a large and flourishing city. (Cheers). Tell her also that the little provinces which she joined together in one great confederation have grown into a mighty and prosperous Dominion, and tell Her Majesty further, that in no portion of her wide Dominions has she subjects more true, more loyal, and more patriotic to her throne than her own Canadian people. (Loud and repeated cheers). Of your estimable wife, Her Excellency Lady Lansdowne, I have nothing but the kindest words to say. By her rare sweetness of disposition, her charm of manner, and her kindness of heart, she has endeared herself to all with whom she has come in contact. (Tremendous cheering). The great regret we experience at Your Excellency's departure is also felt in a like degree for Her Excellency Lady Lansdowne. (Cheers). I am sure I voice the sentiments not only of the citizens of Ottawa, but also of the whole Dominion, when I say that it is the earnest desire and prayer of all of us that Divine Providence may grant to Your Excellency wisdom to your head, courage to your heart, and strength to your arm in administering the affairs of that great Orient Empire over which Her Majesty has called you to preside." (Loud and repeated cheers).

When His Excellency rose to respond, he was greeted with an outburst of wild enthusiasm. Cheer after cheer greeted him; handkerchiefs waved, and several minutes elapsed before the Governor-General could speak, so unbounded was the popular demonstration.

His Excellency said : " Mr. Mayor, Sir John Macdonald and Gentlemen,—You could have paid me no compliment greater or more acceptable than that of asking me to meet this brilliant company at dinner this evening. It is representative of all that is most distinguished and honourable in the society of the capital. I see around me the venerable Premier, who has for so many years been responsible for the conduct of your public affairs. (Cheers). I see his colleagues with whom I have been in constant official intercourse. I see distinguished members of the Privy Council, not of the Cabinet, but whose intimate acquaintance I have nevertheless had the honour of enjoying. (Renewed applause). I see representatives of both branches of the Legislature and of all the most important interests of your city, a city which we regard not only with the respect due to the capital of a great Dominion, but with the affection which nearly five years of constant intercourse has built up in our hearts. It is delightful to us at the close of our sojourn in this country to know that we have become bound to you by something more than official ties, and, sir, when you, speaking in the name of such a body of men as that which I see before me, and with their approval and concurrence, have thought fit to address me as you have addressed me to-night, I may indeed feel that if I have achieved nothing else, I can at least lay claim to that which has in my eyes an estimable value, I mean the sympathy and good will of those amongst whom the greater portion of my life in this country has been passed. And, sir, I never felt more in need of that sympathy than I do now. It is at the critical periods of one's life that the sympathy of friends is essential, and it is through such a period that we are now passing. I can assure you that, in spite of the brightness and exhilaration of the moment, in spite of all that hope, or if you like, ambition, can suggest, the feelings which are uppermost in our minds are those solemn and serious feelings which naturally arise when one is called upon to sever rudely the associations of years, and break with a past which has been peaceful, honourable and happy.

" Of the kind terms in which you have described the way in which I have discharged the duties belonging to my office I scarcely know how to speak. I fear your estimate is coloured by your personal friendship and by that indulgence which is always bestowed upon those who are departing, or who are about to depart from bodily or political life. (Cries of no! no!) A famous Frenchman who was listening to a somewhat superlative encomium passed upon a person who had joined the great majority, is said to have observed that he was ready to give him credit for all the good qualities which were being ascribed to him, '*Pourvu qu'il soit mort.*' (Applause and laughter). But, sir, I am no cynic at the best of times, and I am sure that what you have said has been said from the heart, and from my heart I thank you for your warm and friendly approval of my conduct during my residence amongst you. No one knows better than I do how much has been left undone, or might have been done better, during that time. If you are willing to give us credit for having done our best we shall be content. When I say 'we' I hope you will understand that I am not using the mediæval plural which is usually affected by royalty, but because in speaking of my relations with the people of Canada, and of my gratitude to you, I cannot separate Lady Lansdowne—(great applause)—from myself, and I feel quite sure that, although she is not present with us this evening, she appreciates as thoroughly as I do the significance and value of this mark of your good will. Let me add, too, that no one is better aware than I am of the extent of the assistance which I have received from her and from my small but willing and indefatigable staff. (Loud applause).

And, sir, if my personal and private experience of Canada has been entirely fortunate, I think I may add that I have no reason for complaining of my experience of the public affairs of the country. The years which I have spent in your country have been upon the whole years of peaceful progress—years during which the reputation of your country has advanced, during which it has progressed in arts and manufactures, in education, and in all the conditions essential to the well-being of a great and prosperous community. If you have shared the vicissitudes of fortune which have afflicted other countries you have in my judgment suffered less from them than other nations. If there has been here and there a slight creaking in the machinery of your Constitution, we may, I think, nevertheless venture to say that the structure of Federation has on the whole stood the test pretty well, and that it will, with a little watchfulness, continue to do so. (Applause).

" Upon the other hand, I am far from saying that my term of office has been an uneventful one. I could mention several events, any one of which would in itself be sufficient to mark an epoch in your history. We had, in 1885, that most untoward rebellion in the North-West Territories, to which I will only refer for the purpose of making this observation, that while I believe that any feelings of local irritation, or more wide-spread race antagonism which it may have provoked at the time, will disappear completely, if they have not already done so, there will survive in the recollection of your people, long after the present generation has passed away, the memory of the manner in which your military forces, drawn from all portions of the Dominion, responded to the call which was then made upon them, and of the cheerfulness and gallantry with which they acquitted themselves during a trying and arduous campaign. (Renewed applause).

"While it is impossible to refer to these events without feelings in which pride is mingled with regret, we can recur with unmixed satisfaction to the great national achievement, the great peaceful victory which marked the following year. I mean the completion of the national highway, by which you have united the two oceans which wash the coast of British North America. That achievement is one which stands alone among the great national enterprises which the world has known, both in respect of the physical difficulties which it was necessary to overcome, and in respect of the rapidity and success with which the work was completed. The work is not only one which has fundamentally affected the relations of the different parts of the Dominion to each other, but it has affected those of the Dominion, as a whole, to the mother country and to the Empire, and I am glad to find that it is universally regarded as a most important contribution made by Canada to the strength of the Empire as a whole. (Loud applause). We cannot at present foresee the full extent of the consequences, political and economical, which are likely to accrue to us from its completion. The full results of such an improvement in the arterial communications of the Empire do not make themselves felt all at once. A great arterial road is not complete merely because an engine can run across it from end to end. Although the line has been now open for traffic for upwards of two years, we have yet to see its effects upon the general prosperity of the country when its equipment shall have been completed, its connections made good and developed, and its ocean communications with other parts of the Empire placed, as I hope they soon will be, upon a thoroughly satisfactory footing. (Applause).

" I pass from these to a more recent event, and one upon which I confess I am disposed to dwell with equal pleasure. I mean the attempt which has been lately made to remove the only formidable source of disagreement which has, for many years past, existed between ourselves and the great republic which adjoins us. I have never been one of those who believed that our dispute with the Government of the United States in regard to our fisheries, was one which was likely to lead to a breach of the peace, or to prove in the end, incapable of solution. But, sir, the mere existence of such a dispute, embittering, as it did, our relations with our neighbours, endangering the harmony which ought to unite the whole British race on this continent, and affording a pretext to those who desired to stir up strife between the two powers was a calamity and a scandal to ourselves and to the whole world. (Applause). It is quite true that the final adjustment of these difficulties has not yet taken place. Whether they will be adjusted or not, and if so, what time, does not now depend upon us, but I will take upon myself, to say this, that even if the adjustment be indefinitely postponed, the whole complexion of the question has been radically altered by the negotiations which took place at Washington during the past winter, and by the treaty, ratified or unratified, in which they resulted. Six months ago the positions taken by the Government of the United States on the one hand, and by the Imperial Government and that of the Dominion on the other, appeared to be irreconcilable. As things stand at present, there is, as far as I am aware, no material difference of opinion between the three. Whatever be the action of those with whom the fate of the treaty at present rests, no miscarriage which we can now apprehend can possibly put matters back where they where before the meeting of the plenipotentiaries. (Applause).

" I rejoice to think that in the seventy years which have passed since the Treaty of 1818 was framed our relations with our kinsmen on the other side of the border have undergone a gradual and steady amendment. There is a legend that early in the present century a Colonial Secretary advised the people of Canada to plant a belt of forest trees all along the frontier of the United States in order to keep Canada separate from that unruly people, and ' pure from republican contamination.' (Laughter). That is not, I am happy to say, the policy of the present day. Of all the blessings enjoyed by the dwellers on this continent none is greater than their freedom from the dangerous rivalries and complications such as those which are, at this moment, paralysing industry and retarding prosperity on the continent of Europe. I trust it may be reserved to my successor to see the last shreds of this dispute which we have done our utmost to remove, swept away forever, leaving to us nothing but the frank, generous, and cordial understanding which should unite the English-speaking race upon this continent. (Great applause).

" And now, gentlemen, if I have ventured to mention these matters, I have done so not because I sought to leave on your minds, or on the minds of anyone, the impression that I desired to take any credit to myself in connection with the satisfactory results which have, I believe, in each case been arrived at. It is said that a great English personage, by dint of talking about the battle of Waterloo, succeeded in persuading himself that he had taken part in that engagement. (Laughter). If I live long enough I shall, perhaps, persuade myself that I was in command at Batoche, that I discovered Roger's Pass, and that I took part as a plenipotentiary in the negotiation of the Washington Treaty. (Great laughter). At present, in order to avoid misconceptions, let me state that I am under the impression that my friend Sir Frederick Middleton had the conduct of the North-West campaign (loud applause), that I was not even so fortunate as to drive the last spike of the Canadian Pacific Railway, and that although I certainly sat by Sir Charles Tupper, in spirit, during the Washington negotiations, I am glad to have this opportunity

of bearing witness to the fact that whatever credit is due for
their results belongs to him and to the distinguished British
statesman, who, when the history of these negotiations comes
to be more fully known, will be found to have watched your
interests with an amount of tact and assiduity and determination, which I will venture to say could not have been
exceeded if he had been born within the sound of the Chaud-
iere Falls. (Great applause).

"But, sir, while I wish to disclaim any attempt at obtaining for myself any portion of the credit which belongs to
others, in respect of these events, and while I have never shut
my eyes to the fact that the representative of the Crown, in a
self-governing colony, occupies a position differing very widely
from that of the Governor of a Crown colony, I am, on the
other hand, very glad to find that you are not among those
who have regarded his duties as being of a purely formal
character, and consisting merely in the dispensation of a
certain amount of hospitality, and in the delivery of occasional
speeches bearing a strong family resemblance to each other,
and containing, I am afraid, a good many commonplaces
which must sound wearisome in the ears of those who are
habituated to the more pungent utterances of political discussion. (Laughter and applause). I shall not admit, and I hope
you will not do so either, that a constitutional Governor is one
who does nothing at all. (Hear, hear, and applause). So far
from holding that opinion, I should be myself inclined to say
that while a great colony like yours continues to form a part
of the Imperial system, and I do not see much sign of weariness of that connection on your side or on ours (great
applause), you could not have a much more convenient or
useful connection with the mother country than the office of
Governor-General as it is now constituted. The person who
fills it has altogether exceptional opportunities of serving the
interests both of the mother country and of the colony. He
can have one eye behind the scenes in Downing street, and
another in the Dominion. (Hear, hear). His opportunities
for effecting a good understanding between the two are very
great. My own experience is that, if differences arise, they

arise in nine cases out of ten, from ignorance or misunderstanding of the real position of affairs on one side or the other. You should have in your Governor-General one who is able to speak with equal frankness and with equal knowledge of what he is talking about to either side, and to make it aware of the real requirements and situation of the other. (Loud applause). Holding as I do these opinions, it is most satisfactory to me to find that your verdict is not unfavourable to my conduct.

"It has been my earnest wish during the last four years to co-operate with the members of the Canadian Government in the promotion of whatever measures were most likely to conduce to the general prosperity and well-being of the Dominion, and to leave nothing undone in order to ensure a feeling of mutual confidence and good will between your Government and that of the Queen. I rejoice to think that such a feeling exists at the present time, not only between the Governments of the two countries but between their peoples. I do not believe the general tone of public feeling ever was sounder or more friendly. (Renewed applause). That feeling is, moreover, something more than a mere spurious patriotism which takes refuge in vague and general professions of good-will, but evaporates in the face of the first breath of opposition. The spirit which animates it is eminently thoughtful, independent and critical. (Hear, hear). It takes very little for granted. It is not ready to say that a particular state of things must be satisfactory because it has always existed. It is, on the contrary, disposed to place existing institutions on their trial, and to discuss with the utmost frankness questions which, in days of less intellectual and political activity, would have been gladly shirked and put on one side. Nothing, for instance, has struck me more than the intelligence and ability with which that great group of questions which are involved in the relation of the Colonies and the Empire has been discussed in this country during the last year or two. The public controversies which have taken place upon the political and economical relations of the different parts of the Empire have been of extraordinary interest and have this great advantage, that whether we are on the eve of great changes or whether we may look forward to a long continuance of our present system, whether we find ourselves led in the direction of a closer approximation between the different parts of the Empire or, on the contrary, in the direction of a further emancipation from the already slight ties by which the different parts of the Empire are united, the community is being day by day instructed in regard to these matters, and will, if it is called upon to act, at all events, have no excuse for acting ignorantly and without a full knowledge of the consequences involved. (Applause).

" It would be little short of an outrage if on an occasion like the present, I were to attempt a discussion of questions such as those to which I have referred. I will, however, so far presume upon the indulgence to which a departing friend is entitled, to make one general observation with regard to the standpoint from which they should be approached, that observation is this, that in dealing with problems of this kind, the ultimate factor with which we have to reckon is the public sentiment of two great democratic communities. (Applause). It was once said by President Lincoln, with great truth, that with public sentiment nothing can fail, and that without it nothing can succeed, and that he who moulds sentiment goes deeper than he who enacts statutes. (Loud applause). The influence of sentiment is one which grows every day, which grows at the expense of hard logic and inexorable political economy. (Hear, hear). Before the days of household suffrage, of cheap newspapers and sixpenny telegrams, public questions were disposed of by statesman philosophically, judicially, secretly in their studies or their council chambers. They are now, in nineteen out of twenty cases, virtually disposed of on the platform or in the press. (Hear, hear). I will not now enquire whether the change is one for the better, but it is one with which we have to count. When, therefore, we propose grave and far-reaching changes of policy, involving the future destinies of nations, we cannot bear this change too strongly in mind.

" Will you let me illustrate my meaning by referring to the suggestions which are from time to time made for the establishment of closer and exclusive commercial relations between the Dominion and the great Republic which adjoins us—proposals which are made upon the assumption that in spite of the preference thus given to the latter our allegiance to the mother country is to remain unimpaired, and that her liability to make her cause our own is to stand exactly where it does now. In such cases I confess that the question which I ask myself is not whether such an arrangement would be advantageous to Canada or not, nor what are the motives of those by whom it is proposed. I am content to assume, if you please, that the change considered by itself might be financially a desirable one, and I am willing to give credit to those by whom such proposals are advocated for being every whit as loyal as I am myself. (Hear, hear). I own, however, that I am not without the most serious misgivings when I ask myself whether the public sentiment of the British democracy would stand the strain which the adoption of such a policy by the Dominion would place upon it, and whether it would not be likely to consider the extent, not so much of the material injury which it would be likely to sustain, but of the moral affront to which it was called upon to submit. (Applause).

" I am tempted again to apply a similar test when I am asked what I think of proposals of a very different kind, and leading us in an entirely opposite direction, such as those which are recommended, with the object of establishing between the different parts of the Empire relations, political and commercial, much more intimate and uniform than those which exist between them at the present time. The objects of those by whom such proposals are made, have my warmest sympathy, but, sir, having I suppose a little Scotch blood in my veins, and being therefore of a cautious temperament, I pause and ask myself whether in endeavouring to improve the condition of things, we might not find ourselves again outstripping the public sentiment of the communities concerned and expose their allegiance to a strain greater than it can bear. (Applause). Let me say frankly that, in my opinion, public sentiment in the great possessions of the Crown would be exposed to such a strain if the self-governing colonies were ever to be required to part with any material portion of the freedom which they now enjoy in the management of their own affairs. I have the honour of a pretty close acquaintance with a considerable number of your legislators here, and I will venture to say that there is no feeling stronger in their minds, and in that of their constituents, than the feeling that in purely Canadian affairs the Constitution recognizes the absolute supremacy of the Canadian Parliament. (Loud applause). Now, I do not believe that public sentiment here would tolerate any change depriving it of that authority, or transferring any portion of it to, let us say, an Imperial Chamber sitting at Westminster. You might send your best men to it, but before they had been there six months they would find that the real power remained where it was before, namely, within the Parliament Buildings at Ottawa. (Hear, hear and applause). I would ask you for a moment to consider how the policy of centralizing Imperial business at Westminster would work if you were to push it too hard.

" Take, for example, a great question which is now engaging the attention of the public, and Her Majesty's Government at home, I mean the question of our Imperial defences. There is, I think, room for a great deal of improvement in the existing condition of things. There is no reason why the Governments of the great colonies and the United Kingdom should not agree before hand what measures are to be taken by the military and naval forces at their disposal for the protection of different portions of our Imperial possessions. (Hear, hear). The Australian colonies have lately commenced a very useful movement in this direction by providing themselves with a small naval force of their own, which would under a pre-arranged system co-operate with the Royal Navy in Australian waters. The part to be taken by the British and Colonial forces, respectively, in manning the different positions might, with great advantage, be determined, and there are many other steps of the same sort which will readily suggest themselves to you. But if we are to go further than this and to have a covenant binding, let us say, this country to place a certain number of men at the absolute disposal of the Imperial

Government whenever it is called upon, I say frankly that I do not believe that such an arrangement would work. (Applause). If the safety of the Empire was menaced, and if the people of this country felt that our cause was a just one, you would not choose that moment, when the Empire was in peril, to repudiate your relationship, or to avoid your share in resisting the attack. (Tremendous applause). In such circumstances, I would sooner trust to the spontaneous action of Canada to give me 50,000 men than trust to getting a couple of regiments because you were under a hard and fast bargain compelling you to supply them. (Renewed applause).

"Or, again let us suppose an experiment of the same kind to be tried in regard to the fiscal system of the Empire. I have said the fiscal system of the Empire, but there is no such thing. The fiscal arrangements of the possessions of the British Crown are, at present, chaotic. You have colonies which are free traders, and colonies which are protectionist; you have colonies with *ad valorem* duties, and colonies with specific duties; you have British possessions like India, with only seven articles in its tariff list, and you have possessions like Canada, with a list of four hundred and fifty. Let us suppose that you are going to try your hand at the introduction of a uniform system. You will have two tremendous obstacles to encounter. In the first place, if you are going to propose that the parts of the British Empire shall join hands and adopt a common tariff against other nations, you will have to convince the people of Great Britain that you are not going to lead them into a morass. The United Kingdom does, roughly speaking, at present three-fourths of its trade with foreign countries, and one-fourth with British possessions. Self-preservation is a pretty strong instinct in commercial circles at home, as it is in Canada, and you will find that not a few of our friends will hesitate to disturb the three-fourths of their business which they do with the foreigner on the chance of making the remaining quarter a little larger than it is now. (Hear, hear).

"The case is still stronger if you go into details. It is a matter of life and death to them. Take the great commodity of wheat. Why should not Great Britain admit wheat from the North-West duty free, and tax that coming from foreign countres ? Now, Great Britain only grows one-third of the wheat required for her own consumption ; of the remaining two-thirds she takes every year from foreign countries three-fourths, and the remaining one-fourth from British possessions. From this country it takes only about three per cent. of the whole. We should, I am afraid, find some difficulty in convincing the public sentiment of Great Britain that we should venture to tamper with the larger share of those supplies, and probably increase the cost of every bushel sold in Great Britain for many years to come, for the sake of doing a good turn to those who are at present able to supply us only with a fraction of our requirements. (Hear, hear).

" That is the first obstacle ; let us assume that it has been overcome. There follows an even more formidable assumption, namely, that we have been able to devise a system adjusted so ingeniously as to suit the mother country as well as her possessions on this continent, in Australasia, in Africa and in British India. If you take the trouble to compare the existing tariffs, and if you will remember that these represent the decided preferences of the different communities concerned, you will see what a tremendous assumption that is. But there is worse to come. You have got the whole of the British colonies into line. Are you sure they will stay there ? We all know that there is no such thing as finality in these fiscal arrangements. Circumstances alter, new discoveries are made, new trade communications and connections arise, and your imperial tariff will stand in need of revision and adjustment to circumstances as they alter from time to time. Who is to make this alteration ? We must have an Imperial Council, which might in itself be, no doubt, a very admirable thing. When I look around these tables I feel inclined to submit a list of Canadian representatives which would take away Lord Rosebery's breath, and stagger Lord Dunraven. (Laughter). But of this I am convinced, that the public sentiment of the Canadian people would not permit such an assembly to tamper with what would be regarded here as the

domestic business of the Canadian Parliament. (Loud applause). It would be almost possible to draw in our imagination a humorous picture of the return of the Canadian delegates to their own country after the adjournment of the Imperial Council. They might find themselves in the painful position of having to report that the duties upon some articles in which you were largely interested here, some carefully reared offspring of the Canadian tariff, had been removed or reduced, and they would add that they deplored the decision greatly themselves, but that there had been some log rolling at Westminister and that they had been out-voted, perhaps, because the South African and Australian delegates were anxious that ostrich feathers and opossum skins should be admitted duty free into a foreign country. I suspect that before long they would wish themselves safely back in their own Legislature again. (Laughter and applause).

"I cannot end these observations without expressing my gratitude, not only for your friendly references to the past, but also for the interest with which you have spoken of our future prospects. I rejoice to feel not only that you do not look upon our departure with indifference, but also that we shall carry with us your good wishes in the new career which is about to open for us in another part of the Empire. I feel that I stand in great need of your support in face of the heavy load of responsibility which will shortly be resting upon my shoulders. The post which I am called upon to fill is certainly one of which the responsibilities are heavy. Whether we look at the historical interest of the nations by which it has been inhabited, or whether we consider the vast problems which present themselves to those who are to-day engaged in securing the safety of the Indian Empire, in maintaining peace and order within it, or in taking the necessary precautions to guard the people committed to their charge from the inroads of pestilence and famine, or whether, again, we look forward to those other problems, which as time goes on, and as education leavens and fertilizes these great masses of human beings, and leads them to regard with increasing intelligence and an increasing desire to take part in them, the public

24

affairs of their own country, of this no doubt can arise that no more splendid or interesting field exists for those whose ambition it is to serve their country and the Empire of the Queen. (Great applause).

"And now, Mr. Mayor, it remains for me to thank you once more for your kindness to us, and for all the kindness which we have received at the hands of your citizens. We shall leave you, but nothing can rob us of the memorials and associations which have grown up since we have lived amongst you—memories and associations which we shall preserve amongst the most treasured reminiscences of our lives. (Loud applause). How many and how pleasant will be the Canadian visions which, in years to come, will float across the field of our imaginations when we are far from hence. Visions of the Canadian spring, and of wood and field, bursting, as they are bursting now, into leaf and flower. Visions of summer and of delightful rambles among your mountains and rivers. Visions of autumn, and of hillsides clothed in hues which no eastern splendour could surpass. Visions of winter, with its clear skies, its exhilarating sports out of doors, and within, the bright fire of Gatineau logs, with our children and friends gathered round us. (Applause). Visions of all these and many more will come back to us as we roam unconsciously through the past. But, sir, above all and through all, there will stand out clearly, as it were, in the foreground of the picture, the recollection of the people with whom, during these years, we have lived in the happiest and most unconstrained relations, a people, kindly, hospitable and generous to a fault. (Applause). And of no part of the Dominion shall we carry away pleasanter or more affectionate recollections than of this city, the city which has been our home, and around which there have grown up all those tender and touching associations which belong to the word. We did not know how deeply our roots had struck here until the time came when it was necessary to tear them up. (Great applause).

"Mr. Mayor, I will close what I have to say with a confession. I spent three-quarters of an hour last night in endeavouring to compose a peroration for this speech, but I could not hit upon anything quite to my liking. I have often noticed that a speaker will make you a speech transparent in its sincerity and devoid of affectation until he arrives at his concluding passage. I felt, that to-night anything of a conventional kind would jar with my own feelings, to such an extent that I consigned my peroration to the fire-place, where it ended, as most perorations do, in smoke. (Laughter and applause).

" Under these distressing circumstances, I am going to ask your permission to read to you in lieu of a peroration one or two sentences from a document discovered at Government House in an apartment which will, I understand, shortly be occupied by Lord Stanley of Preston. It is evidently a fragment or a series of fragments of a dairy, and you may be able to aid me with a conjecture as to its authorship. The first entry is dated towards the close of 1883. It runs as follows : ' In for five years of expatriation ; almost wish I had stuck to North Wiltshire ; must make the best of it.' (Laughter). The next entry is in 1884. ' We are making the best of it, and find it very far from unpleasant ; the five years will pass quickly.' Then comes a note in the following year : ' Time passes very quickly and pleasantly. I take back what I wrote about expatriation.' (Loud laughter). After this comes the following in 1886 : ' Time positively flying ; we are beginning to feel quite at home here ; not quite sure that we shall not have to make it six years instead of five.' (Renewed laughter). Then, sir, there comes in 1887 an entry occasioned evidently by some event which exercised a very great effect on the mind of the writer. ' These Canadians are splendid fellows, and have stood by us nobly. We have quite made up our minds to make it six years.' (Great applause). Last of all comes an entry written in rather shaky characters and running thus : ' Why could not D. remain where he was ? It goes to our heart to leave this country and its kind-hearted people. I trust they will remember us—we shall not forget them—while we live.' And, Mr. Mayor, take my word for it, we shall not."
(Tremendous cheers).

When His Excellency resumed his seat he received

another ovation, the cheering and applause lasting for a considerable time.

The Mayor proposed the toast of "The Queen's Privy Council in Canada," remarking that there were present not only members of the Government, but ex-Ministers, leaders of the other great party in the country. (Applause).

Sir John Macdonald on rising received a perfect ovation, cheer after cheer ringing through the room. He said "the toast was a very appropriate one, selected with the best spirit and would be productive of the best effect. (Cheers). The Privy Council was composed of some of the chief men of Canada, not all agreeing in sentiment, but agreeing to disagree, and all anxious for the prosperity of a common country. (Applause). They were cordially united to convey in the most unmistakeable manner a respectful regard for the representative of the Sovereign, whose departure they all deeply regretted. After what had been so well said by the Mayor, it would be out of place to add a single word, with the exception of expressing, as a Privy Councillor, his deep sense of gratitude for His Excellency's kindness and sincere desire for the prosperity of Canada. (Cheers). He paid the distinguished gentleman a high compliment as a constitutional Governor. (Applause). He had displayed great zeal and ability in the discharge of his duty, and a singleness of mind, heart and intellect in everything connected with the interests of Canada. (Hear, hear). He could say that on many occasions he had usefully accepted the advice His Excellency had been kind enough to give. (Hear, hear). He regarded him with the greatest affection and esteem, and he hoped he would be spared to prove himself as graceful in the greater scene to which he had been called. (Applause). He predicted that when he returned to the mother country, after serving well his Queen in India, that he would assume that high position in the councils of the nation, which his distinguished abilities fit him for. (Cheers). At that time he had no doubt he would not forget his love for Canada and the Canadian people. (Hear, hear). He could hardly trust himself to speak of Lady Lansdowne. They all loved her for her amiability and courtesy, and her anxious desire to make everyone feel happy. (Applause). Her Excellency was sincerity itself, and she had told him that the happiest hours of her life had been spent in this country. (Applause). He again and again expressed his deepest regret at the departure of His Excellency and Lady Lansdowne, and sat down amid a perfect hurricane of applause."

Sir Hector Langevin followed in a similar strain. Speaking on behalf of the French-Canadian people, he said "they never had a more popular representative of Her Majesty than Lord Lansdowne. (Cheers). He not only knew what the wants of the people were, but also the wishes of the Queen, and he could truthfully say that from one end of Canada to the other there could not be found one man more Canadian than Lord Lansdowne." (Cheers. He also spoke kindly of Lady Lansdowne, and closed with an appropriate sentence in French. (Applause).

Honourable Mr. Laurier spoke of the pride the French-Canadians felt at living under the British flag. Lord Lansdowne had more than fulfilled all expectations, and would carry away with him the affections of the people he governed so well. His utterances were inspiring and were well received. He sat down amid great applause.

Sir Richard Cartwright followed in a happy speech and was frequently cheered.

His Excellency then proposed in a few felicitious sentences the health of the " Mayor and Corporation of the City of Ottawa," which was received with three times three.

His Worship responded in happy terms, and the festive proceedings were brought to a close by the band playing the National Anthem.

" In its editorial commenting upon the demonstration, the *Citizen* expressed views which, it is safe to say, were fully and enthusiastically endorsed by every one who read them.

" Canada has been exceptionally favoured in the selection of Her Majesty's representatives, since Confederation. Lord Monck, Lord Lisgar, the Earl of Dufferin, the Marquis of Lorne and the Marquis of Lansdowne have each, in their time, maintained that attitude of perfect neutrality towards political parties, that 'subtle and inward balance of sympathy, judgment and ' opinion,' so well becoming, so necessary to those entrusted with vice-regal responsibilities in a constitutionally governed country ; each has, towards Ministers of the Crown, Parliament and People, worthily performed the difficult task of assisting in laying deep and strong the foundation of a great nationality—the future right arm of the British Empire on this portion of the American continent ; each has endeared himself to those Canadians who can appreciate the successful discharge of duties demanding the best and highest elements of statesmanship. Lord Lansdowne, during his administration, has closely identified himself with the social life of the Dominion ; instinct, and a careful training in the political school of the mother country, prompted him, at all times, to sympathise with the every day life, the every day aspirations of the people. Like one of his worthy predecessors, Lord Dufferin, his constant aim appeared to be, to draw all classes towards him. Canada's industrial, commercial, agricultural and philanthropic interests, on all occasions, received his ardent support ; no appeal was responded to in a niggardly spirit ; his purse was open to every local charity; his eloquence heard in advocacy of every national project. Hence, the magnificent demonstration tendered to him last night, was an unstinted and unreserved mark of appreciation, a worthy tribute to a worthy Governor and distinguished man."

Lord Lansdowne was succeeded as Governor-General by the Right Honourable Sir Frederick Arthur Stanley, G. C. B., Baron Stanley of Preston, the second son of the fourteenth Earl of Derby. He was born on January 15, 1841, and received his education at Eton. He was formerly a captain in the Grenadier Guards, and is now Honorary Colonel 3rd and 4th Battalions, Kings' Own (Royal Lancaster) Regiment. He is also a supernumerary A. D. C. to Her Majesty the Queen. He was a member of the House of Commons from 1865 to 1886, when he was raised to the Peerage. On May 31, 1864, he was married to Lady Constance Villiers, eldest daughter of the fourth Earl of Clarendon, K. G. His official experience extends over a great many years, during which time he has served his country in a variety of capacities. He was Civil Lord of the Admiralty, August to November, 1868; Financial Secretary to War Office, 1874-7; Secretary to Treasury, 1878; Secretary of State for War 1878-80; Secretary of State for the Colonies 1885-6, and President of the Board of Trade, 1886-88. During the time he sat in the House of Commons he represented Preston, 1865-8; North Lancashire, 1868-85, and Blackpool division of Lancashire, 1885-6. He was appointed Governor-General of Canada May 1st, and sworn in at Ottawa June 11, 1888.

Immediately after the ceremony, he was presented with an address of welcome by the Mayor (Mr. McLeod Stewart) and the Corporation of the city. His reply was so hearty in manner, so simple in expression, and so natural in every respect, that those who had the pleasure of hearing it felt that they were listening to words which sprang from his heart. Of his predecessor he spoke in warmest praise, saying : " Among the long roll of distinguished men who have filled the high office to which I have been appointed, there is none whose name will be written in more golden letters in the history of this country, than that of Lord Lansdowne after his career of office. He has, I venture to say, endeared himself to all with whom he has been brought in contact. His great abilities, his calm judgment, his knowledge, his courteous manner, have all contributed to make him maintain, as I think he can justly claim to have maintained, the high reputation of his house, and the character of an English statesman. He, I know, felt nothing but unmixed regret in leaving the country where, from the commencement of his sojourn, he had been received with such frank hospitality and with such hearty good will, and although I have been but a few hours amongst you, I think I can say that I have already experienced, aye, even before my arrival, that hospitality, that kindness, that cordiality, which has made the name of every citizen of this Dominion proverbial, and I have fallen even now under a certain amount of the charm which, after riper experience, seems to have settled upon my predecessors."

When His Excellency spoke of the principles which had actuated him in his past political life, he impressed all present with a feeling that, as the Governor-General of Canada, his highest aim would be to discharge the duties of his office in an honest and faithful manner, and to endeavour, by kindness and tact, to cause the machinery of government to move with as little friction as possible. On this point he said, " You have been good enough to refer to other offices which it has been my lot to hold at different times. In all these various situations, it seems to me that there is one principle, and only one, that can dictate with success a career in public life. It is that of endeavouring to address one's self with single heartedness to the problem with which one may be called upon to deal, with an earnest desire to remove all difficulties, with an earnest hope to soften differences, if such may arise, and to endeavour to have before one but one view, namely, that of the public welfare. And when the time comes for me to lay down the great charge, which this day and at this moment I have the honour of assuming, then I will hope I may feel that it is by that rule I have been guided, and it is by the result that I am content to be judged. In the concluding paragraph of your address you refer in graceful terms to the regrets which you assume I feel in leaving the country of my birth and assuming duties elsewhere. I think I have spoken sufficiently already to show you in what spirit your kindness is met. I reciprocate from the depths of my heart those kindly expressions of which you have been good enough to make use, and I trust that, be my career long or short, I may feel when my period of office comes to an end, that I have endeavoured, God willing, to devote to the utmost, my abilities to the cause, to the interests, and to the welfare of your great Dominion."

The impression that Lord Stanley made on his first appearance has deepened and extended as the years of his term of office have rolled by, and when the hour of his departure arrives, that event will be attended with the same feelings of regret that marked the leave-taking of his immediate predecessors, and he will carry away with him the same warm feelings of respect, admiration and affection. More than that it would be impossible to wish him.

Of the three members of the Cabinet who went to England to interest capitalists in the Pacific railway, two—Sir John Macdonald and the Honourable John Henry Pope have joined the great majority, and Sir Charles Tupper alone survives. After serving his country faithfully and zealously for many years, remaining at his post long after failing health warned him that it was time to seek repose, the trusted and loved friend of the Premier, to whom his whole heart was given, John Henry Pope passed peacefully away, surrounded by the members of his family, on April 1, 1889. The House was in session at the time, and the news, which was not unexpected, was quickly conveyed to Sir John Macdonald, who, in a voice so broken by emotion as to be scarcely audible, announced the sad news of the death of his personal and political friend and colleague, and moved the adjournment of the House. In communicating the intelligence to its readers, on the following morning, the *Citizen* bore testimony to the great loss the country had sustained in the following touching words:

"One of Canada's ablest statesmen passed to his long home yesterday afternoon at five o'clock. Many a tear will fall, many a heart will ache, when the news is flashed over the wires that John Henry Pope is dead. Few knew him as he was in the confidences of social life: few, save those who met him at the Council Board, realized the beautiful simplicity of his nature, coupled with giant intellectual faculties; not the mere flashy accomplishments, which charm for the time being; but broad, practical, comprehensive views, manlike courage, untiring industry—in short, lessons learned in the world's great school of human nature, not drawn from the artificial avenues of speculative theory, or from the half-digested opinions of closet students. Essentially a retiring man, who preferred solitude to the attractions of society, Mr. Pope could hold his position in any sphere. He cared for men as he found them, and usually, as he frequently expressed it, made no mistakes in 'sizing them up.' A keen wit, a natural humorist, philanthropic to the deserving, a Ulysses in Council,

the lamented gentleman always commanded the confidence of
his friend and colleague, the Premier, and forced those who
questioned either his ability to grapple with intricate national
questions, or the motives inspiring any action, to ultimately
regard him as the safest and most progressive head who has
presided over a department of Administration since the Union.
In losing Mr. Pope, who as Minister of Agriculture and afterwards Minister of Railways, has worked in unison with him,
Sir John Macdonald loses a devoted friend, an able counsellor,
a sincere Canadian—and Canada is deprived of a man whose
single interest, at all times, was to develop her immense
resources and make her, as he firmly believed she should be,
the greatest Colony attached to the Empire, and eventually,
the greatest portion of the continent of North America.

" The Honourable John Henry Pope, Minister of Railways
and Canals, was born in Cookshire, Province of Quebec, in
December, 1819. He was the son of Colonel John Pope, whose
father was one of those United Empire Loyalists, who came
from the United States, and formed a nucleus of settlers in the
Eastern Townships. Educational facilities being extremely
limited in those days, Mr. Pope received the rudiments of
education at the Common School at Cookshire, after which
he actively engaged in farming. At an early age, he was
elected representative of the Township of Eaton, in the
County Council at Sherbrooke. He was, however, first
attracted towards active politics, by the movement in favour
of annexation, in 1849. The question of annexation to the
United States was, at that time, somewhat favourably looked
upon, and public opinion was strongly towards its becoming
an accomplished fact. Mr. Pope, although then a young man,
took a strong stand against it, organized meetings in various
parts of the country, and upon Sir A. T. Galt resigning his
seat as member for the then County of Sherbrooke, Mr.
Cleveland, of Richmond, at the suggestion of Mr. Pope, was
chosen to oppose the late Judge Sanborn, who came forward
as the annexation candidate. The fight was bitter, but the
election resulted in Mr. Sanborn's return by a very small
majority. It proved, however, the strength of Mr. Pope and

the friends who surrounded him. At the next two general elections, Mr. Pope personally opposed Judge Sanborn, without success. At the election of 1857, however, Judge Sanborn's experience caused a change of sentiment, and he retired in Mr. Pope's favour. He ever since sat as member for Compton, and, although many times opposed, has always been returned by overwhelming majorities.

" The hand of death has pressed the life out of one of the noblest natures, one of the truest friends, one of the best and most successful lovers of Canada, this country ever could, or ever will, boast of. He died as he lived, calmly, unostentatiously. He died with the hand of a loving wife in his own, the voice of a daughter, he cared so much for, sounding in his ears ; the manly words of a son, in whom he placed all confidence, solacing his last moments. He has gone—and with him passes away one of the most devoted stewards of the public demesne, who ever held office under any Canadian Administration."

But while we mourn the loss of these two great men, losses which all recognize as irreparable, we rejoice that the services of Sir Charles Tupper, one of the most able and eminent of Canada's sons is still preserved to us. During his whole life he has laboured to advance the material interests of the country of his birth ; first, in the legislative halls of Nova Scotia, and of later years in the wider sphere of Dominion politics. He has ever been steadfast in his principles and a devoted friend to his leader and to his party. Caring less for self than for the prosperity and happiness of his country he has never hesitated to sacrifice his own claims to advancement when it appeared that some good purpose could be achieved by advancing another. No one could dispute his claims, as Premier of Nova Scotia, to a position of importance in the first Dominion Cabinet, but he cheerfully declined, and yielded his place to another, because he thought that a certain element should be represented, and for three years, as a private member, lent a loyal and powerful assistance to the Government. After that period it was recognized that his country required his services in a more prominent position and he was called to a seat in the Cabinet, since which time no Conservative Ministry was considered complete without him.

Sir Charles Tupper is a son of the late Rev. Charles Tupper, D.D., of Aylesford, N.S., and was born at Amherst on July 2, 1821. He is M.A. and D.C.L. of Acadia College, and D.C.L. of Cambridge. He took his degree of M.D. in Edinburgh in 1843, and returning to Nova Scotia, practised his profession is his native place. In 1846 he married Miss Francis Morse of Amherst. He entered public life in 1855, when he was returned to represent the county of Northumberland with Mr. A. McFarlane, in the Conservative interest, in opposition to the Honourable Joseph Howe and Mr. S. Fulton, the Reform or Liberal candidates. On the change of government, which took place in Nova Scotia in 1857, he was tendered and accepted the office of Provincial Secretary, and in this course he was heartily supported by his constituents. At the general election in 1859 he was again elected for Cumberland, together with Mr. A. McFarlane on the Conservative, and the Honourable Mr. Young on the Liberal side; that county under a new law returning three members. In 1860, the Government being defeated in the House of Assembly by a majority of two, he resigned office and resumed the practice of his profession in the city of Halifax. At the general election, 1863, the province was swept by the Conservative party, the Government sustaining an overwhelming defeat. Dr. Tupper was returned for Cumberland by acclamation, with Messrs. McFarlane and R. Donkin—all in the Conservative interest. In consequence of the decided disapproval and want of confidence expressed by the country, the Government resigned immediately after the elections, and the Honourable J. W. Johnston, now Mr. Justice Johnston, was called upon to form a new Administration. Dr. Tupper was again appointed Provincial Secretary, in the room of the Honourable Mr. Howe, and on appealing to his constituents was re-elected by acclamation. Upon the elevation of Mr. Johnston to the bench, in 1864, Dr. Tupper succeeded him as leader of the Administration, which office he retained until he retired with his Government on the Union Act coming into force. He was created

C.B. (Civil) by Her Majesty in 1867; K.C.M.G., May 24, 1879; G.C.M.G., January, 1886; and a Baronet for his services on the Fisheries Conference, September 13, 1888. He declined a seat in the Dominion Cabinet, 1867; was appointed President of the Council, June, 1870; Minister of Inland Revenue, July, 1872; Minister of Customs, February 22, 1873. When Sir John Macdonald returned to power in 1878, Sir Charles Tupper was appointed Minister of Public Works. In 1879 he was appointed Minister of Railways and Canals and retained that position until 1884, when he was appointed High Commissioner for Canada in London. Just before the elections of 1887 he re-entered the Cabinet as Finance Minister and retained the position for fifteen months, when he was re-appointed High Commissioner. In 1887 he took part in the Fisheries Conference at Washington as one of Her Majesty's Plenipotentiaries, and carried a Bill through both Houses of the Canadian Parliament for the ratification of the treaty. In the fulfilment of the duties of his high office as the representative of Canada in England, Sir Charles has displayed great energy and ability, and to his able advocacy Canadians are indebted for many of the commercial privileges which they now enjoy. At the call of his chief he returned to Canada and took part in the elections of 1891. Being a good speaker, forcible in his arguments, happy in his illustrations and elegant in his delivery, his well stocked mind and intimate knowledge of all political questions that effect the country proved of inestimable value during the campaign. In fact, the history of that memorable contest is altogether imperfect without a full report of his speeches and of the active part taken by him in all the older settled parts of the country, but as the one central idea of these pages is to present a view of the services of Sir John Macdonald, we can only refer in an incidental manner to the work performed by others.

In giving an account of the later years of Sir John's life we have dealt only with the larger questions, and have not gone into that more minute detail that was necessary in referring to former periods. This has been done for the purpose of avoiding all appearance of a desire to become partizan or controversial, and also because in his last great fight were embodied the principles for which he had fought in the preceding years. We feel that this contest, which unquestionably was the cause of his death, cannot be treated in the same way, and that the Life of Sir John Macdonald would be incomplete were we not to present to our readers the issues for which he contended. The next three chapters will, therefore, be devoted to a consideration of the questions involved in the Chieftain's last fight.

CHAPTER XXXVI.

O N February 4, 1891, it was announced that Parliament was dissolved, that nominations for the House of Commons would take place on February 26th, and elections be held on March 5th.

The season of the year selected was unusual and inconvenient, and the period for which members were elected had not yet expired, but the question of trade relations with the United States had assumed so grave a form, and views so extreme and so alarming had been advocated by some prominent and influential men, that it was thought right that the voice of the people should be heard at the polls. The Government, doubtless, felt assured that they could not only rely upon the support of the Liberal Conservative party, but would also draw to them patriotic men of all classes and opinions who, at so serious a juncture in their country's history, might be expected to lay aside party feeling and party traditions and vote for a policy coincident with national honour and independence. During twelve continuous years the country had thriven and progressed under the influence of the National Policy which had fostered and protected every interest effecting the manufacturers, the farmer, the merchant and the workman ; the great Canadian Pacific Railway had been completed from ocean to ocean ; cities and towns had been built up with a rapidity that rivalled the marvellous growth of the American Republic ; new avenues of trade had been discovered ; the bonds of British connection had been more firmly cemented ; and peace, contentment, prosperity and happiness reigned from one end of the country to the other.

The history of these twelve years, and the policy intended to be pursued by the Government in the future, together with an explanation of the policy adopted by the Opposition and its probable result, were laid before the country in a plain but stirring address issued by Sir John Macdonald shortly after the announcement of the dissolution of Parliament. This manifesto was as follows :

To the Electors of Canada :

GENTLEMEN,—The momentous questions now engaging public attention having, in the opinion of the Ministry, reached that stage when it is desirable that an opportunity should be given to the people of expressing at the polls their views thereon, the Governor-General has been advised to terminate the existence of the present House of Commons and to issue writs summoning a new Parliament. This advice His Excellency has seen fit to approve, and you, therefore, will be called upon within a short time to elect members to represent you in the great council of the nation. I shall be a candidate for the representation of my old constituency, the city of Kingston.

In soliciting at your hands a renewal of the confidence which I have enjoyed as a Minister of the Crown for thirty years, it is, I think, convenient that I should take advantage of the occasion to define the attitude of the Government in which I am First Minister towards the leading political issues of the day.

As in 1878, in 1882, and again in 1887, so in 1891, do questions relating to the trade and commerce of the country occupy a foremost place in the public mind. Our policy in respect thereto is, to-day, what it has been for the past thirteen years, and is directed by a firm determination to foster and develop the varied resources of the Dominion by every means in our power consistent with Canada's position as an integral portion of the British Empire. To that end we have laboured in the past, and we propose to continue in the work to which we have applied ourselves, of building up on this continent, under the flag of England, a great and powerful nation.

When, in 1878, we were called upon to administer the affairs of the Dominion, Canada occupied a position in the eyes of the world, very different from that which she enjoys to-day. At that time a profound depression hung like a pall over the whole country, from the Atlantic Ocean to the western limits of the Province of Ontario, beyond which, to the Rocky Mountains, stretched a vast and almost unknown wilderness. Trade was depressed, manufactures languished, and, exposed to ruinous competition, Canadians were fast sinking into the position of being mere hewers of wood and drawers of water for the great nation dwelling to the south of us.

We determined to change this unhappy state of things. We felt that Canada, with its agricultural resources, rich in its fisheries, timber and mineral wealth, was worthy of a nobler position than that of being a slaughter market for the United States. We said to the Americans : " We are perfectly willing to trade with you on equal terms. We are desirous of having a fair reciprocity treaty, but we will not consent to open our markets to you while yours remain closed to us." So we inaugurated the National Policy. You all know what followed. Almost, as if by magic, the whole face of the country underwent a change. Stagnation and apathy and gloom—aye, and want and misery, too—gave place to activity and enterprise and prosperity. The miners of Nova Scotia took courage ; the manufacturing industries in our great centres revived and multiplied ; the farmer found a market for his produce ; the artisan and labourer employment at good wages, and all Canada rejoiced under the quickening impulse of a new-found life. The age of deficits was past, and an overflowing treasury gave to the Government the means of carrying forward those great works necessary to the realization of our purpose to make this country a homogeneous whole.

To that end we undertook that stupendous work, the Canadian Pacific Railway, undeterred by the pessimistic views of our opponents ; nay, in spite of their strenuous and even malignant opposition, we pushed forward that great enterprise through the wilds north of Lake Superior, across the western prairies, over the Rocky Mountains, to the shore of the Pacific, with such inflexible resolution that in seven years after the assumption of office by the present Administration the dream of our public men was an accomplished fact, and I myself experienced the proud satisfaction of looking back from the steps of my car upon the Rocky Mountains fringing the eastern sky.

The Canadian Pacific Railway now extends from ocean to ocean, opening up and developing the country at a marvellous rate, and forming an imperial highway to the east, over which the trade of the Indies is destined to reach the markets of Europe. We have subsidized steamship lines on both oceans—to Europe, China, Japan, Australia and the West Indies. We have spent millions on the extension and improvement of our canal system. We have, by liberal grants of subsidies, promoted the building of railways, now become an absolute necessity, until the whole country is covered as with a network ; and we have done all this with such prudence and caution that our credit in the money market of the world is higher to-day than it has ever been, and the rate of interest on our debt, which is the true measure of the public burdens, is less than it was when we took office in 1878.

During all this time what has been the attitude of the Reform Party? Vacillating in their policy and inconstancy itself. As regards their leaders, they have at least been consistent in this particular, that they have uniformly opposed every measure which had for its object the development of our common country. The National Policy was a failure before it had been tried. Under it we could not possibly raise a revenue sufficient for the public requirements. Time exposed that fallacy. Then, we were to pay more for the home manufactured article than we used to when we bought everything abroad. We were to be the prey of rings and monopolies, and the manufacturers were to extort their own prices. When these fears had been proved unfounded, we were assured that over-competition would inevitably prove the ruin of the manufacturing industries, and thus bring about a state of affairs worse than that which the National Policy had been designed to meet. It was the same with the Canadian Pacific Railway. The whole project, according to our opponents, was a chimera ; the engineering difficulties were insuperable ; the road, even if constructed, would never pay. Well, gentlemen, the project was feasible, the engineering difficulties were overcome, and the road does pay.

Disappointed by the failure of all their predictions, and convinced that nothing is to be gained by further opposition on the old lines the Reform Party has taken a new departure, and has announced its policy to be unrestricted reciprocity ; that is (as defined by its author, Mr. Wiman, in the *North American Review* a few days ago), free trade with the United States, and a common tariff with the United States against the rest of the world.

The adoption of this policy would involve, among other grave evils, discrimination against the mother country. This fact is admitted by no less a personage than Sir Richard Cartwright, who, in his speech at Pembroke on October 21, 1890, is reported to have said : " Some men, whose opinions I respect, entertain objections to this (unrestricted reciprocity) proposition. They argue, and argue with force, that it will be necessary for us, if we enter into such an arrangement, to admit the goods of the United States on more favourable terms than those of the mother country. Nor do I deny that that is an objection, and not a light one."

It would, in my opinion, inevitably result in the annexation of this Dominion to the United States. The advocates of unrestricted reciprocity on this side of the line deny that it would have such an effect, though its friends in the United States urge as the chief reason for its adoption that unrestricted reciprocity would be the first step in the direction of political union.

There is, however, one obvious consequence of this scheme which nobody has the hardihood to dispute, and that is that unrestricted reciprocity would necessitate the imposition of direct taxation, amounting to not less than fourteen millions of dollars annually, upon the people of this country. This fact is clearly set forth in a remarkable letter addressed a few days ago by Mr. E. W. Thomson—a Radical and Free Trader—to the Toronto *Globe*, on the staff of which paper he was lately an editorial writer, which the *Globe*, with characteristic unfairness, refused to publish, but which, nevertheless, reached the public through another source. Mr.

Thomson points out with great clearness that the loss of customs revenue levied upon articles now entering this country from the United States, in the event of the adoption of the policy of unrestricted reciprocity, would amount to not less than seven millions of dollars annually. Moreover, this by no means represents the total loss to the revenue which the adoption of such a policy would entail. If American manufactures now compete favourably with British goods, despite an equal duty, what do you suppose would happen if the duty were removed from the American and retained or, as is very probable, increased on the British article? Would not the inevitable result be a displacement of the duty-paying goods of the mother country by those of the United States? And this would mean an additional loss to the revenue of many millions more.

Electors of Canada, I appeal to you to consider well the full meaning of this proposition. You—I speak now more particularly to the people of this Province of Ontario—are already taxed directly for school purposes, for township purposes, for county purposes, while to the Provincial Government there is expressly given by the Constitution the right to impose direct taxation. This latter evil you have so far escaped, but as the material resources of the province diminish, as they are now diminishing, the Local Government will be driven to supplement its revenue derived from fixed sources by a direct tax. And is not this enough, think you, without your being called on by a Dominion tax gatherer with a yearly demand of fifteen dollars a family to meet the obligations of the Central Government? Gentlemen, this is what unrestricted reciprocity involves. Do you like the prospect? This is what we are opposing, and what we ask you to condemn by your votes.

Under our present system a man may largely determine the amount of his contributions to the Dominion exchequer. The amount of the tax is always in proportion to his means. If he is rich and can afford to drink champagne, he has to pay a tax of $1.50 for every bottle he buys. If he be a poor man he contents himself with a cup of tea, on which there is no duty, and so on all through the list. If he is able to afford all manner of luxuries, he pays a large sum into the coffers of the Government. If he is a man of moderate means and able to enjoy an occasional luxury, he pays accordingly. If he is a poor man, his contributions to the treasury are reduced to a minimum. With direct taxation, no matter what may be the pecuniary position of the taxpayer—times may be hard; crops may have failed; sickness or other calamity may have fallen on the family—still the inexorable tax collector comes and exacts his tribute. Does not ours seem to be the more equitable plan? It is the one under which we have lived and thrived, and to which the Government I lead proposes to adhere.

I have pointed out to you a few of the material objections to this scheme of unrestricted reciprocity, to which Mr. Laurier and Sir Richard Cartwright have committed the Liberal party, but they are not the only objections, nor in my opinion are they the most vital. For a century and a half this country has grown and flourished under the protecting ægis of the British Crown. The gallant race who first bore to our shores the blessings of civilization passed, by an easy transition, from French to English rule, and now forms one of the most law-abiding portions of the community. These pioneers were speedily recruited by the advent of a loyal band of British subjects, who gave up everything that men most prize, and were content to begin life anew in the wilderness, rather than forego allegiance to their sovereign. To the descendants of these men and of the multitude of Englishmen, Irishmen and Scotchmen who emigrated to Canada, that they might build up new homes without ceasing to be British subjects; to you Canadians, I appeal, and I ask you what have you to gain by surrendering that which your fathers held most dear? Under the broad folds of the Union Jack we enjoy the most ample liberty to govern ourselves as we please, and at the same time we participate in the advantages which flow from association with the mightiest Empire the world has ever seen. Not only are we free to manage our domestic concerns, but, practically, we possess the privilege of making our own treaties with foreign countries, and in our relations with the outside world we enjoy the prestige inspired by a consciousness of the fact that behind us towers the majesty of England.

The question which you will shortly be called upon to determine resolves itself into this : shall we endanger our possesssion of the great heritage bequeathed to us by our fathers, and submit ourselves to direct taxation for the privilege of having our tariff fixed at Washington, with a prospect of ultimately becoming a portion of the American Union?

I commend these issues to your determination, and to the judgment of the whole people of Canada, with an unclouded confidence that you will proclaim to the world your resolve to show yourselves not unworthy of the proud distinction that you enjoy—of being numbered among the most dutiful and loyal subjects of our beloved Queen. As for myself, my course is clear. A British subject I was born—a British subject I will die. With my utmost effort, with my latest breath, will I oppose the " veiled treason " which attempts, by sordid means and mercenary proffers, to lure our people from their allegiance. During my long public service of nearly half a century I have been true to my country and its best interests, and I appeal with equal confidence to the men who have trusted me in the past, and to the young hope of the country, with whom rest its destinies for the future, to give me their united and strenuous aid in this my last effort for the unity of the Empire and the preservance of our commercial and political freedom.

I remain, gentlemen,

Your faithful servant,

JOHN A. MACDONALD.

OTTAWA, *February* 7, 1891.

EARNSCLIFFE.

The Finance Minister, the Honourable George Foster, in his address to the electors of Kings, gave his view of the meaning of unrestricted policy, and contrasted it with the policy of the Government. It puts in a smaller space and more comprehensive manner the opinions subsequently expressed by Mr. Blake in his letter of March 5th.

"The policy of the Government has been to assist in developing foreign markets for our natural and manufactured products, and to that end they have liberally subsidized lines of steamers to the West Indies, China and Japan, and the mother country. Proposals for reciprocity with the British West Indies have been made by myself in person, acting for the Government, and I have good grounds for believing that a large and profitable trade may be opened up with these islands for most of our natural and many of our manufactured products.

"In its trade policy with the United States, the Government have always favoured a fair and just measure of reciprocity, and has made repeated propositions looking in that direction. Until lately, however, the United States have made no favourable response.

"Now, however, in the course of diplomatic correspondence, the Government of that country, through its Secretary of State, has intimated its willingness to enter into a conference upon this matter with the Dominion Government, and has declared its readiness to commence this conference after March 4th.

"The trade issue is the great issue in this contest, and it is of the utmost importance that each elector should have a clear idea of the points of difference between the two parties.

"The Opposition declare for unrestricted reciprocity or commercial union with the United States.

"This means and can only mean:

"1. That no tariff duties are to be levied on any products of either country passing into the other.

"2. That Canada is to adopt the tariff of the United States, which is, on an average, twice as high as our own.

"3. That we are virtually to give up the power of making

our own fiscal laws—a thing which no free people has yet been craven enough to do.

"4. That the tariff of the United States is to apply to all British and foreign imports—that is, that while Canada admits United States imports free of duty, she must discriminate against Great Britain and the rest of the world, and virtually prohibit the great part of the imports which now come in therefrom.

"5. That loss and ruin will result to our manufacturing industries, to our seaport towns, to our wholesale business, and, consequently, to our farmers.

"6. That Canada will lose more than half her present revenue, which will have to be made up by direct taxation. I estimate the loss of revenue at $18,000,000 per year. The direct tax necessary to recoup this will be equivalent to $3.60 per head, or $18 for each family of five.

"7. That ultimately the bond which now unites us to the mother land will be severed, and that Canada will become a part of the United States.

"Please consider all that is involved in such a policy, and then contrast it with the policy of the present Government, which is :

"1. To continue to develop home industries, and the agricultural, mineral and other resources of the country on the lines laid down since 1878.

"2. To keep in our own hands the power of framing our own tariff according to our own necessities.

"3. Not to discriminate against Great Britain—our mother land, and the great market for our products.

"4. To raise our revenue by indirect taxation on Customs and Excise, and not by direct taxation.

"5. To meet the United States in a friendly way, and negotiate with them for a reciprocity arrangement on lines that shall be just and equitable, and in accord with the honour and best interests of Canada, so far as it can be done without infringing upon the lines above laid down."

The platform of the Liberals may be said to have been laid down on Wednesday, March 14, 1888, when Sir Richard

Cartwright closed an exhaustive and able speech by moving, as the new fiscal policy of the party, the following resolution :

" That it is highly desirable that the largest possible freedom of commercial intercourse should obtain between the Dominion of Canada and the United States, and that it is expedient that all articles manufactured in, or the natural products of, either of the said countries should be admitted free of duty into the ports of the other (articles subject to duties of excise or of internal revenue alone expected). That it is further expedient that the Government of the Dominion should take steps at an early date to ascertain on what terms and conditions arrangements can be effected with the United States for the purpose of securing full and unrestricted reciprocity of trade therewith."

The leaders of the party did not seem to be united in their views of the policy as expressed in this motion. We find Sir Richard Cartwright addressing a large audience at the music hall at Oshawa, on February 9th in these words.

" If the people wanted reciprocity they could get it, but only on the unrestricted lines which include natural and manufactured products. With unrestricted reciprocity there was almost no limit that could be assigned to the trade that would be built up with the States. For the last dozen years Canada had been simply marking time. No wonder the people were restless and discontented. There could be no reasonable doubt that when Canada came forward with a fair honest, and liberal proposition she would receive fair, honest, and liberal treatment from the States." (Cheers).

C. W. Scott asked : " Does the Liberal party favour discrimination against Great Britain by admitting American manufactures free, and taxing the manufactures of Great Britain ? "

Sir Richard replied : "Certainly we do. I will tell you why. We have a perfect right to manage our own tariff to suit us, the people of Canada. The interests of Canada demand that we should have unrestricted reciprocity with the States. We can only get it by taxing the goods of every country on the face of the earth except those of the States.

That is undoubtedly part of our policy. I am ready to prove that it is for the interest of Great Britain. Every English statesman knows that it is more in the interest of Great Britain to cultivate more friendly relations with the States than to preserve our miserable trade, hampered as it is by our protective tariff. Great Britain has to-day over $800,-000,000 invested in Canada. Her interest in this country as an investor is far larger than her interest in it as a trader. It is far better for her that we should be able to meet the interest on what we have borrowed than that our trade with her should be preserved. I am prepared to prove before any audience, either here or in Great Britain, that it is for the interest of England as well as of Canada that we should have a right to manage our own tariff and maintain our own agent at Washington, which we should have done long ago."

On the evening of the same day (February 9th) Mr. Mercier, the head of the Liberal Government of Quebec, addressed nearly 5,000 people in the Bonsecours market in Montreal, and thus explained his views :

" It was not their desire to do anything rash. They must respect the rights of the manufacturers, but it was their duty to provide for the future. While respecting protection and the National Policy, they had to prepare for the future, so that the doors of the United States might be opened to the agricultural classes. While protesting their loyalty to the Queen and the British Crown, they were adverse to any barriers to their commerce. (Applause). They desired that when their farmers could not find a reasonable price for their produce at home, they might have a free market in the United States ; in short, they wished for free communication as in the period from 1854 to 1866. They then had prosperity and abundance of money, because the farmers were in a position to sell their agricultural products to the Americans. They now wished to remove the barriers that prevented them from doing so." (Applause).

Mr. Mackenzie, the old leader of the party, said " I could never consent to the Zollverein policy (commercial union) for obvious reasons, but I cannot conceive why any one should object to a *favourable* measure of reciprocal trade secured by treaty and not inimical to the interests of Great Britain as the heart of the Empire."

In 1870, while still in the position of leader, he expressed himself in these words : " There is undoubtedly a very great desire for extended intercourse with the United States, and I am quite sure our people are prepared to discuss, in some substantial way that will have some productive result, any scheme which will be submitted by the United States. . . . Your scheme of a continental system has the merit of extreme simplicity, and also that of having had a trial in other countries in Europe. I fear, however, that it would affect prejudicially our relations with the Empire, which, as at present constructed, I, in common with almost all Canadians, desire to see maintained. At the same time I am prepared to have the plan considered, and by anticipation to work out the probable results."

Mr. Mowat, the Premier of Ontario, on several public occasions during the campaign signified his approval of the platform laid down by Mr. Laurier, but expressed his own and Mr. Mackenzie's strong disapproval of commercial union or a Zollverein, and in stirring language, asserted the loyalty of himself and party to the British Crown. He condemned the National Policy and took a very favourable view of the benefits which would be conferred upon both countries by unrestricted reciprocity.

Mr. Longley, Premier of Nova Scotia, was reported to have expressed himself in these words : " Let no person be deceived, unrestricted reciprocity means that we will have to adopt the American tariff against Great Britain."

Mr. John Charlton, M.P., in his address to the farmers of Haldimand, said : " The application of the principle between Canada and the United States would require that the two countries should have the same excise rates and the same tariff upon imports from all other countries ; that the revenue thus collected in both countries should be divided upon conditions to be hereafter arranged ; that the customs line between the two countries from ocean to ocean should be removed."

The Honourable L. H. Davies, of Prince Edward Island, another of the party leaders, is upon record as saying that the immediate consequences of keeping our present outside tariff, under free trade with the States "would be that imports to the United States, instead of being carried to the great ports of the United States, would be taken to the States by way of Montreal. To this the States, whose people are not arrant fools, would never consent. An unrestricted reciprocity, although it would suit us as well as commercial union, was therefore impracticable."

On February 12th, the Honourable Wilfred Laurier leader of the Opposition, issued an address to the electors. In this, after objecting at length to the dissolution, he discussed Sir John's manifesto, accepted the N.P. as the ground of contestation, took issue with the Prime Minister upon his statements of the benefits derived from that policy and arraigned the N.P. upon every claim made in its behalf. The policy of the Reform party he defined as "absolute reciprocal freedom of trade between Canada and the United States," and stated that "the advantages of that policy are placed upon the one consideration that the producing power was vastly in excess of its consuming power, and, as a consequence, the market of the neighbouring nation of 63,000,000 of kindred origin was the best market." He denied Sir Richard Cartwright's proposition that unrestricted reciprocity meant discrimination against England or that the Canadian tariff would have to be assimilated to the American tariff. The loss of revenue that would follow he treats in an airy way as "a far off hazy consequence to be pitted against an immediate result," and to be met by a reduction of expenditure and redistribution of taxation. The charge of "veiled treason" he considered a direct and unworthy appeal to passion and prejudice, and concluded by announcing that the trade question in the present contest must take the precedence of all others and pledging the Opposition to the solution of the same on the basis indicated by him.

On February 17th Sir John Macdonald and Sir Charles Tupper addressed an immense meeting at Toronto. The latter gave an eloquent and elaborate history of the past twelve years, to which justice could only be done by giving his speech in its entirety. He was followed by Sir John who, after an able defence of his course as Prime-Minister, created a profound sensation by laying before the meeting a most treasonable document prepared by Mr. Farrar, editor of the *Globe.* The following description of the meeting is taken from the *Empire* of February 18th :

"There have been many magnificent meetings in Toronto in election contests past, but there has never been one to approach the Conservative gathering of last night in the Academy of Music, when the electors of the Queen City turned out in thousands to welcome Canada's great and only Premier, and the beloved chieftain of her loyal citizens. It is safe to say that it was the greatest political meeting ever held in Canada. Occurring at the height of a most eventful campaign, marked not merely by the presence of the Premier, but also by the assistance of his long-tried and brilliant colleague, Sir Charles Tupper and signalized by two of the grandest utterances ever made before a Canadian public, the meeting was one that will exist without a peer in the political history of the Dominion.

"As was expected, the gathering was of such stupendous proportions that all attempts to accommodate the numbers were practically useless. As the throng from office and workshop were returning home at six o'clock they encountered on the principal thoroughfares a stream of people already flocking townwards. The street cars, even at this early hour, were jammed. Admittance to the Academy commenced a few minutes after six o'clock, when the supporters of Conservatism, who had been fortunate enough to obtain tickets, were admitted by the stage door. That narrow entrance was not even then found equal to the press, and recourse was had to a rear door off Dorset street that led to the basement. At 6.30 the theatre was partially filled, while outside was an immense throng awaiting admittance. A mass of men and women surged and crowded against the main doors, bearing down every obstacle in their way. Police were powerless to make

any orderly arrangement for admittance.   Shortly after seven
o'clock the main doors were opened, the waiting crowd entered
with a rush and a shout, and in a few seconds the whole
building was completely filled.   It was then discovered how
small a fraction of the multitude were accommodated within
the building.   What could be done was done.   Every available
inch of room was occupied.   With the additional chairs 2,000
were seated in the theatre, 300 were crowded on the stage, and
fully 1,000 more were jammed in passages and spaces behind
the seats.   There were nearly 4,000 inside, but outside there
was a mass that numbered between 15,000 and 20,000.   At
7.20 every entrance to the building had to be closed, still
the crowd outside surged and jostled in good nature.   In the
press the large gas lamp in front of the theatre was carried
away, and the rupture in the gas main interfered with the gas
inside the theatre, rendering necessary the use of electricity.

"At 7.35 two carriages drove up in front of the theatre, the
first containing Sir John Macdonald, Mr. W. R. Brock, chairman of the meeting, Col. Fred. C. Denison, and two members
of the reception committee of the Young Mens' Liberal Conservative Club.   Between the pavement and the stage entrance
a solid mass of humanity was wedged, rendering admittance
almost impossible.   Appeals were made to the crowd to clear
an opening for the chieftain, but so dense was the force for
yards on either side that an opening was nearly a physical
impossibility.   At length, after waiting nearly ten minutes,
during which many demands for a speech were made from Sir
John, the chieftain and Mr. Brock managed to make their
way to the door and to enter the theatre.   A few minutes later
and the Premier stood on the platform, surrounded by a sea
of cheering, shouting faces, that could find no way adequately
to express their enthusiasm.   Whirlwind after whirlwind of
applause and cheers shook the building.   Hats, handkerchiefs,
flags were waved in indescribable enthusiasm.   When the
audience were tired of cheering they sang 'For He's a Jolly
Good Fellow.'   It was fully ten minutes before the multitude
had given vent to their magnificent welcome to the Premier.
Nothing could better prove the secure position the noble

chieftain occupies to-day. Premier of the Dominion, he is premier also of the hearts of his fellow-countrymen. When the ovation had at length temporarily ceased, Mr. W. R. Brock, who fulfilled his duties as chairman in a conspicuously able manner, rose to open the meeting, only to be interrupted by the entrance of Sir Charles Tupper, which was the signal for another magnificent ovation of enthusiasm and applause.

"The emblems placed around the theatre added a bright and instructive aspect to the scene. As a background to the stage, crowded with its influential auditors, were the mottoes : 'Hail to Our Chieftain,' and 'No United States Senators Need Apply' ; while appropriately hung between these scrolls were three shields with the words, 'The Old Flag,' 'The Old Leader,' 'The Old Policy.' The stage pillars and boxes were adorned with the mottoes : 'God Save the Queen,' 'Disloyalty is at a Discount,' 'Welcome to the Cabinet,' 'Progressive Legislation,' 'We Welcome Our Leaders,' 'Encourage Home Talent,' 'Canadian Labour for the Canadians.' The railing of the balcony was covered with these bannerets : 'Ottawa, Not Washington, Our Capital,' 'Canada for the Canadians,' 'Ontario, Quebec, Nova Scotia, New Brunswick, Prince Edward Island, Manitoba, British Columbia, N. W. Territories—A Noble Heritage,' 'A Fair Measure of Reciprocity,' 'No Tariff Discrimination Against Great Britain.'

"The stupendous crowd of 20,000 men and women who thronged King street, between York and Simcoe, completely baffled every effort of control. They were there. There was not an inch of room inside the building, yet they were loth to leave, and remained jostling and shoving around the doors until after nine o'clock. Although the magnitude of the multitude inside was great, the floor committee of the Young Liberal-Conservatives worked nobly in endeavouring to handle the throng in the pit and on the platform.

Mr. Coatsworth first addressed the meeting and was followed by Sir Charles Tupper, who made one of the most brilliant speeches of his life, and was rewarded by the hearty applause of a very appreciative audience, which lasted for some minutes after he had resumed his seat. The chairman, Mr.

W. R. Brock, after restoring order, then addressed the
assemblage of citizens in these words : " Ladies and gentlemen,—I want to say one word to this vast audience. We
all admire the Premier of Canada. (Loud cheers). We all
respect the Right Honourable Sir John Macdonald, and the
Liberal Conservatives love John A. (Vociferous cheers).

At this juncture the old man stood up, and as, in the
fulness of his years, he leaned slightly forward there was a
sudden outburst from the audience that fairly shook the
building from its vaulted roof to its foundations. The entire
gathering rose and yelled. Handkerchiefs, hats, umbrellas,
walkingsticks, programmes, and in fact everything within
reach, were waved by the audience. The enthusiastic uproar
was deafening. The grand old hero stood there motionless
as his heart throbbed within his honoured breast. This was
one of the rewards that fall to the lot of a man who has
spent his whole life labouring for the benefit of his race. It
was a proud minute for Sir John. The first words he uttered
after silence had been restored showed that, during the few
minutes of cheering, his memory had carried him back to
younger days when he himself was a citizen of Toronto.
When the cheering had subsided, someone shouted :

" For he's a jolly good fellow."

It's a question whether any Canadian was ever before
honoured by that whole hearted song in such a style. The
words came from nearly every throat, and the soprano voices
intermingling showed that the ladies were doing their share
to honour one of the greatest statesmen of modern times.

From enthusiastic cheering there followed a breathless
silence as the father of Canada addressed the audience. This
address, as a matter of course, dealt in a fuller form with
the questions brought forward in his manifesto, and we will,
therefore, not repeat them but pass on to the Farrer incident.

" How could we expect to make a reasonable treaty with
the United States when these gentlemen of the Liberal party
were—to use a phrase that may be used by some of you,
although I don't use it myself—going one better ? (Cheers
and laughter). We said we must have control of our own

tariff, but they said this is a matter of agreement, and we will come and adopt the tariff. Of course, a tariff once adopted, that tariff can only be altered by the Congress of the United States and the Parliament of Canada. The United States Congress represents 66,000,000 and our Parliament represents 5,000,000 to 6,000,000. The United States is the stronger, and they would wag us, or otherwise the tail would wag the dog, you know. (Laughter and cheers).

"Well, Mr. Chairman, ladies and gentlemen, the conspiracy has been going on and I take the full responsibility of making this statement, that there is a deliberate attempt to induce the United States to favour the present Opposition against the present Government, by holding out to them hopes of annexation. How am I to prove that, you will say. Well, I will tell you how. As you know, the *Globe* is the Bible of the Sir Richard Cartwright branch of the Liberals."

Sir John here gave an account of the transfer of Mr. Farrer from the *Mail* to the *Globe* and continued: "Since then Mr. Farrer has been the ambassador between the *Globe* or Sir Richard Cartwright and Washington. Now, a loyal man brought it to the notice of a member of the Government that this Mr. Farrer,—with his own hand—had prepared a document for the purpose, to be used in the United States. I will read to you the last paragraph of that paper, and you will see the charge that I make, that all this negotiation at Washington is merely leading up to a result which they consider inevitable—the result being the annexation of Canada to the United States. (Hear, hear).

"This documents tells the Americans how they are to force Canada—'You are to grant them nothing; you are 'to try to stop the bonding system; you are to put a tax 'on everything that Canada produces.' In fact, the document points out every possible way in which Canada and its trade can be injured and its people impoverished, with the view of eventually bringing about annexation. The writer pays me a great compliment. He says annexation cannot make great progress as long as I am at the head of affairs. (Hear, hear, and cheers). But then, he says, I am seventy-five years old. (Laughter). Now, gentlemen, you laugh at their attempts to bulldoze us into this position, and I am inclined to laugh myself sometimes ; but this document shows that there is a treasonable conspiracy in Canada—(Hear, hear)— and it is a treason that is to be met by every man, no matter what his proclivities may be, no matter whether he reckons himself a Liberal or a Conservative, a Conservative Liberal or a Liberal Conservative ; so long as he is a British subject, every man who feels his obligation as a Canadian will visit— I was going to say with his vengeance—with his righteous indignation any party that would be guilty, directly or indi- rectly, of a conspiracy of this kind.

"I know the responsibility of what I am saying ; but I will read you the document, and I think you will say that I am justified in characterizing it as I do. It is a rather long document, and I will read its concluding paragraph, which alludes particularly to the fisheries of the Maritime Provinces, as the feature in which Canada can most easily be hurt. What I shall read is a copy taken from the original galleys and printed from the types of Hunter, Rose & Co.; and I have got the original.

"'A word in conclusion about the situation in the maritime 'provinces. Outside of Halifax, the people, as a body, are 'well disposed towards the United States. The fishermen's 'phrase, that they should like "to see Gloucester moved east," 'in order that they might enjoy higher wages, commends 'itself to the majority. Sir John Macdonald secures the 'election of a Tory majority from Nova Scotia only by a 'system of largesse and corruption carried on without attempt 'at concealment. A constituency which returns an Opposi- 'tion member is forthwith excluded from sharing in the rail- 'way subsidies and other appropriations lavished on the rest. 'The fishermen have a saying that a Nova Scotia member 'on the wrong side at Ottawa is "a spare pump in a dry ship." 'In Prince Edward Island, where it is impossible to spend 'public money except on a few wharves and lighthouses, the 'people return a solid Liberal contingent to Ottawa. The 'islanders are exceedingly friendly to the Americans, and it

'is said by one who knows the state of feeling there, that
'fully seventy per cent. of them would vote for full reci-
'procity or for annexation, provided the question were sub-
'mitted to them free from any entangling issues of a local
'character, and that the Ottawa Government abstained from
'the use of bribery. It is felt by all that Sir John's methods
'of reconciling these provinces to the vast economic loss they
'sustain from being severed from their natural market in New
'England, cannot survive the man himself. No one else
'could employ them with equal skill or success. He is now
'seventy-five years old.

  " ' The fishery question owes its existence, not to the
'people, but to the fish merchants and vessel owners. The
'traders in other lines would be glad to see the widest privi-
'leges extended to the Americans, whose custom was once,
'and might be again, an important factor in the business of
'the provinces, more especially since the decay of the inshore
'fisheries has rendered it all the more essential that the coast
'population should be permitted to resume their former
'relations with the visitors. The influence of the fish mer-
'chants is far reaching. They control the newspapers, and
'to some extent the politics of the province. The headland
'question, the dispute over the right of Americans to enter
'the Bay of Fundy, which was terminated by the arbitration
'in the case of the vessel *Washington,* and other points of
'controversy, were all pressed by them in the hope, to which
'they still cling, of being able to force Congress into yielding
'free fish. If their minds could be disabused of this notion,
'and they were made to see that free fish was not procurable
'through coercion, we should soon hear the last of the cry
'that to grant commercial privileges to the Americans would
'be to surrender an invaluable franchise.

  "'The imposition by the United States of a tonnage tax on
'all Nova Scotia vessels laden whole or in part with fish, would
'speedily put an end to seizures and, indeed, to the whole
'controversy. Another ready way of bringing the Govern-
'ment and all concerned to their senses, would be to suspend
'the bonding privilege, or to cut the connection of the Cana-

'dian Pacific with United States territory at Sault Ste. Marie.
' Either of these methods would rouse the full force of western
'Canada influence against the Government. It would be
'better still to oblige Britain to withdraw her countenance
'and support from the Canadian contention, as she did in
'1871. That would secure the end desired without leaving
'the United States open to the charge of being animated
'by hatred of Canada, on which Sir John Macdonald trades.

"'Whatever course the United States may see fit to adopt
'it is plain that Sir John's disappearance from the stage is to
'be the signal for a movement towards annexation. The
'enormous debt of the Dominion ($50 per head), the virtual
'bankruptcy of all the provinces except Ontario, the pressure
'of the American tariff upon trade and industry, the incurable
'issue of race, and the action of the natural forces making for
'the consolidation of the lesser country with the greater have
'already prepared the minds of most intelligent Canadians for
'the destiny that awaits them ; and a leader will be forth-
'coming when the hour arrives.'

" I think you will agree with me that there is somewhere
and among some people a conspiracy to drive Canada into
the arms of the United States, by inducing the United States
to be as obstructive as possible and as annoying as possible to
this country. The abolition of the bonding privilege, under
which we have free intercourse, and every device that can
possibly hurt Canada, is suggested in this paper ; and we are
told that all the intelligent people of Canada think so ; that
these things must bring about annexation, and that the leader
will be found when that time comes. Gentlemen, that is the
position we have to face in Canada at the present time. Here
we have a Government and a people, and I believe an
electorate, as will be shown in a few days, that fully values the
privileges we have got, that believe we will be losers and not
gainers by such a union, and we believe that we have enjoyed
as great an amount of freedom as any country in the world.

" I believe that we are as happily constituted as any country under the sun, believing that here there is social freedom,
there is individual freedom, there is political freedom, and

there is an absence of those disintegrated and treasonable qualities which threatened the peace and prosperity of the country. We have no such questions as the negro question, which was looming up so disastrously in the United States, to bother us ; we have no large nuclei assemblage of foreign anarchists ; you saw what they did at Chicago a while ago. We have no such thing as elected judges, where the people elect men who will decide according to the wishes of the majority. We look up to England and to English tradition for our guidance ; we have everything to lose, much more than wealth, much more than money's worth, we have everything to lose in being severed from England; we have everything to gain by the benign influence of Her Majesty's Government, a free Queen over a free people, but governed by principles of religion, by principles of equality and by principles of morality which a democracy never had and never will have. (Applause). And will the people of Canada submit to such a thing ; will they submit to men going off to a foreign country, aye, and raising money for the purpose of driving the people into annexation ?

"I have no idea that the people of Canada will do that. Why, Mr. Chairman, look at the fate of Poland. Poland a free country, a gallant people, a great people, the greatest soldiers in the world, one of the finest races in the world ; that country was finally conquered by corruption. The people rose in arms, and under their great general they fought against enormous odds, but at last they were overcome, and when the gallant Pole fell on the field of battle his last words were, ' Finis Polina '—that is, 'the last of Poland.' Now, we will not have war just yet, but, if we submit to this kind of foreign intervention, if we allow American millionaires or speculators to come into this country, to be traitors among our ranks, to spend foreign gold for the purpose of buying up our people, 'why, then we can say like the Polish general, ' Finis Canadia ' —this is, ' the end of Canada.' But there is no fear of that. (No, no). But if it should happen that we should be absorbed in the United States, the name of Canada would be literally forgotten ; we would have the State of Ontario, State of

Quebec, and State of Nova Scotia, and State of New Brunswick ; every one of the provinces would be a state ; but where
is the grand, the glorious name of Canada which we now have
in one, and which we are now so proud of? It would, indeed,
be this in the end.

" All I can say is that not with me, or not by the action of
my friends, or not by the action of the people of Canada, will
such a disaster come upon us. I believe that this election,
which is a great crisis, and upon which so much depends, will
show to the Americans that we prize our country as much as
they do, that we would fight for our existence as much as they
fought for the preservation of their independence. (Hear,
hear). That the spirit of our fathers, which fought and won
battle after battle, still exists in their sons ; and if I thought it
was otherwise, I would say the sooner the grass was growing
over my grave the better, rather than that I should see the
degradation of the country which I have loved so much, and
which I have served so long." (Loud and prolonged applause).

After the Premier had resumed his seat, and the cheering
had subsided the entire audience sang " God Save the Queen."
The gathering dispersed after three cheers for Sir John and
Sir Charles.

After the meeting the grand old man held an informal
reception on the platform.

Those who had thought that the greatest statesman of the
continent was yielding at all to the advance of years, were
agreeably surprised. As the great chieftain stood before the
admiring gathering his eye glistened with all its wonted fire
and acuteness, his voice rolled out distinctly, emphasized by
that appealing stress that age alone can give. His speech
possessed the same wonderful force of statement as ever, and
was adorned with the same pointed allusion and anecdotes.
The inspiration of his words seemed greater than ever before,
as he made a great and stirring appeal to the people of Canada
to preserve their country for themselves and for the glorious
empire, and not to hand so fair a heritage over to an alien
nation. Old Conservatives who have heard Sir John in every

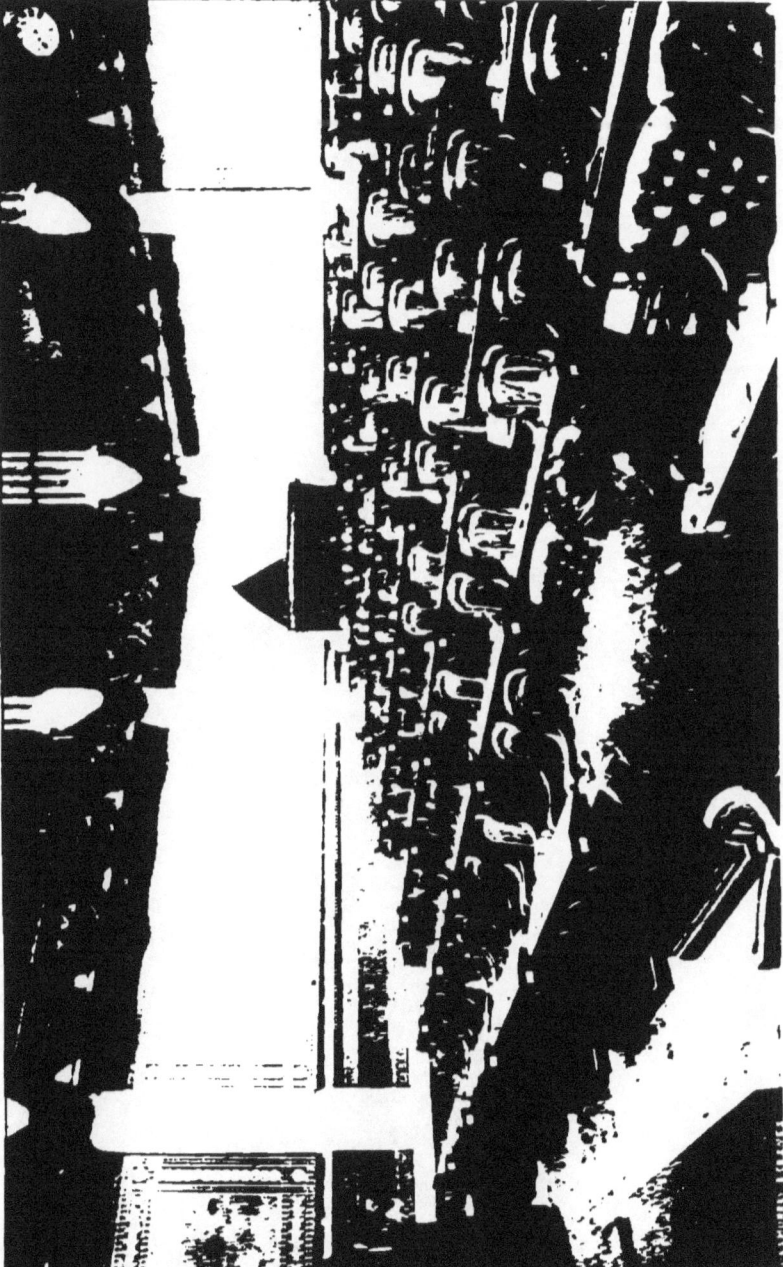

INTERIOR OF HOUSE OF COMMONS.

campaign for nearly the last half century said that his speech was one of the greatest he had ever made.

How feelingly, how gracefully, how sweetly, did Grace Fenton describe that meeting months afterwards, when the loved leader lay dying, as the result of his over-exertions in that last campaign :

' It seemed as though a premonition of this evil day touched lightly the hearts of that vast audience, for never have I heard a welcome so thrilling as that accorded to the Premier.   It broke in great waves over the house, falling and rising again and again, spontaneous, irrepressible, magnetic ; and through the volume of sound poured a certain vibrant note that told of something deeper than mere outward good-will.   It was a note of tenderness ; it was as though the very hearts of the people had leaped into their throats and thrilled into welcome.

" And I think he who has been the hero of a thousand enthusiasms felt the warmth and sympathy of this his last Toronto greeting, and was touched and cheered thereby.

" The fur overcoat he loved to wear lay thrown across the back of the easy chair from which he had risen ; a cluster of roses drooped near by, the light flashing through a glass water ewer sent scintillating sparkles across his face, a little pale and weary with fatigue, and his words dropped into stillness —the intense stillness of a vast audience.

" How he has loved his country, how he has worked for it, sparing nothing of personal sacrifice, that he might accomplish its welfare.   Loyal always, faithful always, fighting all detraction with a happy optimism that worked its own realization.

" And now that he is resting, oh mothers of Canada, let us teach our sons to carry on the labour in the spirit of loyalty with which he has imbued !

" And if it be that dark days come, when patriotism pale or honour falter, let his be the name to conjure with, whose magic shall stir our hearts and strengthen our hands."

On the day after their great reception at Toronto, Sir John Macdonald and Sir Charles Tupper left for Hamilton.   Crowds

of people assembled at the stations along the way anxious to
see the distinguished statesmen. As the train approached
each place long and loud welcoming cheers were sent up,
handkerchiefs were enthusiastically waived and men tried to
climb over each other to grasp them by the hand. When the
city of Hamilton was reached another splendid demonstration
awaited them. The platform was thronged with people who
cheered vociferously when Sir John and Sir Charles stepped
out off the car. As the carriages drove through the streets the
busy crowds along the way stopped to cheer and waive their
hats. Flags were flying everywhere from big buildings and
factories. All was, however, but a faint indication of the
tremendous demonstration prepared for the evening, of which
the following description is taken from the *Empire :*

"Before it had yet become dark the pretty central city
park, the Gore, famous all over the Dominion, was lighted up
with innumerable and various coloured gas lamps. The effect
was magnificent, particularly when the wide and handsome
thoroughfare, King Street, gradually became packed with the
marshalling hosts of a mammoth procession. Column after
column of torchlighted forces wheeled into line from the
neighbouring streets. Prancing horses and caravans of all
descriptions bearing transparencies of political portent, followed. Drays and pleasure vans carrying the cheering and
happy employees of the prosperous manufactories of the city
swept past the multitude. They marched and countermarched;
they played and they tooted their horns ; they cheered and
they shouted till the listening spheres paid back the great
acclaim. But this was not sufficient. Fireworks were started,
and a first-class line of fireworks they were. This kept up for
an hour and a half. There were not less than 30,000 people
out on the streets, and it may be added that no city in the
world could turn out people more orderly, good humoured or
better dressed. Hamilton did credit to Canada and to her
citizens. That was the object of the great demonstration and
it was demonstrated beyond doubt or question.

"When the marshal had brought affairs to an orderly
termination in the vicinity of the park and got their torches

into marching order, it could be seen at a glance that the
finest political procession ever organized in this country was
under way. As far as the eye could reach the darkness of
night was pierced by the light of myriads of torches, and an
incessant discharge of Roman candles and rockets illuminated
the line of march. Ten bands headed that number of detach-
ments of the industrial army which marched in their rear,
proud to have the opportunity of doing honour to the grand
old chieftain whose policy had fostered the industries which
gave them employment. Numerous transparencies, bearing
appropriate mottoes, were carried on lorries or borne on the
shoulders of the processionists.

" The meeting held in the Palace Rink was gigantic in its
dimensions. The building is seated to accommodate 2,500.
but as almost all the seats had been reserved for the ladies,
2,000 of the intellectual voters of the city had to find standing
room as best they could. The building was filled up before
seven o'clock, although the meeting did not open till after
eight. Thousands were crowding around the building during
the interval preceding the arrival of Sir John Macdonald. The
police arrangements for admitting by private entrance only
those who had tickets, were perfect, and contributed in a great
measure to the orderly manner in which the people were able
to gain admission. Both inside and out the immense assemblage of people was remarkable for orderliness. Enthusiasm,
of course, ran high, in fact nothing could excel it. The hall
was decorated profusely with British and Canadian flags.
The back of the platform was covered with an immense Union
Jack.

" When Sir John entered there was an outburst of enthusiasm which, for its magnificence, was not even excelled by the
ovation which the grand old chief received in the city of
Toronto. The ladies stood up and waived their handkerchiefs
and cheered with all the power of their voices, while the wave
that rolled from the back portion of the hall seemed as if it
would lift the roof off.

" It was a happy thought which made provision in the
Arcade Hall for an overflow meeting. It gave opportunity

for a fraction, at least, of the people who could not obtain admittance to the Palace Rink, to hear Sir John and Sir Charles. Doors opening on the Arcade from James Street were guarded by policemen, and kept closed until the procession was over, by which time an immense and impatient concourse had gathered on the street waiting for admission, and when the doors were opened so tremendous was the rush that the front and side windows of the *Globe* office were smashed to pieces by the surging crowds. In five minutes the hall was packed to suffocation. The wide cornice even was climbed upon by large numbers of adventurous young men who were unable to obtain room for their feet upon the floor of the hall. Such an ovation as Sir Charles Tupper and party received upon entering the hall, and later in the evening the veteran Premier and his body guard, it is no exaggeration to say, has never before been tendered to any men, politicians or otherwise, in Hamilton, not excepting even the demonstrative welcome extended the same gentlemen in 1878. When Sir Charles entered the hall the assemblage stood up and yelled itself hoarse, and the war horse of Cumberland advanced to the platform between ranks of most enthusiastic supporters who welcomed the honoured patriot. When the enthusiasm had subsided sufficiently for J. W. Nesbitt, Q.C., to be heard, that gentleman made a few introductory remarks, burning with patriotic fervour, and introduced Sir Charles to the audience. Never did statesman address an audience more perfectly in accord with the sentiments eloquently expressed than the one Sir Charles faced. Each patriotic utterance was received with loud acclaim in token of ready acquiescence, while every reference to the traitorous designs of our political opponents was followed by correspondingly vigorous demonstrations of disapproval.

" Sir Charles had not completed his brilliant address when Sir John, accompanied by Senator Sanford, A. McKay, M.P., T. H. Stinson and Alexander Turner, entered the hall. The assemblage could not be restrained and the speaker had to discontinue while the veteran chieftain made his way to the platform.

" If the crowd had been excited before, the appearance of Sir John caused it to go wild with enthusiasm. It seemed as though the cheering and waving of hats and handkerchiefs would never cease. Ladies were as enthusiastic as men, and if they did not succeed in displaying it to the same degree, it was not for the lack of will, but because of less vigorous lung power.

" Sir John having rested sufficiently after his lengthy effort at the Palace Rink, addressed the Arcade audience. Although pleading fatigue at the commencement as a reason for the intention to make a brief speech, the aged chieftain warmed up to his subject as he progressed and spoke for about three-quarters of an hour."

The next day Sir John and Charles Tupper went on to London where the people were described as simply wild with excitement. In the evening they addressed another monster assemblage of people, the following description of which is taken from a private letter :

" A portion of the Drill Hall, where the meeting was held, was apportioned to the ladies, no gentlemen allowed in. In the rest of the hall the general public could fight it out for breathing room. Seats had been provided for 4,800. The hall was full before six o'clock. The torchlight procession did not start from Sir John's car until a quarter to eight. Can you imagine the hall after the procession arrived ? Hundreds pushing and yelling like madmen to get into a place already packed. Sardines in a box are comfortable compared with that jam. When Sir John rose to speak, a large Union Jack, about three feet long by two feet wide, made of flowers, the same on both sides, attached to a staff about six feet high covered with smilax, was presented to him—a gift from the 'loyal Conservative ladies of London.' It was very beautiful ; the ensign on one side was all geraniums, the reverse side carnations, and the Jack in the corner made of flowers of the proper colour. The ladies attended in force, all armed with small flags, which they waved like crazy children, until the excitement was so great that many of them stood upon their chairs and joined in the cheering of the crowd behind them. Sir Charles told me yesterday morning that of all the meetings he had ever attended he had never seen such a grand and enthusiastic one. The streets were running with water and slush, and it was raining hard, but the crowd did not seem to know it, and they waded through everything with apparent enjoyment."

Among the signs displayed on the walls of the drill-shed were the following :

"Welcome to Sir John, Canada's Greatest Statesman."

"Canada for the Canadians."

"Sir John, You Can Trust London to Send You Back Honest John Carling."

"The Old Policy, the Old Flag, the Old Leader."

"Canada Shall Not Be Governed by Washington.'

"London Will Not Favour Annexation."

"We Will Preserve the Farmer's Home Market."

"No Sympathy With Treachery or Treason in London."

"Welcome to Sir Charles, Who Thrice Saved the Canadian Cattle Trade."

"This, My Last Effort, for the Unity of the Empire."

"Canada's Noble Heritage Will Not Be Sold For a Mess of Pottage."

"No U. S. Senators Need Apply."

"No Discrimination Against Great Britain."

At the close of the meeting the great procession was re-formed, and, accompanied by the Seventh Fusiliers band and the Forest City band, escorted the carriages of Sir John and his party back to the Tecumseh house. This procession along the streets at 12.30 o'clock, with thousands of exuberant citizens on the way-side, was the crowning feature of one of the grandest political gatherings ever held in the city of London.

The following day, Saturday, Sir John made a marvellous effort for a man of his years. In the morning he spoke at Stratford. At one o'clock in the afternoon he made an address of nearly an hour at St. Mary's. He spoke briefly at Guelph, and arrived in Brampton about seven. Here he spoke for fifty minutes in support of Mr. W. A. McCulla. His voice was hoarse, but when he warmed up to the subject he spoke with vigour and roused great enthusiasm. He arrived in Toronto about ten Saturday night, going at once to the Queen's, where he enjoyed a well-earned rest.

In the early part of the following week Sir John Macdonald proceeded to his old home, Kingston, and on the evening of February 24th, addressed the greatest political gathering ever held in that city, which was thus described by the *Daily News*.

" It began to rain about five o'clock, after which a windstorm arose and blew violently for some time. Towards evening the rain came down harder, and later the night became very dark, so black that it was feared the inclement weather would have an effect upon the welcome to Sir John Macdonald, but it didn't, as the facts will show. , The meeting was announced to take place at eight o'clock, but as early as 6.30 crowds began to collect in front of Martin's Opera House. It kept increasing rapidly, and ten minutes later the doors could not stand the test, the crossbar was pressed from its fastenings, and, the door yielding to the pressure, the crowd rushed in. At seven o'clock the house was crowded, even the standing room being occupied. Such an early crowding of the hall was never known before. The manager of the opera house says he never experienced the like. Many ladies called at the opera house during the day and asked if they could have seats reserved. The hint was taken, and soon the large stage was cleared of its scenery and seats were secured from other halls sufficient to seat 350 ladies. They were admitted by a back door, and so eager were they to gain admittance that by 7.15 the stage was crowded by them also. At 7.30 the ways leading to the opera house were jammed, and people were again gathering on the streets.

" The immense audience which crowded every available part of the house—from the upper gallery to the orchestra seats, and even the fly galleries above the stage—represented all classes and creeds, and was most enthusiastic throughout the proceedings.

" Many hundreds were turned away, unable to gain admission."

The next day Sir John proceeded to Napanee and there addressed a large meeting characterized by the same hearty enthusiasm with which he had been everywhere received in his triumphal tour since the Toronto meeting, and was presented with an address.

On his return he received from England a most complimentary resolution from the Primrose League, which afforded another evidence that, while he possessed the confidence of the people of Canada, he also held and increased the warm regard and appreciation of those in the mother country, who had followed his long patriotic career. The address was as follows :

To Sir John Macdonald, Premier of Canada :

We, as loyal subjects of our Queen and supporters of the British Empire, send you warmest greetings and heartfelt thanks for the patriotic stand you have so nobly made in defence of the maintenance of the Empire ; and, although for the time being, dangers may menace that unity between Canada and the mother country, we feel that the patriotism of our fellow-countrymen in Canada will not allow them to swerve from their duty to the heritage of glory handed down to them in trust for posterity, but that they, like ourselves in the Old Country, will fight shoulder to shoulder against that veiled treason which has for its object the disintegration and dismemberment of our Empire, which has stood immovable amid the ages of man and the downfall of nations.

We feel sure that the energy of character, skill, daring and indomitable valour exercised by our forefathers in England and the colonies will stimulate us, whether in Canada or in England, to rally round the flag of our Empire, upon whose dominions the sun ne'er sets, under whose folds have been developed a degree of national felicity and comfort more rich and uninterrupted than has ever been enjoyed by any other empire in the world's history.

We feel satisfied that with such guides as yourself the future of our Empire is safe, and its progress secure. We therefore pray that your valuable life may be long spared to still carry out your noble work in defence of our national principles of empire and liberty.

Signed on behalf of the members of the Clarendon Habitation (No. 1642) of the Primrose League, in public meeting assembled.

J. W. D. BARRON.

President and Chairman of the Meeting.

HYDE, CHESHIRE, ENGLAND,
    Tuesday, February 17, 1891.

When Sir John Macdonald went eastward to Kingston, Sir Charles Tupper went westward to Windsor, where he received a demonstration that for numbers and enthusiasm was not excelled in the election campaign. The meeting was held in the Essex Music Hall which was jammed to the doors. In a speech of great power and earnestness Sir Charles dealt with the questions of the day, and added to the sensation caused by Sir John Macdonald's speech at Toronto by giving still further evidence of the existence of a conspiracy to compass the ruin of the country. This evidence consisted of the production of correspondence between Mr. Wiman, Mr. Farrer and Mr. Hitt, Chairman of the Foreign Relations Committee of the House of Representatives and was composed of the following letters :

TORONTO, *April 22, 1889*

MY DEAR MR. WIMAN :—Our Ottawa man will send a good summary of your speech, so that on our account you need not go to the trouble of preparation. At present the C. U. movements is at a standstill. First of all, the Jesuit agitation, which is here to stay, has to some extent supplanted it. Secondly, the general belief is that the Republicans would not listen to any such scheme. Thirdly, a very large number of people are inclined to think that we had better make for annexation at once, instead of making two bites of the cherry. Lastly, the old parties here are rapidly breaking up, and when Sir John goes we shall be adrift without a port in sight, save annexation. Moreover, although the Liberals have taken up C.U., they are not pushing it with any vigour. For these reasons the *Mail* has, in the slang of the day, given the subject a rest. There is really no use talking it up to a people whose politics are in a state of flux, and whose future is wrapped in doubt. I saw Mr. Hoar, while at Washington, and told him just what he says I did, namely, that the smaller forces favour annexation, and will favour it all the more if C.U. be withheld. It seems to me, and I have talked the thing all over lately with Maritime members, as well as with Manitobans, that C.U. would only delay the coming of the event those people most desire. Hence, in the provinces referred to, C.U. does not take hold, whereas annexation will always demand a hearing. In Ontario the Jesuit campaign has brought that aspect of things home to thousands who would not look at C.U. The littleness and halfheartedness of the Liberals is also very disheartening. Then, again, the truth is that every man who preaches C.U. would prefer annexation, so that the party is virtually wearing a mask. Can't you come round this way and have a talk ? Yours very truly,

(Signed) E. FARRER.

HOUSE OF REPRESENTATIVES,
WASHINGTON, D.C., *April 25, 1889.*

Erastus Wiman, Esq., 314 Broadway, New York.

DEAR SIR,—I am greatly obliged to you for sending to me the proof slips of the " North American " article, and have been much interested also in Mr. Farrer's letter, which surprised me somewhat, as I did not think from his conversation, which gave me a very favourable impression, that he would be so easily discouraged. The reasons he gives existed before the Commercial Union movement began with greater force than to-day. The Republicans as protectionists, it was apprehended, would be against it. They are not. Their representatives vote for it, their newspapers have received it kindly, and often with warm approval. The Jesuit agitation, which has taken the place of Commercial Union in his mind, is largely sentimental and will probably not last long. The other, C.U., is a business question that concerns each citizen, and in a way which he does not understand at first, but sees more and more clearly the more he talks intelligently about it. There is some logic in what F. says, of not making two bites of a cherry, but going for annexation at once, but I think he is misled on that point in a way that often occurs. Where a man is thinking much on a point and discussing it, he is liable to narrow his horizon to those within his reach, and his own mind, and perhaps those he meets, having passed on by discussion to distant results, he takes it for granted that the wide world, which is so wonderfully slow, has kept up with him and has the same results in sight. We must be very patient with the slow moving popular mind. If the Canadian public of farmers, artisans, lumbermen, miners and fishermen can be, in three years, argued up to the point of voting Commercial Union, and giving sanction to the movement in Parliament, it will be great progress. Slow as such movements are the comforting thing is that they never go backward. To you personally it ought to be in your moments of reflection a consolation that long hereafter when this ball which you set rolling has gone on and on and finished its work, everyone may then look back and see and appreciate the services done to mankind by the hand that set it in motion. I shall look with interest for what you say in Ottawa. The *North American Review* article will have a powerful tendency to keep our public men from scattering away on annexation next winter, and I hope we can get the offer of Commercial Union formulated into law. I return the proof slips of the article and the letter of Mr. Farrer's. Very truly yours,

(Signed)

R R. HITT.

P.S.—Just received yours of yesterday with Goldwin Smith's ; it reads admirably.

THE FUNERAL LEAVING THE PARLIAMENT BUILDINGS

CHAPTER XXXVII.

THE policy of protection, to which Sir John Macdonald
referred in his manifesto, is contained in the resolution moved by himself in the House of Commons on March
7, 1878.

"Resolved, that this House is of opinion that the welfare
of Canada requires the adoption of a National Policy, which,
by a judicious readjustment of the tariff, will benefit the
agricultural, the mining, the manufacturing and other interests
of the Dominion ; that such a policy will retain in Canada
thousands of our fellow-countrymen now obliged to expatriate
themselves in search of the employment denied them at
home ; will restore prosperity to our struggling industries now
so sadly depressed ; will prevent Canada from being a sacrifice market ; will encourage and develop an active interprovincial trade, and moving (as it ought to do) in the direction
of a reciprocity of tariffs with our neighbours, so far as the
varied interests of Canada may demand, will greatly tend to
procure for this country eventually a reciprocity of trade."
And his statement that "almost, as if by magic, the whole
face of the country underwent a change. Stagnation and
apathy and gloom—aye, and want and misery, too—gave
place to activity and enterprise and prosperity. The miners
of Nova Scotia took courage ; the manufacturing industries
in our great centres revived and multiplied ; the farmer found
a market for his produce, the artisan and labourer employment at good wages, and all Canada rejoiced under the quickening influence of a new found life," finds ample justification

and verification in the records of the past twelve years. A comparison of 1878 with 1890 shows the following marvellous national growth and increase :

	1878	1890	Increase
Miles of railway........	6,143	13,988	7,845
Tons of shipping........	23,102,551	41,243,251	18,140,700
Letters and post-cards carried by P.O. Dep..	50,840,000	113,580,000	63,140,000
Deposits in chartered and savings banks.....	$88,995,126	$197,892,452	$108,900,326
Money orders..........	$7,130,000	$11,970,862	$4,777,862
Bank note circulation...	$29,786,805	$47,417,071	$17,631,266
Production of coal (tons)	1,152,000	3,000,000	1,848,000
Value exports of Canadian cheese...........	$3,997,521	$9,372,212	$5,374,691
Value exports of Canadian cattle...........	$1,152,333	$6,949,417	$5,797,083
Value exports of Canadian sheep...........	$699,337	$1,234,347	$538,010
Value exports of manufactured wood.......	$13,908,629	$20,659,348	$6,750,719
Value exports of home manufactures	$18,182,647	$25,530,003	$7,347,356

The railway system, as will be seen, has more than doubled its mileage, but to get a better idea of the expansion, we must look at the amount of capital which has been invested, the traffic that has sprung up, the earnings and the working expenses. All these have increased more than 100 per cent. since the initiation of the National Policy, the figures being :

	1878	1890
Passengers carried...............	$6,443,924	$12,151,051
Tons of freight carried	7,883,472	17,928,626
Paid-up capital	$360,617,186	$760,576,446
Gross earnings....................	$20,520,078	$42,149,615
Working expenses	$16,100,102	$31,037,045

The shipping in 1890 was nearly 18,000,000 tons greater than 1878, so that to find employment for this increased tonnage, the water borne trade of the country must also have expanded to the extent of nearly eighty per cent.

During the same period of time our foreign trade has also increased in a marked manner. For the five years—1874-78

—previous to the introduction of the National Policy, the total foreign trade, imports and exports, amounted to \$940,308,362. For the next five years—1879-83—it was \$983,375,079. For 1884-88 it was \$999,164,938, and the returns for 1889 and 1890, (\$423,021,488), without allowing for any further increase, indicate that the amount up to 1893 will aggregate \$1,056,553,720. Sir John Macdonald went out of power at the end of the year 1873, when the imports and exports, for the year ending June 30, 1874, aggregated \$217,565,560. For the next five years they stood as follows :

To June 30, 1875	....	\$200,957,262
" " 1876	....	174,176,781
" " 1877	....	175,203,355
" " 1878	....	172,405,454
" " 1879	....	153,455,682

He returned to power at the end of 1878, and, early in 1879, introduced the National Policy. For the next fiscal year, ending June 30, 1880, the total trade amounted to \$174,401,205. In 1881 it went up to \$203,621,663, and since then it has only twice been below \$200,000,000. For 1890 it was \$218,000,000.

Of this foreign trade the principal part of our exports went to Great Britain.

Fiscal Year ending June 30th.	VALUE OF EXPORTS BY COUNTRIES.	
	Great Britain.	United States.
1879	\$36,295,718	\$27,165,501
1880	45,846,062	33,349,909
1881	53,571,570	36,866,225
1882	45,274,461	47,940,711
1883	47,145,217	41,668,723
1884	43,736,227	38,840,540
1885	41,877,705	39,752,734
1886	41,542,629	36,578,769
1887	44,571,846	37,660,199
1888	40,084,984	42,572,065
1889	38,105,126	43,522,404
1890	48,353,694	40,522,810
Total	\$526,405,239	\$466,440,590
Average for twelve years	\$43,867,103	\$38,870,050

These figures disclose how unwise would be a policy that would encourage unrestricted reciprocity with the States, and discrimination against the mother country.

There is also to be taken into consideration the interprovincial trade which has grown immensely of late years. This trade may be said to have become important only since Confederation. In the *Empire* of December 28, 1889, appeared a letter from the pen of Mr. George Johnson, Dominion Statistician, from which the following facts are gleaned :

" Previous to 1854 the trade between Canada, then composed of the Provinces of Ontario and Quebec and the Maritime Provinces, was small but growing. Then came the reciprocity treaty with the United States, and this diverted into United States channels so much of what scanty interprovincial trade did exist that the value of the direct trade between the provinces in 1865—the last year of the treaty—was less by half a million of dollars than that in 1853—the year immediately preceding that in which the treaty came into operation, while in the last few years of the treaty the total trade between the Maritime Provinces and Canada averaged not more than $2,000,000 a year.

" In 1866 the Grand Trunk established a line of steamers between Portland and Halifax and St. John, which effected a considerable increase in the trade, so that in the first year of our confederated life its value had increased to over $4,000,000, while the trade with the North-West was still practically nil.

" The opening of the Intercolonial Railway in 1876, the completion of the Canadian Pacific Railway five years in advance of the stipulated time, and its extension from Montreal to St. John and Halifax in 1889, afforded such increased facilities that, aided by the fostering influence of the National Policy, the trade increased by leaps and bounds. The interchange of commodities between Ontario and Quebec is immense, and the interprovincial trade between the Maritime Provinces themselves is also very great, but there are no official figures, and exact estimates are difficult to make, so that Mr. Johnson, in his paper, regarded Ontario and Quebec as one division and the Maritime Provinces as another division.

Adding all of Canada, west of the Lake of the Woods, as a third division, he gives these totals as the value of the inter-provincial trade actually in sight :

Eastward from Ontario and Quebec............. $28,000,000
Westward from Maritime Provinces............... 26,000,000
Amount carried by U. S. Railways 1,500,000
Between Eastern and Western Canada. 24,500,000
                                                ————————
                Total......................... $80,000,000

As evidence of the rapidity with which this trade is increasing Mr. Johnson gives the further facts, that "the tonnage of vessels from the Maritime Provinces to the port of Quebec increased in 1887 by thirty-three per cent. over 1886, and by forty-seven per cent. over 1885. The wonderful development of this interprovincial trade will be further revealed by a glance at the following table of freight carried by the Inter-colonial Railway :

Year	Flour, Barrels.	Grain, Bushels.	Lumber, Feet.	Live Stock, No.	Other Goods, Tons.
1878....	637,778	331,170	56,626,547	46,498	375,025
1882....	792,095	560,253	78,356,418	73,479	647,561
1886....	739,091	843,949	116,253,382	70,246	759,320
1890....	1,094,193	2,597,951	209,904,071	80,065	917,039

And it is an unquestionable fact that this class of trade is the very best we can have. It is better than exports to a foreign country ; the purchases on both sides are made because of necessity, and if we could not afford the mutual supply the goods would come from abroad. As it now is, our own railways and vessels carry the merchandise, and Canadian labour handles it. The profits, too, remain in the land."

An English writer says, that " home trade, home production, home consumption, are three times the bulk and value of foreign trade," but American writers place a much higher value upon them. It is, however, self evident that a market at his own door is the best possible one both for the farmer and the manufacturer, and that the greater the numbers of the latter who consume but do not produce articles of food, and who require raw materials for their business, the better must it be for the farming interests. It is equally true that it is in the best interests of the manufacturer to find a market for his finished productions as near at hand as possible.

"In 1890," said Mr. Blue, sec Bureau of Industry reports, "$440,000,000 worth of produce was raised by the farmers of Canada. Of this, $400,000,000 worth was consumed in Canada, only $13,000,000 went to the States, which, with a deduction of $5,000,000 imported here, left only $8,000,000 worth actually sold in the United States. The city of Toronto consumed that much itself. Who dare say in view of this that we require the American market for the consumption of our products?"

The farmer's best market is, of course, the home market and the problem for our statesmen to solve is where will he find the readiest sale for his surplus productions after the home market has been satisfied? This foreign market is naturally Great Britain, a country that buys annually nearly $500,000,000 worth of articles such as we produce, not the United States that has over $350,000,000 worth of the same articles to sell.

The Canadian farmer has only to look at the vast quantities of produce consumed by Britain to realize where an inexhaustible market for Canadian farm products lies. The prices realized there are good, and such articles as cheese, meats and fruits as our farmers now send are among the best paying products of Canada.

The British imports yearly of the very articles our farmers can readily supply are as follows :

Cheese	203,765,508 lbs.
Eggs	93,222,585 doz.
Butter	189,326,409 lbs.
Oats	54,247,997 bush.
Barley	41,563,229 bush.
Wheat	108,646,763 bush.
Beef	110,447,975 lbs.
Bacon	427,358,151 lbs.

What other market in the world can make such a showing as this?

Does it follow that the United States is our "natural" market because it is our nearest? Is not an over-crowded country like Great Britain, which cannot feed its own population, more of a "natural" market than an essentially agricultural country, such as the United States, which produces and exports everything that our farms can produce and export? Is a big farm on one side of the concession line the natural market for a smaller one across the way because it is nearer than the market town, or because the owners find it convenient to occasionally trade horses, or interchange seed?

And if proximity makes the United States the natural market for Canada, Canada must also be the natural market for the United States? Are they not anxious to secure this "natural" market? In the May number of *The Forum*, the Honourable Roger O. Mills, Democratic member of Congress, and author of the Mills' Tariff Bill introduced in 1888, has an article on reciprocity in which he urges closer trade relations with Canadians, because, that under reciprocity their trade with us would double in one year. Doubtless it would and perhaps more than that, but it would displace our own natural products or manufactures to the same extent and Canadian producers would have to leave off producing those articles they could not raise or make at equally low rates, with the result that our whole farming and manufacturing systems would have to be revolutionised to conform with the altered conditions.

The United States exports hundreds of millions of dollars worth of precisely the same articles that our farmers raise. Therefore, if they become our customers it cannot be because they do not raise enough for their own wants.

Many of the articles which they buy from us we see figuring in large quantities in their exports to Great Britain, and they, therefore, must buy in Canada as the cheapest market and sell in England as the dearest market, and pocket the commission made as middlemen.

The following table shews the exports of the United States in cattle and their produce and in farm produce for the year 1890:

Cattle	Number	394,836	$31,261,131
Hogs	"	91,148	909,042
Horses	"	3,501	680 410
Sheep	"	67,251	243,077
All other and fowls		......	120,725
Bones, hoofs, etc		......	271,533
Barley	Bushels	1,408,311	754,605
Corn	"	101,973,717	42,658,015
Cornmeal	Barrels	361,248	896,879
Oats	Bushels	13,692,776	4,510,055
Oatmeal	Pounds	25,460,322	784,879
Rye	Bushels	2,257,377	1,279,814
Wheat	"	54,387,767	45,275,906
" flour	Barrels	12,231,711	57,036,168
Eggs	Dozens	380,884	430,151
Apples	Barrels	453,506	1,231,436
Hay	Tons	36,274	567,558
Hides and skins		....	1,828,635
Beef, canned	Pounds	82,638,507	6,787,193
" fresh	"	173,237,506	12,862,384
" salted	"	97,508,419	5,250,068
" other cured	"	102,110	9,223
Tallow	"	112,745,370	5,242,158
Bacon and hams	"	608,490,956	47,056,760
Pork, pickled	"	79,788,868	4,753,488
Lard	"	471,083,598	33,455,520
Mutton	"	256,711	21,793
All other meat products	"	....	931,770
Butter	"	29,748,042	4,187,489
Cheese	"	95,376,053	8,591,042
Seeds, clover, timothy, etc		....	2,543,521
Tobacco leaf		....	21,149,869
Beans and pease		261,212	558,317
Potatoes		406,618	269,693
Vegetables, canned		....	231,265
Wool		231,042	33,543

Total.............................$344,675,715

A prominent member of the Liberal party made a speech at the Auditorium, Toronto, on February 13th, in which he endeavoured to prove that the Canadian farmers were not prosperous, that they were overwhelmed by mortgages on their property and suffering great injury by being excluded from the United States market. His statement on this point was endorsed by the *Globe* on February 19th, in these words : " In fact the value of farm lands have greatly diminished and the amount of mortgage thereon much increased throughout a very large portion of this Dominion since 1879." On the other hand the report of the Ontario Bureau of Industries for 1890, showed an average mortgage indebtedness (chattel and farm) on Ontario farm property of less than nine per cent. of its value, as compared with a mortgage indebtedness of fifteen per cent. of its value in 1878.

The following table shows that the farmers of Ontario are steadily increasing in wealth and prosperity :

	Farm Lands.	Buildings.	Implements.	Live Stock.	Total.
1882	$632,342,500	$132,711,575	$37,029,815	$80,540,720	$882,624,610
1883	654,793,025	163,030,675	43,522,530	100,082,365	961,428,595
1884	625,478,706	173,386,925	47,830,710	103,106,829	949,803,170
1885	626,422,024	182,477,905	48,569,725	100,690,086	958,159,740
1886	648,009,828	183,748,212	50,530,936	107,208,935	989,497,911
1887	636,883,755	184,753,507	49,248,297	104,406,655	975,292,214
1888	640,480,801	188,293,226	49,754,832	102,839,235	981,368,094
1889	632,329,433	192,464,237	51,685,706	105,731,288	982,210,664

Some years ago (1886) the report of the statistican, American Department of Agriculture, contained, amongst other details of state indebtedness, the following regarding New York, which is generally considered to be the wealthiest state in the union :

" There are a large number of farms, which were purchased a few years ago and mortgaged, which now would not sell for more than the face of the mortgages, owing to the depreciation of the farming lands, which, on an average, is fully thirty-three per cent. in ten years. Probably one-third of the farms in the state would not sell for more than the cost of the buildings and other improvements, owing to the shrinkage. . . . The wages for farm help have been, for several years, thirty-three per cent. more than the business could bear."

The report sums up by stating that :

" The result of the investigation in New York shows that three-tenths of the farms are mortgaged, and that one in twenty of the farm proprietors is hopelessly in debt."

We have here, in contrast, the American official report regarding the condition of the farmers in the State of New York and the Canadian official report regarding the condition of the farmers of Ontario, the former declaring that the farms in New York have decreased thirty-three per cent. in ten years, and that one third would not bring more than the cost of the buildings and improvements, the latter declaring that Ontario farmers are $100,000,000 better off than they were eight years ago. Even this large amount does not fully represent the advance made, for it must not be forgotten that during that space of time the cost of farm implements has fallen very much.

If there is any farming community in the United States that ought to be prosperous it is the State of Illinois, where the farms lie all around the great city of Chicago, affording a market of over a million consumers of the minor products of the farm, and yet, excluding chattel mortgages, they owe over $147,000,000, the mortgage incumbrances increasing twenty-three per cent. between 1880 and 1887, or twice the ratio of increase in the value of the land.

In the report of the Illinois Bureau of Labour Statistics for 1888 it is stated that " there are 8,082,794 acres of Illinois land under mortgage, besides the mortgages on 237,336 lots and on chattels." It appears that there were filed in 1887 a total of 125,923 new mortgages for the immense sum of $117,152,857. The report winds up by saying : " Averaging the total mortgage indebtedness, as estimated by the state administration, it makes a debt of $520 for every head of family in the state, while the new debt contracted in 1887 alone makes $146.25 for each head of family. . . . The condition of Kansas and other western states is even worse."

An American writer, Mr. J. R. Elliott, has published a book on American farmers, in which he says :

" One who has been familiar with the past history of the farm homes of a country, who has known of the struggles and triumphs of the early possessors of these properties, cannot but be saddened when he sees them, one after another, abandoned,

INTERIOR OF ST. ALBAN'S CHURCH ON DAY OF FUNERAL, SHEWING CATAFALQUE
AND SIR JOHN'S SEAT DRAPED.

the lands to become the pasture domain of more successful estates, or to be entirely given over to the public common.

"Large tracts of country—away from the towns and cities—in the old states and provinces of America are thus being transformed ; and not only are these manifestations of failure on the part of our old farms to hold their own against the conditions of the times not confined to the old states, but are rapidly extending over the continent.

"Through the Boston *Advertiser,* a rather conservative journal, we have the following graphic picture of the desolation which already reigns over portions of Massachusetts, once the settlements of happy and prosperous farmers :

"'Throughout the State of Massachusetts, away from the 'cities and the large towns, may be met, besides oral reports, 'traces of farms once yielding a support to their occupants, but 'now abandoned. The signs of former tenancy are to be found 'in conditions varying from the indications of recent occupancy 'to those of a generation or longer ago. Sometimes the 'dwelling house has a look of neatness, in its white paint and 'green blinds, not yet yielding much to the weather. The 'barns, waggon sheds, corn cribs and other outbuildings will be 'blackened of course, from exposure of their unpainted surface 'but yet have in them wear and utility. But the stillness of a 'solitude haunts the place and the sign, affixed to a tree, " For 'Sale," stirs in the practical observer the suspicious question, 'Why ?

"'The storms of several decades have worn the paint away. 'The clapboards are darkening in the weather. The mortar 'has crumbled from between the bricks in the chimneys, 'so that you see the light of the sky through the crevices. 'Some of the panes in the windows are broken. The front 'door hangs ajar. The wind sighs through the empty wood-'shed. The outbuildings, first to go, are falling in. Acres of 'land, once cultivated, lie around. The sign announcing the 'place as being for sale is broken, and hanging by a single nail, 'and the words are almost untraceable.

"'Another scene will represent a ruin. The roof has 'tumbled in. The charming prospect of hill and dale and

'wood and setting sun is now never more to be shut out from
'the front door, where once the busy housewife may have
'sometimes glanced, for the door is swung far back and gaping
'on the scene, and no one is there to push it to. At some
'time or other the barn fell down, and the boards and timbers
'are rotting from the repeated dryings and wettings. It is a
'scene of desolation. The suggestiveness of former tenancy
'imparts to it a melancholy, such as a mere old cellar or the
'traces of a stone underpinning do not have. These, too, may
'be found sometimes in the midst of lonely woods, where the
'trees have grown up in the fields formerly ploughed and
'sowed, so that the owner is already counting on their value
'at some lone sawmill. But where the remnant of a frame is
'standing, it suggests the farmer's hopes, the housewife's
'counsels, the ploughboy's whistle, once known here, now gone
'forever.

" ' Large areas are now offered for sale. The prices asked
'for the land are low compared with the prices asked for land
'in the places where the population is growing.'

" A writer in the *Grange Homes,* of Boston, mentions seeing
farms sold in Vermont for less than the cost of the buildings
upon them. He pertinently suggests the query : ' The fathers
'among the hills were poor, but they cleared away the forests,
'raised and educated families and built homes. Why do the
'buildings now sell for less than they are worth, with 100 or
'200 acres of land thrown in to make the trade? Yes, why are
'these lands being abandoned? Why are the farmers becoming
'mere tenants? Why are mortgages settling down on the old
'farms of America?'"

At page 40 Mr. Elliott says :

" It is admitted now on all sides that farm industry is not
progressing in New England ; rather, fast losing ground."

At page 42 he goes on :

" The decadence of the agricultural interest in New Hampshire and Vermont is now the object of official investigation.
Mr. B. Valentine, Commissioner of Agriculture for Vermont,
finds that good areas of tillable land can be bought in his state
at prices approximating those of western lands. Two hundred

acre farms, with 'fair buildings,' good orchards and plenty of timber, are being sold for less than $1,000. In some counties large tracts of land of fair quality can be be bought for $3 or $4 per acre. Town Clerk Fuller, of Vershire, Vermont, says : 'We have many abandoned farms in different parts of our 'towns, with good buildings on them, that could be bought for '$5 or less per acre. All this land was once occupied by 'thrifty and prosperous farmers.'

"In forty-five agricultural townships in Connecticut the decrease of wealth in the eleven years 1865-76 amounted to $1,893,172 ; between 1876 and 1886 the decrease ran up to $2,741,520. Out of 603 farmers interviewed 378 show a yearly loss. As we travel away from New England to more western lands we meet the same cry—the decline of agriculture. The report on the financial affairs of the farmers of Nebraska (1887-88) shows that of 215 farmers, over fifty per cent. stated that they were losing money."

And at page 47, on the same subject, he says respecting the state of Michigan :

"The opinion of the labour commissioners of Michigan, that the mortgages upon the farms of that state operate as a 'mammoth sponge' upon the labours of the owners, is the growing feeling of the majority of the farmers all over America—the older parts at least. The farms of Michigan surround the great iron industries of the west. The state now contains large centres of population, and its lands are fertile and productive, and yet the farmers are evidently on the downward track."

Following up this question of mortgages, at page forty-nine he gives the following picture :

"The picture given of life on Saturday in a Kansas town is certainly a startling one : 'It matters not how dull the 'town has been during the week, on Saturday the streets are 'crowded with people ; on that day chattels are sold to satisfy 'the overdue mortgages. At present these sales are numerous 'in the west, outside of the corn belt, and a very large portion 'of these do not realize sufficient to pay the mortgages. 'Teams, waggons and horned stock, which six months ago

'were considered ample security for a loan of from $100 to
'$150, frequently fetch at public auction twenty-five per cent.
'less than the price of the mortgage.' "

At page sixty-three he quotes an authority well known
throughout the whole continent, as follows :

" The Honourable David A. Wells says : ' A few years
'ago the inhabitants of Ludlow, formerly a most prosperous
'town in Windsor county, Vermont, memorialized the legis-
'lature to the effect that there were twelve deserted farms
'within the town (townships) limits, and asked permission to
'guarantee to any person who would lease and work them
'exemption from taxation, local and state, for a considerable
'term of years.' He also states : ' All over New England
'farms in abundance can now be purchased for less than the
'cost of the improvements upon them—yes, for less than the
'cost of the construction of their stone walls.' "

Our extracts are already lengthy, but let us call another
witness, no less than Judge Nott, of the U.S. Court of Claims.
Writing to the New York *Post* on November 11, 1889, he
says :

" Midway between Williamstown and Brattleboro' a few
years ago I saw on the summit of a hill against the evening
sky what seemed a large cathedral. Driving thither I found
a huge, old-time two storey church, a large academy (which
had blended in the distance with the church), a village with
a broad street, perhaps 150 feet in width. I drove on and
found that the church was abandoned, the academy dis-
mantled, the village deserted. The farmer who owned the
farm on the north of the village lived on one side of the broad
street, and he who owned the farm on the south lived on the
other, and they were the only inhabitants. All of the others
had gone to the manufacturing villages, to the great cities,
to the west. Here had been industry, education, religion,
comfort and contentment, but there remained only a drear
solitude of forsaken homes."

The same story as to the wretched condition of the
American farmers was brought out in the evidence given
before the Committee of Ways and Means of the United

States Congress, before the adoption of the McKinley Tariff. It has all along been said by the leading American statesmen that the McKinley Bill was not meant to injure Canada but simply to afford relief to their own farmers by giving them protection against outside competition, and thus somewhat improve their condition. That this assistance was necessary, and, therefore, that no efforts of Canada will induce the Americans to allay the strictness of that Bill, was amply proved before this Committee. The American farmers are in such sore straits that even with the great market of 65,000,000, of which we have heard so much, they demand to be protected from all competition which will further increase the immense surplusage of farm produce which must seek a foreign market. In reading this evidence it must be remembered that it was given by Americans before the American Congress, and was published for the information of their own people, without any thought of Canadian elections. Let our farmers read the story and say if they are willing to reduce themselves to the same condition.

If unrestricted reciprocity were brought about our farmers might expect to occupy a position similar to that of the farmers of the State of New York, brought about by the competition with western prairie fed cattle. The following is taken from the New York *Times* of February 13, 1891:

"Never before was the market value of beef cattle so low. At the present prices prevailing no farmer can feed cattle without such a loss as to wholly neutralize the value of the resulting manure, to which he has been in the habit of looking for a part of his profit. Just now the feeding of cattle is the most unprofitable part of agriculture, and thus the ancient maxim that it was the most important part of the farmer's vocation becomes wholly obsolete. The reason is not far to seek. The low price of western dressed beef has reduced the value of stock to this inadequate point. Sides of beef are retailed from the refrigerator cars at six and seven cents a pound, or less when competition is to be destroyed. The western cattle are fed on the public lands, which are free to the use of stock owners without any charge. Thus, the ranging of stock comes into disastrous competition with farmers whose lands represent large investments and which are taxed on this basis. Good steers fed on farms have been sold at two cents and less per pound. This low price does not pay the cost. And as there is no other product which helps to make up this loss, feeding is stopped, and the grain and hay formerly used in this way is thrown upon an already overloaded market."

While the farmers of the United States are much less prosperous than those on the northern side of the border line, the wretchedness and misery in the large cities is something terrible to behold. Read the following headlines taken from two consecutive members of the Chicago *Herald* in the early part of this year 1891 :

IN SAD NEED OF HELP.

THOUSANDS HUNGRY AND COLD.

Many Touching Cases Where Deserving People Are Struggling to Secure the Bare Necessaries of Life Discovered by the "Herald's" Relief Corps.

ARE IN DESPERATE STRAITS.

Men Seeking for Work While Their Families are Starving.

CHILDREN CRYING FOR FOOD.

Relief Afforded a Worthy Family Which Was on the Verge of Starvation.

IN UTTER WANT AND MISERY.

Many Families on the North Side Are Suffering the Pangs of Hunger.

AID FOR THE HUNGRY.

ASSISTANCE FOR CHICAGO'S POOR.

Many Contributions Being Received by the "Herald's" Corps That Will Go Far Towards Relieving the Distress Throughout the City.

HELPLESS AND STARVING.

Pitiful Condition of Many Children and Sick Men and Women. in the Polish Quarter.

Families Slowly Starving While They Vainly Seek for Work.

MANY CASES OF SUFFERING.

Families Hungry and Cold and Sorely in Need of Help.

The Rochester, Buffalo, New York, Philadelphia and Detroit papers reveal the same deplorable state of affairs among the poor of these cities. The following is the summing up of a long article in the Detroit *Sun*:

"The poverty in all our great centres of civilization, as well as throughout the landlord and mortgage cursed frontiers of our land is, year by year, growing more terrible and more general.

"In the city of New York there are over 150,000 people who earn less than sixty cents a day. Thousands of this number are poor girls who work from eleven to sixteen hours a day. Last year there were over 23,000 families forcibly evicted in that city, owing to their inability to pay their rent. One person in every ten who died in New York in 1889 was buried in the Potter's field. Those are facts which may well give rise to anxious thoughts."

Do we ever hear of such hardships, wretchedness and misery in Canada?

The effect that unrestricted reciprocity would have upon our trade and commerce was very forcibly put by Mr. Van Horne, President of the Canadian Pacific Railway, in a letter addressed by him to Senator Drummond, and published by the latter in all the leading papers. Being an American by birth, education and training, and having spent the best years of his life in that country, it may fairly be presumed that his thoughts and aspirations would be strongly in favour of closer connections with the United States, and that he would appreciate, as fully as any man could, the advantages which would flow from unrestricted reciprocity. When, therefore, we find him coming forward and giving expression to the strongest opinions against that policy, and backing his views with statements, the truth and force of which must strike every thoughtful person, we are compelled to give him the greatest possible attention. The first of these letters was written in reply to one from Mr. Drummond, and was as follows :

MONTREAL, *February* 21, 1891.

My Dear Mr. Drummond:

You are quite right in assuming that the statement in the letter enclosed in your note of to-day is untrue. I am not in favour of unrestricted reciprocity or anything of the kind. I am well enough acquainted with the trade and industries of Canada to know that unrestricted reciprocity would bring prostration or ruin. I realize that for saying this I may be accused of meddling in politics, but with me this is a business question and not a political one, and it so vitally affects the interests that have been entrusted to me that I feel justified in expressing my opinion plainly. Indeed, since opposite views have been attributed to me, I feel bound to do so. No one can follow the proceedings in Congress at Washington, and the utterances of the leading newspapers of the United States, without being struck with the extraordinary jealousy that prevails there concerning Canada—jealousy growing out of the wonderful development of her trade and manufactures within the past twelve years. It was this jealousy that prompted the Anti-Canadian features of the McKinley Bill. It was represented and believed at Washington that the Canadian farmers largely depended on the United States for a market for many of their chief products, and that their loyalty could be touched through their pockets, and that it was only necessary to " put on the screws " to bring about a political upheaval in Canada, and such a reversal of the trade policy of the country as would inevitably lead to annexation. I have found it necessary to keep well informed as to the drift of matters at Washington, because the interests of the Canadian Pacific Railway have been threatened by all sorts of restrictive measures ; and from my knowledge of the feeling there, I do not hesitate to say that if the result of the pending elections in Canada is what the authors of the McKinley Bill expected it would be, another turn of the screw will follow. No comfort is to be found in the recent disaster to the Republican Party in the United States. It was not the anti-Canadian features of the McKinley Bill that caused this, but it was the heavily increased duties on many articles, the manufacture of which, at home, was intended to be forced. This increase of duties came at a time of general depression among the farmers and working classes, and it was resented by them. Trade relations with Canada had nothing to do with it. They were not thinking of us. Putting aside all patriotic considerations and looking at the question of unrestricted reciprocity from a strictly business standpoint,

What, in the name of common sense, has Canada to gain by it at this time? Thousands of farms in the New England States are abandoned; the farmers of the Middle States are all complaining, and those of some of the Western States are suffering to such an extent that organized relief is necessary. The manufacturers everywhere are alarmed as to their future, and most of them are reducing their output, working on short time and seeking orders at absolute cost, so that they may keep their best workmen together. We are infinitely better off in Canada. We have no abandoned farms and no distress anywhere, and there is work for everybody who is willing to work. Our neighbours' big mill pond is very low just now, but our smaller one is, at least, full enough to keep us going comfortably. His pond requires twelve times as much as ours to fill. It is not necessary that a small boy should be a school-boy to know what the result would be if we were to cut our dam. Our pond would at once fall to the level of the other. Even if we were suffering from hard times we could gain nothing by unrestricted reciprocity. No man of sense would seek partnership with one worse off than himself because he happened to be hard up. You can't make a good egg out of two bad ones. The Canadian Pacific Railway is far away the largest buyers of manufactured articles in Canada. It buys dry goods and groceries, as well as locomotives and cars; it buys pins and needles and millinery goods, as well as rails and splices and spikes; it buys drugs and medicines and clothing, as well as bolts and wheels and axles. It buys almost every conceivable thing, and it is necessarily in close touch with the markets at home and abroad. It has built up, or been instrumental in building up, hundreds of new industries in the country, and it is the chief support of many of them, and its experience with these markets and these industries justifies my belief that unrestricted reciprocity with the United States, and a joint protective tariff against the rest of the world would make New York the chief distributing point for the Dominion instead of Montreal and Toronto; would localize the business of the ports of Montreal and Quebec, and destroy all hope of the future of the ports of Halifax and St. John; would ruin three-fourths of our manufactories; would fill our streets with the unemployed; would make Eastern Canada the dumping ground for the grain and flour of the Western States to the injury of our own North-West, and would make Canada generally the slaughter market for the manufactures of the United States, all of which would be bad for the Canadian Pacific Railway as well as for the country at large; and this is my excuse for saying so much. I am not speaking for the Canadian Pacific Railway Company; nor as a Liberal or a Conservative, but only as an individual much concerned in the business interests of the country, and full of anxiety lest a great commercial, if not a national, mistake should be made.

(Signed) Yours truly,

W. C. VAN HORNE.

Sir John Macdonald concluded his last appeal to the Canadian electors in these words :

"I commend these issues to your determination, and to the judgment of the whole people of Canada, with an unclouded confidence that you will proclaim to the world your resolve to show yourselves not unworthy of the proud distinction that you enjoy—of being numbered among the most dutiful and loyal subjects of our beloved Queen. As for myself, my course is clear. A British subject I was born—a British subject I will die. With my utmost effort, with my latest breath, will I expose the 'veiled treason' which attempts, by sordid means and mercenary proffers, to lure our people from their allegiance. During my long public service of nearly half a century I have been true to my country and its best interests, and I appeal with equal confidence to the men who have trusted me in the past, and to the young hope of the country, with whom rest its destinies for the future, to give me their united and strenuous aid in this my last effort for the unity of the Empire and the preservance of our commercial and political freedom."

Some Liberal speakers stated on the platform that their party had been called disloyal because they desired free trade with the United States, but that was hardly correct. It is permissible for any political party to advocate any trade policy which they honestly believe to be in the interests of the country, without laying themselves open to reproach, but loyalty, as taught by Sir John Macdonald and as understood by all true Canadians, is to believe in British connection, to be proud of our share in the glorious history of the mother country, to desire to perpetuate the institutions and principles which there prevail, to consider that Canada owes gratitude and allegiance for benefits received in the past and to be prepared to resist any efforts which may result in weakening the ties which bind us to the old land from which we sprang. With his "utmost effort," with his "latest breath" Sir John opposed those.

"Who fain would lop, with felon stroke,
The branches of our British oak,

> And, wronging the great Canadian heart
> Would deem her honour cheaply sold
> For higher prices in the mart,
> And increased hoard of gold.

and encouraged the people of this country to feel and to proclaim to the world that,

> "Our pride of race we have not lost,
> And aye it is our loftiest boast
>   That we are Britons still!
> And in the gradual lapse of years,
> We look, that 'neath these distant skies,
> Another Britain shall arise,—
>   A noble scion of the old—
> Still to herself and lineage true,
> And prizing honour more than gold."

This feeling is not confined to Conservatives ; it animates
also the wisest and best men of the Reform party, but, unfortunately, there are others whose views are distinctly and
emphatically in favour of courses antagonistic to our present
relations with Great Britain and in favour of new ties with the
United States, who, while not exactly identified with that
party, are in antagonism to the Conservative party. These
men sneer at loyalty, disbelieve in patriotism, make light
of our allegiance to the British Empire, and lose no opportunity of working with tongue and with pen to destroy the
noblest sentiments and aspirations of our national lives. They
slander and belittle our country, proclaim Confederation as a
fraud, and the establishment of Dominion unity as a dream ;
prate of corruption, debt and taxation, and hold up absorption
into the United States as the only panacea for the evils under
which we lie, a policy which all true Canadians regard as dis-
graceful, disloyal and contemptible in both its inception and
its advocacy. And, although these views may have no importance in the eyes of the people of the country as a whole, and
may not even commend themselves to the Liberal audience to
which they are addressed, it is quite certain that signs of
approval and applause given to persistent detractors of our
national position and future prospects—even if conceded only
as an act of courtesy—are not calculated to impress outsiders

with an idea of intense loyalty. But we do not believe that
these persons voice the views of that great party. We prefer
to accept them as laid down by the *Globe* in its issue of March
4, 1887 :

"The value of Canada's political status is not to be
measured in dollars and cents. Who that loves British connection will appraise his feeling in money? Where is the
U. E. Loyalist who will name a price at which he would
be willing to see Brock's monument and the field of Lundy's
Lane under the flag of those against whom his ancestors
fought? Where is the French-Canadian willing to sell out
the pride with which he thinks of the battle-ground of
Chateauguay?

"Are young Canadians of so poor a spirit that they will
speculate in their patriotism and national aspirations? We do
not believe it. Those who reckon Canadians as five millions
of stomachs make a profound mistake. Unreasonable they
may be called, but the sort of unreasonableness that keeps
people from subordinating their affections or sentiments to
their pockets has been universally defined as Honour.

"Can Canada satisfy its demands and yet enter into the
customs union that we think would be profitable? The question is surely one to be discussed in a larger spirit than some
of our contemporaries display.

"One unfortunate result of division of Canadian parties on
fiscal lines has been to imbue the people largely with the false
and dangerous notion that political institutions are not of the
first importance. Compared with the preservation of our
responsible Government the scale of our tariff is of little
moment. It should be thought of as nothing more than
a scheme of taxation to provide for the main concern—the
maintenance of our institutions. By treating the tariff as an
end instead of a means, the doctrine that self-government is
not priceless has been insiduously, perhaps unintentionally,
inculcated."

"The loyal and patriotic people of Canada can draw
a deep breath of relief this morning, and humbly and
reverently return thanks to the Almighty Dispenser of all good

that He so touched the hearts of the people that they rose in their might and entered a vigorous protest against the traitorous attempt to betray the country to a foreign nation."

These were the words with which the Ottawa *Citizen* commenced the announcement to its readers of the result of the election, and there is no doubt that it found a response in the bosoms of many who eagerly looked for the first news of the contest. It was a desperate struggle from the first, and, from the nature of the issue, was watched with great eagerness by the outside world, and more especially by Great Britain and the United States. It was interesting, as well as amusing, to note the results as calculated by the different papers. The *Empire* put the Government majority at forty-two ; and, from that point, it descended through other Conservative papers to thirty-two, the figure of the Montreal *Gazette*. Of the Opposition papers, the *Mail* conceded twenty-nine ; the *Globe* twenty-seven ; and so on down to the Ottawa *Free Press*, which would not allow more than four. The New York *Times* gave only one. Then the figures ran the other way, the Quebec *Telegraph* claiming a majority of twenty for the Liberals, and the *L'Electeur* five more. Many men, especially from the Province of Quebec, were claimed by both parties, so that the question could not be decided until a vote was taken. By the division on Mr. Cameron's franchise motion, and subsequent declarations by members, it was ascertained that the Government could rely on a majority of about thirty-one in a full House.

The result of the first vote may be tabulated as follows :

	Conservatives.	Opposition.	Majorities.
Ontario	48	44	4
Quebec	30	35	..
Nova Scotia	16	5	11
New Brunswick	13	3	10
Manitoba	4	1	3
British Columbia	6	0	6
N. W. Territories	4	0	4
P. E. Island	2	4	..
			38

Less Opposition majority in Quebec and P.E.I. 7

Total Conservative majority 31

This indicates a majority of four in Ontario, the leading province in the Dominion, and an overwhelming majority in every other province except Quebec and Prince Edward Island.

Sir John Macdonald had a magnificent personal victory in Kingston. His majority of seventeen in 1887 being increased to four hundred and eighty-three. The defeat of Mr. Colby in Stanstead was one of the most regrettable incidents of the campaign. He was a representative of great ability, of whom his Province had reason to be proud.

CITY BUILDINGS KINGSTON, ON DAY OF FUNERAL.

(The Clock in Tower was presented by Sir John and Mr. Counter in 1857.

CHAPTER XXXVIII.

Sir John's strength gives way under the great strain of the campaign—He ha! the attack of nervous and physical prostration—Which is followed by paraly ... " and hemorrhage on the brain—Sad scenes in the House of Commons when' the nigh approach of death is announced—His hour of rest had come Canada's grief—Memorable scenes when Sir Hector Langevin announces his death—Mr. Laurier's noble tribute—Lying in state The funeral at Ottawa—The journey to Kingston—Lying in state in the City Hall—To Cataraqui cemetery—The final scene—Movements to erect monuments to his memory—Memorial services in Westminster Abbey—A memorial to be erected in St. Paul's Cathedral—Lord Dufferin's tribute—Lines by Mrs Rothwell.

> Life's race well run,
> Life's work well done,
> Life's crown well won,
> Now comes rest.

THE extraordinary exertions made by Sir John Macdonald during the election would have been creditable to a young man, but for a man past seventy-six years of age, they were simply marvellous. He, however, over-estimated his strength, and when he arrived at Kingston was quite unwell and very much exhausted. His medical advisers enjoined complete abstention from work, but his energy and anxiety impelled him to break through their kindly restrictions, and in a day or two he was actively participating in the campaign. After the election was over he returned to Ottawa, and it was hoped that he would then take a rest and thereby secure a sufficient return of strength to be able to meet Parliament and undergo the fatigues of the session. Had it been possible for him to have done this, or had he been willing to leave his post and go away for a holiday, he might have recovered and been spared to his country for some time to come, but the labour of preparing for the session, following so soon after the excitement and bustle of the campaign, was too much for him. When Parliament opened he was able to attend and direct proceedings, but it was evident to all that he was not himself. An unusual appearance of weariness was perceptible at times, and it was observable that he was physically weak although his mind was clear and bright as ever. He was always cheerful, however, and moved about among his supporters

ating them with anecdotes, or saying some kindly word.
r a few days his place was vacant and it was rumoured
he had experienced a fit of exhaustion similar to that
h overtook him at Kingston. A week or so later he was
n in his place still looking unwell, but apparently better.
last appearance in the House was on Friday, May 22nd,
nen he was in good spirits, jocular and full of life. The next
evening he gave a large dinner party. During the early part
of the next week it was known that he was not so well, but
nothing serious was apprehended. On Monday he was suffering from a slight cold, but attended to business at Earnscliffe.
On Wednesday his symptoms became more unfavourable, and
Dr. Powell, his regular physician, expressed a desire for a
consultation. Sir John agreed and Drs. Ross and Stewart of
Montreal were sent for. The physicians met on the following
day, and after examining their patient, issued this bulletin :

EARNSCLIFFE, *May 28, 1891.*

Sir John Macdonald has had a return of his attack of physical and
nervous prostration, and we have enjoined complete rest for the present
and entire freedom from public business.

R. W. POWELL, M.D., *Ottawa.*
GEO. ROSS, M.D., *Montreal.*
JAS. STEWART, M.D., *Montreal.*

While it was recognized that it would be unlikely, if not
impossible, that Sir John would be able to take his place again
during the session, a hopeful feeling was experienced that his
immense vitality would enable him to recover, and that a
period of thorough rest would so recuperate his strength that
he could once more resume the duties of his high position.

On Friday morning re-assuring tidings were conveyed in
the following bulletin, which was posted in the hotels and all
places of general resort :

EARNSCLIFFE, *May 29, 10 a.m.*

The Premier passed a quiet and comfortable night, and this morning his physical strength shows distinct improvement since yesterday.

(Signed)   R. W. POWELL, M.D.

At 10.30 Sir John Thompson had an interview with him
for about half an hour. Although all business had been for-

bidden by his physicians, the Premier could not refrain from following his old routine and during the day gave directions with regard to certain matters that required attention. At two o'clock a cablegram of enquiry and sympathy was received from H.R.H. the Princess Louise, to which he dictated the reply : " Thanks for your gracious message. Am improving." At three o'clock, when the House met, the excitement had somewhat abated, and at four o'clock, when Dr. Powell called, he found Sir John sitting up and seeming better. In answer to enquiries he was telling how he felt and what nourishment he had taken, when the terrible stroke of paralysis came, and he sank back unconscious. Further medical aid was at once summoned, but hemorrhage on the brain had succeeded the paralysis and the doctors feared that death would ensue in a few hours. The sad news was conveyed to Sir Hector Langevin in a note from Sir James Grant, and by him communicated to the House of Commons.

Never in the history of Parliament was there a more affecting scene than that which followed the motion for adjournment. As the Premier's old companion, his own eyes full of tears, announced the nigh approach of death to one whom they all revered and loved, sympathetic glances and sympathetic words were exchanged by political friend and political foe, every face was a picture of sorrow, and the dimmed eyes of his old friends showed that the loss of their leader would be a personal bereavement, while among his opponents nothing was heard but the kindest words of the stricken statesman, the greatest admiration for his abilities, and the deepest regret at the prospect of his death.

But the end was not to be yet. The dauntless spirit struggled hard, and when the last bulletin was issued that night all hope was not destroyed :

EARNSCLIFFE, *11 p.m.*

Sir John's condition still continues very precarious. Loss of power of speech. Respiration and circulation weak. Rests somewhat better than during the afternoon.

Takes a moderate degree of liquid nourishment.

(Signed)

R. W. POWELL, M.D.
J. A. GRANT, M.D.
HENRY P. WRIGHT, M.D.

And so it went on for seven days and nights, the vital forces gradually lowering, until, at 10.15, of the evening of June 6th, he calmly and peacefully passed away. His hour of rest had come, and the soul of the great statesman, the revered chieftain, winged its way into eternity.

We will not try to express the grief with which the sad news was received from one end of Canada to the other. The task has been better performed by more able pens, and we will, instead, quote the words of his friend and faithful follower, Mr. C. H. Macintosh, M.P. for Ottawa, in the *Citizen* of June 9th :

"'O, friends! our chief State-oracle is mute!' He who served Canada faithfully and well, has been called to his long home : Sir John Macdonald is no more, but his name will be revered by generations yet to come, and a nation's tears consecrate the spot, where soon will rest another distinguished mortal who has put on immortality. It is hard to part from those we love ; doubly bitter from those whose friendship has been enjoyed, whose character has been esteemed, whose splendid abilities reflected glory upon the entire commonwealth: Many hearts will ache, many eyes be dimmed, when the sad news is flashed throughout the Dominion, that Sir John Macdonald is dead : that the hand ever raised in defence of his country's interests is cold and still ; that the tongue, ever eloquent in a great cause, is pulseless and silent forever. Tremblingly, we pay this tribute to one whose inestimable services to his party and whose patriotic devotion to Canada, commanded the respect of every civilized community in the world. Tremblingly, we chronicle the irreparable loss which the wisdom of Providence has ordained, and, bowing submissively to the decree, bid farewell to him who, but a few days ago, was employing his great mental faculties in solving the problem of how best to promote the welfare, the happiness, the future comfort of millions who placed implicit confidence in his statesmanship, and were unswerving in their fealty to his principles. He who

> " Hath run his bright career,
>   And served men nobly, and acceptance found,
> What can he better crave, than then to die,
>   And wait the issue, sleeping under ground ?"

" True, indeed, the poet's words, but the lesson is hard to learn, the burthen heavy to bear. We know, but scarce can realize, that the voice is hushed, the hand still, the heart cold ; that never more can praise or censure, eulogy or blame, pass beyond the precincts of the dark and silent tomb. Vain it is to boast ' of fleeting things, too certain to be lost'; we know the blow must fall, we know the parting must come ; but, human-like, dream that the day is long and the Angel of Death far off. It is not for man to pierce the mysterious labyrinth, or to discover the dread secrets beyond the silent shores ; affliction comes, and teaching the lesson of humility, brings us nearer the realms of kindliness, charity and forbearance. We realize how vain are human pursuits, how flimsy the world's rewards, what mockery its greatest honours, how short its most potent enjoyments. As the cradle is pushed aside, and life's trials, vicissitudes, triumphs and successes follow in rapid review, it seems but a fleeting moment ere we stand beside a grass-covered mound—mourning what was, but what has ceased to be. The Here and Hereafter, the Sunshine and Sunset, never lose sight of one another."

When the announcement was made to the House of Commons the scene was one not soon to be forgotten. The Chamber was hung with emblems of mourning, the empty chair of the dead Premier being heavily draped, and on his desk lay a beautiful floral shield, the tribute of his loyal followers in the House. As Sir Hector Langevin rose to speak, the deepest silence prevailed, and when, struggling in vain to stifle his emotions, sobs choked his utterance, many members bowed their heads on their desks, or sat erect with tears rolling down their cheeks, while spectators in the gallery wept audibly. The tribute of Mr. Laurier was a noble one, most eloquent and touching, and evidently proceeded from his heart. The following are some of the speeches delivered in the House :

Sir Hector Langevin—"Mr. Speaker, as the oldest Privy Councillor, it falls to my lot to announce to the House that our dear old chief, the First Minister of Canada, is no more. After a painful illness of two weeks, death put an end to his earthly

career on Saturday last. To tell you, Mr. Speaker, my feelings
under the circumstances is more than I can do. I feel that by
the death of Sir John Macdonald, Canada has lost its greatest
statesman, a great patriot, a man of whom any country in the
world would be justly proud. Her Majesty, our gracious
Queen, never had a more devoted and loyal subject than the
grand old man whose loss we all deplore and regret from the
bottom of our hearts. For nearly fifty years he has directed
the public affairs of this country. He was, among the fathers
of Confederation, the most prominent and distinguished. He
put his whole soul into that great undertaking, knowing full
well that the confederation of all the British North American
provinces would give to our people a country and institutions
to be proud of, and to the Empire, not only a right arm, but a
great and safe highway to her Indian and other possessions.
He told me more than once how grateful he was to the people
of Canada to have allowed him to have consummated that
great work. The fact is his love for Canada was equal to that
he had for his own mother country.

"When the historians of Canada write the history of the
last fifty years, they will have to write the life of Sir John
Macdonald, and in writing his life they may not agree with all
his public acts, but they cannot fail to say that he was a great
man, a most distinguished statesman, and that his whole life
was spent in the service of his country, dying in the midst of
his official duties, not having a day's rest before he passed to a
better world. I need not express, Mr. Speaker, my own personal feelings. Having spent half of my life with him as
his follower and his friend, his departure is the same as if I
lost half of my existence. I remember how devoted he was,
not only to the old Province of Canada, but how chivalrous he
showed himself to the Province of Quebec, and especially to
my French-Canadian countrymen. He had only a word to
say, and instead of being at the head of a small band of
seventeen Upper Canada members, he would have had all the
representatives of his province behind him, but as he told me
several times he preferred to be just to his French com-
patriots and allies, and the result was that when Confederation

came the Province of Quebec had confidence in him, and on his death-bed our great chief could see that his just policy has secured peace and happiness to all. Mr. Speaker, I would have wished to continue to speak of our dear departed friend, and have spoken to you about his goodness of heart, the witness of which I have been so often, but I feel that I must stop, my heart is full of tears. I cannot proceed further. I therefore move, ' that, in the opinion of this House, the mortal remains of the Right Honourable Sir John Macdonald, G.C.B., should be publicly interred, and that this House will concur in giving to the ceremony a fitting degree of solemnity and importance.' "

Mr. Laurier.—" Mr. Speaker, I fully appreciate the motion which the honourable gentleman has just proposed to the House, and we all concur that his silence under the circumstances is far more eloquent than any human language can be. I fully appreciate the intensity of the grief which fills the soul of all those who were the friends and followers of Sir John A. Macdonald at the loss of the great leader, whose whole life has been so closely identified with their party, a party upon which he has thrown such brilliancy and lustre. We on this side of the House, who were his opponents, who did not believe in his policy, nor in his methods of Government, we take our full share of their grief for the loss, which they deplore to-day is far and away beyond the ordinary compass of party strife. It is in every respect a great national loss, for he is no more who was, in many respects, Canada's most illustrious son, and who was, in every sense, Canada's most foremost citizen and statesman.

" At the period of life to which Sir John A. Macdonald had arrived, death, whenever it comes, cannot come unexpected. Some few months ago, during the turmoil of the late election, when the country was made aware that on a certain day the physical strength of the veteran Premier had not been equal to his courage, and that his intense labour for the time being had prostrated his singularly wiry frame, everybody, with the exception perhaps of his buoyant self, was painfully anxious lest, perhaps, the angel of death had touched him with

his wings. When a few days ago, in the midst of an angry
discussion in this Parliament, the news spread in this House
that of a sudden his condition had become alarming, the
surging wave of angry discussion was at once hushed, and
every one, friend and foe, realized that this time for a certainty,
the angel of death had appeared, and had crossed the threshold
of his home. Thus we were not taken by surprise, and although
we were prepared for the sad event, yet it it almost impossible
to convince the unwilling mind that it is true that Sir John
Macdonald is no more, that the chair which we now see vacant
shall remain forever vacant, that the face so familiar in this
Parliament for the last forty years, shall be seen no more,
and that the voice so well-known shall be heard no
more, whether in solemn debate or in pleasant and mirth-
ful tones. In fact the place of Sir John A. Macdonald
in this country was so large and so absorbing that it
is almost impossible to conceive that the politics of this
country, the fate of this country, will continue without him.
His loss overwhelms us. For my part, I say with all truth,
his loss overwhelms me, and it also overwhelms this Parliament as if, indeed, one of the institutions of the land had given
way.

  " Sir John A. Macdonald now belongs to the ages, and it
can be said with certainty that the career which has just been
closed is one of the most remarkable careers of this century.
It would be premature at this time to attempt to divine
or anticipate what will be the final judgment of history
upon him, but there were in his career and in his life features
so prominent and so conspicuous that already they shine with
a glory which time cannot alter. These characteristics appear
before the House at the present time such as they will appear
to the end in history. I think it can be asserted that, for the
supreme art of governing men, Sir John Macdonald was gifted
as few men in any land or in any age were gifted, gifted with
the most high of all qualities, qualities which would have shone
in any theatre, and which have shone all the more conspicuously the larger the theatre. The fact that he could congregate together elements the most heterogeneous, and blend

them into one compact party and to the end of his life keep them steadily under his hand, is perhaps altogether unprecedented. The fact that during all these years he maintained unimpaired, not only the confidence, but the devotion and the ardent devotion and affection of his party, is evidence that besides these high qualities of statesmanship to which we were the daily witnesses, he was also endowed with that inner, subtle, undefinable characteristic of soul which wins and keeps the hearts of men.

"As to his statesmanship, it is written in the history of Canada. It may be said, without any exaggeration whatever, that the life of Sir John Macdonald, from the date he entered Parliament, is the history of Canada, for he was connected and associated with all the events, all the facts, with all the developments which brought Canada from the position Canada then occupied—the position of two small provinces having nothing in common but the common allegiance, and united by a bond of paper and unity and by nothing else—to the present state of development which Canada has reached. Although my political views compel me to say that in my judgment his actions were not always the best that could have been taken in the interest of Canada. Though my conscience compels me to say that of late he has imputed to his opponents motives which I must say in my heart he has misconceived, yet I am only too glad here to sink those differences, and to remember only the great services he has performed for his country ; to remember that his actions displayed unbounded fertility of resource, a high level of intellectual conception, and, above all, a far-reaching vision beyond the event of the day, and still higher, permeating the whole, a broad patriotism to Canadian welfare, Canada's advancement and Canada's glory.

"The life of a statesman is always an arduous one, and very often it is an ungrateful one. More often than otherwise his actions do not mature until he is in his grave. Not so, however, in the case of Sir John Macdonald. His career has been a singularly fortunate one. His reverses were few and of short duration. He was fond of power, and, in my

judgment, if I may say so, that was the turning point of his
history.   He was fond of power and he never made any secret
of it.   Many times we have heard him avow it on the floor of
this Parliament, and his ambition in this respect was gratified
as perhaps no other man's ambition ever was.   In my judgment even the career of William Pitt can hardly compare with
that of Sir John Macdonald in this respect, for, although
William Pitt, moving in a higher sphere, had to deal with
problems greater than ours, yet I doubt if, in the management of a party, William Pitt had to contend with difficulties
equal to those that Sir John Macdonald had to contend with.

"In his death, too, he seems to have been singularly
happy.   Twenty years ago I was told by one who, at that
time, was a close personal and political friend of Sir John
Macdonald, that in the intimacy of his domestic circle he was
fond of repeating that his end would be as the end of Lord
Chatham, that he would be carried away from the floor of
Parliament to die.   How true his vision into the future was,
we now know, for we saw him at the last with enfeebled health
and declining strength, struggling on the floor of Parliament
until, the hand of fate upon him, he was carried to his home to
die, and thus to die with his armour on was probably his
ambition.   Sir, death is the supreme law, and although we see
it every day in every form, although session after session we
have seen it in this Parliament, striking right and left without
any discrimination as to age or station, yet the ever recurring
spectacle does not in any way remove the bitterness of the sting.
Death always carries with it an incredible sea of pain, but the
one thing sad in death is that which is involved in the word
separation—separation from all we love in life.   This is what
makes death so poignant, when it strikes a man of intellect in
middle age.   But when death is the natural termination of a
full life, in which he who has disappeared had given the full
measure of his capacity, has performed everything required
from him, and more, the sadness of death is not for him who
goes, but for those who love him and remain.   In this sense I
am sure the Canadian people will extend unbounded sympathy to the friends of Sir John Macdonald, to his sorrowing

children, and, above all, to the brave and noble woman, his companion in life, his chief helpmeet.

"Thus, Mr. Speaker, one after another we see those who have been instrumental in bringing Canada to its present state of development removed from amongst us. To-day we deplore the loss of him who, we all unite in saying, was the foremost Canadian of his time, and who filled the largest place in Canadian history. Only last week was buried in the city of Montreal another son of Canada, one who, at one time, had been a tower of strength to the Liberal Party, one who will ever be remembered as one of the noblest, purest and greatest characters that Canada has ever produced—Sir Antoine Aimé Dorion. Sir Antoine Aimé Dorion had not been in favour of Confederation. Not that he was opposed to the principle, but he believed that the union of these provinces at that day was premature. When, however, Confederation had become a fact, he gave the best of his mind and heart to make it a success. It may indeed happen, sir, when the Canadian people see the ranks thus gradually reduced and thinned of those upon whom they have been in the habit of relying for guidance, that a feeling of apprehension will creep into the heart, lest, perhaps, the institutions of Canada may be imperilled.

"Before the grave of him who, above all, was the father of Confederation let not grief be barren grief, but let grief be coupled with the resolution, the determination, that the work in which Liberals and Conservatives, in which Brown and Macdonald united, shall not perish, but that, though united Canada may be deprived of the services of her greatest men, yet, still Canada shall and will live. I agree to the motion."

After the adjournment of the House a Conservative caucus was held, at which the members were arranged in groups of four to act as a guard of honour over the body of the Premier from the time of arrival at the Parliament Buildings until the hour set for the funeral. Each quartette went on duty for an hour and a-half, when it was relieved by the next group.

Early on Tuesday morning all that was mortal of Sir John Macdonald was brought to the Senate Chamber, and the

casket opened, that those who chose might gaze for the last
time on the well-known features. Near the head was placed
a table on which were arranged the insignia of the various
orders which had been bestowed in recognition of high and
valuable services. The floral tributes, composed of the rarest
and most beautiful flowers, formed one continuous bed and
filled the room with their aroma. Conspicuous amongst these
was one of circular form fashioned out of rare white roses and
small sprigs of trailing fern, "from Her Majesty Queen Victoria in memory of her faithful and devoted servant." The
dead Premier lay dressed in the uniform of an Imperial Privy
Councillor, his sword by his side, and his cocked hat across his
breast. The face looked so peaceful and quiet that it brought
to mind the beautiful lines of the " Poet Priest of the South,"
which were said to have been the favourite verses of Sir John.
He was especially fond of the first and the last two stanzas :

> " My feet are wearied and my hands are tired,
>   My soul oppressed ;
> And I desire, what I have long desired,
>   Rest—only rest.
>
> *   *   *   *   *
>
> 'Twas always so ; when but a child I laid
>   On mother's breast
> My weary little head, e'en then I prayed,
>   As now—for rest !
>
> And I am restless ; still 'twill soon be o'er ;
>   For, down the West,
> Life's sun is setting, and I see the shore
>   Where I shall rest ! "

At 10.15 Lord Stanley arrived, attended by Major Colville,
military secretary ; Viscount Kilcoursie, Capt. Walsh, Lt.-Col.
Smith and Lt.-Col. Macpherson, A.D.C's., and closely followed
by Major General Herbert and Capt. Streatfield, A.D.C., and
the members of the late Ministry.

Lord Stanley walked first, bearing in his hands an immense
wreath of white roses and maidenhair fern, to which was
attached a card with the words, " In loving memory from
Stanley of Preston and Constance Stanley," a last loving
tribute of respect, which he reverentially laid on the casket.

With eyes brimming over with tears His Excellency gave one long, lingering look at the face of the statesman whom he had learned to love and to value, and then, with mournful step and downcast head, passed silently out of the chamber.

After the Ministers, Senators and Members of the House of Commons, the general public were admitted, and from that time until late into the night, and all next morning until the hour of the funeral, one continuous line of sad faced men and women passed through the chamber. The funeral took place the next day, and in the history of the Dominion there has never been seen so large or so impressive a cortege. At one o'clock the bearers entered the Senate Chamber, and lifting the casket shoulder high the solemn march began. The two senior whips, Messrs. Taylor and Trow, bearing the Queen's wreath, and Messrs. Daly and Pope, M.P's, carrying their Excellency's wreath, headed the procession. Then followed the mourners. Next were the dignitaries of the State. Guards lined the corridors and stair-way leading to the main entrance, where the black plumed hearse stood in waiting, and as the chieftain's form passed through the portals of Parliament for the last time and under the canopy of mourning drapery which covered the high groined archway, the tower bell pealed forth a solemn stroke ; the bells in every church in the city seemed to take up the sound, and like a monster chime rung by a master hand, the solemn funeral dirge was tolled in unison. So from the dim chamber where he lay in state they bore their chieftain out into the glorious sunlight where the multitude were gathered.

At 1.15 the procession got under way and slowly, solemnly, the vast concourse moved out upon the street, through the eastern gate, in the following order :

Squad of Dragoon Guards, four abreast.
Band of the Governor-General's Foot Guards.
Band of the 43rd Battalion.
Militia Officers in Uniform.
Two cars of Floral Tributes.
The Hearse, drawn by four horses.
The Pall-bearers, being Members of the late Cabinet.

Carriage containing Mr. Hugh J. Macdonald, " Little Jack," Lieut.
Col. J. Pennington Macpherson and Rev. Dr. Williamson.
Carriage containing Dr. Powell, Mr. Fred. White, Mr. Joseph Pope
and Mr. George Sparks.
Carriage containing His Excellency the Governor-General and Col. Sir
Casimir Gzowski, representing Her Majesty the Queen.
Lieutenant-Governors.
The Senate.
Judges of the Courts of Law.
The Commons.
Officials of the House of Commons.
Parliamentary Press Gallery and Pages.
Consular Corps.
Provincial Legislatures.
Law Associations.
Medical Associations.
The Deputy Ministers.
The Grand Trunk Railway Officials.
The Canadian Pacific Railway Officials.
Officers of the Militia, not in uniform.
The Mayor and Corporation of the City of Ottawa.
Other Municipal Bodies.
Liberal Conservative Associations.
Deputations from Cities and Towns.
Citizens.

At St. Alban's Church the casket rested on a bier, consisting of two mahogany pedestals covered with a banner of
purple and gold, placed beneath a handsome baldachino of
purple silk. The service was conducted by the Rev. J. J.
Bogert, assisted by Venerable Archdeacons Lauder, Bedford-
Jones and others. Many eyes were suffused when the choir
chanted the tenth verse of the 90th Psalm : " The days of our
age are three score and ten, and though men be so strong that
they come to four score years, yet is their strength then but .
labour and sorrow, so soon passeth it away and we are gone."

The chanting of the psalms over, the choir and congregation together sang Bishop Heber's beautiful hymn :

Now the labourer's task is o'er ;
 Now the battle day is past ;
Now upon the further shore
 Lands the voyager at last.
Father, in Thy gracious keeping
Leave we now Thy servant sleeping.

The reading of the beautifully appropriate fifteenth chapter of Corinthians, with its message of resurrection and immortality, was marked by a most curious coincidence. Just as Venerable Archdeacon Lauder, the reader, reached the passage "We shall not all sleep, but we shall be changed, in a moment, in the twinkling of an eye, at the last trump (for the trumpet shall sound)," a movement at the door led the military to believe that the service was over, and a trumpeter outside sounded the "assembly," the notes reverberating through the church and startling the congregation. After an anthem and the reading of the committal portion of the burial service, the choir sang Stainer's "Sevenfold Amen" and the "Nunc Dimittis," "Lord now lettest Thou Thy Servant Depart in Peace," and the congregation moved out of the church, followed by the solemn strains of "The Dead March in Saul."

The procession was reformed on Daly Avenue, and proceeded by way of Rideau and Wellington Streets to the Canadian Pacific Railway station. The earlier part of the day had been intensely hot and oppressive, the sun beating down from a cloudless sky with blistering intensity on the heads of the thousands of mourners, but now a change took place, the sky grew overcast with black and threatening clouds, the air became murky and, before it could be realized, the storm of rain burst down in a blinding deluge. As the head of the procession reached Parliament Hill, a vivid flash of lightning lighted up the sky, and a peal of thunder rent the air, drowning the beating of the muffled drums, as if nature, too, desired to join in bidding a last farewell to him whose mortal body was being borne away forever from the scenes of his triumphs and his usefulness.

The train which was to carry Kingston's son back to his old home was waiting at the depot, draped in black, and decked out with trappings appropriate to its mournful mission.

The hearse drew up at the gangway, the bearers gently lifted out the casket, and, as the body of the Premier was slowly borne into the funeral car, the pall-bearers stood bareheaded on either side, and the hushed silence which fell upon the multitude was only broken by the solemn music of the band playing, soft and low, the sweet and tender strains of " Nearer My God to Thee." Nothing could have rivalled in intensity of pathos the solemn scene and its accompaniment of sad, sweet music. A throb of deep emotion thrilled the crowd, and a deep sigh of sorrow that arose as died away the last mellow notes of music, seemed like the echo of a great Amen.

It took nearly twenty minutes to transfer the immense pile of floral offerings to the car, and while this was in progress many friends pressed around the bereaved relatives and offered their personal condolences. Now everything was in readiness, the gangway was removed, the mourners boarded the cars, softly the notes of the Dead March ascended, the whole vast multitude, moved by a common impulse of sorrow, uncovered their heads, and sobs and sighs were heard on every hand. So the burial train moved out.

The interior of the funeral car was heavily draped with crape, which covered sides and ceiling and flowed in waves out upon the floor. Heavy fringed drapery was carried around the sides, and the ceiling and dome were worked out with rosettes in black cloth. In the centre of the floor stood the biers on which rested the coffin ; while occupying the sides and almost the entire floor space, were the floral tributes offered in loving memory of the illustrious dead.

The journey was one of impressive solemnity, not only because of the deep feeling of those on the train, but as well because of the many timely tributes of respect and manifestations of sorrow from the people along the route. It was a journey the like of which has never been seen in Canada, the counterpart of which may not occur again in a lifetime. Sir John had many times been the central figure of a triumphal progress through the country among the people he so well loved and served, and on those occasions the crowds that assembled at every stopping place bore testimony to a political popularity that was as hearty as it was continuous. But, to-day, Sir John dead, carried in pomp from the scene of his parliamentary triumphs to the home of his youth and to his grave, attracted not the huzzas of the multitude, but the deep, tearful grief of a nation. The massed mourners of the capital were not more indicative of the general feeling than the solitary farmer who stood at the roadside, and, as the train sped by, reverently uncovered his head at the sight of the emblems of woe. The thousands upon thousands who took their places in the funeral cortege in Ottawa bore testimony to Canada's grief at the loss of her greatest statesman ; but that testimony was not more striking than the deputations who met the train at the stations of the country towns along the route, and offered their tribute of respect and regret. It was an historical journey. Perhaps it might be called the last great triumphal progress of the grand old man's earthly career—for, though it was a funeral train, the tributes of grief of the people made it assuredly the crowning glory of a long life well-spent.

It was 10.20 p.m. when the train arrived at Kingston, at which time there were fully 10,000 people assembled in the streets near the station. As the train ceased to move the clock over the Town Hall began to toll. "A" battery was present under the command of Captain Gaudet, and formed two lines from the train to the City Hall. At a signal from Chief of Police Horsey, eight constables stepped forward and received the casket. The spectacle, as the procession moved from the train towards the buildings under the vivid glare of the electric light, was solemn in the extreme.

The body was carried into the City Hall and placed on a bier, over which was a canopy with four plumes over the four corners, and crape over all. The floor was covered with snow-white duck with a deep border running around the room. On the stage near the head of the casket was a full length portrait of Sir John, as a young man, heavily draped and surrounded by masses of beautiful flowers. The cover of the casket was at once removed and the awaiting thousands allowed to view the face of their old friend. Entering at one door and retiring by another, confusion was averted, and the living stream was allowed to pass by until after midnight, when the doors were closed, and the room left in charge of the guard of honour, which was composed of the cadets of the Royal Military College under Captain Moran.

Before five o'clock the next morning people began to make their way into the mortuary chamber, for a last gaze on the features of him whom all Kingston knew so well. As morning advanced the crowd of pilgrims increased, until at times the crush became so great that the doors had to be closed. Thousands of visitors poured in from the adjacent country, and by every train and boat, and nearly all wore mourning or mourning badges. Numbers who were personal friends lingered at the casket; all were reverential, and many were deeply affected. Here the late Premier had spent his earliest years; had gone to school with other lads; had passed the days of his youth; had dwelt in manhood's prime; had made his first steps in that brilliant career which the old limestone city had watched for nearly half a century, until he had attained such an eminence that her citizens were proud of the glory which he had reflected upon them. It was here that he had formed those early tender ties which twine closest around the heart, and here were scores of friends who had never faltered in their loyal support and sympathy from the hour that he was first induced to offer himself as their representative. To Kingston he had always turned with a feeling of warm affection felt for no other place in the wide Dominion, and it was peculiarly fitting that to his old home he should be brought to receive the last sad honours, and to be laid beside the dear ones who had gone before. The blow was felt in Kingston with a sorrow that no other place could feel, and the old city mourned her son with an intensity of grief that showed how large a place he had filled in her heart. But not alone were her citizens permitted to give their tribute of tears to his memory, for, from the far Pacific on the west to the Atlantic on the east, they came, the representatives of tens of thousands of friends in far off places, to do him honour. Cities, towns, villages, urban and rural constituencies sent their quota of delegates, and all professions, classes and creeds were present to take part in the greatest and most solemn pageant Canada had ever witnessed.

At two o'clock the funeral cortege was organized in front

of the old historic city hall, and moved off in order corresponding to that which had been arranged in Ottawa.

As the procession moved along Princess street, headed by the Gananoque Carriage Company's band, playing Mendelssohn's funeral march, the dense crowd made way, and all heads were uncovered in respectful sympathy. Up Princess street and away out through the tollgate and beyond the city the mournful cortege wended its way, the houses all along the line, even out in the country, displaying their tokens of universal bereavement. The great chief who had followed near and dear ones, and many an old friend, over this road was now being borne to his last resting place in the beautiful cemetery of Cataraqui. At last the lovely spot is reached and the vast crowds cluster on every point of vantage to get a view ; the bearers raise the casket on their shoulders and, followed by the mourners, make stately progress to the new made grave. The bell in the little stone church behind the pine trees tolls its plaintive knell, the multitude upon the hillside reverently bare there heads, and the form of the beloved statesman sinks into its narrow bed, whence it shall only rise when the last trump shall sound. The Venerable Archdeacon Jones read the solemnly beautiful service of the English Church, and as the mournful words, " Earth to earth, ashes to ashes, dust to dust," were wafted over the solemn stillness of the scene, and the yet more impressive rattle of the earth on the coffin lid told that forever from mortal sight had passed John Alexander Macdonald, the matchless leader, the true patriot, the warmhearted friend, those whose family ties had been severed, and the colleagues who stood sadly looking on, were not alone in their grief, for in that vast concourse there was hardly an eye that was not dimmed with tears.

The sad duty over, the vast concourse turn sorrow-stricken from the grave, gathering fragments of stone, leaves and other small things, to bear away as mementoes, the sighing pine trees sing a soft hymn of requiem, and, once more silence reigns in the city of the dead.

And while Canada mourned the loss of her greatest son, and thousands gathered round his grave, the solemn death bell of Westminster Abbey called the people of England together to join, in spirit, in the sad and solemn obsequies. Her Majesty, the Queen, and all the Royal Family were represented. The Marquis of Lorne, Lord Knutsford, Lord Kimberly, Lord Aberdeen, the Speaker of the House of Commons, and a large number of other distinguished people were present, and here, within the majestic pile where reposes all that is mortal of England's greatest, noblest and truest sons, men whose influence on the field, in legislative halls, on the bench, in church and in state, have made her what she is, the parent of free nations and the home of liberty ; in the presence of a sympathetic audience which filled every available place in the choir and the transepts, a memorial service was held, and the tears of the motherland flowed in unison with those of her greatest colony. The significance of such a ceremony, in such a place, may be gathered from the comments of the London *Times :*

" Westminster Abbey yesterday offered a spectacle which is without precedent in the long and varied annals of that venerable building. A congregation, eminently representative of all ranks and classes of Englishmen, from the Sovereign downwards, assembled to take part in a solemn service held in memory of Sir John Macdonald, and to testify to the strength and sincerity of the sympathy felt in this country with our fellow-subjects in Canada. Many a great Englishman sleeps within the Abbey, and many a requiem sung within its walls has awakened mournful echoes in the hearts of English-speaking peoples beyond the seas. But this is the first time that a great sorrow, primarily falling upon our fellow-subjects abroad, has awakened in the mother country a sentiment so strong as to demand and receive expression in the ancient church that is consecrated by so many of our proudest associations. Our roll of heroes would be sadly curtailed were we to remove from it the names of those who did their work in foreign lands and laid broad and deep the foundations of empire on which self-governing communities have since based the fabric of their liberties. But the great soldiers and administrators, whose reward was sealed and perfected by their final

SIR JOHN'S GRAVE, CATARAQUI CEMETERY, KINGSTON

entry into the national Pantheon, have always hitherto been the servants of England, directly responsible to the English people ; and the conscious aim of their work, whatever might be its indirect issues, has been to extend the power and add to the greatness of their fatherland. Sir John Macdonald has primarily laboured for the greatness of Canada, has been the devoted servant of the Canadian people, and has sought at their hands the guerdon of faithful service. It is in the character of a Canadian statesman that he is now honoured and mourned by the people of this country as they have been wont to honour and mourn men whose lives were given to their own service. Because he was a Canadian statesman his bones may not mingle with those of our illustrious dead, but the service at the Abbey is the outward sign of a profound conviction that the great Canadian is also a great Englishman, and that his service to the Dominion ranks him with the most distinguished of those who have served the mother country."

Even before the last scenes had taken place, movements were originated in the cities of Toronto, Montreal and Kingston to erect monuments to his memory. As might be expected, the latter place was prompt and energetic in action. The citizens aimed at a memorial that would be national in character and extent, and organized committees in outside places to assist in carrying out the scheme. Many eminent persons, including Her Royal Highness, the Princess Louise, have lent their names. In the autograph volumes now being circulated for the signatures of subscribers to the fund, is a preface from the able pen of Principal Grant, of Queen's College, which fitly describes the characteristics of Sir John Macdonald :

"Though dead the ideas that inspired him live. He believed that there was room on the continent of America for at least two nations, and he was determined that Canada should be a nation. He believed in the superiority of the British Constitution to any other for free men, and that the preservation of union with the mother country was necessary to the making of Canada. He had faith in the French race, and believed that a good understanding between

French and English-speaking Canadians was essential to the national welfare. The people followed him not only as a leader but as an actual embodiment of those fundamental ideas. No one charged him with exaggeration when he said, concerning himself: ' There does not exist in Canada a man ' who has given more of his time, more of his heart, more of ' his wealth, or more of his intellect and powers, such as they ' may be, for the good of the Dominion of Canada.' They accepted his last public utterance : ' A British subject I was ' born ; a British subject I will die,' as the confession of their own faith. To the doing of his work he brought great qualities, and all were laid unreservedly on the altar of his country. The combination of imaginative power and insight, with a just appreciation of the necessities of the present, made him a statesman. In virtue of a quick judgment and extraordinary grasp of detail he was a supreme man of affairs. Those who knew him best, knew him to be also essentially just, humane, and God-fearing. He loved power, but the people believed that he sought it that he might minister to the country and not to himself. Canadians will not let the memory of this great man die."

Mr. Henry Olger, an intimate friend and supporter in Kingston, expressed his views in the following terse and graphic terms :—

" I can think of no man whose qualities it would be more difficult to capture in words than those of Sir John Macdonald's, there was that in him which refused to be defined. A history of his acts and words, all that he has done and said, would not make him known to those who never came in personal contact with him. There was in him some indescribable charm that acted by presence, seemingly without means or argument, a sort of intellect of the heart which pleased and convinced, and drew and bound men to him. He was ' organized victory.' "

Steps have also been taken to erect a fitting memorial in St. Paul's Cathedral, in grateful recognition of the distinguished services rendered by Sir John Macdonald to the British Empire, and we cannot more appropriately conclude our task than by quoting the tribute paid to his memory by the Marquis of Dufferin and Ava, the chairman of the committee formed to carry out this purpose :

"We are assembled here to do honour, not to a consummate party leader, or a skilful tactician, but to a great Imperial statesman, who, as the trusted Minister of the Crown, and the chosen representative of the Canadian people during so many years, used his great abilities and industry and zeal to promote the best interests of Her Majesty's Canadian subjects, and to maintain unimpaired those ties of interest and affection which, I trust, are long destined to bind the peoples of Canada and Great Britain in a fraternal union. I cannot help desiring to bear my personal testimony to those engaging and lovable qualities which endeared Sir John Macdonald to every representative of the Crown that was sent over from this country to assume the reins of government. His equable and genial temperament, his delicate courtesy, his genuine kindness, his considerate frankness, rendered him one of the most charming and satisfactory public men with whom I have ever had the good fortune of being associated in the conduct of public business. Above all things this must be placed to the record of his great qualities, that he always showed a proud eagerness to take upon himself the responsibility of whatever line of action the head of the Canadian Government may have pursued on his recommendation, to shield him from any popular resentment to which that action may have given rise, and at the same time to show a most scrupulous anxiety to avoid the slightest appearance of sheltering either himself or his party behind the prestige or the authority of the Crown.

" A firm friend, a most generous and placable opponent, a charming companion, an affectionate husband and a most tender father, Sir John Macdonald, after a long life spent in the service of his country, has descended to the grave mourned by his Sovereign and all her representatives, passionately regretted by his personal friends and adherents, respected even by those who most differed from him in political opinions, and universally honoured by the Canadian people. In these circumstances it seems to me only natural that Canadian lamentations should find an echo in English hearts, and that we on this side of the water should desire to mark our appreciation, our reverence, and our love of one who so nobly fulfilled his duty, and has left us all so bright and honourable an example.   During the last half-century in the four quarters of the globe there have been colonial statesmen of first-rate ability endeavouring to advance the fame and the material interests of England and of Englishmen, but amongst them to my mind no name will shine with more conspicuous brilliancy on the page of history, both in regard to the length of his service and the success of his administration, than that of Sir John Macdonald."

> Into the darkness of the pitiless grave
> We stretch dumb hands, as we would rive again
> From his fierce clutch Death's last and greatest prey
> . "We will not, cannot lose him !"   Such the cry
> That rose in anguish from the million hearts
> Who counted up those agonizing hours,
> And throbbed response to every parting pang
> Of his, their guide, their father, and their friend,
> Not ours to choose ; another will than ours
> Is done.   We stand before the eternal gates,
> And know the bolts are drawn for evermore.
>
> What shall we say?   How speak, when every breast
> Is vibrant to the sting of hopeless loss ?
> Like infant babble fall the trembling words
> Which strive to voice a grief that has no name,
> Or praise of him whose fame transcends all praise.
> Silence best fits the time when the bowed face,
> Manhood's stern sorrow, and the nation's tears
> Are our first tribute to the nation's dead.
> Not the cold tomb receives him ; he is shrined
> In the warm hearts of half a continent.
> Vainly shall marble rise ; his monument
> Is the broad land he built, and loved, and died for.
>
> For not more surely on the hard-fought field
> Of victory falls the soldier (thinking nought
> Of self but all of duty) in the cause
> He has sworn faith to—never martyr sealed
> More surely his devotion—than did he,
> Who for the space of half an age gave brain,
> And soul, and tireless thought, his best, his all,

To one sole purpose, his dear country's good,
Lay down his life in service for her sake.
He stood beside her birth-bed ; fondly held
Her baby hand when her first steps were trod ;
Saw her first maiden blush, her budding powers ;
And at the last, for that she needed him,
Spared not one hour of toil till Death's stroke fell.

But, oh bereaved people ! while ye hold
The peace of heart-break by the new filled grave,
Hearken the words he left ye, echoing back
From those far courts we may not penetrate—
Alike our consolation and command.
Hoard them as priceless treasures in your souls,
Write them in fire and brass that all may see,
Ring them through mart and hall that all may hear,
Bind them as frontlets on your children's brows—
" I have loved Canada with a passionate love."

Oh land, not all bereft while these *his* words,
Live to inspire thee—while his works remain
Undying witness of his care for thee,
And his great memory, undimmed, endures
While one stream leaps, or one green hill shall wave
Through all the fair land that he loved so well.
See thou prove worthy of his gift to thee.
Hold fast his hope for thee—lift up thy head-
And tread unfaltering in that forward road
His hand still points thee though it guides no more.